Forgotten

A NOVEL BY

JEANNE HARDT

Gina —
Those we love
are never forgotten!
Enjoy!
Jeanne
Hardt

I'd like to dedicate this book to my
mother-in-law, Joyce, who will *never* be forgotten ...

Chapter 1

This is what I'll miss . . .

Billy gazed at Paulette and her chocolate-colored ringlets. Her chin rested in her hands, framing her chubby five-year-old cheeks. She was lying on her belly listening intently to their mama read the same Christmas story she'd read for as long as he could remember.

"God bless us, everyone." She closed the book and sighed.

The glow from the fireplace added the warmth they needed on the cold December night.

"Read it again, Mama!" Paulette chirped.

Billy laughed at her enthusiasm. "You have to go to bed or Santa will never come."

"Your brother's right." His mama shifted her eyes to his father, who held Christina—his ten-year-old sister—on his lap. "We got time for the Bible story, don't we, Douglas?"

"Of course." He smiled and readjusted Christina, who'd almost fallen asleep.

"I'll get it!" Richard jumped to his feet. He lifted the old Bible from the end table and brought it to their mama. His nine-year-old brother had more energy than all of them put together.

His mama held the book to her chest. "Mrs. Moss would be happy knowin' we still read her Bible." She leafed through the pages until she found the appropriate chapter.

As she read, Billy's mind drifted. He had other things to think about. Growing up in such a fantastic home, he'd never wanted for anything. But special wishes were granted at Christmas. This year was different, though they attempted to pretend otherwise.

It was impossible to shut out the soldiers wandering around the perimeter of the house. For the last year, they'd been an undeniable presence. He'd often overheard his mama praying the war would end so they'd leave.

"What's swaddle clothes, Mama?" Paulette asked.

"Reckon it's what they called blankets. His ma wanted to keep him warm."

"Oh." Paulette grinned at Billy, then stood and plopped down on his lap. She laid her head on his shoulder and cuddled close.

Since the day she was born she'd been special to him. He loved his sister, Christina, as well as his brothers, Donald and Richard, but Paulette tugged at his heart.

Being the eldest, he took his role seriously. He'd be fourteen in two months. His father already treated him like a man—allowing him to do things his siblings weren't permitted to. Including choosing his own bedtime.

When the story ended, Paulette was asleep. He carried her down the hallway to her room, followed by his father, with Christina clutched close.

Though the house was large enough to allow a room for each of them, the girls shared a room. Billy assumed when they grew older that would change.

I hope I'm here to see it happen.

He tucked Paulette beneath the sheets, covered her with a patch-work quilt, then kissed her on the forehead. She didn't stir. Neither did Christina when his father put her in bed.

They crept from the room. His mama was waiting in the hallway. "Are *you* goin' to bed?"

"Yes'm."

She opened her arms and he moved into her embrace. "I love you, Billy."

"I love you, too, Mama." She kissed his cheek and he returned it, then went to the living room where his brothers were wrestling on the floor, grunting and moaning.

"You'd better quiet down," he said. "You don't want to wake Grandmother."

"We won't," Richard said, laughing, while Donald held him in a headlock.

"Don't break his neck," Billy scolded.

They arose from the floor, glanced one last time at the Christmas tree, then hurried off to bed. Their laughter carried all the way down the hallway.

Billy sat in a chair close to the fire. The house could be frigid with its tall ceilings and large rooms. Fortunately, it had been a mild winter. The soldiers were undoubtedly grateful. They'd had enough to battle without having to fight nature itself.

His mind returned to heavier thoughts. The idea of the war troubled him. Most of Tennessee fought for the Confederacy, but *his* loyalty was with the Union army. Living in Memphis made it difficult. Union soldiers had taken over. At one point, Confederates had tried to push them out. They'd failed. But since then, there'd been a heavy presence of Union soldiers in the city.

Because the Wellesley estate was enormous, the army made use of it, pitching their canvas tents. His mama didn't approve of him talking to the soldiers, so he'd sneak away whenever he could. He had no doubt what he needed to do. The cause couldn't be more just.

The flames danced before his eyes.

Angel . . .

She'd always been as much a part of his life as his siblings, but she wasn't free. He *needed* to fight. For her.

"Billy?"

He looked up at his father. "Yes, sir?"

"Are you all right?" He sat beside him. "I thought you were going to bed."

Putting his palms toward the heat of the flames, Billy hesitated, not wanting him to know what actually troubled him. "I am. I was just . . . thinking."

"About Christmas?"

"It's hard to think about Christmas during a war."

"Yes, but you handled yourself well with your brothers and sisters. We're trying to make the holiday as normal as possible. We don't want to frighten them."

Billy gazed at the fire. "Paulette's so little she doesn't remember a time when the soldiers weren't here."

"They should be gone soon. There's rumor the South is ready to surrender. If Lincoln has his way, slaves will be set free."

"Why do you need a law to give them their freedom?" Billy focused on the flames. His words came out icier than he'd intended.

"You know I've never treated them like slaves. They have their own homes and freedom to go about as they please."

"But they *aren't* free." Billy looked him in the eye. "You should pay them for what they do."

"We give them a place to live. Food. Everything they need. Where do you think they'd go if they were freed?"

"Wherever they choose."

"Perhaps they'd stay. I think they're happy here."

"Maybe. But it'd be their choice." Billy stared intently at the man he respected more than anyone.

"You're becoming a man, Billy. A very *good* man." He smiled and stood. "Now, you'd best get to bed. Richard will be waking everyone as soon as day breaks."

"Yes, sir." He didn't move.

"Billy . . ." His father gripped his shoulder. "I'm proud of you."

He finally managed to smile. "Thank you, sir. Merry Christmas."

"Merry Christmas." He gave him a pat, then walked down the hallway to his room.

Billy envied his parents. They were able to warm themselves in the comfort of each other's arms on these cold winter nights. The thought of leaving the fire and crawling between icy-cold sheets wasn't appealing. Maybe Biscuit—the male tabby cat—would be on his bed, and there'd be a small warm spot to lie under.

He moved to the mantel and lifted the wooden angel from its place. The features were intricate and the wood smooth. It was his mama's favorite treasure, carved by her father when she was a child. It had inspired Angel's mama to give her the name. At least, that was the story he'd been told.

A less exquisite figurine stood beside it. An angel carved by his brother, Donald, who'd been learning the craft from their great-uncle, Harper. It had lopsided wings and a broken halo.

He chuckled and fingered the odd carving. Donald had more to learn.

With his plan tumbling through his mind, he trudged to his room. He just needed to decide *when* to do it.

I hope I don't break Mama's heart. Maybe one day she'll understand.

His father had said he was proud of him. He intended to do something worthy of it.

Chapter 2

"Billy! Wake up! Ada made cimmanon bread!" Paulette shook his shoulders with all the strength a five-year-old could muster.

He opened his eyes. Paulette's were wide with excitement. "*Cimmanon?*" He grinned at her mussed brown hair, no longer donning perfectly-formed ringlets. "That's my favorite."

"C'mon, Billy!" She tugged on his pajamas. "Santa came!"

Swinging his legs over the side of the bed, he stood and took her tiny hand. She pulled him down the long hallway to the living room, where the warm fire blazed.

"Hard to believe you slept through Richard's yelpin'." His mama laughed.

He chuckled and moved to an empty seat by the fire. Ada handed him a steaming cup of apple cider. "Thank you, Ada. Merry Christmas."

"Merry Christmas, Billy." She winked and walked away.

She'd been their head cook his entire life. He'd never seen her as a slave. Just like Bessie—Angel's mama—as well as Angel and Jeriah, the stable hand. They'd all share Christmas dinner together. Once a year, they disregarded status and sat down together as family.

Normally, he'd have been on the floor with his siblings, anxiously waiting gifts to be passed. Something held him back this year. Maybe he was getting too old, or as he'd told his father—the war made it difficult for him to feel like celebrating.

It didn't take long for them to open their gifts. The girls received dolls, Donald was given a new pocket knife, and Richard received a leather pouch filled with assorted glass marbles.

When his father placed a large box in Billy's lap, his mama winced. He opened it quickly and found what he'd wished for. A Kentucky long rifle.

Holding it up and away from him, he thanked his father and looked apologetically at his mama. He could shoot, but didn't have a gun of his own. He'd hunted with his father for years and had asked for one many times, but his mama had always said no.

"You must be very careful," his grandmother said. "That's a man's gift."

He crossed to where she was sitting. "I will." He kissed her cheek. "Merry Christmas."

His mama frowned. "I still don't like it. Just be careful. Promise you won't shoot any birds, or cats, or dogs. Or . . ."

"I won't, Mama." She didn't have to say it. She didn't want him to shoot a man. But if the time came where he was forced to, would he?

There were other gifts; socks, candy, and items of clothing. He received a much-needed coat with a matching wool hat.

After the presents were opened, he returned to his room and quickly changed out of his nightclothes. Even though his brothers and sisters remained in theirs, he didn't want to risk having Angel see him that way.

"Billy." His grandmother patted the arm of her chair, as he re-entered the family room. "Come sit by me."

He did as she asked. "Are you warm enough?" He tucked the lap blanket around her knees. Mary Wellesley was a small woman, but very able for her age. However, she frequently got chilled. He suggested she leave her hair down around her shoulders for warmth, but she insisted it was improper at her age and kept her gray hair neatly twisted atop her head.

She nodded. "I'm fine, but I'm worried about you. You're not yourself."

He turned away and focused on the Christmas tree. It felt like many Christmases before. He should be happy, but his heavy heart wouldn't allow it. "I'm all right."

"Talk to me when you're ready. I'll always listen."

Without looking at her, he nodded. Somehow, she'd always been able to look into his heart. He had great respect for her. After his grandfather died, she'd kept their business going with the help of his father. When the war started, their textile mill thrived. Unlike many others in the south, they hadn't suffered financially.

His spirit lifted at the sound of an all-too-familiar laugh. *Angel.*

She stood in the hallway admiring Paulette's new ragdoll. Then her eyes shifted in his direction. Her face lit up with an even brighter smile than she'd had for his little sister.

She'd changed a lot in the past year and looked nothing like the other slaves. Her skin was fairer, though still dark, and her hair was long and wavy. Like Paulette's, it was the color of chocolate. No doubt she'd grow into a beautiful woman. The older he became, the more he appreciated that fact.

His grandmother nudged him, prompting him to stand and cross the room. "Merry Christmas, Angel," he said with a nod.

She pulled him into a hug. "Merry Christmas, Billy."

Though she was closer in age to Donald, the two of them were inseparable—his best friend.

She squeezed him a little tighter, then released him and stepped back, smiling all the while.

Ada handed her a cup of cider. "Cinnamon bread's in the kitchen. Still hot, too."

Without hesitating, Angel headed for the kitchen. Billy followed her.

Ada bustled along behind them and took her place at the stove stirring a large pot filled with cider. As she stirred, her overly-large bottom wiggled.

Billy glanced at Angel. They both grinned, then Angel lowered her eyes and bit her lower lip.

She's embarrassed . . .

When they were younger, they'd tease Ada about her size. She'd brush it off and laugh. As they grew up, they understood it wasn't polite to say such things. Their shared memories retained everything. Happy recollections Billy never wanted to forget.

"That's a lot for our family," he said, looking into the pot.

"Your mama wanted 'nuff for the soldiers. Said it's for Christmas. I gots even more to heat. Your daddy'll take this to 'em soon."

He patted her shoulder, then joined Angel at the kitchen table. She pulled apart pieces of cinnamon bread, popped them into her mouth, then licked the sticky glaze off her fingers.

"It must be good," he said, laughing.

She broke off a piece and waved it in front of his face. "Try it an see."

As he opened his mouth, she placed it on his tongue. He snapped at her playfully.

"Billy Denton!" she scolded, followed by a giggle.

Chewing the bread and enjoying every bit of it, he wiggled his brows. "That'll teach you to feed me. I'm not a baby."

She leaned back and silently stared at him. The way she looked at him made his heart skip a beat. That had never happened before.

"Why are you looking at me like that?" he asked quietly, not wanting Ada to hear.

She leaned in. "You've changed."

"So have you."

"Is that bad?"

Slowly, he shook his head. "No."

They stared at each other, until his father entered the kitchen and disrupted the moment.

"Is it ready?" The man peered into the pot.

"Yessa," Ada replied.

Taking two towels, he grabbed the handles of the heavy container and headed for the back door.

Billy jumped to his feet. "I'll help you." Ada handed him a ladle. He quickly grabbed his coat before going outside. Thankful for the distraction from Angel, he needed to do something to steady the beat of his heart.

Several large canvas tents were scattered about the gardens. They used the biggest one for food storage and preparation, the others for officers. Enlisted men slept in smaller ones, usually occupied by two or three men. Those tents were everywhere. Nearly eighty soldiers camped at the Wellesley estate.

He admired the blue Union uniforms and the men who wore them. He'd become especially close to Matthew Grey, a young soldier from Massachusetts who was only sixteen. He'd lied about his age to enlist, but said he'd felt compelled to do it. Billy understood . . .

The men lined up with metal cups in hand, anxiously awaiting the hot cider. Appreciation showed on their faces.

Matthew nodded to Billy's father. "This is very good. Thank you, sir."

"It's the least we could do. Perhaps it'll make your Christmas merrier." He smiled at Matthew, then turned to Billy. "I'm going to get more."

"I'll be in soon," Billy said, and his father walked away.

Matthew took another sip. "Your stepfather's a good man."

"Yes, he is."

"You're lucky. Somehow, he managed to convince the officers to camp out here. With a house like yours, most would've moved in. The man has some kind of pull."

Billy wasn't sure what he'd done to keep them out, but with money most anything was possible.

Matthew led him away from the other soldiers. "Are you still gonna do it?"

He nodded. "I have to."

"When?"

Nervously, he looked around not wanting to be overheard. "After the new year. My family celebrates on New Year's Eve. We stay up until midnight, then everyone sleeps late the next morning. I'll leave then."

"Remember . . . go to Clifton. You can get there in three days, long as you have a good horse. There's still Union soldiers there."

"Tell them I'm eighteen, right?"

"Yes."

"At times like this I wish I had my brother's height." Billy's stomach churned. "Will they believe me?"

Matthew gripped his shoulder. "If you say it's so, they'll believe it. I've seen soldiers younger than you playing drums, leading troops into battle. They'll take anyone willing to fight."

Joining his rolling stomach, his heart pounded. "I can fight."

"It's not as easy as you think. I've seen horrible things."

Billy grabbed his arm. "I *can* fight. I'm not afraid."

"You *should* be. War's an ugly thing."

"But *you* joined. Why shouldn't I?"

"I didn't say you shouldn't. Just know what you're getting into."

Billy stared at the ground, then slowly raised his head. "I won't change my mind."

Matthew drank down the rest of his cider, then nodded toward the house. "Go back inside. It's Christmas. Enjoy your family while you can."

Matthew was right. Besides, Angel was waiting.

* * *

The pained look on his mama's face, wrenched Billy's heart. "Rosie'll be here soon," she said. "Uncle Harper's bringin' her."

Rosie had been important to his mama when she'd first moved to Memphis, and they'd remained friends. It would be Rosie's first Christmas without Toby, her son who'd died in the war. He, too, had been born a slave. When the opportunity came to fight, he'd grabbed it without reservation. Now Toby's mama had no son.

If I die, at least Mama will have Donald and Richard.

She reached out to him. "Be sure an say sumthin' nice to her. She's havin' an awful time."

"I will, Mama." The sorrow in her eyes almost caused him to reconsider leaving. He didn't want to hurt her.

But then the sounds coming from the kitchen affirmed what he had to do. Angel was working hard, like she'd done for as long as he could remember.

I won't change my mind.

The formal dining room table had been set for Christmas dinner, with fine china and crystal. His mama and sisters had decorated the room with fresh green boughs and red ribbons. But his favorite part of the holiday was the aroma coming from the kitchen.

Turkey with cornbread stuffing, green beans cooked with ham, whipped potatoes, and piping hot dinner rolls were only part of the menu. Rosie would be bringing corn pudding and chess pie.

He crossed the room and looked out the tall windows into the garden. Soldiers mulled around the property. They didn't appear to be doing much at all. Being Christmas, maybe the officers were giving them a day of rest.

His mama came up beside him and promptly pulled the drapery. "I hope you don't mind. It makes me sad seein' 'em out there."

"I understand."

She wrapped her arm around his shoulder. "I pray it all ends 'fore you're old enough to fight."

He couldn't respond. So he stood there enjoying the warmth of her presence, saying nothing.

"Mama," Richard said, running up to her, "Rosie's here."

She took a deep breath, squeezed Billy's shoulder, then walked away.

Relieved, he made a small part in the curtain.

One day soon I'll wear that uniform.

Chapter 3

Angel had enjoyed helping with dinner preparations, but was glad when she could finally take her seat. Billy had saved the spot beside him.

Happiness surrounded her. Even Rosie had managed to smile when Paulette wrapped a napkin around her doll declaring it *swaddle* clothes.

She couldn't quite understand why Harper, Mrs. Wellesley's brother, didn't live at the estate. He was getting old, and it seemed he'd be happier there, but for some reason he liked living in his house on the river.

The best part of the entire day was having Billy so close to her.

"I have a gift for you," he whispered, leaning in.

"I have one for you, too."

They'd finished their meal, so they scooted their chairs back and she followed him to the living room.

They sat on the floor beside the Christmas tree, and he handed her a paper-wrapped package. The gift was flat and rectangular.

She grinned. *A book.* She loved to read and took advantage of the estate library every chance she could. Years ago, Mrs. Denton had given her free reign, and she'd been told to read to her heart's content.

She held the present to her chest. "Did you find one that's not in the library?"

He beamed. "Open it."

She peeled away the paper and ran her hand over the leather cover. "It's beautiful. But there's no title." She flipped through the pages and found them blank. "I don't understand."

He produced a smaller package from beneath the tree. "This goes with it."

She tore it open. It held a quill and bottle of ink.

"I know you want to write. Now you can." He licked his lips. "Don't you like it?"

"It's the finest gift I've ever gotten." Tears welled in her eyes. "Thank you, Billy." Setting the book aside, she wrapped her arms around him and hugged him tight. As she slowly released him, she peered deeply into his eyes. She'd never noticed just how green they were. Green with flecks of gold. "Christmas eyes," she whispered.

"What?"

"Your eyes. They're green. Like Christmas."

"I have my father's eyes." He gazed at the tree. "My *real* father."

Hearing the pain she recognized whenever he mentioned the man, she laid her hand on his. "I like green."

"I like brown." He met her gaze.

Her stomach fluttered. Should she move closer or run away? *What's wrong with me?*

Confused, she did neither, and instead handed him his Christmas gift. "I made it myself," she said, rolling her eyes.

He grinned, took the package, and untied the ribbon. As he unfolded the long knit scarf, he found the gloves inside. "Blue. My favorite color."

Her heart danced when he wrapped the scarf around his neck. "It'll keep you warm."

"Thank you, Angel. I love them." He put the gloves on, then patted his hands together.

She swallowed the lump in her throat, as he pulled her close and hugged her. *I love you.* When he released her, she sat up straight. *Where did that thought come from?*

In a few short months she'd be thirteen. Not old enough to be in love. Then again, she'd always loved him. He was her best friend.

"Angel?" He removed the gloves and unwound the scarf.

"Yes?" *Why's he so serious?*

"I . . ." He looked away from her.

With compassion, she set her hand on his leg, causing him to jump. His reaction surprised her and she jerked away. "I'm sorry, Billy."

"No. Don't be sorry. I just . . ."

"What?" She leaned in, making a point *not* to touch him.

"There's something I want to tell you, but I can't yet." His brows furrowed and he bit his bottom lip. "You'll come to our New Year's Eve party, won't you?"

"Course. I always do."

"Good." He sighed. "I'll tell you then." He glanced over his shoulder. "We'd better join the others." Rising to his feet, he extended his hand.

She took it, allowing him to help her stand. Once she faced him, their hands remained locked together. Her heart skipped a beat when his thumb moved along her skin.

He squeezed her hand. "Promise me you'll write in the book. Write whatever comes to mind. It can be a journal or a book of poetry. Whatever you want. Someday, I'd like to read it."

"If I write a diary, I won't let you read it."

"I understand." He laughed, then paused and let out a long breath. "But . . ." Again, his expression changed. "I want you to write something about all of us. Something to help us remember growing up here."

"Sumthin' 'bout you?" She nudged him with her shoulder.

"About *us.*"

The house seemed unusually quiet. For a moment, she stopped breathing and did nothing more than look into his Christmas-green eyes. As quickly as it stopped, it started again. The fire crackled, and Paulette's laughter erupted from the other room.

"Paulette must be telling another story," he said. "C'mon."

She followed him to the dining room.

* * *

Billy's mama pulled her robe tight around her body and stared into the fire. "Another Christmas come an gone."

"You sound sad, Mama." He stood beside her.

"Broke my heart seein' Rosie 'thout Toby. He meant everythin' to her." She lovingly stroked his hair. "Just like I feel 'bout you." Her fingers stopped, still entwined around several strands. It likely reminded her of *him*. He had William O'Brien's red hair, but fortunately *her* features.

He was glad to have time alone with her. Everyone else had gone to bed, and his father was settling the boys down for the night.

"Am I so different from your other children?"

"You was my first. That makes you special." She smiled and nodded toward the sofa. They sat side-by-side, then she took his hand. "Your pa . . ."

His heart thumped. She *was* thinking of him, not Douglas Denton. It was rare she spoke about his *real* father. "Yes?"

"Your pa was much older than me. Wanted a son so bad he was willin' to marry me. Didn't care I was poor and paid no mind to the way I talk."

"Mama, you talk fine." She often chastised herself for the way she spoke, but it was something he loved about her; a unique quality that made her even more endearing.

She looked sideways at him and patted his leg. "He gave me everythin' I needed. Best of all was you."

He swallowed hard, feeling even guiltier about what he planned to do. "Then he died before I could ever know him." He stared vacantly forward.

"Sometimes things happen we don't understand." She soothingly rubbed his back. "I reckon you was always meant to be raised by Douglas."

"Someone who won't teach me to drink and gamble." He immediately wished he hadn't said it. She cast her eyes downward, breaking his heart. "I'm sorry, Mama. But it's hard to understand. Having a father who cheated at cards and was hung for it isn't easy to accept."

"He loved you. That much I can tell you. More than anythin' he wanted us to be happy. Douglas loved you, too, from the first time he held you. An you was just a tiny baby."

"He's been a good father."

She sighed, long and steadily. "A very good *father*." She forced the word as if foreign. The corners of her lips rose just enough to resemble a smile.

"I could never call him *Pa*. And you were never *Ma*. It didn't fit."

"You was swayed by Angel goin' all over the house sayin' *Mama, Mama*. She was a mama's baby for sure."

"So it was Angel who got me calling you Mama?" He laid his head on her shoulder. "I like it better than *Ma*."

She cradled his head, then turned and kissed his forehead.

"Mama?" He felt comforted against her. "Can I ask you about Angel?"

Her body went rigid. "What do you wanna know?"

"Is she a Negro, or is she white?"

She hesitated. "Reckon since she's a slave, she's a Negro."

He faced her. "What if her mama had died and she'd been raised by her father? Wouldn't she be considered, *white*? And would she be free?"

"Dang, Billy." She quickly covered her mouth. It was rare to hear her curse, and it made him chuckle.

She swatted his arm. "It ain't funny. You know how long I've tried to stop sayin' that word?"

"It's not such a bad word. I've heard worse."

"Where you been hearin' worse?" Her eyes widened.

"Well . . ."

She stood and placed her hands on her hips. "It's them soldiers, ain't it? I told Douglas they was a bad influence on y'all. I wish they'd never come."

"They're good men." He rose and laid a calming hand on her arm. "What they do isn't easy. You should be grateful."

She dropped her hands to her sides. "Reckon I am. They're fightin' for what's right."

A lump rose in his throat. That was his point. "Mama, about Angel . . ."

"I'm listenin'."

"When she's old enough, who will she marry? A Negro or a white man?"

She stared at him. "Slaves can't marry."

"What if she were free?"

"Even if she was, she ain't even thirteen."

"I-I know—but—can't you answer my question?"

She looked upward and twisted her mouth. "Reckon she'd marry who she loves. But most folks wouldn't take to her marryin' any white man. It just ain't done."

"She's *half* white."

"Reckon so, but she lives with her ma. An Bessie's as dark as can be. You can't change the color of your skin."

"No . . ." he whispered. "And you can't change your heart."

"What? I didn't hear that last part."

"It was nothing. I'd better go to bed. It's been a long day." Though his questions weren't answered the way he'd hoped, he kissed her cheek and walked down the hallway to his room.

His mind reeled as he crawled into bed.

If Angel was free would things change? Could she choose her husband, white or Negro?

A damp nose pressed into his cheek, followed by a loud purr.

"You're a multi-colored cat." He stroked Biscuit's fur. "Your life is much less complicated."

Biscuit rubbed his furry face along his chin, then curled into a ball and shut his eyes.

Billy's eyes remained wide open.

Chapter 4

"Seventeen, eighteen . . ." Richard's counting grew quieter the further Angel and Billy went.

"C'mon," he said, tightening his grip. He led her up the staircase to the second floor. In his other hand he held a lantern, lighting their way through the dark house.

The twenty-seven room house, with three stories and an attic, made hide-and-seek quite challenging. But it had always been a favorite game.

Both nervous *and* excited, she'd let Billy lead her anywhere.

"Where we gonna hide?" she asked.

"The attic. Richard hates going up there. It scares him."

"He ain't the only one," she muttered.

He flashed a grin. "I'll protect you. Besides, there's nothing to be afraid of. Only dusty old trunks filled with clothes and Grandmother's trinkets."

"Just don't leave me." She squeezed his hand a little tighter.

"I won't."

As they climbed to the third floor, she shivered. "You sure you wanna go there? It's so cold."

"I'm sure." He put his arm around her. "I want to be somewhere we won't be heard."

Not heard?

The way he'd said it, made her believe he had more in mind than playing the game.

Even wearing one of her heavy winter dresses, the frigid air seeped through every bit of the fabric and chilled her to the bone. How could Billy be so warm? He constantly radiated heat.

He held her closer as they ascended the much narrower stairwell to the attic. The door creaked, causing her to tremble. "I don't wanna stay here long, Billy. Even with you, I don't like it up here." Visions of cobwebs, spiders, and mysterious shadows filled her mind.

He gave her a reassuring smile and led her through the door. "I'll try to be quick, but you may not like what I have to tell you." His smile changed. The dim light from the lantern cast an eerie shadow across his face. Swallowing hard, she followed him.

He pointed to an old trunk and set the lantern beside it. After sitting, he reached out to her. His hand was covered with sweat and his breathing, uneasy. He cleared his throat. "Angel?"

Wishing she could stop her body from trembling, she scooted closer to him. "What's wrong?"

He twisted his fingers together. "I'm leaving."

Instantly, her chest tightened. "Leavin'?"

"Promise you won't tell anyone." He faced her. "Can I trust you to keep this to yourself?"

His face was so close his breath warmed her cheeks. "Course you can. You're my best friend. But where are you goin'?"

He took her hands, pulled them to his mouth, and breathed on them. "They're so cold." Again, he blew out his warm breath.

"Billy, tell me where you're goin'."

"I can't."

She jerked free from him. "Why? If you ain't gonna tell me, why'd you bring me up here?"

"To say goodbye. I'm joining the Union army."

Every bit of air was sucked from her body. "No, you can't!"

He grabbed her hands and held them firmly. "I look at you and know I have to do this."

"Me? Cuz I'm a slave?" His nod told her everything. "I've never felt like a slave! I belong here." She licked her dry lips. "We could a done like some a the others and left when the war started. But we *wanted* to stay." Tears filled her eyes. "Don't go! What if I never see you again?" Any fear she'd had of the attic was nothing compared to the thought of him going to war.

He pulled her to his chest. His rapidly beating heart thumped against her. "Shh," he whispered. "I'll be fine. I'm fast and smart. I won't let anyone hurt me."

Lifting her head, she looked into his eyes. "You can't be sure a that." Her chin quivered. "Your mama's heart will break." She stared at him, trying to reach his mind with her eyes. "Don't do this."

With a single finger, he pushed back a strand of hair from her face. His gentleness made her heart flutter. "I have to." He breathed slow and steady, and his face inched closer to hers. Never had he been so close.

"No, you don't." Her body warmed from the inside out.

"Yes, I do." His tongue came out of his mouth, moistening his lips.

She didn't back away. For some time she'd thought about kissing him. Ever since she'd seen her mama and Jeriah locked in an embrace and watched their lips move together, she'd wondered what it must feel like.

"Billy," she rasped. His full warm lips covered hers, causing her already rapid heart to beat even stronger.

His arms encircled her and brought her tight against him. She was no longer cold.

As he pulled away, she sensed deep sorrow. In a moment she'd never forget, she wanted to be happy. But the thought of him leaving made happiness impossible.

His head whipped around. "Did you hear that?" He rose to his feet.

She stood quietly, tilting her head toward the door. *Footsteps.* She grabbed his hands. "Billy . . . please? Change your mind."

"I'm leaving tonight." He spoke with urgency, as if every word were his last. "I'm taking Cotton. He's fast and strong. I have my rifle and plenty of ammunition. I've left a letter for my parents. They should find it in the morning." He framed her face with his hands. "Promise me you won't tell them tonight. I need time to get away."

It took every ounce of strength she had to nod her head. "I promise."

"Thank you."

The attic door swung open. Richard lurched forward and swatted her arm. "You're it!" He laughed, then turned and ran away.

"Angel . . ." Billy took her hand and held it to his chest. "I'll never forget you." He gave her a simple kiss.

Numbly, she followed him out the door, down the flights of stairs, and back to the living room where everyone had gathered. She carried the burden of a secret. One which she didn't have to hold for long, but by holding onto for any length, would cause pain.

Across the room, Billy lifted Paulette off the floor. "Where were you hiding?" He tickled her under the arms.

She giggled and squirmed in his grasp. "Behind the drapery in the dining room. Richard saw my feet!"

"You always hide there." He laughed and released her, then glanced at Angel. There was pain behind his laughter.

Paulette put her hands on her hips. "You was hidin' with Angel. Was that fair, Mama?"

"I don't know," Mrs. Denton said, bending down to her level. "I ain't sure 'bout the rules."

Billy put his arm around his mama, then kissed her on the cheek. "I was helping Angel hide. But Richard tagged her, so I wasn't much help at all."

Tears bubbled up inside Angel. She wouldn't let his family see her cry. How could she explain herself? "Excuse me," she said and ran from the room.

* * *

Billy understood, but couldn't follow her. If he intended to carry out his plan, this was part of it. He had to let everyone go and walk away.

His bags were packed. Cotton wasn't used to traveling at night, but he could lead him in the dark. He was a young strong horse. White as the cotton he'd been named for.

"She must gotta use the outhouse," Paulette said, pointing in Angel's direction.

He forced himself to chuckle. "Yes, Paulette. But you shouldn't talk about such things."

Paulette tipped her head and wrinkled her nose, then giggled and covered her mouth.

At least Angel returned for the final countdown to midnight, though her red swollen eyes indicated she'd cried for quite a while.

Her mama hovered close.

What had Angel told her?

If she hadn't kept his secret, Bessie would have already told his mama.

Bessie took Angel out the door, following shouts of *Happy New Year*. Before they left, Angel glanced at him, then whipped her head around so quickly he couldn't comfort her with a smile.

Later, as he tucked Paulette under the covers, the ache in his heart grew. He traced her tiny face with his finger. How much different would she look when he saw her again?

"I'll miss you," he whispered, then kissed her cheek.

He paused and turned to Christina before leaving the room.

"'Night, Billy," she mumbled, then rolled onto her belly.

"Happy New Year." Had he masked his sorrow?

This had been their routine for as long as he could remember. Would his parents forgive him for changing it?

He walked with his father down the hallway. Laughter from Donald's room filled the air.

"Your brothers have always been a greater challenge than you were," his father said with a grin. "Let's help your mother get them to sleep."

"You may have to sit on them," Billy said, laughing.

When they entered Donald's room, his mama sat perched on the side of the bed. "Too many sweets again," she said, shaking her head.

"I'm waiting!" Richard yelled from further down the hallway.

His mama kissed Donald on the forehead. "Go to sleep now."

He nodded toward Billy. "Why don't *he* hafta go to bed?"

Billy crossed his arms over his chest. "I'll be in bed soon enough."

"Hey!" Richard yelled. "I said I'm waiting!"

Donald rolled his eyes. "Better go kiss Richard, Mama. He won't quit yelpin' 'til ya do."

"*I'll* go kiss him," Billy said. He grinned and fled from the room, with his parent's laughter following him.

"No!" Richard covered his face. "I don't want *you* kissin' me!"

Billy knelt on the edge of his bed and playfully tickled him. "Then quit yelling."

"All right!" Richard yelled, then calmed. "Don't kiss me, Billy. I'm too old."

Billy sat back and smiled at his little brother. "Yes, you are." He looked over his shoulder, then leaned toward Richard. "Do you know how lucky we are to have such good parents?"

He nodded, then wrinkled his nose. "Why you being so serious?"

"Just . . . appreciate them." Billy shrugged. "And always be good to Mama."

Richard punched his arm. "I am! You're acting strange."

With his words still hovering in the air, their parents walked into the room.

"Time to turn out your lantern," their father said. "You need to sleep."

"Father's right," Billy said. "Happy New Year, Richard."

Richard replied with a loud yawn, then lay down once he received the goodnight kiss he'd been waiting for from their mama.

When they left Richard's room and his parents told him goodnight, Billy held onto his mama longer than normal. He even gave his father a hug, using the New Year as an excuse.

"I love you," Billy said, nodding to both of them in turn.

They responded accordingly, as they had many times. It may have been an end to a routine for them, but they were words he'd hold in his heart forever.

Chapter 5

"Steady now, Cotton." Billy took the horse's reins and spoke as softly as he could.

The crisp air had a bite to it, making him even more grateful for the scarf and wool coat he'd received for Christmas.

He placed a saddle across Cotton's back and strapped it into place. The horse fidgeted and pawed nervously at the ground.

"I know you don't like the saddle, but we have a long way to go."

He hoisted a pack onto his back, filled with extra clothing and food he'd snuck from the pantry. Small amounts of dried meat, bread, and a canteen full of water were all he could carry. Hopefully it would be enough to get him to Clifton.

He'd tucked a little cloth bag filled with money he'd been saving, into a pocket on the inside of his coat. Most importantly, he had his rifle. He'd had the opportunity to fire it, which pleased his father. They'd made plans to hunt, but that'd never happen. At least not anytime soon.

"Billy?"

He jerked around, his heart pounding in his chest. Angel stood in the stable doorway. He patted Cotton, then hurried toward her. "Why are you here? What if someone saw you?"

She stared at the ground and didn't move.

When he reached her, she was trembling. "You're freezing. You need to go back inside."

Shaking her head, she looked up into his eyes. Though the night was dark, the moonlight illuminated her dark features.

"Angel, please? I don't want you to catch cold."

"Don't go, Billy. I—I don't want you to." Her voice shook, and she sniffled.

He brought her into his arms and held her close. "Don't cry. If the soldiers are right about the war, it'll be over soon. Then I'll be home and you'll be free."

"Promise you'll come home." She nestled against him.

"I promise." He lifted her chin with his fingers. He hadn't stopped thinking about their kiss in the attic. It had been better than he'd ever imagined and over much too quickly.

He cupped his hand against her cheek. "Think of me every day and write in your book." He kissed her forehead, then moved his mouth to hers and pulled her closer, encouraged by her willing response. At that moment, he didn't want to leave, but also realized he was out of line kissing her this way. His parents would never approve.

He took a deep breath and stepped back.

She grabbed his hand and pressed an object into his palm. When he looked at it, he recognized the tiny angel Donald had given her. It had been his first attempt at carving an angel, and they'd thought it looked more like an unusual winged bug.

"Take this with you." She placed her hand over his. "When you look at it, think a me."

"I don't need this to remind me of you."

She sighed. Her warm breath floated like a misty fog into the frigid air. "I still want you to have it. But someday I want it back."

He nodded. "Go inside. I don't want you to get sick. I have to go."

She kissed him quickly on his cheek, then sped away and didn't look back.

He tightened his grip around the tiny carving, then returned to Cotton and swung up into the saddle. Looking one last time around the stable, the ache in his heart grew. Cotton's stablemates snorted and pawed as if knowing something was out of the ordinary.

"C'mon, Cotton." He gave him a gentle nudge. The dark road ahead appeared foreign, though he'd ridden it many times. He had a long way to go, and there was no turning back.

* * *

Angel couldn't sleep. Tossing and turning, she tried to justify keeping her word to Billy. She'd promised to keep his secret, but as every minute passed, he was further away. Her heart tightened as if being crushed inside her chest.

She wiped the tears from her eyes to keep them from falling onto her pillow.

Morning would come. His parents would find the note he'd left behind. Then she'd have to admit she knew he was leaving.

Or did she? She sat upright. *I can pretend I didn't know. Then they won't be mad at me.*

The perfect solution.

With her mind at ease, she sank back into the bedding. A relieved smile curled the corners of her lips. It'd be much easier than bearing the burden of being a part of his plan. Besides, she'd tried to convince him to stay. It wasn't her choice to have him go. It had all been his idea.

Her eyes closed. It'd be dawn soon. Billy was gone. The house would seem larger than ever. Nothing would be the same again.

* * *

"Angel, wake up!" Her mama shook her shoulders.

Angel's eyes popped open. "What time is it?"

Her mama opened the drapery and Angel squinted at the bright rays piercing her eyes.

"Near nine o'clock!" She faced her with hands on her hips. "Ada an me had to fix breakfast 'thout you. Ms. Denton say I should let you sleep. You was up late."

"Yes'm. Sorry 'bout breakfast." She sat up, immediately alert. "What 'bout Spot?"

"Don't worry none. I milked Spot. That cow din't like my cold hands, but I took care a her."

"Thank you, Mama. I promise I'll do the milkin' this afternoon." She flipped the blankets from her body and swung her legs onto the floor. "I'll get dressed an help you clean up."

"That's my girl. Seems Billy was tired, too. He ain't up. Not like Billy to miss a meal!" She chuckled and walked toward the door.

Angel's heart raced. *They don't know yet.*

Once her mama left, she quickly changed from her nightgown into a simple day dress. The heavy blue fabric kept her warm with its long sleeves and high collar.

Though it was only a short distance from the slave quarters to the main house, she put on a wool coat. She walked quickly across the stone path to the back door, which led to the kitchen. She'd grown used to this life. Billy saw it differently, but she was content.

Placing her coat on a wooden peg beside the door, she grabbed a long white apron and tied it around her waist. She then positioned a scarf around her head to cover her long hair.

The stove in the kitchen had been lit for hours. It warmed the room with not only heat from the fire but also the pleasant aroma of baked bread.

Ada looked up from a pan she was scrubbing and grinned. "Sleep good?"

She nodded, then grabbed a broom and began to sweep.

Her mama was slicing potatoes and placing them into a stew pot. "Ain't never known you to be at a loss for words. Sumthin' new for 1865?"

"I'm just tired, Mama." She sighed. "1865 . . ."

Running footfalls in the hallway made them stop what they were doing.

"Douglas!" Mrs. Denton's shrill cry made her cringe.

Her mama set aside her paring knife. "Sumthin' ain't right!" She rushed to the hallway, followed by Ada.

Taking a deep breath, Angel traipsed behind.

"Where's Douglas?" Mrs. Denton asked, grasping her mama's arm. Panic covered her face, but Angel's eyes were drawn to the piece of paper in her hand.

Billy's letter.

"Reckon he's out with the horses," her mama replied. "I'll go find him, Ms. Denton."

Ada led Mrs. Denton to the kitchen table and helped her sit. Within moments, the children were there, and Angel could do nothing more than watch and wait.

When Mr. Denton came in with her mama, his eyes were wide with fear. "Cotton's gone. Jeriah's out looking for him."

"Tell him not to bother," his wife whispered and extended the piece of paper.

"What's this?" He took it from her. The concern on his face grew, drawing his brows together.

Tears trickled down Mrs. Denton's cheek. "A letter from Billy." She covered her face and sobbed.

The sound seeped into every part of Angel's being. She could scarcely contain her own tears, but held them in. She couldn't let on she knew.

As Mr. Denton read aloud the words Billy had obviously chosen carefully, Angel sunk into a chair at the table. Her body trembled. Even the reassuring hand of her mama gave no comfort.

He stopped when Mrs. Wellesley entered the room. "Mother," he said with a pained expression. "You'd better sit down."

How much worse could this get? She'd never seen Mrs. Wellesley so pale. Angel's stomach churned as he continued reading.

"And more than anything, I pray you'll understand my reasons for leaving and can find it in your hearts to forgive me . . ." He lowered the letter to the table.

With a trembling hand, Mrs. Wellesley picked up the letter and blankly stared at it.

"Why?" Mrs. Denton sobbed. "Douglas . . . you gotta go after him!"

No longer able to hold back tears, Angel turned to the man, waiting to hear what he'd say.

Jeriah walked in and cleared his throat. "Ain't no sign a Cotton."

"Billy has him," Mr. Denton said, pointing to the letter. "He's joining the army. Probably been riding for hours."

Angel remained quiet. Yes, he'd been riding for hours. Yet she'd said nothing . . .

Jeriah's eyes passed from Mr. Denton to her and didn't move. Her throat went dry.

"If'n you go after him, where would you look?" Jeriah asked.

Angel breathed a sigh of relief when he shifted his gaze.

Mr. Denton struggled to find the right words. "I don't . . . I don't know. He could be anywhere by now."

"Mama?" Paulette's tiny voice quivered. "I wanna see Billy."

"I know, sweetheart." Mrs. Denton soothed her with a soft voice that shook with every syllable. "Your Pa will find him."

"Cora?" Mr. Denton extended his hand.

She arose from the table, took his hand, and he led her away. They were immediately followed by Mrs. Wellesley and all four children.

Angel watched them leave, then turned to her mama, wide-eyed. "Where are they goin'? What 'bout Billy?"

"They needs to work through it. Mista Denton will figger things out." She took Angel's chin in her hand, lifting her face. "Baby girl, don't cry. They'll find Billy."

"How?" She erupted into an all-out bawl, and gasped, struggling with each sob. "Mr. Denton said he could be anywhere. Anywhere! Oh, Mama!" Grasping her mama's waist, she buried her face into the fabric of her dress.

Jeriah sat beside her and placed his hand on her shoulder. "Now, now, Miss Angel. Things is gonna be fine. I'll hep Mista Denton. We'll find Billy."

She shifted her grasp from her mama to Jeriah's neck and continued bawling. Nothing could stop her. Not her mama's soothing voice or the reassurance from the man she'd always looked to as a daddy. Billy didn't want to be found, and she believed in her heart he never would be.

"Is there sumthin' you know 'bout this?" Jeriah asked, gently patting her back.

She pretended not to hear him and didn't answer.

"Miss Angel?" He spoke firmer. She couldn't avoid him.

Wiping away tears with the back of her hand, she sat upright and looked him in the eye. "Course not. How could I know such a thing?" Her chin quivered and again tears flowed readily.

Ada bustled across the kitchen floor and handed her a cup of water. "That's right, Jeriah. How could the child know that boy was gonna leave?"

"Angel." Her mama pulled up a chair and took hold of her hands. "Baby? Did you know?"

She'd never lied to her mama, at least not about anything of any importance. She'd been taught to tell the
truth, even if it was hard.

She forced out the words. "No, Mama. I didn't know."
Her face contorted as her crying commenced. Not only
was she grieving the pain of Billy's absence, but lying to her
mama crushed her already broken heart.

Chapter 6

Bitter, bitter cold. It stung Billy's face with an icy bite he wished he could escape.

He'd driven Cotton hard all night, stopping briefly for water. For now, he'd stay close to the road, but soon people would come looking for him and he'd have to veer off into the woods.

The sun was rising and he decided to take a short rest.

"C'mon, boy." He led Cotton off the road into a thicket.

Though the ground was hard, cold, and covered in a thin hard layer of snow, they were fortunate it wasn't raining, snowing, or worse. He'd seen ice storms and prayed he'd be spared from that torment.

After tying Cotton to a tree, he gathered as much pine straw as he could to make a bed. Nothing like the down mattress he'd left behind, or having Biscuit to warm him.

Wrapped in a wool blanket, he curled into a ball and shut his eyes. Even with Angel's scarf and gloves, he still shivered.

I wanted this. He refused to regret his decision. But how had his mama reacted when she read his letter? With thoughts of her inevitable tears, he fell asleep . . .

Brrr . . .

Snowflakes melted on his cheeks, and his eyes popped open. *How long did I sleep?*

Cotton nervously pawed the ground; steam blowing from his nostrils.

"Yes, it's time to go."

The instant he removed the wool blanket, the frigid air covered him like a new layer of skin. With quivering fingers, he took off one glove and pulled a piece of dried venison from his pack. Then it struck him. He'd not considered food for Cotton. Had they been home, Jeriah would've fed him oats and hay. But here . . .

"I'm sorry, boy." He stroked Cotton's nose. "Let's find something for *you*."

There was little grass and few leaves on the low-lying bushes. Cotton nosed at the ground and resorted to munching on small sticks. The horse seemed to be looking at him with displeasure. He'd have to find something more. Without Cotton, he'd never make it to Clifton.

"Let's go on, boy."

He'd always been good at direction, knowing how to follow the rise and fall of the sun. Clifton was almost directly east of Memphis and the road was well-traveled. He could easily hear approaching horses and could leave the road at a moment's notice. If necessary, Cotton could outrun any horse.

I wonder what the encampment will look like.

Most likely it would be similar to the one at home. At night they'd probably gather around a campfire and share stories of battles and brave deeds.

Campfire . . .

He puffed out his chest and nudged Cotton's sides. A great adventure lay ahead. He was more than ready to get it started.

* * *

The pen trembled in Angel's hand. She'd done what Billy had asked. *Everything* he'd asked her to do. She'd kept her word and hadn't told anyone he'd left last night.

Now she'd write in the book he gave her.

January 1st, 1865. Billy left today.

Tears welled in her eyes. A single drop smudged one of the words. She wiped it away, but it left a mark. Forever there, to remind her of her sadness. Though she needed no reminder. It was constant. Ever present and tearing her apart from the inside out.

I don't know when he'll be home again. I miss him so much. Why does it hurt so bad?

She stopped.

Because of her difficulty dealing with Billy's absence, her mama had allowed her to stay in her room until she was ready to work.

Even Mrs. Denton had dismissed her from daily chores, but then walked away and shut herself in her own room. She'd hated seeing the look in her eyes. Eyes revealing a greater loss than her own. *Did I betray her?*

Shortly after the war started, Angel had overheard a visitor chastising the Denton's for using slave labor. But because it wasn't outlawed, Mr. Denton abided by his mama's wish and kept them. Mary Wellesley had always had slaves and didn't believe the mill could run without them.

That's why Billy left. He wanted to prove his grandmother was wrong.

Setting aside her book, she flopped down onto her bed and stared upward. Her head throbbed after shedding so many tears. She lay there and listened to the wind whistling through the tiny cracks in the wall.

She pulled a heavy quilt up to her chin. "Where are you, Billy?" She closed her eyes.

Was he warm? Safe? Her lip quivered, and silent tears fell.

* * *

He'd never stolen anything before. Billy handfed the hay to Cotton, feeling guilty with every bite the horse took. He left a coin atop one of the hay bales in the barn, but wasn't eased.

I should've asked to buy it.

But asking would raise suspicion. He couldn't afford being found out. Not so close to home.

"This'll have to last for a while." He patted Cotton's side. "I can't do that again."

Knowing his horse was getting nourishment made him smile. He didn't mind going without, but Cotton needed every ounce of strength. They had another full day of riding ahead.

The long ride gave him plenty of time to think. Every thought drifted back to Angel—the most beautiful girl he'd ever seen. After sharing more than one kiss, he was smitten.

He'd known of young men who'd married at fourteen. A few years ago, he'd have thought them foolish. Now he understood. He wanted to share everything with her.

When I get home, I'll marry her.

"Foolish thought," he muttered. "They'll never allow it. They'll say I'm too young, but that won't be the reason they'll object."

He urged Cotton down the road. "Be glad you're a horse. If we bred you to a mare as black as night no one would care."

Hay in his horse's belly did a world of good. He had the energy to gallop at a steady rate for a number of miles. Billy appreciated the warmth Cotton radiated—almost wishing he was riding bareback in order to feel the heat on his legs and backside.

They stopped frequently for water in nearby streams, but the water he was looking for was the Tennessee River. Clifton sat on its edge. Once he spotted the river, the city would be close.

He'd stayed on course, traveling almost perfectly east and veering only slightly to the north.

Finding it much safer to travel by day and sleep at night, he guided Cotton off the main road into a heavily wooded area before the sun set.

The day had been warmer than the previous two, though not warm enough to bring heat back into the tip of his nose. He wound his scarf across his face and gathered bedding for the night.

"Tomorrow we should be sitting by a fire and eating real food." His teeth chattered. "That is, *I'll* be sitting." He stroked Cotton's mane. "You'll probably be nuzzled up with a warm mare."

The rumbling of his stomach affirmed they needed to get there quickly. He'd run out of food. Water was plentiful, but it didn't satisfy hunger.

Since they were far from home, he considered building a fire, but the butterflies in his belly cautioned him otherwise. He could survive one more night, then everything would be better.

* * *

No longer butterflies—*ravens*—flapped their vicious wings, turning Billy's insides into complete chaos. His throat was dry, and his empty stomach churned. If he were to vomit, nothing would come up but a scarce amount of water. It had been a day and a half since he ate the last morsel of venison in his pack.

Cotton had also lost most of his energy. When the ferryman guided them aboard, he chastised Billy with a single glance. "Got money for a ferry, but can't tend your horse?" He sneered and took Billy's coins.

He fumbled for the right words. "I—I had to get to Clifton quickly. Got a telegram. My uncle's hurt. He—He's at the army encampment."

"No excuse," the man grumbled under a dark, scruffy beard. "That's a fine animal. Deserves better than the likes a you."

Much to his relief, the man remained silent for the rest of the ride across the river.

The ferry jerked to a halt and the man tied it off at the docking post. Billy held onto Cotton's reins and led him off, hoping the man wouldn't speak.

"I'll buy him from ya," the man snarled, then spat over his shoulder.

Billy wasn't about to be intimidated. "He's not for sale." He didn't look at the man and continued onto dry land.

"You steal that horse?" the man yelled.

Courage finally crept through his veins. He turned sharply to face the despicable man. "He's mine! My father gave him to me!" His chest heaved with every breath.

The man rubbed his chin, spat, and didn't utter a word.

"Do you know where the encampment is?" Billy stood rigid and threw his shoulders back.

"Behind the Presbyterian church." The man moved to the rudder to begin the trip back across the river.

Knowing the weight of his body would weaken Cotton even more, Billy kept the reins in his hands and feet on the ground. His heart calmed the further he got from the ferryman. He shouldn't have let the man upset him. He had to keep his wits about him or no one would believe his story.

What if he asks around about my uncle? He'd never been good at lying, but he'd have to become an expert quickly. *All right, William Casey O'Brien, get yourself ready . . .*

* * *

January 4th, 1865. Three days.

Angel couldn't write another word. She'd cried away every tear her body held, and now she felt . . . *numb.*

Convinced Billy's leaving was her fault, she'd had a hard time facing Mrs. Denton. The woman hadn't left her room much since New Year's Day. She'd overheard her mama and Ada talking about how Mr. Denton feared she was becoming sick from grief.

He and Jeriah had been gone for two days following a trail. They'd returned home cold and discouraged, which caused Mrs. Denton to retreat even further.

"Them other children needs her," Ada had said, and her mama agreed.

Did Billy think all this through?

He couldn't have. If he'd seen what it would do to his mama, he'd have never left.

A loud knock made her jump. Closing the book with ink not yet dry, she hopped off her bed and opened the door.

Her mama paraded into the room in one swift motion, then turned and faced her with an expression capable of wilting flowers.

Angel prepared for an inevitable scolding. "Mornin', Mama," she squeaked out.

Her mama's petite frame became enormous. She inhaled deeply and raised her chin in the air. "Mornin'? It be nearly time for dinner!"

She started to respond, but was cut off short.

"I don't care if'n Ms. Denton say you can stay in your room! They's work to be done. I's tired a you sittin' in here weepin' an carryin' on. I said you could wait 'til you was ready to work, but I din't mean for all eternity!" She threw her hands in the air and continued her rant. "I had to milk Spot again! Poor cow was mawin' sumthin' fierce! Ada had to get the eggs from the coop. We din't mind heppin', but they's no excuse for this!" She moved toward her with a finger pointed sharper than a knife. "Billy ain't dead! Stop mournin'!"

"B—But . . ." Her chin quivered and she choked back renewed tears.

"They ain't no buts 'bout it." Her voice had softened. She placed her hands on Angel's shoulders, then kissed her forehead. "I loves you, but I can't stand back an watch you grieve. Bad 'nuff I hasta worry 'bout Ms. Denton. Don't forget what happened to Sophie."

How could she? When Benjamin—one of the mill slaves —left the estate, Sophie cried for days and stopped eating. Everyone said she'd died from a broken heart.

"I won't forget, Mama." She licked her dry lips. "I know Sophie was your friend."

"An you're my baby. You means more to me than any slave or free man on this here earth. If Billy has any sense, he be back." She stepped away and tipped her head. "You shore Billy din't say nothin' to you 'bout leavin'?"

Nervous laughter bubbled out of her. "No, Mama."

"No?" She pursed her lips, then rubbed a finger across her nose. Turning, she walked toward the door. "Come hep with dinner."

"Yes, Mama." She blinked slowly, watching her mama leave. *She doesn't believe me.*

It'd always been a habit of her mama's—rubbing her nose when she felt uncomfortable with a conversation.

I'd better start actin' right, or she'll ask more questions.

Chapter 7

Every step reverberated in his ears, yet the thumping of Billy's heart was even louder. A tingling sensation crept down his back. There were eyes on him.

Cotton nudged him with his large wet nose and blew out a blast of air from his nostrils.

He patted his only friend. "It's all right, Cotton."

Clifton wasn't what he'd expected. At one time it had probably been beautiful. Even now, the leafless trees were towering and majestic, lining the river and scattered throughout the city. But everywhere he looked there were burned out houses and very few people.

To his relief, a man walked toward him carrying a load of wood.

"Excuse me." Billy found his voice. "Can you direct me to the Presbyterian Church?"

The man's eyes shifted between him and Cotton. "You one a *them?*"

He forced a smile. "Yes. Or . . . I will be soon enough."

The man spat at his feet and continued on his way. *What is it about spitting?* He wasn't used to such rude people. He'd just have to keep going and hope to find someone helpful.

In a sudden burst of energy, Cotton reared up with a startled whinny. Before Billy could react, he was immobilized in the strong grip of a very large man. "Don't hurt my horse!"

Another man appeared from nowhere and jerked on Cotton's reins. He struck with his front legs, and the man stumbled backward onto the ground.

"Damn horse!" The man stood, brushed off his pants, and adjusted his hat.

Billy's heart thumped. He'd recognize that uniform anywhere. *Union blue.*

"What'd you expect?" Billy spoke amidst fear. "He's trying to protect me." The arms holding him grasped even tighter, taking his breath.

"Who are you?" the man with the vice grip asked.

Billy swallowed hard. "William O'Brien. I—I came here to enlist." Though the man was hurting him, he wasn't about to let him know it and forced out each word.

"Did ya now?" The man's mouth was nearly inside his ear.

"Y—Yes. I want to fight."

The man released him and crossed to the other, erupting with laughter. "Fight? You?"

Adding to his agony, the other man joined in. Being spit at had been easier to handle.

Able to breathe again, Billy stood his ground and grabbed Cotton's reins. "Why are you laughing? I'm quite serious."

The strong man laughed even harder. "Did ya hear the boy, Taylor? He's *quite* serious!"

"I'm not a boy! I'm eighteen and I can fight as good as any man." Planting his legs solidly with his feet spread apart, Billy positioned himself for a fight, bringing up his fists.

Taylor shook his head and advanced toward him. "Eighteen?"

Billy gulped. The man towered over him—about the size of his father—a solid six feet and three inches. "Yes." He stood tall and puffed out his chest.

Taylor erupted into a different kind of laughter, this time patting him firmly on the back. "You've got nerve, boy." He looked at the other man. "Calm down, Duffy. He's no threat."

Duffy had the curliest black hair Billy'd ever seen. It poked out beneath his Hardee hat. "Boy may not be a threat, but that stallion is gonna cause trouble."

"He's hungry!" Billy feared what they might do and pulled Cotton closer.

Taylor shook his head and grimaced at Duffy. "The way you're acting, you'd think it was *you* he'd kicked. If I hadn't jerked back he'd have busted my ribs. Like the boy said, he was trying to protect him." Patting Cotton's side, he motioned his head up the road. "Let's take them to the camp. Captain Granger can decide what he wants to do with them."

Duffy smacked his lips, gesturing to Cotton. "May wanna eat 'im." He had the nerve to laugh.

The man probably *had* eaten a horse or two. Billy's ribs still ached from his crushing hold.

"Don't worry—*William*, is it?" Taylor asked. "I won't let him eat your horse. He likes showing his muscles. But unless Captain Granger tells us otherwise, we have to keep you both alive. For now." He flashed a grin.

What have I gotten myself into?

A nervous laugh emerged from his dry throat. "Yes, it's William, but folks call me *Will*." The lie came out easier than he'd expected. "My horse is Cotton."

"Well, *Will*, I'm Sergeant Taylor and that brute ahead of us is Duffy." Taylor's remark prompted Duffy to turn and give him a gesture Billy'd never seen before accompanied by a sneer. "Don't mind him." Taylor chuckled. "He's not an officer and he's fairly harmless."

"Tell my ribs," Billy said, rubbing his ribcage. "I think Duffy's stronger than Cotton."

Duffy glanced over his shoulder. "Boy's growin' on me."

Cotton raised his head and snorted.

"I still may hafta eat his horse," Duffy added, then increased his pace.

* * *

"I assume you searched him," Captain Granger said, studying Billy.

The man was what he expected in an officer; well spoken, sharply dressed in a well-tended uniform, and respected by the other soldiers. Not as tall as Taylor, but he had broad shoulders and a large build. His face was framed with grayish-black sideburns.

"Didn't strip him naked, Captain," Duffy said. "Gave him a good pat-down. Found a rifle and ammunition in his gear. Not much else."

He'd come to realize Duffy enjoyed aggravating him. Not wanting to give him any satisfaction, Billy stood erect and faced the captain squarely.

The man circled him. "And the stallion?"

"Took him to the church. Stabled him with the other horses." He winked.

Captain Granger saw the gesture and shook his head. "That will be all, Duffy. Tell Sergeant Taylor I want him here in fifteen minutes."

"Yes, sir." Duffy saluted, then turned sharply and left.

Though the air outside was brisk, the interior of the large canvas tent was warm. An earthy scent filled Billy's nose. He held his breath waiting to see what the captain would say, and a trickle of nervous sweat dripped from his brow.

"At ease," Captain Granger said.

The command made him smile, already feeling like a part of the company. "Yes, sir." He pulled his shoulders back, wishing once again he was taller than five feet and five inches.

The captain stepped back and crossed his arms over his chest. "Why are you here?"

"To enlist, sir. To fight." He remained rigid. His heart pounded.

"You understand the war's nearly over? Why now?"

"Why not . . . sir?" He looked down. Maybe it hadn't been the best answer.

"How do I know you're not a guerrilla?" He rubbed his chin. "Why should I trust you?"

"If you don't trust me, why'd you dismiss Duffy?"

The captain's eyebrows rose and the corners of his mouth curled upward. "You remind me of my son. But he's only fourteen. Not *eighteen* as you are."

Choosing to remain silent, Billy stood still. Though he didn't take his eyes off the captain, he took in the surroundings; the bookcase filled to capacity, the neatly-folded uniform on the shelf beside the perfectly-made cot, and the picture of a woman on a table close to his pillow.

His stomach grumbled and caught the captain's attention. "How long since you've eaten?"

"Nearly two days, sir."

"I thought as much. I'll see to it you're fed, then I want you to return home."

Billy's heart raced. "No!" The word slipped out before he could stop it. "Please, sir . . . I don't have a home to go to."

"No home?"

He shook his head. "My father died when I was a baby. My mother recently passed." Stopping momentarily to digest the horrific lie he was concocting, he breathed deeply and pressed on. "All I have left is my horse. Please don't send me away."

The captain pulled out a chair. "Sit down, son. You're looking a might shaky."

He gladly complied. "Thank you, sir." Nervously, he wrung his hands.

The flap of the tent parted, drawing their attention.

"You asked to see me, Captain?" Taylor stepped inside and saluted. Glancing in Billy's direction, he offered a genuine smile.

"Yes, Sergeant. I'm placing Mr. O'Brien in your care. See to it he's fed and has a place to sleep. I've not yet made up my mind what to do with him."

"Yes, sir." He took a deep breath. "Sir, there's a slight problem with his stallion."

"Cotton?" Billy jumped to his feet and crossed to Taylor. "What's wrong with my horse?"

The captain cleared his throat. "Sit down, Mr. O'Brien." His firm tone demanded action.

Billy sat, but his heart couldn't be stilled.

"Go on, Sergeant." Captain Granger cast a sideways glance at Billy.

Taylor removed his hat and scratched his head. "One of the mares is in heat. The stallion acted in a natural way. One of the men tried to pull him away and the horse tried to bite him. They determined it was best to let him finish his business."

"Can he be controlled?" The captain crossed his arms. "We can't have a biting stallion upsetting the other horses —or the men, for that matter."

Billy couldn't remain seated. "I can control him!" He gulped when the captain glared at him and quickly added, "Sir."

"It appears you can't control *yourself*." Lowering his arms, the captain tilted his head, contemplating. He returned his attention to Taylor. "For tonight, let the horse be. Perhaps now he'll settle down. It will give me time to decide what to do with both of them."

This wasn't how things were supposed to happen. *What did I do wrong?*

"Sir?" Though Billy's heart continued to pound, he had to try.

"Yes, Mr. O'Brien?" Captain Granger spoke with little-remaining patience.

"I'm sorry about my horse, but he's young and spirited, and—"

"And that's the problem. He's too much like his master."

I remind him of his son. He thinks I'm too young.

"Please, sir? I can do better. I'll do whatever you ask. I—I just want the chance. I want to be a soldier." Angel's image flashed before him. He couldn't fail her. "Please?"

The captain stared without a response, then turned away. "Sergeant, get him some food."

"Yes, sir." Taylor saluted. He then motioned to Billy, pointing to the open flap.

With a heavy heart, he followed him.

Chapter 8

"I reckon the floor's clean 'nuff," Ada said, shaking her head.

Angel looked up. Her arms had been moving back and forth, but her mind wasn't focused on the instrument in her hands.

"Sorry, Ada." She placed the broom in the corner. "Want me to peel potatoes?"

Her mama bustled into the kitchen with an armful of wood. "'Til her mind's right, don't let her handle no knife." She proceeded to the stove.

Angel plopped down at the kitchen table. "What can I do?"

Her mama huffed. "Long as you been alive, an you cain't think what's to be done? They's a basket a laundry needs tendin' for starters." She fed wood into the stove, stoking the flame.

"Don't feel like doin' laundry." She mindlessly traced the pattern of the wood grain.

Her mama was at her side in a flash. "What'd you say?"

She sat upright. "Sorry, Mama. I—I don't feel good."

Her mama sat beside her. "I knows how you been feelin'. Trust your mama, baby girl. Work will get your mind off Billy."

"It's not the same 'round here with him gone."

"I know." She stroked Angel's cheek. "But I believes in my heart he be back."

"Your mama's right," Ada added, while vigorously scrubbing potatoes. "He be back."

It was late afternoon. Four days since Billy had left. The house had never been so quiet. Mr. Denton was at the mill, the children were having lessons in the library with their private teacher, and Angel assumed both Mrs. Denton and Mrs. Wellesley were in their rooms, resting.

She missed hearing laughter, but more than anything she missed her best friend.

A smile warmed her face, remembering his kiss. No, he was more than just a friend.

Her thoughts of him were those of a woman, not a girl. Though not yet thirteen, in many ways she was already a woman. Her woman's time had come for the first time six months ago. Maybe that was what he'd seen in her. The *change* that made her different.

"Much better!" her mama exclaimed. "Look at her, Ada! She be smilin'!"

Ada waddled across the floor, dripping water from her hands. "Praise the Lawd!" She kissed her on the forehead. "I missed that smile."

Angel was about to respond when she caught sight of Mrs. Denton standing in the doorway. "How are you feelin' today, Mrs. Denton?"

She was pale and weak, not having eaten much since Billy left. "Ada, I'd like some tea."

"Yes'm," Ada replied, and began preparing the water.

Mrs. Denton sat beside Angel. "Bessie, I need to talk to you an Angel."

Her tone caused Angel's stomach to knot. This wouldn't be pleasant.

Her mama must have sensed it, too. When she joined them, her eyes were wide and she immediately started rubbing her nose. "Yes'm?"

"Bessie, we've known each other for a long time now. I trust you more than most anyone. An Angel—you grew up here. I hafta believe I can trust you, too."

"Yes'm," Angel said with a weak smile.

Mrs. Denton rested her hands on the table, looking like she might cry. "'Fore Billy left he had a talk with me. At the time, I figgered he was askin' questions, just to be askin'. But when I think back on it, I reckon it had sumthin' to do with him leavin'."

Angel's heart skipped beats, anticipating what was to come. Then Mrs. Denton turned and looked directly into her eyes. *I'm gonna be sick.*

"Did sumthin' happen 'tween you an Billy?" The woman's eyes didn't move.

Lord, what do I say? A whimper popped from her throat. She tried to cover it with a cough.

"Angel?" Her mama's stern voice shook her to her core, but when she didn't respond, she turned her attention again to Mrs. Denton. "What did Billy say?"

"He wanted to know if Angel was a Negro or white." She stood and hovered over them. "And . . ." She took in a large amount of air. "Whether she'd marry a white or colored man."

What? Was he thinkin' 'bout marrying me?

"She ain't even thirteen!" Her mama exclaimed. "Why was he askin' such things?"

The pained look in her mama's eyes tore Angel apart. But she had no idea what to say.

"Angel?" Mrs. Denton spoke much softer. "What happened 'tween you an Billy?"

Her mama grabbed her hand tightly. "You tell Ms. Denton."

Unable to hold it in any longer, Angel burst out, "He kissed me!" She then laid her head on the table and hid her face with her hands.

"Do what?" her mama gasped. "You has no business kissin' anyone! 'Specially Billy!"

"Why?" Suddenly, nothing mattered anymore. She was determined to speak her mind. "Cuz he's white?" Her voice quivered. "What 'bout you? You did more than *kiss* a white man!"

An abrupt slap across the face silenced her. Tears formed, but she tried not to cry. Her mama had never struck her before.

"Oh, baby. Forgive me." She arose from her chair and moved to her, wrapping her arms around her.

Mrs. Denton stood, choking back tears. "You reckon it's time to tell her 'bout her pa?"

At the mention of her daddy, her mama's body tensed. The look of horror she directed at Mrs. Denton was one she'd never seen before.

"No, Ms. Denton," she muttered with a rapidly shaking head. "No."

"What 'bout my daddy?" Angel asked, disregarding her mama. Perhaps the slap across the face had made her less sympathetic.

Her mama stood, all the while shaking her head. "Don't make me tell, Ms. Denton."

"If it's 'bout my daddy, I need to know. I *deserve* to know." Her mama had told her very little about the man, aside from the fact he was white and died before she was born.

"No," she mumbled again, then bolted out the back door.

Ada set a steaming cup of tea on the table. "Here's your tea, Ms. Denton. Is it a'right if'n I sees to Bessie?"

Mrs. Denton nodded silently. "Thank you," she added, in a whisper.

Tempted to follow her mama, Angel glanced toward the door, but then returned her focus to Mrs. Denton. "Can *you* tell me 'bout my daddy?"

"It ain't my place to tell you anythin', Angel." She sipped her tea and looked over the top of the cup. "When your ma's ready, she'll tell you."

"But, you said . . ."

"I said I reckon it's time you know."

How the conversation had turned from her and Billy to her parents, she wasn't sure. But she couldn't be more grateful the focus was off her. "Then, I reckon I should go talk to Mama."

She started to rise but Mrs. Denton grabbed her hand. "Billy left cuz a you, didn't he?"

Feeling her chest tighten more than the grip on her hand, Angel panicked. "I—I . . ."

The woman's eyes dropped and her body folded into itself. "If I said you was free an you could leave, would you?"

Angel's chin quivered. "You want me to leave?" Her words came out in gasping breaths.

"Angel, please answer my question. If you was free, would you go?"

"I don't wanna leave." She couldn't hold back tears. "This is my home. Y'all are my family. Please don't make me go!"

Mrs. Denton's eyes filled with pity. "I was gonna give you your freedom. It's what Billy wanted." Her shoulders shook and her tears flowed freely.

"Please don't cry, Mrs. Denton." Angel attempted to soothe her with a gentle hug. "I tried to talk him into stayin'." The words left her mouth without thought, and the moment she spoke them Mrs. Denton became rigid.

"What?" She pushed her away. Slowly. Steadily.

Angel sucked in her breath, covering her mouth with her hand. Not knowing what to say, she fled from the kitchen, following her mama's footsteps.

Her feet couldn't carry her fast enough. She stumbled on the stone path and nearly fell to the ground. Vision blurred by never-ending tears made the short span difficult to follow. Bursting into her home, she raced to her bedroom and slammed the door shut.

Not long after, Mrs. Denton's voice—mixed with her mama's—erupted from the other room. Forcefully stopping her own blubbering, she arose from the bed and put her ear to the door.

"She knew!" Mrs. Denton yelled and sobbed simultaneously. "She should a told us! We could a stopped him!" She'd never heard Mrs. Denton raise her voice this way.

"Now, Ms. Denton." It was Ada's voice. "You needs to calm down."

"No! Cuz a her my boy could die!" Her frantic words nauseated Angel.

She was about to open the door to confront her, when Mrs. Denton cried out. The sound made her freeze. "She's just like her pa! Sneaky and connivin'! If I hadn't killed him, he'd a gotten rid a her an I'd still have Billy!"

Angel stumbled backward and fell onto the bed. *Mrs. Denton killed my daddy?*

Without having time to digest what she'd heard, her mama's loud voice made everything worse. "How could you? Angel's in her room! She heard every word you say!"

"Good!" Mrs. Denton screamed. "'Bout time she knew the truth 'bout her pa!"

Her mama's agonized sobs made listening unbearable. "You know what he did to me. It wadn't my fault. It ain't Angel's fault neither. She's a good girl."

"A good girl would a told what she knew. We've done ev-erythin' for her. I ain't never gonna trust her again." Mrs. Denton's voice had calmed, but her words were even more hurtful.

Angel couldn't take it any longer. Rising on shaky legs, she opened the door to face the women she'd always looked up to and respected.

Scared to speak, she pushed the words from her lips. "He asked me not to tell."

All three women stared at her, so she repeated it louder. "Billy asked me not to tell. All I did was keep my promise."

Her mama was beside her in an instant, wrapping her loving arms around her and holding her close. "I'm sorry, baby."

"Oh, Mama." She seemed frail and helpless. It tore her heart in two. "Mama? Is it true? Did she . . ." She glanced at Mrs. Denton, who'd gone silent as soon as she'd entered the room. "Did Mrs. Denton kill my daddy?"

Her mama led her to the sofa "It's true. But she had every right. He was . . . tryin' to have his way with her. *Be* with her. You understan'?"

When Angel's cycles started, her mama had explained why she was bleeding and what men and women did together. Having told her the reason was to make babies, she couldn't understand why he'd want to do that with just anyone.

"But, why? I thought he wanted to make a baby with *you* and that's why you had me. I thought you meant sumthin' to him—that he loved you."

"Marcus Giles loved himself. Used women for pleasure. He wadn't a good man."

It couldn't be true. She believed her parents had been in love.

"Am I like him?" Angel asked Mrs. Denton, who immediately shifted her gaze.

Her mama took her face in her hands and peered into her eyes. "You're *nuttin'* like that man. You're good. You're my Angel."

Mrs. Denton walked out the door, slamming it shut.

Angel shuddered. "I hurt her, Mama. I didn't mean to. I was only doin' what Billy wanted."

Her mama rocked her back and forth. "She be fine in time. She be hurtin' an needs someone to blame. Ms. Denton's a good woman. What your daddy done was wrong. But that was him, not you. You gots a good heart." She let out a long slow breath. "You shouldn't a lied to me."

"I'm sorry, Mama. But Billy—"

Her mama stopped her with a single finger across her lips. "I understan'."

For a time they said nothing. But then, Angel had to ask. "What did Mrs. Denton mean when she said he was gonna get rid a me?"

Her mama's eyes closed. Tears trickled from her lids onto her cheeks. "We was on a boat." She opened her eyes, but looked somewhere far away. "He was gonna throw you in the river when you came. Mista and Ms. Denton brought me here. Saved us both."

"He'd a drown me?"

Her mama nodded and swallowed hard. "I would a jumped in the water after you."

Angel had a new respect for her mama. And none whatsoever for the memory of her daddy.

Chapter 9

"You can sit there." Sergeant Taylor pointed to an up-ended log.

Billy would have sat on the ground if need be. Anywhere close to the blazing fire. While trying to get comfortable, he inhaled the aroma of wood smoke and roasting meat.

If it hadn't been for Captain Granger's threat to send him home, he'd have been happy. He was surrounded by soldiers. The scruffy faces proved a good shave must be hard to come by—or maybe they didn't see the need. Whiskers weren't a problem for him, but lack of them was further proof of his youth.

Everyone seemed at ease; some laughed and told stories. One man even played a harmonica.

"What are they roasting?" Billy pointed to the fire. There was meat skewered on the ends of bayonets. He'd never imagined they'd be used to roast meat.

"Rabbit." Taylor gestured to the largest. "Those smaller ones are squirrels."

"Oh." His stomach longed for Ada's pork roast.

Taylor cast a sideways glance. "They're making do until supplies come from Nashville. When we first arrived here, meat wasn't a problem. Local farmers had plenty."

"You bought their livestock?"

Taylor chuckled and shook his head. "We're at war, Will. We foraged what we needed."

Foraged? It sounded like stealing. No wonder the locals treated him poorly. The soldiers at the estate were different. *Why didn't they forage our livestock?*

"You don't approve?" Taylor asked.

"It's not that . . ." What would he say? "I never thought about it that way. Helping yourself to whatever you need." *Taking hay for Cotton was hard enough.*

Taylor stood. "Come with me."

Billy followed him, slightly confused. "I thought we were eating at the campfire."

"Officers have privileges others don't. Since Captain Granger told me to feed you, I'm taking you to the mess tent. Unless you'd prefer a greasy squirrel over sweet potatoes and corn mash."

"I thought you were waiting for supplies?"

"We are. For the men. Stores are always set aside for officers."

Billy gladly went with him. Not only was he given a hot sweet potato and mash, but also bread and beans. They sat comfortably in wooden chairs, though Taylor wasn't eating.

"Much better than squirrel," Billy mumbled, shoveling in food. Every tidbit that touched his tongue tasted like the finest food he'd ever eaten. "Why aren't you eating?"

"I'm not an officer. But there's more if *you* want it."

"Won't the other men be angry I'm eating in here?"

"Captain's orders. I'll be honest with you, Will." Taylor leaned in. "You'll most likely be sent from camp tomorrow. The other men won't have time to be angry."

He instantly lost his appetite and set down his spoon. "I don't understand. Why doesn't the captain want me?"

Taylor folded his hands and looked directly at him. "The war will be over soon. I'm sure you noticed how relaxed the men were at the campfire. They're biding their time until orders come telling them they can go home."

"There's no guarantee it'll be over soon. I know there are places the Confederates are fighting hard. That's where I want to go. Somewhere I can make a difference."

"Are you that anxious to be killed?" Taylor's brow wrinkled.

"No. I just need to be a part of this." Why'd everyone seem to think he'd die? He stared at the remaining food on his metal plate and pushed it around mindlessly with his spoon.

Taylor leaned back in his chair. "Are you eighteen? Truthfully?"

He'd come to respect the man, but Billy couldn't risk changing his story. "Yes, I am. Turned eighteen this past month."

"A Christmas baby?"

"Seventeenth of December." He made a mental note of this detail he might have to repeat.

Rising to his feet, Taylor cleared his throat. "I'll do what I can for you. For now, eat. You'll need your strength regardless of what you're asked to do."

"Yes, sir. Thank you, sir." *There's still hope.* "Sir? What do I do when I'm finished?"

Taylor grinned. "Go back to the campfire. You may learn some things from the other men. For starters, call me *Sergeant*, not sir. I'm not an officer."

As Taylor walked away, heat filled Billy's cheeks. Yes, he had things to learn and he certainly needed his strength. But he'd never return home. Not now. If Captain Granger wouldn't let him stay, he'd find another encampment. He wouldn't stop until he became a soldier.

* * *

The sun was setting. Along with lack of light, the temperature plummeted. To add to Billy's discomfort, random drops of frozen rain pelted down from the sky. Fortunately, they stopped falling as quickly as they'd started, but far-off rumbles of thunder threatened worse weather.

He'd done as he was told, and after cleaning his plate, walked with a full stomach and a heavy heart to the campfire. Self-conscious, he had no doubt some of the soldiers were whispering about him. Ignoring the glances and stares, he focused on the crackling fire and its warmth.

He opted to sit on the ground with his back resting against a log. Though surrounded by twelve other men, loneliness weighed him down. *What am I supposed to learn from them?*

Several soldiers left randomly, then returned appearing more cheerful than when they'd left. They patted each other on the back and chuckled, while speaking with voices so low only they could hear. What had they been doing that made them so proud of themselves?

"That white stallion yours?"

Billy looked up. The soldier who'd asked the question didn't seem much older than him and had actually smiled.

"Yes, he's mine." Panic struck, and he started to stand. "Is he all right?"

The man held up a hand. "Don't get up. He's fine. Had to tie him up, but he's been fed and watered." He sat down beside him. "I'm Jackson. Folks call me Jack."

"I'm Will." It was the first time he felt like an equal.

Jack extended his bayonet into the fire. Something other than meat had been wound around the end.

"What are you cooking?" Billy pointed to the weapon.

"Dough." He laughed. "Reckon it'll be bread or a biscuit when it's done."

"Is it good?"

"Nah," he smirked. "But it fills the hole in my gut."

Another soldier on the far side of the campfire stood to give his place to someone else. Once again the returning man received a congratulatory *pat on the back.*

Billy pointed. "You know what that's all about?"

"Jessica." Jack shook his head.

"Jessica?"

"She's one a them *soiled doves.* Came from Nashville. The men can't get enough of her."

He'd never heard of a soiled dove, but was afraid to show his ignorance. "I didn't think women were allowed in camp."

"Women aren't." Jack chuckled. "Jessica's sumthin' special. Or so I've heard. I haven't tried her myself."

"Tried her?"

Jack nudged him. "You know—*poked* her."

Billy's stomach flipped. Though he'd never heard that crude reference used before, it wasn't difficult to figure out what he meant.

"Oh." He lowered his voice and spoke through the side of his mouth. "She's a prostitute."

Jack pulled his bayonet from the flames, then removed the hot bread with careful fingers. "Course she is. But she don't like to be called that. Reckon she figgers she's doin' us a service. Her part to help win the war." He nodded toward the men who'd enjoyed her services. "War can be hell, but they're smilin'."

Jack was right. The men looked happy. But Billy'd always been taught it was something two married people did. Something he might do with Angel one day.

"Damn, that was good!"

Duffy. Unlike the other men, every word Duffy uttered was meant to be heard by everyone. The soldiers erupted into laughter when he grabbed his crotch and strutted toward the fire. "Jess won't never be the same again!"

This could *not* have been the lesson Taylor wanted him to learn. Billy knew nothing about Jessica, but pitied her having been bed by Duffy.

"Hey!" Duffy's obnoxious voice stung his ears. "William O'Brien!"

If Billy could have melted into the ground and disappeared, he would have. Hoping Duffy would leave him alone, he chose not to respond.

Jack prodded him, but he shook his head and Jack backed down.

"I said . . . *Little Willy!*" Duffy laughed heartily, then looked at the men next to him. "Not a problem *I* have!" Again, he grabbed his crotch, and the men hooted.

Was he the only one that found Duffy offensive? Adding to his distress, the man circled the campfire and made his way toward him.

"Has Taylor's pamperin' made ya deaf?" Duffy poked his rump with his foot.

"I didn't think you were speaking to *me.*" Billy tried to keep his voice from shaking.

"I don't see any other little Willies 'round here."

He'd had enough and stood to face the unbearable man. "What's your problem with me?"

Duffy took a step back and chuckled. "No problem. Just like messin' with ya." Billy nearly fell to the ground when he draped his muscular arm around his shoulder. "Think of it this way. I'm breakin' ya in. You should thank me."

Feeling like the center of attention, Billy tried to back out of Duffy's grasp, but he pulled him in closer. "Wanna try sumthin' good, boy?"

Trying to control his breathing, Billy said nothing.

The heat from Duffy's breath covered his ear. "Wanna meet Jessica? Become a *real* man?"

"Private Duffy!" Taylor's voice couldn't have been more welcome.

He released him immediately.

"Jackson," Taylor commanded. "You'll be sharing your tent with Mr. O'Brien. I'm sure he's tired. Go to supply and get him a gum blanket, then show him where he'll be sleeping."

"Yes, Sergeant," Jack said, jumping to his feet.

As quickly as Taylor arrived, he was gone again.

Billy brushed past Duffy and followed Jack away from the campfire. The instant chill in the air stung, but he was glad to be away from the intolerable man.

* * *

After the horrible encounter with Mrs. Denton, Angel didn't want to return to the main house. Honestly, she doubted they wanted her there. The slave house had never been more appealing. Though the rooms were small and the furnishings simple, it was home.

She shared the house with her mama and Ada, and at one time Sophie and a mill worker named Esther. Shortly after Sophie died, Esther ran away, giving the three of them their own rooms. She enjoyed having a place to call her own.

Might as well get it over with. Angel opened the back door, hoping the Denton's were elsewhere.

She set down the pail of still-warm milk and was overcome with a rush of energy—a mixture of commotion and loud voices.

"As much as you can fit in the bag," Mr. Denton said, pointing to a large leather satchel.

Ada was bent over in the pantry pulling out canned goods.

Everyone was in the kitchen, even Jeriah.

Her mama approached her, filled with excitement. "Baby, they knows where Billy went!"

"What?"

Paulette tugged at her sleeve. "Daddy's gonna get Billy!"

Bending down, Angel picked her up and hugged her. "I know you miss him. I miss him, too."

Mrs. Wellesley paced in the doorway. "Hurry, Douglas. Billy could be frozen by now!"

Mr. Denton stopped what he'd been doing. "Mother, please. Don't say such things in front of the children."

"Forgive me." She hurried down the hall to her room.

Paulette wiggled out of Angel's arms. "Daddy? Billy won't be frozed, will he?"

"No, sweetheart." He bent to her level. "Your brother's smart and knows how to take care of himself. I'm sure he and Cotton are fine." He kissed her cheek, then she rushed into her mama's open arms.

"Where are you goin'?" Angel managed to ask.

Mr. Denton glanced at her, but didn't respond. He finished placing items in the bag.

"We's goin' to Clifton," Jeriah said. "Mista Denton got one a them soldiers to talk."

"Where's Clifton?"

"More than three days ride."

Angel's heart sank. *Three days?* It would be almost a week before they'd return.

A week to worry.

"Is there anythin' I can do to help?" she asked, but no one responded.

Mr. Denton hoisted the pack onto his back. "Let's go, Jeriah. We're wasting daylight."

"Be careful," Mrs. Denton said with tear-filled eyes. She then stood on her tip-toes and kissed her husband. "Bring Billy home."

"I'll do everything I can." He nodded to Jeriah.

Angel's mama held onto Jeriah's arm. She'd never seen the two of them show their affections around the Denton's and watched in awe as she kissed Jeriah firmly on the lips. "I love you." Her voice trembled.

The room fell silent.

Jeriah gaped at her. "I loves you, too, Bessie." He followed Mr. Denton out the door.

After they left, the kitchen emptied, leaving Angel alone with her mama and Ada. It was the way she'd hoped it would be when she first came in, but now it felt cold. Completely vacant.

"Why you lookin' so sad?" her mama asked. "They knows where Billy is. In no time they be bringin' him home."

Angel refused to cry, no matter how much her body longed for it. "Did you see how the Denton's looked at me? Or, *didn't* look at me? They hate me. I know they do!"

"Hate's an ugly word, baby girl. They be angry, but they don't hate you."

Though she wanted to, Angel didn't agree with her mama.

"Put a smile on your face, Angel. In a week's time, Billy'll be home an everythin' will be fine again." Her mama's face twisted into a playful grin. "'Cept we'll hafta see 'bout that kissin'. Cain't have that goin' on. You're too young."

Not wanting to talk about what she and Billy would or wouldn't do, she decided to change the conversation. "What 'bout that kiss with Jeriah, Mama? What was that all 'bout?"

"Don't know what came over me." She covered her mouth and giggled like a girl.

Ada burst out laughing. "*I* does! That man's fine! Got my heart pumpin' just watchin' you!"

"Shame on you, Ada!" She swatted her with a towel.

Watching the two of them made Angel laugh. Her mama was right. Billy'd be home in a week. Until then, she'd stop feeling sorry for herself and write in her book.

Chapter 10

Numerous campfires dotted the grounds known as Stockade Hill. All were surrounded by soldiers who gave Billy little regard as he passed by them on his way to Jack's tent. The naked trees scattered throughout the encampment offered little shelter.

"We're the smart ones," Jack said with a laugh. "It's fixin' to rain sumthin' fierce. We'll be in my tent 'fore it comes down."

With his newly acquired gum blanket draped over his shoulders, the winter air didn't penetrate Billy's clothing. Heavy cotton on one side and rubberized on the other. Perfect for keeping him dry and warm.

Jack's tent was a small dog tent, open on both ends. Nothing like the enclosed tents the officers stayed in.

Before entering, Jack lifted his face to the weather. "Wind's comin' from the west. I'm throwin' an extra gum over that end." He nodded to the far side of the tent.

"You stay dry in here?"

"Dry as possible. Be glad you chose our side. Most grey-backs don't have tents."

Billy'd been carrying around his pack all day, hoarding it like his life's blood. When Duffy searched him, he'd feared he'd keep it, but handed it back after examining the contents. However, his rifle had been confiscated. Hopefully he'd get it back, too.

"That looks warm," Jack said, eying the wool blanket Billy pulled from his pack.

He smoothed it on the rock-hard ground. "It is, but not like the gum blanket."

"Put the gum over you in case the rain blows in." Jack set the lantern he'd been carrying at the enclosed end of the tent, then settled into his bedroll.

Billy wound his scarf around his neck, then removed his coat and rolled it into a ball to use as a pillow. Smelling the strong scent of rubber, he pulled the gum blanket up around him and lay back. If it wasn't so cold, he'd be enjoying this experience.

Jack dimmed the lantern, then lay back with a sigh. "Can't figger out why you're here, Will. I can't wait to go back to Kentucky. Been here eighteen months. I miss my Sally."

"Your wife?"

"Not yet. Just started courtin' 'fore I joined up. She's why I ain't done Jessica."

Having no intentions of going anywhere near Jessica himself, Billy understood. "I think that's good. I was always taught it's supposed to be done with your wife."

"Me, too. My folks didn't like me courtin' Sally, but when I knew I was enlistin' I asked to. Her folks didn't care. She has eight sisters. I reckon they like the idea of gettin' rid a one of 'em." He started to laugh, but then suddenly fell quiet. "'Fore I left," he whispered. "Sally gave herself to me. Said she was afraid she'd never see me again."

Having Jack confide something so private sealed their friendship. "That's why you want to go home? To marry her and make it right?"

"I got to." He let out a long breath. "She had a baby. I got a son. Heard 'bout him in a letter."

"Then I hope for your sake the war ends soon." Billy couldn't imagine what he must be feeling. He missed Angel more than anything, but to miss out on the birth of a child?

Angel . . . He jerked upright and grabbed his coat, blindly searching the pockets.

"You all right?" Jack asked.

Billy calmed when he felt the small wooden angel in his grasp. "I am now. Thought I'd lost something." Balling up his coat again, he lay back down.

"Will? You think what I done with Sally was wrong?"

Billy rolled onto his side and faced Jack's shadowed figure. As if on cue, frozen rain beat hard against the canvas. "You probably should've waited, but you can't change it now. Do you love her?"

"More than anythin'."

"Then I don't think it was *completely* wrong. I understand how it could happen."

"Do *you* have a girl waitin' for you?"

Closing his eyes, he pictured Angel. "No. I don't have anyone anymore."

"That why you're here?"

"Yes." He couldn't say more. "Jack? What happened here? Most of the houses I saw were burned."

"We're at war. Plain an simple. Most a the folks in Clifton sided with the rebels. Didn't want us here. But this place is important—what with the river an all. General Forrest brought a raid here in sixty-two. Union drove him out and we've kept a company here since."

"The Union army burned the houses?"

"Course they did. Like I said, this is war. If folks didn't surrender, we burned 'em out."

The rain came down harder and the wind picked up causing the sides of the tent to billow. The icy breeze filled the tiny dwelling.

"Jack? Have you ever had to kill anyone?" Billy dreaded the answer.

After a long drawn out minute, Jack sighed. "More than one," he muttered. "We best go to sleep. Long day t'morra. Cap'n likes to drill us early."

Incapable of closing his eyes, Billy stared into the darkness listening to the rain. He had more questions, but it seemed tonight Jack had nothing more to say.

* * *

The aroma of Ada's cinnamon bread filled Billy's nose. Maybe he'd find Angel in the kitchen waiting for him.

Paulette's laughter rang through the house, and Christina told her to lower her voice.

A wet nose nuzzled his ear. "Biscuit! That tickles!" Billy moved his hand to push the cat away, but it was met by something other than fur.

"Wake up, Will!" Jack yelled, grabbing his hand. "Cap'n Granger wants to see ya!"

The dream vanished. The reality of a sore back from sleeping on hard ground took over.

"C'mon, Will!" Jack persisted. "The cap'n don't like to wait."

Reluctantly, he got out from under the warm blanket and put on his coat. Blinking into the morning sunlight, he realized the rain had stopped. The air was fresh, but still bitterly cold.

Once he got on his feet and outside the tent, he stretched and yawned. Then he wiggled his toes, which had remained tucked inside his boots throughout the night. He should've taken them off for bed, but was afraid of frostbite.

The captain was as wide awake as the first time he'd met him. Perfectly groomed and ready for whatever the day might hold. Billy assumed in the captain's eyes *he* was unacceptable.

Not knowing if it made any difference, he attempted to smooth his clothing and ran his fingers through his hair. What he got from the captain in return was a single raised brow.

"Rough night?" Captain Granger scanned him from head to toe.

Billy stood rigidly straight. "No, sir. But I believe I could use more sleep."

"Couldn't we all?"

"Yes, sir." He swallowed the lump in his throat.

Captain Granger folded his arms over his chest and breathed deeply. "Your stallion bit one of my men this morning."

Feeling like his knees would buckle at any moment, Billy waited for the inevitable.

"You'll need to take the horse and leave camp, Mr. O'Brien." The captain paused, searching his face. "Or we'll have to take measures to settle your horse."

"Settle him, sir?" His dry throat indicated this wasn't a good thing.

"Yes. Aside from Duffy having him for dinner, castration would calm him. Although I admit I'd hate to see that done to such a fine animal."

It was the last thing he wanted done. Cotton was supposed to be bred to their mare in the spring. His father had high hopes for their offspring. *Why'd I take Cotton?*

"Sir?" All hope disappeared. "I'll take him from camp. I don't want him altered."

"Where will you go?"

Billy's eyes focused on the floor. He shrugged and shook his head.

Aside from the puff of air escaping from the captain's nostrils, the tent was silent.

"I believe I may have something you can do for me," Captain Granger finally said. "But you'll need your strength. It won't be easy."

Billy became instantly alert. "I can do whatever you need me to, sir." Pulling his shoulders back, he regained his posture.

Captain Granger paced the small expanse of the tent, mumbling something under his breath. He stopped abruptly, then turned to face him. "See to your horse. Take him out. Ride him. Do whatever it takes to tire him so he'll leave the mares alone for one night."

"And then?"

The captain raised his hand in a gesture he'd seen from his mama. Billy shut his mouth tight.

"And then, get a good meal and go to bed early. You'll have a long ride ahead of you."

A long ride? "Where will I be going, sir?" He hoped he wasn't out of line asking.

"I'll give your orders in the morning, Mr. O'Brien."

Billy closed his gaping mouth.

"That will be all, Mr. O'Brien." Captain Granger motioned him out of the tent.

He managed an inaudible, "Thank you, sir." As he exited, he could scarcely stay on his feet.

The captain will be giving me orders? I'm going to be a soldier.

* * *

The change in Cotton was unmistakable; re-energized from good hay and oats.

Approaching cautiously, Billy reached a hand to his nose with the intention of stroking him. Cotton stomped a front hoof and snorted, jerking his head up.

"What's wrong, boy?" His actions were peculiar.

"He smells the mare," a voice said from behind him.

Turning, Billy faced a young, stern-faced soldier. He held up a bandaged hand.

Billy stared at it, wide-eyed.

The man grunted. "He bit me."

"He never bit anyone before. *Ever.*"

"He wasn't mature. He's old enough now for breeding and it's all he wants to do. Don't you know anything about stallions? You had no business bringing him into camp." The man went by, scowling at Cotton as he passed.

"I'm sorry he hurt you." The man didn't acknowledge his apology.

It was good he was leaving tomorrow no matter where he'd be sent. Neither he nor Cotton was welcome here.

He spoke soothingly to his horse and fed him a handful of oats. The stench of manure filled the air and stung his nose. Though inappropriate to board animals in the church, the soldiers didn't seem to be bothered by it. To accommodate the horses, they'd removed bricks around the front door to enlarge the entrance. War showed no respect for religious property.

It didn't take long to regain Cotton's trust. He saddled him and had him running at a full gallop. Feeling suddenly free, the cold no longer bothered him.

When they returned to the church, Jack was waiting. He took the reins as Billy dismounted. "Captain Granger made him my responsibility tonight. Guess you'll have the tent to yourself."

"Sorry, Jack."

"Don't be. Once you get used to the smell, it ain't bad. It's warmer than the tent."

"Maybe I should stay here with you."

"If you want. Right now, the cap'n wants you back on the hill."

Billy scratched his head. "Know where he's sending me?"

"Nope." Jack led Cotton to a nearby stall. "All I know is he wants you at the camp for now."

Billy's stomach grumbled. Going to the camp wasn't such a bad idea. "I'm glad you're tending my horse. I don't think that other soldier likes him."

"I might not neither if he bites me."

"Don't stick your hand in his mouth," Billy said with a grin. "I'll come back later."

The brisk walk up the hill increased his appetite. The aroma of meat was welcome. Approaching his campsite, he looked for Taylor. Unfortunately, Duffy caught his eye.

"Willy!" the man hollered. "I thought ya left!" He clapped his hands together, then rubbed them briskly—as if warming up for some kind of mischief.

Billy breathed deeply. "Not yet. I'll be leaving tomorrow."

In a now-familiar fashion, Duffy draped his arm over Billy's shoulder. "Too bad. I like havin' ya 'round." Guiding him toward the fire, Duffy nodded to a horizontal log long enough for both of them to sit. "If you're hungry I got some rabbit I'll share."

Unsure why Duffy was being nice, he hesitated before accepting.

"Ah, come on now, Will. I even salt 'n peppered it."

"All right." Billy reluctantly sat.

Much to his surprise the rabbit tasted good. And when Duffy produced a jar filled with canned peaches, he was glad he took his offer.

Duffy nudged him as he devoured the sweet fruit. "I won them peaches playin' cards."

"They're good. Thank you for sharing."

"*You* ever play cards?"

That was one thing Billy promised his mama he'd never do. A fact he wouldn't share with Duffy. "Rarely." He hoped the subject would drop.

"You any good at it?"

His heart raced. Other men were listening. "It's been a long time since I played."

Duffy slapped his leg. "Then you're overdue!" He winked at one of the other soldiers. "We got a game tonight in Jenkins' tent. Cap'n Granger don't mind what we do after hours. Long as we behave ourselves. Right, Jenkins?"

Jenkins was the man whom Duffy had winked at. *They're setting me up.* When Duffy searched him, he'd found his money bag. Though it had been returned with his other belongings, Duffy knew Billy had money to lose.

"I don't think I should," Billy said as boldly as he could. "I have to get to bed early."

"A young man like you?" Duffy shook his head. "Nah . . . I figger you're scared a losin'. Ain't that right, Jenkins?"

Jenkins took a drag from a cigar, then blew a ring of smoke into the air. "Bet the boy don't know how to play."

Billy's heart thumped even harder. "What game are you playing?"

"Poker. Five card stud."

He'd heard of the game. It couldn't be too difficult. He could watch them play a few hands and learn. But he wouldn't bet. He couldn't risk losing his money.

"Oh, yes. Poker." Forcing a smile, he looked at Jenkins. "It's been years since I played. I may have to watch a few hands to remind me how it goes."

Duffy's shoulders shook with laughter. "How it goes!"

Billy fumed. "I'll play! I'm sure I'll remember." His chest tightened. *Dang! What have I gotten myself into?*

A firm slap on the back nearly sent him headlong into the flames. "Good boy!" Duffy yelled. "After supper, we're gonna show you the time of your life!"

Billy couldn't change his mind now. He'd be a man and learn how to gamble.

Chapter 11

Captain Granger had instructed Billy to be at his tent at sunrise for orders. First he had to get through the night. He wished he'd been able to get word to Jack that he'd be late.

Duffy escorted him to Sergeant Jenkins' tent. It wasn't as large as the captain's, but big enough for a small table and four chairs.

Jenkins was already seated when they arrived, puffing on his foul-smelling cigar. A cloud of smoke hovered at the pinnacle of the tent. Billy's breath caught the moment he stepped inside.

"Where's Langford?" Duffy asked.

"Should be here any minute," Jenkins replied. "He's bringin' the juice."

A mischievous smile covered Duffy's face.

What kind of juice?

"Have a seat, Will." Jenkins motioned to a chair.

Cold sweat covered Billy's skin. He should've never agreed to play.

"Cigar?" Jenkins asked, extending one in his direction.

"No, thank you." Breathing the smoke from Jenkins was bad enough.

"I'll take one of those," a man said, parting the flap of the tent.

Duffy patted him on the back.

Must be Langford. The man was short and plump, with a bulbous nose accentuated by a mustache. The rest of his face was scruffy, but he kept his beard trimmed short.

"You must be Will," Langford said, grinning.

Billy nodded. The grin turned his stomach.

Jenkins handed Langford a cigar, which he immediately lit.

"Did ya bring it?" Duffy rubbed his hands together like an over-anxious child.

Langford chuckled, then reached into his coat pocket and removed a large flask. "Wouldn't be poker without it!" Undoing the cap, he took a long swig, then passed it to Duffy.

Duffy took an even longer drink. "Ah!" He shook his head. "Almost better than Jessica!"

The men laughed as Duffy passed the drink to Jenkins. "Didn't backwash, did ya, Duff?"

"Never do! 'Sides, it wouldn't hurt ya if I did. Juice is strong enough to kill any kind a bug I might be carryin'."

"Better give some to Jessica next time." Langford bumped Duffy's arm with his fist.

Duffy scowled, but then they both erupted into laughter.

After Jenkins took his drink, Billy knew what was coming. They passed the flask to him. Everything he'd been taught was flying right out the flap of the tent. Licking his lips, he tilted the flask and took a large swallow.

Dang, it burns! His chest tightened. He sputtered and coughed.

"Good stuff, ain't it, Will?" Duffy asked, chortling all the while.

"Yep," he choked out, only to regret it.

"Take another swig." He pushed the flask against Billy's lips.

This time, it went down smoother, but the burn remained. When Duffy offered a third drink, Billy shook his head and handed the flask to Langford.

He had to keep his head on straight to get through the game they were already playing. Knowing alcohol could cloud his mind, he'd have to limit it. But a small amount couldn't hurt.

Jenkins shuffled the cards, but no money had been laid out.

Maybe this is a friendly game with no betting involved.

Langford produced a box of Lucifers and emptied them onto the table He divided them into three equal portions. "Safer than putting coins on the table." He leaned toward Billy. "Duff's been known to sneak a few when we aren't watching."

"Why only three piles?" Billy pointed to the Lucifers.

"The *sergeant* is dealing," Duffy said, nodding toward Jenkins. "Besides, he has a wife to go home to when this blasted war's over."

She must not approve of gambling.

Jenkins shuffled the deck one more time, took a drag from his cigar, then with a sly grin dealt the cards. He laid a card face down in front of each of them, then one card face up.

"Good card, Will." Duffy pointed to his six of diamonds. "Gonna look at your down card?"

Noticing the other men had glanced at theirs without showing them, he did the same. He had an eight of spades. Good or bad, he didn't have a clue.

Billy was given the option to bet after Duffy tossed two Lucifers into the center of the table. Deciding he had nothing to lose, he did the same.

"What the hell," Langford muttered and called the bet.

Another round of cards face up. This time Billy got a four of hearts. Once again everyone cast their Lucifers to the center of the table.

After two more rounds, four cards each were face up on the table, and they still didn't reveal their down cards. Duffy seemed excited about his two nines and his king and queen of hearts.

On the final round of betting, Langford dropped out, but Billy chose to remain. Though he didn't know whether his four, six, eight, jack and queen were worth anything.

Puffing out his chest, Duffy revealed his hold card—a nine—giving him three-of-a-kind. "Show us what you got Willy-boy!"

Frowning, Billy laid down his cards.

"Damn!" Duffy threw up his hands. "You see that? Boy was foolin' us. Had a corn-frogger and knew he had us beat."

Billy stared at the cards. A nervous chuckle wormed its way out of him. *A corn-frogger?*

"What?" Langford yelled.

"Right there!" Duffy pointed to Billy's cards. "A four, six, an eight. All off suit." He shook his head. "Perfect corn-frogger."

"You're right, Duff," Langford said. "One a the hardest hands to get and young Will opens with it. You play a mean hand, son."

Billy was unsure what to do or say, but grateful he'd been so lucky.

Jenkins puffed out another plume of smoke, then motioned toward the center of the table. "Take your Lucifers, Will."

"Oh. Of course." Billy pulled the pile toward him, adding it to his stack.

"And this," Langford said, and handed Billy the flask. "Win a round, you get a drink."

Not a good thing. Deciding to make it a small one, Billy tipped the container, barely letting the alcohol touch his lips. As he was about to hand it back, Duffy tipped it high. Since it wouldn't be polite to spill it, he drank it down.

"Much better!" Duffy nodded with approval, then returned the flask to Langford.

With all of the other men smoking and the foreign beverage in his belly, Billy was becoming nauseated. Not to mention—light-headed.

Jenkins dealt another round, then several more. The game couldn't be more complicated. Every time Billy thought he had a losing hand, some strange combination of cards made him a winner.

Hoping to lose a round and not have to drink, he was grateful when Duffy was dealt two aces. In a previous round, Billy had won with two aces and was told they were the best possible pair. With only a pair of twos, he sat back and waited for Duffy to take the Lucifers.

"Crap!" Duffy threw his cards in the air. "How'd ya do it, boy?"

"What? You have a pair of aces. You won."

Duffy tapped him on the chest. "You're sly, Will. Like a fox. Don't pretend you didn't know you had tater eyes."

"Tater eyes?"

"Course ya do! Look at them deuces. One's a club and one's a spade. Tater eyes! Beats a pair a aces every time! Damn!"

The flask was passed once more to Billy. At least the alcohol was keeping him warm—on the inside. His fingers were so cold he could barely hold the cards.

"Quittin' time," Jenkins announced. He drew the cards toward him.

Thank God! The stench of manure would smell like roses after being enclosed in cigar smoke for the past two hours.

"We know who won tonight," Langford said with a grin. "Look at that stack of Lucifers."

Billy scooped up his *winnings* and tried to stand. The room tipped to the left and his legs buckled. Plopping back down in his seat, he received a familiar pat on the back.

"Don't fret none, Will," Duffy said. "We're gonna take you to your winnin's."

"What?" Billy tried to get him into focus.

"Have a good time," Jenkins said. "I'm turning in."

The next thing Billy knew, Duffy was on one side of him and Langford on the other, hoisting him to his feet and out of the tent. Things were no longer tipping, they were spinning.

"I'm going to be sick," Billy muttered, and stumbled. His insides made their way out and he heaved.

"Reckon he shouldn't a won so many hands?" Duffy asked. He and Langford both chuckled.

Even with their laughter, Billy felt better after emptying his stomach.

Duffy handed him a canteen. "Rinse your mouth real good."

Billy just wanted a bed, but the water was refreshing. Though no longer queasy, his vision wasn't clear, and the world tipped on its side.

How could anyone enjoy alcohol when it made him feel so horrible?

What was I thinking? He'd come here to prove himself. Now he'd done the things he swore he'd never do. *Oh, my head hurts.* "Are you taking me to the stable?"

"Nope," Duffy said. "Some place better."

"Jack's waiting for me. He'll wonder what happened to me."

"Jackson's a grown man. He'll understand."

Still unable to stand, the two men continued their escort. "Where are we going?" This part of the encampment looked unfamiliar to him, set off in a grove of trees.

Langford parted the flap of a tent similar in size to Jenkins'. A peculiar scent filled Billy's nose. Sweet and spicy. Much different from the smoke that had permeated his clothing.

"I thought you weren't coming." A female voice, as unusual as the aroma surrounding him, arose from a small figure standing in the center of the tent. She was wrapped in a bundle of blankets. "I've nearly froze waiting for you."

"You'll be plenty warm soon enough," Duffy said.

They pulled Billy across the floor of the tent to a large mattress and released him. He tumbled onto the bedding. With his face buried in the blankets, the scent intensified.

"Who is this?" the woman asked.

"He won tonight," Langford said with a laugh. "Be good to him, Jess. He's a tad bit drunk."

Oh, Lord. I'm in Jessica's tent.

Unable to lift his head from the mattress, Billy lay there like a dead man.

Jingling coins pounded his brain like banging drums. "That's enough for the whole night," Duffy said. "Make sure he gets his money's worth."

Closing his eyes, Billy wished he was anywhere but here. Gambling, alcohol, and . . .

Jessica the prostitute. Let me die now.

He moaned, making Duffy laugh. "Willy boy!" he taunted. "Jessica will give you a better night than Jackson. May not sleep, but you won't never forget it!"

The men's obnoxious laughter filtered into the tent, though they were some distance away. When Billy realized what would be expected of him, his heart thumped, taking away his breath.

"You need to move over." Jessica prodded him with her foot. "I'm freezing."

This was the first real mattress he'd seen since his arrival at the encampment. If a woman hadn't wanted to lie down beside him, he'd have appreciated it.

Feeling as if the bed was spinning in circles, he rolled onto his back. She promptly lay down and pushed her body against his. Then she pulled the blankets over the top of them.

She wriggled against him and draped a bare arm across his chest. *Is all of her naked?*

"This will never do." She worked the buttons of his coat.

"What are you doing?" The lump in his throat and tightness in his chest indicated he didn't need an answer.

She giggled and continued to undress him.

His body surged with energy. Sitting upright, he scooted away from her. The pounding of his head no longer mattered.

"You are shy!" she chirped, and hugged the blankets to her body. She sat, grabbed a lantern, and turned up the flame. She peered at his face. "You are just a boy."

"I'm eighteen." He crossed his arms over his chest. "I'm not a boy."

The heavy blankets surrounded her body, but in the flickering light he caught a glimpse of her breast as she adjusted herself on the bed.

He tried not to stare, but he'd never seen a woman's bare breast. He couldn't help himself. Swallowing hard, he shifted his gaze.

"You like what you see?" She fluttered her long lashes, then licked her full lips. Next to Angel, she was the most beautiful woman he'd ever seen.

Setting aside the lantern, she pulled her long dark hair forward. It cascaded down her body, thankfully covering her breasts. "It helps keep me warm," she purred, while running her fingers through her lengthy locks. "But I'd rather *you* do that. It's what I've been waiting for." She cupped his cheek, then inched closer, raising her body up for a kiss.

Before he could say a word, her mouth covered his, moving in a way that asked for more. Her hands were on him, once again tugging at his buttons.

"No," he forced himself to say. Breathing hard, he was no longer cold.

"No?" She pulled away.

He rubbed his temples. "I didn't know you were the prize for winning the game."

"How could you not know? I'm always the prize." The way her lower lip protruded, he believed she was truly disappointed. Perhaps even insulted.

"Jessica." He couldn't take his eyes from her face. "I think you're beautiful—"

"Then what are you waiting for, Willy?" Lurching forward, she kissed him, then followed it with a seductive nip on his lower lip.

He'd given in to gambling and drinking, but he'd *not* give in to her. "No!" He spoke as firmly as he could. "And please, don't call me Willy. It's Will."

She sat back and cinched the blankets snugly around her. "Why do you tell me no? Every man wants me." Her tone became smug. "I think you're afraid. You've never had a woman."

"I'm not afraid. But I won't do *that* with just any woman. I'm waiting for one I love."

She was silent. Had he insulted her further? "Why do *you* do this? Wouldn't you rather be with one man? Someone *you* love?"

"Are you judging me, Will?" Now, she'd become defensive.

"No." He shook his head and reached for her hand. It was icy cold, so he pulled it to his mouth, cupped it inside his own hands and breathed on it.

Her demeanor softened. "You're different from other men."

He chuckled, causing his head to thump. "That's a compliment. Especially if you're comparing me to Duffy."

"He thinks a lot of himself." She giggled. "But I *do* appreciate his hair. It covers his entire body. He's very warm."

He'd rather not have known that, but at least she was opening up and talking. Conversation might keep her from expecting other things.

Her accent perplexed him. "Where are you from? I've never heard anyone talk like you."

"You ask a lot of questions." She hugged her knees. "Most men don't want to talk."

"I'm not like most men." *I'm not even fourteen yet.*

"No, you are not." Coyly, she tilted her head and bit her lower lip. "Mother was French. My father, I don't know. I was raised around many people and picked up their ways of speaking."

"I like the way you talk. My mama has a good friend who's French. Strangely enough, she used to be a prostitute."

She stiffened. "I don't like that word, but it's better than whore. I think of myself as a lover."

"But what you give isn't love." Even in the dim light he knew he'd hurt her. *I shouldn't have said it.*

She pulled her hand away. "What do you know about love?"

"I've watched my parents. And, there's someone . . ." He stopped. Why was he telling her the truth? What if she told Duffy? Or Captain Granger?

"Someone?"

Somehow he believed he could trust her. "Angel. Her name's Angel."

"And your *Angel* would be hurt if she knew you were with me?"

"Of course. Isn't there someone *you* care about?"

Her silence accentuated the whistling of the wind through the trees. Grateful they were in an enclosed tent, he waited for her answer.

"Years ago," she finally said. "But he died. And now, I can't expect to find love again. So I make money giving the only kind of love I know how. It makes men happy and helps me forget my loneliness."

The sorrow in her words compelled him to hold her, but it wouldn't be wise. After all, she was completely naked beneath the covers and he couldn't deny his attraction.

"Why not?" He dismissed his other thoughts. "Why couldn't you find love again?"

"What man would share his life with a woman who's shared her bed with the world?"

"Francine found a man who loved her regardless."

"Francine is your mother's friend?"

"Yes. They met on a steamboat. My father was the pilot and owner. Francine *worked* on the boat." He jiggled his brows, which prompted her to giggle.

"And your mother told you this?"

He nodded. "When I was old enough to understand. Francine was different than other women who came to visit. When I asked about her, Mama told me. I believe she wanted to make me aware of women of your profession so I wouldn't be taken advantage of."

"She is wise." She rested her head on her knees like a child waiting for the end of a fairytale.

"Eventually, Francine married the cub pilot who took over after my father died. But when the war started, the Confederates took the boat. It was sunk in battle several years ago. Broke Mama's heart. The *Bonny Lass* meant a lot to her. I was born on it."

He was rambling, but talking seemed to help clear his head. How he was able to talk so easily to this stranger surprised him. Somehow he wanted to help her.

"But Francine found love?" The dreaminess in her tone was different than anything he'd heard from her.

"Yes. They live in St. Louis. It's been several years since we saw them. They manage a home for orphaned children."

She smiled, then her eyes widened. "Will? Could *you* love someone like me?"

His pulse quickened. "If my heart wasn't already taken I could."

She took his hand and pulled it toward her. "I want to look at your palm."

"Why?"

"Just let me." She turned his hand over, then traced the lines with her finger. "I was taught long ago to read the lines. This is your lifeline."

Her gentle touch sent chills down his back.

"Hmm . . ." Her mouth twisted. "The line breaks, but then begins again. It's very unusual."

"What does it mean?"

She shrugged. "I'm not good at this. I should have paid more attention to my grandmother. She was a seer."

He'd heard of seers, but didn't believe in them. "Since your grandmother isn't here," he paused and grinned at her. "What do *you* think? Will I live a long life?" Her fingers tickled his skin, causing his throat to become dry.

"This line is for love and family." She raised her eyes to meet his. "It is the boldest line on your hand. You will live long enough to have children."

She lowered his hand and rested it against her breast. "Do you feel my heart, Will?"

He gulped. Yes, he could feel it beating against his hand beneath her warm, soft, *full* breast. "Yes," he squeaked out, but didn't move his hand.

"Lay with me, Will," she whispered. "Just hold me. Hold me like you would hold your Angel. Please?"

She dimmed the lantern, then faced him in the darkness.

He didn't want to refuse her. Simply to hold her and nothing more.

He unbuttoned his coat and removed it. "Put this on."

"Why?"

"Because I don't dare feel you. But I'll hold you." He held up the coat. She allowed the blankets to drop from her body long enough to put it on.

He lay against down-filled pillows, and she nuzzled into him with her coat-encased arm draped across his chest. They pulled the blankets up to their necks and basked in each other's warmth.

"Thank you, Will," she sighed, and wriggled even closer. Her fingers moved in a circular motion over his chest. "Are you certain this is all you want from me?"

Closing his eyes, he pictured Angel. One day *she'd* be in his arms. "Yes, I'm sure."

A small whimper came from her throat, then she let out a long breath and stilled her hand.

He breathed in her essence. Even her hair smelled sweet.

How could a woman so fine be with men like Duffy?

He placed a small kiss on the top of her head, then lay back onto the pillow. Morning would come much too soon.

Is this what Duffy wanted all along? Was he trying to ruin his chance of becoming a soldier?

I won't let him.

Jessica's faint breathing relaxed him. Duffy had been right, he'd never forget this night. A smile crossed his face and his headache subsided. He drifted off to sleep wondering what dreams awaited him.

Chapter 12

A single shot rang out and Billy fell. His dark red blood stained the frozen ground. Helpless and unable to move, Angel screamed.

"Billy!" Her voice shook the walls, bringing her mama instantly to her side.

"Baby, wake up!" She shook her hard, jarring her from the nightmare.

Her body trembled. "Mama, they killed Billy!"

Pulling Angel against her breast, she soothed her with tender words while stroking her hair. "Hush, baby. Billy's fine. He be home soon."

Angel's rapidly beating heart began to slow, comforted in her mama's arms. "It seemed real." Tears trickled down her cheeks. "Billy was shot. He was lyin' on the ground. There was blood . . ." She closed her eyes tight, trying to erase the vision.

"Don't think such things. I don't understan' what you're feelin' for Billy. You're too young to be thinkin' 'bout lovin' a man. An Billy ain't even a man just yet."

This wasn't a conversation Angel wanted to have. *Ever.*

"An don't you go changin' the subject to me an Jeriah. We's grown-ups. You ain't."

"Mama, it's the middle of the night." Her tears dried and the nightmare faded.

"Yep. An we's both wide awake."

Faking a yawn, Angel stretched her arms over her head. "I'm tired, Mama."

"No, you ain't. Even if you is, I want you to listen to me. An listen good."

"Yes'm." She knew that tone.

"When Billy comes home, I don't want you bein' alone with him."

"But—"

"No matter how young or old you is, Billy will always be white. You ain't."

She opened her mouth to object, but her mama stopped her. "Yes, your daddy was a white man, but it don't matter none. White folks won't never let someone like you mix with their kind. That's the way it be. So you hafta get any a those kind a thoughts outta your mind. One day I pray we's free an I can marry Jeriah. Then you can find you a good colored man to love."

Angel decided to take the easy way out. "Yes, Mama." She gave her a kiss on the cheek and lay down. "Can I go back to sleep now?"

Even in the shadows, Angel could tell her mama was rubbing her nose. "Reckon so. Near time to get up, but you can sleep, baby."

"I'll do better since I know Billy's comin' home. I promise."

Her mama bent down and kissed her forehead. "No more bad dreams."

The door creaked as she left the room. Afraid to shut her eyes, Angel stared into nothingness. Not only haunted from her nightmare, she'd also become angry. It wasn't her fault her daddy was white and her mama was colored. Why should it matter? She'd never given it much thought until Billy had kissed her. She wished she'd never told.

* * *

A cold chill crept across Billy's bare chest, waking him from a deep sleep. As his eyes slowly opened, he gazed downward.

His shirt had been opened wide. Jessica was leaning over him, placing tiny kisses on his skin. When her mouth moved to his nipple and she circled it with her tongue, every part of him quivered.

"What are you doing?" He grabbed her face in his hands and raised her head. She looked even more beautiful in the daylight. His heart raced and it seemed she wasn't done.

A broad smile covered her face. "Telling you good morning." She licked her lips, then bent down and resumed her kisses.

"But—I said I'd hold you. Nothing else." Knowing he should throw her aside didn't help. Afraid to touch her, he put his hands over his face. He couldn't deny he was enjoying this.

She giggled. "Then do nothing. I'll do it all."

Angel . . . Angel . . .

Moving his hands into his hair, he glanced down again. "Where's my coat?"

She motioned her head sideways. "The wool made me itch. I removed it while you slept. You didn't seem to mind."

"What are you doing now?" Her hand slid down his torso. Lower and lower . . . "Dang!"

"I'm touching you." She giggled. "Your body is telling me what it wants."

"No!" He grabbed her arm as cautiously as he could while trying to avoid other parts of her body. He had to stop the movement of her hand.

Reveille sounded, changing everything. He hopped from the mattress and hurriedly buttoned his shirt, tucking it into his overly-snug trousers.

She stood, pulling one of the blankets with her. "I think I found your weakness, Will." The devilish grin she flashed made him wonder if she could ever be anything else.

Trying not to look at her exposed flesh, he took her hands. "Jessica, you could make any man weak." He looked her straight in the eye and gulped. "You could also make him fall in love with you. I promise, love would be better than all this."

In the sunlight, her tent was simple. Aside from the mattress, there was one chair and a large trunk he assumed held her clothes. How could this be worth giving herself to strangers?

She stepped closer and peered into his face. She was small. Not even five feet tall. "You were kind to me." Brushing his cheek with her fingertips, she inched even closer. "You have freckles and red in your hair. You're a handsome young man, but I do not believe you're eighteen."

"I will be. *Soon*." The way she looked at him took his breath. "Jessica, don't stay here. Go where people don't know you and start over."

She shook her head. "What would I do for money?"

"There must be other things you can do." Raising his brows, he waited for a response.

"I can cook. But I'm much better there." She pointed to the bed, then took a final step, closing the gap between them.

Her erotic scent surrounded him. No, he wasn't anywhere close to being eighteen, but with her it would be easy to behave as a man.

Her arms encircled him and she rested her head on his chest.

"Willy!" Duffy's unwelcome voice broke her spell.

"Damn him," she muttered.

The flap of the tent flew open and Duffy stepped in. "I ain't payin' for no mornin' quickie!"

"What?" Billy stared at the wretched man.

"I paid for an all-nighter. Not whatever you was fixin' to do."

"Duffy!" Jessica yelled. "Get out! I was telling him good-bye."

Duffy took a step back, staring at both of them. "I ain't stoppin' you."

"Out!" Jessica pointed her finger and stomped her foot.

"Damn whore's got an attitude," Duffy mumbled, and lifted the flap to exit.

In two swift strides, Billy crossed the tent. He grabbed Duffy's arm. "Don't call her that!"

"What the?" Duffy dropped the flap to face him. "She gotten under your skin, boy? It must a been some night!"

Looking past him, he glared at Jessica. "Give him a good ride, Jess?"

Billy drew back his arm, and before he thought it through, he planted his fist in the side of Duffy's jaw. The man stumbled back, but didn't fall. Expecting him to hit back, Billy braced himself and brought up his fists.

"Puppy's got a bite!" Duffy exclaimed and burst into laughter. Then instead of launching his fist into Billy, he smacked him on the back. "Made a man outta ya, Will. Knew I could."

He didn't know what to say. Jessica snuggled against him.

Duffy shook his head. "Tell her goodbye, then get yourself to the cap'n's tent. He sent me to fetch ya." He left without another remark.

"You stood up for me," Jessica said, nestling her head into his shoulder.

Though he assumed her to be in her twenties, she reminded him of his sisters. He'd have done the same for them. "You didn't deserve to be talked to that way."

He had to go, so he gently pushed her aside.

His pack lay near the opening of the tent. In his drunken state, he hadn't recalled it being there. But what he needed wasn't in the pack. He hoped it was still in his coat. Lifting it from the floor, he reached into the deep pocket. Relieved, he withdrew the cloth bag.

"Here, take this." He placed a handful of coins in her palm. "Go somewhere and . . . *cook*."

"But—"

"You're afraid." He closed her fingers over the money. "I'm afraid, too. But that won't stop me from going wherever Captain Granger decides to send me. You can do it, Jessica."

"I don't know what to say." Her lashes fluttered, framing her big brown eyes.

"You don't have to say anything."

She smiled, then crossed to her trunk. "I don't know what this is, but it fell out of the pocket when I took it off." She gave him Angel's wooden figurine.

"Thank you." He clutched it to his chest, then let out a large breath. "I can't lose this."

"What is it?"

"A gift." Opening his hand, he stared at it. "From Angel."

"A bug?" She wrinkled her nose.

Laughing, he tightened his fist around it, then placed it with the bag of money in his pocket. "My brother's still learning how to carve. It's supposed to be an angel."

"Oh." She rose up and kissed him. Her kisses were unlike those he'd shared with Angel. This kiss was that of a friend.

"I hope to see you again someday, Will."

"Me, too." He opened the flap to leave, but stopped. "My name's actually Billy."

With wide batting eyes, she blew him a kiss.

Not knowing why he'd told the truth, he hurried away. Yes, he was afraid, but he'd proven to himself how much he loved Angel. Still, he'd never forget Jessica. He'd been given a chance to taste gratification. But the only satisfaction he wanted would be found in Angel's arms.

* * *

Billy's feet were planted solidly on the floor of Captain Granger's tent. After several minutes passed without the captain saying even one word to him, he couldn't help but clear his throat, hoping for some sort of acknowledgment.

"I'll be with you momentarily," the captain grumbled.

When he'd first arrived, the captain had pointed to the place where he now stood and proceeded to write something on a document at his table. Though he'd tried to read it over the man's shoulder, it was hidden from view.

Captain Granger folded and sealed the document and rose to his feet. He circled him, all the while shaking his head. "I'm disappointed in you, Mr. O'Brien."

Not the words he wanted to hear. Tempted to speak, he kept his mouth shut, remembering his previous scolding.

Leaning toward him, the captain sniffed. "Duffy told me you spent the night with Jessica. The perfume on your clothing confirms he told the truth." He sniffed again. "I also smell cigar smoke." Stepping back, he folded his arms across his chest in an all-too-familiar fashion. "You had an eventful night, didn't you?"

The words stuck momentarily in his throat. "Yes, sir."

Captain Granger chuckled. "Is that all you have to say? You usually have much more."

Billy's shoulders slumped. It appeared Duffy had won. "I played cards, sir. I was trying my best to fit in with the other men. Somehow, I was lucky enough to win. I didn't know Jessica was the prize."

"I see. Do you play cards often?" The captain stared at him while rubbing his chin.

"N—No sir." He couldn't lie. Especially with the way the man was looking at him.

"Duffy's an exceptional player with a fondness for Jessica. I'm surprised you were able to beat him."

"I was lucky, sir. I had good hands. Even managed a corn-frogger and tater eyes. The men said they were difficult to get."

The captain covered his mouth and chuckled. "Damn, that Duffy."

Not understanding why he found it funny, Billy kept his eyes to the floor. "Am I in trouble, sir?"

"No, Mr. O'Brien, you're not. But I'll be having a long chat with Private Duffy." He motioned to a chair. "Please sit. You look tired."

"Thank you, sir." It felt good to sit, but he wouldn't let on that he *was* tired. "I slept last night, sir."

"With Jessica?" Captain Granger took the chair beside him.

"Y—Yes, sir. But it's not what you're thinking. I didn't . . ." The heat rising in his cheeks caused sweat to bead on his brow.

"You didn't *what*, Mr. O'Brien?" The captain drummed his fingers on the table.

"I didn't—well—*you know*—with Jessica." He wiped his brow with the back of his hand.

Captain Granger nodded and smiled. "As long as you slept. That's what concerns me." Folding his hands on the table, he looked into his eyes. "When you leave my tent, go to the officer's mess. You're to eat a full breakfast, then I've instructed them to fill your pack with food. You're also to take a gum blanket and I'll be returning your rifle."

"Where am I going, sir?" Scared to hear the answer, he closed his eyes.

"I'm taking a risk with you, O'Brien. I'm sending you to Fort Morgan in Mobile, Alabama."

His heart thumped. "Alabama, sir?" With wide eyes, he gaped at the captain.

"You *do* know where it is, don't you, O'Brien?"

"Of course I do. But why so far away?"

His head tipped to the side. "You said you wanted to go somewhere you could make a difference. You're a capable rider and I need that stallion out of my stables. With enough food, you should have no difficulty reaching the fort in four days' time." He handed Billy the sealed document. "This is a letter for General Canby. When you reach the fort, give it to him. It will tell him who you are as well as some very important information about Confederate movement. Private messenger is the only trusted means of delivery."

His stomach did acrobatics. "Why me?"

"Because no one will believe you're a soldier. You'll not be in uniform and you'll keep your wits about you. If you're captured, God forbid, you're to claim ignorance. And most importantly, destroy this letter. Eat it if you have to."

He gulped, unable to speak.

The captain placed his hand on Billy's shoulder. "I believe you can do this, Will. And when you do, Canby will make you a soldier. Do you understand?"

His head bobbled up and down. "Yes, sir. This is my test. A way for you to know I'm telling the truth about what I want to do."

Captain Granger stood. "I wish you success, Mr. O'Brien."

Billy jumped to his feet and saluted. "I'll make you proud, sir."

The captain returned his salute, then motioned him out of the tent. "Jackson will tell you how to get there. Oh, and this is very important . . ."

"Yes, sir?"

"Remember these words. *The fox is coming home.* Knowing them will get you to General Canby. But only say them when you reach the fort. Have I made myself clear?"

"Yes, sir." Taking a deep breath, he smiled at the captain, then patted the document in his breast pocket—right beside the wooden angel.

Now his real adventure would begin. In less than a week, he'd be a soldier.

Chapter 13

"Good mornin', Mrs. Denton," Angel said. She placed a cup of tea in front of her. Offering a generous smile, she hoped it'd be returned.

"Mornin', Angel." She stood and walked away, taking her tea with her.

Angel slumped into a chair. How would she ever regain her trust?

"Give her time," Ada said. "It'll be fine when the men comes back."

Angel frowned, too depressed to do much else.

"Get off your tail and hep Ada," her mama scolded. "Hard work's what you need."

"What can I do?" Angel shrugged and stood.

Her mama rolled her eyes. "Here we goes again. Baby girl, I's worried 'bout you." She pointed to the door. "Go to the men's house. Tell Bo we needs more wood for the fire. He be heppin' with the horses while Jeriah's gone. If he ain't there, you'll find him in the stable."

"Yes, Mama." Grabbing her coat, she headed out the door.

Any other time, Bo'd be working at the mill. He shared the men's house with Jeriah and two other mill slaves. Most of them lived in barracks beside the mill.

Bo was younger than Jeriah, but at least ten years older than her. He'd always been nice, but rarely around to talk to. Billy, on the other hand, had constantly been there. Until now.

Women weren't permitted in the men's house and vice-versa. She knocked on the door and waited for an answer. When none came, she headed to the stables.

She had to pass the encampment on the way. Not only was it a constant reminder of the reason why Billy left, but more than once the soldiers had called out to her. She'd ignored them, but the sounds they'd made caused her insides to twist. At least they'd never come near her.

Today they left her alone.

The sun shone bright in the sky, but January was never a warm month in Memphis.

"Bo?" She peered into the open gateway.

The huge stable housed ten horses, three buggies, and a carriage, as well as tools and riding gear. A separate area was set aside for Spot, the milk cow.

"In here!" His voice came from a far-off stall.

She made a point to watch her step while walking across the straw-covered ground. Following the sound of his voice, she approached the last stall. He had a shovel in hand removing waste.

"Oh, my," she said, pinching her nose.

He laughed. "A fresh one." He shoveled the pile into a wheelbarrow.

"Reckon you must be used to it," she choked out, then backed away from where he was working. "Mama asked me to have you chop some wood for the stove."

"Tell her I'll be there soon as I finish this." He pushed the shovel under another pile.

Lowering her hand from her nose, she smiled at him. Even though he was filthy, he'd always been good-looking. He was taller than Billy and had very broad shoulders; muscular from all the physical labor. "You'll be glad when Jeriah's back, won't you?"

He shrugged. "I dunno. I kinda likes workin' with the horses. Even shovelin' the shi—" He stopped. "I means— the *manure*—ain't bad." He looked at the ground. "Sorry, Miss Angel. Ain't used to bein' 'round you women folk. Men talks different."

Biting her lip, she giggled. "That's all right. I won't tell." As she started walking back to the main house, she turned to look at him one more time. He happened to be looking at her with a very large grin, resting his gloved hands on top of the shovel.

When she walked through the door, into the kitchen, she still wore a smile. "Bo will be here soon as he finishes in the stable." She crossed to the sink and began washing the dirty dishes.

Her mama tapped her on the shoulder. "What happened out there?"

"Nothin', Mama. Reckon gettin' out in the fresh air helped."

"More like seein' Bo's fresh face," Ada laughed.

"He's nice, Ada," she said, while scrubbing a pot. She wasn't about to look at her. "He made me laugh." It felt good.

"I'll be shore an thank him," her mama said. "I's tired of your whimperin'."

Honestly, she was tired of it, too. *Billy wouldn't like me cryin'.*

Her hands flew over the dishes. Her mama was right; hard work helped. She placed the last dish in the cupboard, ready to write.

* * *

January 6th, 1865. I laughed today.

She dipped the pen into the inkwell.

It had always been Billy who made me laugh. Well, sometimes Ada. Pausing, she smiled. When Billy read this, he'd understand what she meant.

Today, Bo made me laugh. He was shoveling manure and said a word he shouldn't have.

Since she'd been allowed to sit in on Miss Banks' lessons, at least she could read and write. Billy also gave her private lessons when she struggled with the work. He'd been more patient than Miss Banks and told her he wouldn't give up until she could read every book in the library.

Billy should be home in less than a week. I have a lot I want to tell him. Until he was gone, I didn't realize how much he means to me. I don't ever want him to leave again.

I'm promising myself to smile more. Mama deserves a happy child. Besides, I heard frowning creates wrinkles. I don't want wrinkles.

She blew on the ink before closing the book. Then she puckered again, this time kissing the cover. For now it'd have to do.

* * *

"I'm glad he didn't bite you," Billy said, as Jack saddled Cotton. "Maybe he's gotten that mare out of his mind."

Jack stepped back. "He hasn't. I put her on the opposite end of the church and tied him up for the night." He crossed his arms and let out a loud sigh. "He ain't much different than you, Will."

"What's that supposed to mean?"

"All that talk 'bout waitin' for marriage an you spent the night with Jessica."

What could he say without saying too much? "It wasn't like that." Throwing his pack over Cotton's back, he prepared to mount.

Jack grunted. "Right."

Billy swung up into the saddle. "Jessica's a nice woman. She shouldn't be here."

"Neither should I. Can't take much more a this."

"Are you upset because you think I bed her?"

Jack scratched his head. "You spent the night with her. You know how hard it's been stayin' away from her? Never thought waitin' for Sally would be so tough. But I'm a man and there's things men need to do. Course, I don't hafta tell *you* that."

"I didn't have Jessica. Stay true to Sally. You'll be home with her before you know it."

He doubted Jack believed him, but had no way to prove himself. How Jack felt wasn't as important as the task at hand—proving himself to General Canby.

"Since you're goin' south, there should be more grass an such for Cotton. It'll get warmer the closer you get to the bay. Just keep goin' straight south 'til you see the water. Fort's right there." Jack patted Cotton's side prompting a whinny. "I put some oats in a bag for you."

"Thank you."

Jack looked at the ground, then raised his head. "Sorry I got mad. Reckon I was jealous."

"It's all right." Looking around the interior of the converted church, his heart began its usual pounding. All he had to do was nudge Cotton's sides and he'd be on his way. "Take care of yourself and that son of yours."

Jack beamed. "I will. Sometimes I forget I'm a pa."

Pa. The word made him smile and think of his mama, then his thoughts turned to his stepfather. His only *real* father. *Time to make him proud.*

"C'mon, Cotton!" They left the security of Clifton.

Chapter 14

Captain Granger had made sure Billy had everything he needed. His belly, just like Cotton's, was full of oats, as well as bacon, canned peaches, and bread. His pack had been filled with hardtack and jerky, as well as a canteen of fresh water and the gum blanket the captain promised. Most importantly, his rifle had been returned, and he'd strapped it to Cotton's side.

He wore Angel's gloves and secured her scarf around his neck. The inside pocket of his coat held his remaining money, Angel's figurine, and the letter for General Canby.

He followed the river for a short distance, but had to leave it behind as it turned west. Luckily, he found a well-traveled road heading south that would be easy on Cotton.

Since he was simply a *traveler* heading to Mobile to see his *sick uncle,* he saw no need to hide from others on the road. If questioned, his story was in place. Depending on the color of a man's uniform, he'd alter it to fit his purpose.

"You're going to be a real war horse, Cotton." He prompted him to move faster with a gentle kick. "No more mares for you. At least for now." Maybe they'd be home by spring.

Home. Only a week had passed and he was already forgetting what it had been like to be there.

"We'll be there again one day." Sitting taller in the saddle, he patted his pocket.

The fox is coming home.

* * *

The hair stood up on the back of Billy's neck. His stomach flipped like a one-winged bird. Someone was watching him.

Tied to a tree not far from him, Cotton tossed his head and pawed the ground.

He'd led him off the main road and into a thicket to take a short rest and have a bite to eat. The rustling of nearby branches caused him to hold his breath and wait. It didn't take long before he heard the snap of twigs and the rasp of a heavy breather.

Swallowing the lump in his throat, he pulled his rifle from its sheath on Cotton's side; silently sliding it one inch at a time. His heart beat out of his chest. The air coming from his nose hissed in his ears. Surely no one else could hear it.

He raised the rifle and pointed it toward the rustling branches. "Stop now or I'll shoot!"

"Don't shoot me, Mista!"

Lowering the rifle, Billy hurried toward the sound and found a young boy huddled on the ground hiding his face in his hands. He pitied the scarcely clad child, who trembled from head to toe. "What are you doing out here?"

Peeking out between his fingers, the boy slowly stood. "I's sorry if'n I scared you. But I's hungry. I seen you had food."

After traveling for a day and a half, Billy had been enjoying the times he'd stopped for a meal, even allowing himself to build a fire. He had a large number of Lucifers—thanks to Duffy's poker game—and since he wasn't trying to hide from anyone, saw no reason not to enjoy the heat of the flames. The child needed that warmth and a good meal.

"What's your name?" The boy was most likely a runaway slave.

"Leroy." He rolled his eyes.

It made him smile. "Leroy?"

This time, the boy curled his lip. "I don't like it neither. Masta gave me the name."

"What would you like to be called?"

The boy grinned from ear-to-ear. "Joe."

"Alright then, *Joe*, you can call me O'Brien." He dug a piece of jerky and a few soda crackers from his pack and handed them to Joe, who devoured them; scarcely chewing. "There's more, Joe, but you need to slow down." It was like talking to his little brothers.

"Ain't eaten for long time. Heard you talkin' to your horse an figgered you was nice. You always talk to your horse?"

"Only when there's no one else around." Billy motioned to a nearby log, close to the campfire. Joe perched next to him. "Where'd you run from?"

"Don't make me go back!" His eyes glistened with tears ready to fall. "Let me stay. I do anythin' you say."

How could he allow him to stay? He had a mission to complete. Joe would slow him down.

His mind reeled, and his heart softened. Maybe it wouldn't be such a bad thing. Joe could easily fit into his story. Since he'd be going deeper into slave states, if they were stopped, he could tell them he was returning Joe to his uncle. Was it too far-fetched?

"How old are you, Joe?"

"I's six." Joe stuck his nose into the air. "How old you be?"

He hated that question. "I'm eighteen. Twelve years older than you. And if I let you stay with me, you have to do exactly what I tell you. If you don't, I'll leave you on the side of the road."

"Do I hafta ride your horse?" His eyes widened, pointing to Cotton.

"Yes, you'll have to ride with me. We have a long way to go. Walking would take too long." Billy extinguished the campfire so they could leave.

Joe stood beside him, still shivering in his ragged clothes. He timidly approached Cotton. "He be big."

"You're small." Billy laughed and lifted him onto Cotton's back. Before mounting behind him, he handed him a sweater from his pack. "Wear this over your clothes. It'll help."

Joe threaded his skinny arms into the sleeves and popped his head out the neck hole. "It be too big, Brian." He'd simplified his name to *Brian* and he didn't have the heart to correct him.

The sweater swallowed his tiny frame, but he didn't have anything else for him to wear. He pushed up the sleeves so his hands were free. "I know it's too big, but it's better than freezing."

"I like green. I likes your blue gloves, too."

"You can't have those. If your hands get cold, pull the sleeves back down."

"Yessa."

At least he had someone to talk to. Joe seemed harmless enough and even helped him stay warmer in the saddle. Admittedly, the little boy helped ease the absence of his siblings.

There had to be more to his story. Hopefully there wasn't an angry master on his trail who'd accuse him of stealing his property. *Property. Just like Angel.*

They rode hard, trying to make up lost time. Though he wasn't on a schedule, Billy wanted to reach the fort quickly. He'd let the general decide what to do with Joe. Someone of that rank would be fair about such things.

Sitting behind the little boy had its disadvantages. Smelling his soiled clothing was unpleasant, but also made him realize how long it had been since *he'd* bathed. Jessica hadn't complained, so he hoped he wasn't too ripe.

As the sun set to his right, he knew he was on course. It was time to give Cotton a rest, and the limp body of the six-year-old nestled against him needed a good night's sleep.

"Wake up, Joe," he whispered, while jostling the boy.

His body jerked. "Don't beat me!" He whimpered and flailed his arms.

What has he been through? "Wake up. You're safe with me."

His big brown eyes opened wide. "Brian?"

"Yes. We've stopped for the night. Time to make a fire and have some supper." He held Joe steady on Cotton's back, then dismounted and brought the boy to the ground.

"Supper?" Joe's face brightened. He clapped his hands, proving his dream had been forgotten.

While Joe gathered kindling, Billy retrieved a pot from his pack and went looking for water. He set up a campsite and in no time they had a blazing fire and water heating in the pot.

"What you gonna put in the water?" Joe asked, scratching his head.

"If the pot was bigger, I'd put you in there." He winked at the boy.

"You'd eat me?" Joe jumped up, looking as if he'd bolt.

Billy laughed. "Sit down. The water's for washing."

The boy's surprise turned instantly to horror. "Washin'? Why?"

"You're dirty, and so am I."

Kicking at the ground with one foot, Joe's mouth twisted "Don't look dirty."

"Maybe I don't, but if I smell half as bad as *you*, then I am."

Joe lifted the over-sized green sweater to his nose. "It don't smell."

"*You do.*" No child would talk him out of this. *So much like Richard.*

After helping Joe scrub in all the appropriate places, Billy cleaned himself. He was determined to make the best impression possible for General Canby.

He'd set aside some water to mix with the flour and baking soda mixture sent with him. After making soft dough, he found a stick to wrap it around and extended it over the fire.

"What's that?" Joe asked, wrinkling his nose.

"Dough," Billy grinned. "But it'll be a biscuit when it's done."

"I likes biscuits with jam."

"So do I. But all we have is the biscuit."

"Can I try?" Joe pointed to the stick.

Billy placed it in his hands. "Don't put it directly in the flame. Hold it over the top."

"Huh?"

"Like this." Billy raised the stick out of the flames.

With his chin raised high and his shoulder's back, Joe began to whistle, happily rocking his head back and forth while he browned the perfect biscuit.

He may have landed in Billy's lap, but this little boy had been no accident. Taking care of him took away his fear. Could angels come in the form of a little Negro boy? Yes, he believed they could.

* * *

"I know it's the middle of winter but I could a sworn I heard birds chirpin' when I woke up!" Angel hung her coat in its usual spot. "I slept good, had good dreams, even gave Spot a good brushin'."

The silence following her cheerfulness took her aback. Ada was bent over the sink scrubbing bread pans, and her mama stood in the archway between the kitchen and the main house, staring down the hallway.

Angel looked one more time at Ada, who was wiping her eyes with her sleeve.

"Mama? What's happened?" Angel rushed to her.

When she turned to face her, she, too, had been crying.

A knot twisted in Angel's belly. "Mama?"

Her lower lip quivered. She led Angel to a chair at the table. "Baby . . ." She closed her eyes, shaking her head. "Billy . . ."

Angel's heart stopped. "Mama?" She clutched her chest, afraid to take a breath.

"It ain't what you think." She framed Angel's face with her hands. "But it ain't good."

"Tell me."

In the silence that followed, a familiar sound came from down the hallway. Mrs. Denton was crying, too.

The joy in Angel's heart disappeared. She swallowed hard. "Tell me, Mama."

"Ms. Denton gots a telegram. When Mista Denton an Jeriah got to Clifton, Billy wadn't there. The cap'n had already sent him away. Seems Cotton was causin' trouble with the mares."

"Sent him away?" No. Billy was supposed to be coming home.

Her mama nodded. "Hard to knows everthin' from a telegram, but the men ain't comin' home 'til they goes to Mobile."

"Mobile, Alabama?"

"That's right. They's gone to find him. They knows where he was goin', but we don't know when they be back." She stroked Angel's hair. "The children don't know. Ms. Denton wants to tell 'em later. They's missin' their daddy. This'll be hard on 'em."

Ada placed her arm over Angel's shoulder. "I knows how happy you was, thinkin' Billy be home in a few days. Your smile heps us all. Billy be home soon. Don't stop smilin'."

"*You're* not smilin', Ada."

"Don't matter none." She pulled a handkerchief from her apron pocket and blew her nose. "I's never been an *angel*. That's your job."

Were angels always expected to smile? Sometimes her name felt like a burden. Something she couldn't live up to. But her mama gave it to her for a reason and when Billy said it, it made her warm from the inside-out. How long would it be before she heard him say it again?

"We needs to get breakfast done," her mama said, rising. "Them children will be hungry, even if Ms. Denton ain't."

"*I'm* not hungry," Angel said.

"You hep fix it, you don't hafta eat it." Though her mama looked down on her with sympathy, she spoke with firmness.

"Yes, Mama." She'd do as she was told, but how could she keep the promise she'd made to herself? She didn't feel like smiling and she certainly didn't want to write in her book.

What if they don't find him and he never comes home?

"After the Denton's eat, you takes a plate to Bo," her mama instructed. "Since Jeriah ain't comin' home anytime soon, Bo be heppin' with the horses for a time." Her face wrinkled and her shoulders shook.

Thinking only of herself she'd not considered her mama. "I'm sorry, Mama." She jumped to her feet and embraced her. "I know Jeriah will be fine. He's with Mr. Denton. They'll be home before you know it."

They clung to each other. "I love you, Angel. We'll get through this."

Feeling more like a grown woman than ever before, Angel kissed her cheek. "Yes, we will."

Maybe things wouldn't be so bad. Billy'd have a lot more to tell her when he got home. And after this, maybe her mama and Jeriah would stop hiding their feelings and they could be a real family. Especially if they were given their freedom. *That's what Billy wanted. I want it, too.*

* * *

"Where we goin', Brian?" Joe asked. Cotton traveled along at a slow canter.

Billy stared straight ahead. "Mobile." After two days of traveling with Joe, he was exhausted.

"Ain't never heard of it." Joe wiggled in the saddle. "When we gonna eat?"

Food had become scarce. With the extra mouth to feed, they'd run out before reaching Fort Morgan. "Soon." He'd forego his own meals to make sure the boy ate.

He'd been grateful they'd seen little activity on the road. A few eyes followed them when they rode through small towns. At least no one bothered them. Apparently, they didn't pose a threat.

The weather had gotten warmer, just not warm enough. He was no longer able to see his breath, but remained bundled in his wool coat, hat, and gloves. Constantly worried about Joe, he wrapped his scarf around his little head and neck.

Cotton fared better than Billy. The ground offered vegetation for him to nibble and fresh water was plentiful. Billy's stomach rumbled, but as long as his horse and his *charge* were nourished, he was satisfied. Soon he'd have plenty to eat.

Joe munched on the remaining crackers. "I's still hungry, Brian."

"I know." He wished he knew how much further they had to go. Four and a half days had passed, so they had to be close. "I'll try to shoot a squirrel for dinner."

"Huh?" Joe squinted and wrinkled his nose. "I ain't never ate no squirrel."

"They're better than nothing."

As Cotton plodded along, Billy could have easily closed his eyes. Even though he'd slept, it had been restless and dreams weren't good. This had been too easy, and it made him uncomfortable.

They rounded a corner and his weariness slapped him in the face. Before he could turn around, he was face-to-face with a greyback.

In all the conversations he'd had with Joe, he'd neglected to tell him what to do if they came upon soldiers. Maybe it was a good thing. Joe didn't know his mission and he wouldn't know what should or shouldn't be said.

Breathing deeply, Billy urged Cotton forward, reminding himself to keep his wits.

A shredded quilt partially covered the man approaching them. He looked far worse than any of the soldiers in Clifton; thin, threadbare, and completely unkempt.

When the man produced a rifle from beneath the blanket, Billy's heart raced.

Remember your story.

Joe craned his neck backward, looking at Billy with eyes as large as saucers.

Billy gave him a reassuring squeeze. "Everything will be fine," he whispered.

"Where ya headed?" the soldier asked, then spat on the ground. Though thin, the man was tall with hardened features. Not someone to be crossed.

Billy squared his jaw. "Mobile."

"What fer?"

"My uncle's ill. I'm going to see him."

"That yer nigger?" The man stared at Joe, then moved his eyes to Cotton and licked his lips.

Joe's heart beat rapidly beneath Billy's arms. "He belongs to my uncle. I'm returning him."

"He a runaway?"

What should he say? Joe's punishment could be brutal. "Yes, but I've disciplined him. It won't happen again."

With a gentle nudge to Cotton's ribs, Billy urged him on.

Cotton took a step, only to be stopped by the soldier. "Didn't say you could go."

"Why? My uncle's waiting." Sweat beaded on his brow. Had the man noticed?

This was one time he wished his horse would rear up and bite, but it would probably make matters worse. He patted Cotton's side hoping he didn't sense danger.

The man took a step back, then raised his rifle. "Get off the horse."

Joe trembled. Billy's mind reeled, deciding what to do. He could jab Cotton with his heels and he'd bolt, but they'd likely be shot. "I don't understand, sir." *Stay calm.* "We need to be on our way."

"I said, get off yer horse!" The man raised his gun even higher and with his finger on the trigger took aim.

Billy had no option but to dismount. Joe remained in the saddle shaking beneath his saggy green sweater, his face partially hidden by the blue scarf.

"Get yer nigger down." The man nodded toward Joe, but kept the rifle in the air.

No other soldiers were in sight. This man appeared to be a lone picket making his own rules.

"He's tired. Can't I leave him on the horse?" Billy tried to smile but his lips twitched as he pushed them upward.

"I ain't gonna tell ya again. Get 'im down." The man turned his head to spit, then took aim again at Joe.

"C'mon, Joe," Billy said, calmly. "It'll be all right." He lifted him off the horse and set him down, all the while keeping his eyes on the man and his rifle.

The greyback jerked his head and pointed up the road. "Over there. An get on yer knees."

Without thinking, Billy moved his hand to his coat pocket, drawing the man's attention.

"What are ya doin?" the man yelled. "Get yer hands in the air!"

Complying, he raised his hands, then nodded to Joe. "Joe, do like me."

"Yeah, *Joe*. Listen to yer master." The man snarled and spit.

The tears in Joe's eyes broke Billy's heart. Dropping to his knees, he motioned for Joe to kneel. "Why are you doing this?"

The man led Cotton to a nearby tree and tied him. He tucked his rifle beneath his arm while rummaging through Billy's pack. Finding the Kentucky rifle, he sneered. "I reckon yer a Yankee. Ya talk like one. An that little nigger boy ain't yers. Yer too nice to 'im."

"I'm no Yankee. I told you, I'm returning Joe to my uncle." Watching the man sort through his belongings made his stomach churn.

"Damn," the man chuckled. "Done found me a gum!"

"Take it. I don't need it. I'll be home soon."

The man faced him with a scowl on his face that proved he had other things in mind. "Don't count on it. I aim to take ya to the sergeant. He don't take to Yankee spies." He stroked Cotton's sides. "Damn fine horse."

This couldn't be happening. He'd gotten so close.

The note . . . Eat it if you have to . . .

With the soldier facing the other direction, Billy reached for his pocket while keeping his eyes focused on him. Angel's carving rested in his grasp, so he slipped it inside his glove. He reached further for the note.

"Brian?" Joe's little voice squeaked out.

"It's all right, Joe." Though he'd said it more than once, he could tell the little boy didn't believe him. The fear in his eyes said everything.

"I ain't goin' back to the masta." Before Billy could stop him, Joe stood and sprinted toward the trees.

The man's head jerked up. He stepped away from Cotton and repositioned his rifle.

"No!" Billy yelled, jumping to his feet. He sprung at the man, but he'd already pulled the trigger. The blast from the gun pierced Billy's ears, but the sound of Joe falling to the ground shattered his heart.

Billy encircled the man's waist and wrestled him down. In his weakened state he was no rival for this soldier. Billy grunted and panted, fighting for his life.

The man easily slipped out of his grasp. He stood and hovered over him. His eyes held more hatred than he'd ever seen. His face contorted. He ground his rotten teeth and snarled. "He won't run away again! Neither will you!"

In one swift motion the man raised his gun and turned it around. Thoughts raced through Billy's mind as the butt of the rifle came straight toward his head.

Angel . . .

Chapter 15

An entire week had passed since the arrival of the telegram. Angel ate less and less.

"You're gonna shrivel away to nothin'." Her mama pushed a bowl of oats toward her.

Angel stared at the food, picked up a spoon, and swirled it through the mush. "I can't."

"Do I need to feed you like a baby?" She sat beside her. "Ain't doin' no good not eatin'."

"We should a heard sumthin' by now." Slumping down in the chair, Angel tipped her head back and closed her eyes.

"Yes, we should." The words came from Mrs. Denton. She crossed to the stove and dished herself a bowl of oatmeal.

Angel sat upright, completely alert.

"You needs to let me do that for you, Ms. Denton," Ada said.

"I'm able to get my own oats, Ada." She smiled and sat.

"You feelin' better this mornin', Mrs. Denton?" Angel asked. She waited for a cold response.

"You need to eat, Angel." She took a bite of oats. "You're gettin' too thin."

"Yes'm." She forced a bite into her mouth.

What had changed her? Had she heard good news? Angel dare not ask. Bringing up Billy always ended with an argument or tears.

"Want some tea, Ms. Denton?" Ada asked.

"Yes. Thank you, Ada." She continued eating.

Her mama had been staring at the two of them. Mrs. Denton returned her gaze. "Have *you* eaten, Bessie?"

"Yes'm." She didn't move.

"I wanna have a talk. Why don't you sit down?"

Her mama complied, but nervously rubbed her nose.

Mrs. Denton took a breath. "I miss Douglas, an I ain't gotta tell you how much I miss Billy." She looked at Angel. The anger she'd seen before was gone, replaced by grief.

Angel confirmed her understanding with a nod.

"I've been hard on you," she continued. "An I'm sorry. One day when you're a ma, you'll understand. No matter how old your babies get, you still wanna protect 'em."

Angel sniffled. "I'm sorry, too. I didn't mean to hurt you."

Mrs. Denton stretched her hand across the table. "I know you didn't. Your ma's right 'bout you. You're a good girl an I was wrong to say them things 'bout your pa. Can you forgive me?"

Holding Mrs. Denton's hand wasn't enough. Angel hopped out of her chair and went to her, wrapping her arms around her. "There ain't nothin' to forgive. I know how much you love Billy. From now on, I won't keep any-thin' from you."

She held Angel tightly. "You're growin' up. Some things I don't hafta know. But . . ."

Just when Angel had started to feel better, her voice changed. "But?" She returned to her seat.

"I need you to promise me that when Billy comes home you'll be his friend an nothin' more."

Just as her mama had asked. And though her heart told her otherwise, she did what was best. "Yes'm. I promise."

Her mama nodded. "That's my girl."

Rising to her feet, Mrs. Denton took her empty bowl and handed it to Ada. "The children will be up soon. The oats tasted extra good this mornin'. Not sure what you did, but I liked 'em. I know the children will, too. I'll come back an have my tea when they eat."

Ada beamed. "It be cinnamon, Ms. Denton."

As Mrs. Denton walked out of the kitchen, she turned and looked at Angel one last time. "I'm only tryin' to keep you from bein' hurt. It's best for everyone."

Angel tried to smile. *How can it be best for everyone . . . especially me an Billy?*

Didn't their feelings matter at all?

Her mama stood and crossed to her. "You're gonna be thirteen soon. You gots lotsa time for others to care 'bout. Billy will always be your friend."

"Yes'm."

"Now. Finish your oats, then go check on Bo. Make shore he's keepin' them horses up." She patted her cheek, then went to help Ada.

Check on Bo.

Her intentions were obvious. But Bo wasn't Billy. Besides, he was much too old for her. He probably saw her as a child, not the young woman she was. And though she liked looking at him and enjoyed talking to him, her heart had already been taken. No one could ever change that. Not her mama, not Mrs. Denton, and certainly not Bo.

Chapter 16

Why was it so hard to open his eyes? He forced them open only to regret it.

It's too bright . . . He shielded his eyes from the piercing light. Everything was white.

Fabric swished. Someone brushed by him. Sounds were muffled and unclear. And to make matters worse, his head pounded, causing him to moan. *What's on my forehead?*

"Don't touch that." A gentle hand moved his arm away from his face. A female who sounded more like a child than a woman. She rested his arm across his chest. "I'll be right back."

He squeezed his eyes shut again. Seeing was too difficult. *My head hurts . . .*

He started to raise his arm, but laid it down again heeding her words.

What's happening? His rapidly beating heart and dry mouth affirmed his fear.

As he lay still, his hearing sharpened. There were other people near him speaking softly. Footsteps approaching got louder and louder. Not the same as before. Much heavier, like that of a man. He slowed his breathing, attempting to remain calm.

A large hand grabbed his wrist. At least a minute passed. "Your pulse is strong." The man released him but didn't move. "Can you open your eyes?"

Again, he struggled to raise his lids. "Too bright." The sound of his own voice startled him, and from the way the man jumped, he assumed it had startled him, too.

"Talking?" the man asked with a chuckle. "Hannah, you didn't tell me he was talking."

"He wasn't." There was a smile in her voice.

"Where?" He couldn't finish his question, but it didn't matter.

"You're my miracle for today," the man said.

Hannah giggled. "I told you he'd be fine, Daddy. I mean . . . *Dr. Mitchell.*"

"Forgive my daughter," Dr. Mitchell said. "She's a big help, but sometimes forgets protocol."

"Protocol?"

The doctor cleared his throat. "Never mind. I'm Dr. Mitchell and this is Hannah. And from what we've been told, your name is Brian. We'd like to know more so we can contact your family."

"What?" He couldn't have been more confused. "Who's Brian?" His eyes were open now, adjusted to the light. All of the white transformed into high painted walls with tall windows, sheet-covered beds, and hospital uniforms. His heart eased. They were trying to help him.

Dr. Mitchell had a kind face, though the bags under his eyes, beneath wire-rimmed glasses, indicated he needed sleep. His well-groomed mustache danced sideways, as he tilted his head and licked his lips. His eyes narrowed. "I assumed it to be your name. The little boy we're treating didn't want to be separated from you. He called you Brian. We thought he belonged to you."

"Belonged to me?" None of this made sense.

"He's a slave. We nearly lost him, but he's recovering. I had to break hospital rules treating him here. Our administrator frowns on mixing Negroes with white patients."

Trying to sit up caused his head to pound even harder. The doctor pushed him back into the bedding with a firm, but gentle hand.

Now, not only pain, but *fear* gripped him once again and he trembled.

"Hannah," Dr. Mitchell whispered. "Leave us for a while."

The girl had large blue eyes and blond hair in ringlets beneath an overly-large nurse's cap. She wore white, but couldn't be old enough to be a nurse. She frowned as she walked away.

"She's been looking after you," the doctor said. "Made you her pet project."

He stared at the man.

"I'm sorry. I can see you're frightened. Since this war started, I've lost my bedside manner."

"War?"

Dr. Mitchell let out a long pronounced breath. "What do you remember?"

He lifted his hand to his head, only to have the doctor lower it again. He tried to clear his mind and think. "Nothing."

"Nothing?"

He closed his eyes and pushed his head further into the pillow, but then winced from an unexpected jolt of pain. "I know you're a doctor and I must be in a hospital." Opening his eyes, he lifted his hand in front of his face. "I know this is my hand, but—I don't know who *I* am."

The doctor took it and gripped it tightly. "You were badly injured. We don't know how you got here, or who brought you. You were found on the hospital steps with the little boy."

"The one who called me Brian?"

"Yes. If he'd died, we wouldn't have a name for you."

Brian? It seemed completely foreign, although there was something about it . . . "And it was because of me you treated him at all? Is that right?"

"You misunderstood. I'd have treated him regardless. But I have to answer to someone who doesn't share my feelings."

This doctor's a good man. "Has he told you anything else?"

"I'm afraid not." Dr. Mitchell frowned. "Aside from being shot, he's terrified of something. We hoped you'd be able to tell us."

"He was shot?"

"Grazed his neck. If the bullet had gone slightly more to the right he'd have choked on his own blood."

Somehow he knew men weren't supposed to cry, but he couldn't stop tears from pooling in his eyes. "Was *I* shot?"

The doctor shook his head. "No. You were hit in the head. *Hard.* And the injury on the *back* of your head indicates you must have struck it on the ground when you fell. Whoever did this wanted you out cold. It's a miracle they didn't kill you. You're very lucky."

Lucky? He didn't feel lucky. He blinked and tears trickled down his cheeks.

Dr. Mitchell patted his shoulder, then stood. "Get some rest. I know this is a lot for you to digest. We'll talk more later." He walked away.

How could he sleep? Aside from his throbbing head, his heart ached. How could he know what a doctor was and yet not know who *he* was? He could name every item in the room; bed, window, pillow, even sunlight. The doctor was a man and his daughter a girl. And the other people in the room—aside from being *patients*—were men. So how could he have names for all of these *things* but not one for himself?

Pinching his eyes shut, he tried to remember. It only made his head pound harder. The bandage above his eye must be covering the wound.

Evaluating the rest of his body, he made a mental note of every part. Those he could name as well; neck, shoulder, arm, chest, hips, legs, and feet.

Fingers and toes, too. Aside from his head, nothing hurt but his heart.

Somehow, he managed to sleep. When he woke, the room was dark. Looking toward the door, a light flickered in the hallway. "Nurse!"

A tall brunette came in waving her hands. "Shh . . ." She placed her finger to her lips. "You'll wake the others."

He carefully turned his head. There were three other men in beds like his. His hands shook, as he turned his attention back to her. "What's wrong with me?"

"It's all right, Brian. I'll get Dr. Mitchell." She walked away.

Brian? Yes, that's the name they gave me.

The trembling in his hands spread to his arms, then his entire body. He wasn't cold, so why was he shaking?

Dr. Mitchell entered the room, took a seat beside him, then placed his hand on his forehead. "Fever," he said to the nurse who'd followed him in. "Get some ice."

She rushed from the room, then returned holding a cloth bag.

"You're fortunate it's winter. Ice is easy to come by." Dr. Mitchell placed the bag on the uninjured side of his head. "I need to bring your fever down. If this doesn't help we may have to cover you completely."

Brian breathed hard and didn't attempt to respond.

"Take deep breaths," the doctor instructed. "Try to relax."

Doing as he was told, he eventually stopped trembling.

The doctor pushed a cold metal cup against his lips. "Drink," he said. "It'll help the pain."

He'd do anything to make it all go away; the pain *and* the fear. Whatever he gave him sent him drifting back to sleep.

When he woke for the second time, bright rays of sunshine beamed through the window. The bag of ice was nowhere near him and his body was still. His stomach grumbled.

A different nurse entered his room. This one was short and plump. Her hair was streaked with gray and her chubby cheeks were bordered with deep wrinkles. "Feeling better I see!" she chirped, then pulled him into a sitting position. "It's good you're awake. I need to change your bedding. It's much easier when you're not in it."

Flipping the blankets from his body, she shifted his bare legs over the side of the bed. "In the chair with you." Placing one arm around his waist, she hoisted him from the bed and plopped him into the wooden chair beside it.

Strangely, nothing hurt.

As she stripped the bed, she hummed, then looked over her shoulder and grinned. "What's wrong? You act as though I've not done this before." She resumed humming.

He thought hard. No, he'd never seen her before. She wasn't someone he'd forget. "Ma'am?" He swallowed, moistening his dry throat. "I don't know you."

"Silly boy!" She tittered. "I've not only changed your bed the past three days, I've changed *you*!"

A rush of heat covered his face, which only prompted her to giggle harder. As she bent over to smooth his sheets, her large bottom nearly hit him in the face.

"All done!" she chimed, then pinched his cheek. "Your face is as red as your hair." Winking, she lifted him to his feet and returned him to the clean bed.

Dressed in a simple hospital gown—and thankfully a pair of underdrawers—he pulled his blankets up to his neck and lay against the pillow. Feeling no pain, he touched his forehead. The bandage was still there. "Nurse . . ."

"Primrose," she said, grinning.

"Nurse Primrose, I'm very hungry."

She clasped her hands to her chest. "That's music to my ears!" She left the room, humming once again.

"You have an admirer."

Brian faced the man who spoke. It was the first time he'd realized there were now only two of them in the room. The other beds were empty. "I do?"

The man nodded toward the door. "Nurse Primrose. She only hums when she takes care of *you*. She doesn't find *me* so appealing."

When the man lowered his blanket, Brian gasped, seeing he had only one arm. "I . . ."

"Don't feel bad. I get that reaction all the time." He took his one hand and rubbed it across the stub on his shoulder. "It doesn't hurt anymore. Dr. Mitchell's good at what he does. Has the hospital record."

"For what?"

"Cuttin' off limbs. He can do it faster than any other doctor."

His appetite plummeted. "Why would he be cutting off limbs?"

"I nearly forgot. You're the one who doesn't remember anything. Wish I was you. I'd give anything to forget the war." He covered himself again, hiding the wound.

Brian would give anything to *remember*. Wouldn't it be better to be without an arm or leg than to have no memory? "Was *I* in the war?" It had to be the only explanation.

The man rubbed his chin. "You look kind a young. But you might a been. From what I've heard, no one knows where you came from." He shrugged. "My name's David. I'm glad you're awake. I was gettin' lonely without anyone to talk to."

"I'm . . . *Brian*."

"Brian!" A small Negro boy jumped on his bed, climbed on top of him, and flung his arms around him taking his breath. "They told me you was awake and you wasn't sick no more!"

When he didn't reply, the boy sat back on his heels but remained on his chest. "Why you lookin' at me like that? Din't you miss me?"

"Who are you?" *The boy Dr. Mitchell spoke of?*

"I's Joe!" He placed his hands on his hips. "They hit your head hard. Din't they, Brian?"

"Who did?"

His face fell. "Don't wanna talk 'bout that."

The little boy stayed atop him, giving no indication he intended to leave. Brian noticed a small bandage on his neck and pointed to it. "Is that where they shot you?"

"I say I don't wanna talk 'bout that!"

Brian sighed with relief when Dr. Mitchell entered the room, followed by Nurse Primrose. She carried a tray of food that smelled wonderful. His appetite had returned.

"I heard you're hungry," Dr. Mitchell said with a smile. His eyes shined behind his glasses, as he rubbed his hand across the top of Joe's head.

Joe laughed, but didn't move.

"Yes, I am." With great effort, Brian moved Joe to the side, then scooted up in bed and propped the pillow behind his back. The little boy didn't seem to mind being moved, and continued to stare at him.

"The food be better than yours," Joe said, wrinkling his nose. "They ain't cooked no squirrels."

"Squirrels?" What had he done with this child?

Dr. Mitchell pulled up a chair and took his wrist. When he finished checking his pulse, he placed his hand on his forehead. "You'll be ready to leave the hospital in a day or two. I want to be sure you get some food in your belly first."

"Leave?"

"Yes. Your fever's gone and your wound is nearly healed. We have to make room for other patients. Unfortunately, we never know when we'll have another influx of soldiers."

The war wasn't over. "Where will I go?"

The doctor folded his arms over his chest. "Still no memories?"

"No, sir." Since Joe seemed determined to stay in his room, Brian decided to try and get some information from him. "Joe, do you know where I live?"

He shook his head. "Uh-uh. You never told me. You just said we was goin' to Mobile."

"Where did *you* come from?"

"I ain't tellin'!" He hopped off the bed and fled the room.

Nurse Primrose placed a cloth napkin around Brian's neck and patted his cheek. "Don't worry about that child. He'll be back. He has nowhere else to go from what we've gathered. And—he likes the food." She began spoon-feeding Brian a bowl of chicken soup.

The soup tasted delicious, but he felt foolish. "Can I please feed myself?"

She pouted, then handed him the spoon, followed by the bowl. "I'll come back later to help you relieve yourself."

David snickered.

"That's also something I can do myself." *What else did she do to me while I was sleeping?* Maybe he didn't *want* to remember.

Dr. Mitchell had sat silently until she left. "She's a good nurse. She means well. Likes to mother all of you young men."

"As far as I know she could *be* my mother." Self-pity consumed him.

"I know of a boarding house in town not far from the hospital. They have a room for you if you want it."

"I don't even know where I am."

"You're in Mobile, Alabama. Which—if Joe's telling the truth—is where you were going when you were injured. This is Mobile City Hospital. Does that sound familiar?"

He thought hard and took another bite of soup. "I wish it did."

"I've seen only one other case of severe memory loss. He eventually recovered, but it took time."

"How long?"

The doctor paused. "Years."

Years. "Is there anything I can do to help it?"

"Nothing in particular. Something may simply trigger a memory. Seeing someone you know, or even hearing a certain name. The mind is peculiar. You'll have to be patient."

Obviously, he had no other choice. "Thank you for telling me about the boarding house, but how can I go there without money?"

"How do you feel about work?"

Though he had no memory of it, it didn't scare him. "I can work. As long as you say I'm strong enough."

"You are."

"But what can I do? I don't know if I know how to do anything." *I sound so foolish.*

Dr. Mitchell chuckled. "We'll have to see. You might surprise yourself."

"What 'bout me?" Joe's big brown eyes peered around the door frame.

Dr. Mitchell glanced at Joe, then returned his attention to Brian, questioning him with his eyes. "He says he belongs to you."

Brian set the bowl of soup on the tray beside his bed. "Are you sure he and I were together?"

Joe took a step into the room and leaned against the wall, tapping his feet like a nervous cat.

"When you were brought in, you were both nearly naked. Whoever brought you took your clothes. Even your boots. They left you in your underclothes. And—oddly enough—you were wearing gloves and Joe had a scarf wrapped around his neck that matched them. The scarf was covered in blood and we had to dispose of it, but we still have the gloves and what was inside."

"Inside?"

The doctor opened the drawer of a small bed stand. He held up a little figurine and gave it to him. "It was in your hand."

Brian studied the small wooden thing. "A bug?"

"I don't know. It *looks* like a bug." Dr. Mitchell peered at it. "Maybe even an angel."

"An angel?"

"Whatever it's supposed to be, it must have meant something to you."

So the only things in his possession were a pair of gloves, a wooden bug, and a Negro boy named Joe. His life had become a mystery.

Chapter 17

Dr. Mitchell smiled and handed Brian some clothes donated by a local church.

"You've been more than kind to me," Brian said.

The doctor sat. "I wish I could do more. I know you have a family somewhere missing you. It's hard for me to imagine what I'd do if any of *my* children were missing."

Brian began dressing, thankful to be shedding the hospital gown. "How can you be sure I have one?"

"You're well-spoken. Obviously educated. And you have the hands of someone who hasn't done a lot of manual labor. I doubt very much you're an orphan."

Joe sat in a chair in the corner of the room swinging his legs. "I's ready to go, Brian. I's tired a sleepin' in the basement."

Brian had gotten to know him better over the past two days. The little boy was growing on him. Though he couldn't recall how Joe came into his possession, he wasn't going to leave him. He'd brought him to Mobile, so it seemed they were meant to be together.

"Soon, Joe." Brian buttoned his shirt. The sleeves were about two inches too short, but at least he was covered. And unlike Joe's clothing, it didn't swallow him whole.

David cleared his throat. "I'll miss having you as a roommate."

"You'll be going home soon," Dr. Mitchell said. "I'm certain that makes you happy."

"Yes, sir."

"Where's home?" Brian asked, then sat on the edge of his bed.

"Jackson, Mississippi." David rose up and scooted against the wall.

Brian didn't know where it was, but smiled and nodded.

Through the course of their conversations, he'd learned about the war. It was a war between the North and the South and had lasted for four years already. Slavery was a key issue, but David had told him he believed it was more about money than anything else.

Hard to comprehend. Not knowing which side he'd been fighting for was the oddest thing of all. Since he owned a slave and was going to Mobile, he assumed he'd been fighting for the South. But it didn't feel right.

There was much he needed to know. Who'd hurt him and why hadn't they killed him? "Dr. Mitchell? When my memories return, will I remember everything?"

The doctor removed his glasses and polished them with the tail of his white coat, then gave him a stern look. "There's no guarantee your memory *will* return. I pray it does, and I hope that *when* it does you'll remember everything. But don't have unrealistic expectations."

"I won't," he whispered.

A pair of boots accompanied the clothing. When he put them on, they were too big. "Any chance I'm still growing?"

The doctor smiled broadly, then offered some cotton to stuff in the toes. "Since I don't know how old you are I can't answer that."

Joe hopped from his chair. "He be eighteen!"

Brian stared at the child. "How do you know that?"

"You told me." Joe rolled his eyes and placed his hands on his hips.

"I'm sorry, Joe. I didn't remember." He readjusted his cotton-stuffed boots.

"You don't member nothin'! I told you I was six an you said you was eighteen. Twelve years older than me." He returned to his chair, shaking his head.

Dr. Mitchell's brows rose. "Well, now. At least we know your age. Being eighteen, you may or may not grow. If you were a few years younger I'd say it was probable."

Brian sighed. At least he knew *something*. "Is there anything else you can tell me, Joe?"

Joe wrinkled his nose and looked toward the ceiling. "You had a big white horse."

"There wasn't by any chance a white horse on the steps of the hospital with us, was there, Doctor?" Brian's sarcastic tone made him smile.

"I'm afraid not." His smile quickly vanished. "They took your clothes. A horse is much more valuable. I'm sorry, Brian."

Joe stood and crossed the room. "You hepped me, Brian." He wrapped his skinny arms around him. "You took care a me." He tilted his head back and looked up into his face. "Are we goin' to see your uncle now?"

Brian's heart raced. "My what?"

"Your uncle! You said we was goin' to Mobile to see your uncle."

"If you have an uncle in the city," David said. "He shouldn't be hard to find."

Dr. Mitchell's face brightened as he patted Joe on the head. "Joe may have helped us more than he realizes. I'll put a posting in the newspaper. If your uncle was expecting you, there may be others he told you never arrived. Some-one is bound to make the connection."

A ray of hope beamed into Brian's heart. If only his un-cle could find him and help him remember. Somehow, he knew he'd piece it all together. Maybe one day soon.

It was time to leave. The doctor had made arrangements for them to stay at the boarding house. He'd even set up a meeting for Brian with a woman who needed help with her café. He wasn't guaranteed a job, but had been told the woman would be willing to talk to him.

Joe was another matter. He'd be able to stay with him at the boarding house, but he wasn't sure what he'd do with him while he worked.

"You're going to need this." Dr. Mitchell placed money in Brian's palm.

"No. You've done more than enough already." He tried to return it, but the doctor refused.

"When you start working, you can pay it back. Would that make you feel better?"

He nodded. "Yes, sir. Thank you."

"I'm glad I didn't miss you!" Hannah rushed in with the brightest smile he'd seen all day. She was wearing a regular day dress, covered by a long blue coat. A matching hat sat atop her curls. She was a pretty girl. *One day she'll be a beautiful woman.*

"I was just about to leave," he said.

"*We* was just 'bout to leave," Joe corrected him.

"I made these for you," she said, then handed him a tin filled with pastry.

They smelled wonderful. *Cinnamon.* "Thank you, Hannah."

She coyly tipped her head and grinned. "You're welcome."

Joe tried to reach into the tin, but Brian stopped him. "Later, Joe. We'll take them to the boarding house." Joe pouted, but complied.

"Brian." Dr. Mitchell placed a hand on his shoulder. "Come back and see me in a week. *Sooner* if you have any problems. Pain. Headaches. After you leave here, I'm still your doctor."

"I will. And if I remember everything and find out I'm rich, I can pay you back even sooner." He wiggled his brows and laughed.

Dr. Mitchell chuckled, then sobered. "I hope you *do* remember. Rich or not."

"*I* wants to be rich!" Joe interjected, once again brightening their mood.

Hannah walked with them down the hall to the front desk. Brian was asked to sign a release document. He looked up at Dr. Mitchell. "How can I sign this?"

"If you don't know how to write, put an *X* there." Dr. Mitchell pointed to the document.

"I remember how to write, but do I just sign, *Brian*?"

"For now it'll have to do." The doctor offered an encouraging smile.

Brian. He scrolled the name perfectly; still, it didn't feel right. As if his hand had never written the word. It shouldn't bother him, but it did. *I want to remember.*

With Joe holding his right hand and Hannah's pastries in his left, he walked out the front door of the hospital.

He stopped and gulped. Concrete steps fanned out to the street below. He took several steps, then turned to look behind him. A long row of tall white pillars adorned the front of the hospital making it look like a Greek temple. He counted at least fifteen columns. *Magnificent.*

But how do I know what a Greek temple looks like?

Joe tugged on his hand. "C'mon, Brian! We gots to go!"

Brian hoped his new memories had been retained so they could reach the boarding house. He visualized the doctor's directions in his mind.

Every step he took led him further away from the security of the hospital. He didn't want to fail, but knew nothing about his life. He felt like a newborn baby starting life at eighteen. No one should have to live like that.

Joe squeezed his hand. "It's a'right, Brian. I's gonna take care a you."

A six-year-old would take care of him. His life couldn't be more upside-down.

* * *

At the end of the two-level stairway, Brian turned right. They passed Sylvia's Pantry, then went on a short distance until he found the boarding house. He'd wait until tomorrow to go to Sylvia's, which was where Dr. Mitchell had said a job might be available. The small café, with its curtained windows, appeared harmless, so why did his heart pound when he passed it?

The bare branches of tall-reaching live oak trees hovered over them, lining the street. Magnolias were scattered here and there as well as a few evergreens.

He shook his head. *I know what kind of trees they are. I must've grown up here.*

Counting the number of houses he passed, he reached number seven on the right.

Two-story red brick house bordered by a white-washed fence. The sign reading *rooms for rent* affirmed he'd come to the right place.

"C'mon, Joe." He gave a gentle tug on the boy's hand. "Let's see what they have for us."

Even though Joe had been in a hurry to leave the hospital, he froze and planted his feet on the stone pathway. "I cain't go in there." The boy was trembling.

"Why?"

"White folks live there."

"You're with me. They'll let you stay."

Joe scratched his head and wrinkled his nose. "You sure?"

"Dr. Mitchell told them about *both* of us. They know you're with me."

With a hand in the middle of his small back, Brian urged him forward. When they reached the door, Joe circled behind him and hid behind his legs.

A middle-aged woman opened the door. She had a tightly twisted auburn bun atop her head and even tighter pinched lips. Her dress was plain, covered by a knee-length white apron.

With slowly blinking eyes, she peered down her long pointed nose at him, then tilted her head, attempting to look at Joe.

"Dr. Mitchell sent us," Brian said.

"I've been expecting you." She continued to peer toward Joe, who went further into hiding.

"He's shy, ma'am." Brian tried to produce him, but he wouldn't budge.

"Wait here," she said, and retreated into the house. In moments she returned. "Will this help?" She extended a cookie.

Without hesitation, Joe grabbed it. Seconds later it was gone.

"There are more in the house, but you'll have to come inside to get one." Her voice was as sweet as he assumed the cookie had been. "There's plenty for you, too." She smiled at Brian.

The interior of the house matched the woman to perfection. Nothing elaborate. Simple colors. Tidy. To add to its appeal, the air smelled like vanilla. She'd probably just baked the cookies.

"This is the common room," she said, waving her hand. It had a large stone fireplace, two stuffed sofas, and two over-stuffed chairs. "You're welcome to use it at any time." She paused and looked at Joe. After a tentative smile, she returned her attention to Brian. "That is *you* may use this area. I'm afraid the boy will need to stay in your room. I'm making an exception allowing him to stay here at all. We normally don't house Negroes."

Brian didn't know what to say.

"If you read," she continued, "there are books on the shelves. All I ask is that you're careful with them and return them as soon as you're done reading."

She led them down a short hallway. "Your room is at the end. We have a back door you should use from now on. Considering the boy."

Because of Joe? Brian's heart fell. The woman spoke sweetly, yet her words were unkind. This didn't feel like home. But for now, they had no other option.

She turned a glass knob and pushed open the door to their room. Like the rest of the house, it was simple but comfortable. Twin beds had been pushed against the walls to his right and left, covered with patched quilts in colors of green and brown. Straight ahead was a window with light white drapery. A shared bed stand stood below it. The stand held a hurricane lantern and nothing more. The white walls were bare. The room couldn't have been plainer.

She pointed to the window. "The sun shines through in the morning and warms the room. You'll find extra blankets in the wardrobe if you need them."

The tall oak wardrobe was in the corner of the room to his left. On the opposite side of the room was a wooden stand holding a ceramic wash basin and water pitcher.

Her head dipped downward and she gestured toward the back door. "You'll find the outhouse through there. But . . ." She huffed and raised her head. "I'm afraid the boy will have to use the chamber pot. It's in the cabinet beneath the bowl and pitcher. I can't allow him in the outhouse."

"Why?" The common room had been understandable. The outhouse was another issue.

She licked her tight lips. "The other tenants wouldn't approve. After all, he's *colored.*"

"I'm aware of that, ma'am."

"So, you must understand it's not done. As I said, I'm making an exception allowing him to live here. Please don't make me regret my decision." Spoken as sweet as ever, but if they didn't abide by her rules she'd probably throw them out on the street.

"Yes, ma'am."

"Good." Her smile was one of satisfaction. "I'll leave you to get settled." She turned to go. "Oh, supper is at six o'clock sharp." She eyed him. "*You* may eat at the common table. You'll have to bring food to the room for the boy."

Brian wanted to flee. He glanced sideways at Joe. *We have nowhere to go.* "Ma'am?"

"Yes?"

"What do we call you?" No introductions had been made.

"Miss Harrison," she said, raising her chin.

"Thank you, Miss Harrison . . . for the room and all." At least they had a place to sleep, but his stomach churned with each polite word he cast her way. "I'm Brian and this is Joe."

"I know," she said, and walked away.

Joe crossed to the bed on the right and plopped down. He bounced up and down a few times with his hands splayed over the quilt. "Feels nice, Brian. I ain't never had my own bed before."

Brian set the pastry tin on the bed stand, then dug into his pants pocket and pulled out the carved bug. He rubbed it between his fingers before setting it down. The wood felt smooth. Someone had taken time to carve it. *Maybe I carved it myself.*

He sat on the other bed. "I don't know if I did or didn't have a bed of my own, but I think I can sleep here."

"Reckon your uncle will come for us?"

"I hope so." He lay back and rested his head on the pillow. His uncle *had* to come. Hopefully sooner rather than later. For now they'd have to make do. Tomorrow, he'd meet Sylvia and try to secure a job. With luck, there'd be something for Joe to do. He couldn't imagine leaving him locked in this little room all day long. *Not with that woman managing the house.*

* * *

Joe promised to stay in their room until Brian returned.

Surely he won't run away. Every time he tried to ask the boy how long they'd been together, he clammed up and wouldn't talk about anything. *Maybe one day . . .*

After standing in front of the building for more than ten minutes, it was time to stop thinking about it and go in. If only he had some decent clothes to wear. What would she think of him wearing a shirt too small and pants so long he had to roll them up at the bottom? At least he'd washed. His smell shouldn't offend her. With a breath of courage, he opened the door.

Though he'd already eaten breakfast, the smell of bacon filled the air and made his mouth water. Six tables dotted the floor, each with four chairs. A longer table was at the far end of the café. There he counted ten chairs. Thirty-four people could eat at full capacity. Seems he remembered a bit of math. Presently only two tables had patrons. Five people total.

Standing just inside the doorway, he couldn't move.

A tall young woman approached him wiping her hands on a towel. "Can I help ya?" A form-fitting apron covered her long blue dress, worn over a rather plump form. Her blond hair had been pulled up and held beneath a scarf. She had a kind face, but wasn't what he'd call *attractive.* With a crooked nose and very thin lips, her face was out of proportion.

Had he been staring? "I'm looking for Sylvia Watson."

"Ya found her." Her accent surprised him, but he liked it.

"I'm sorry. I expected you to be older. Dr. Mitchell said you own this café."

Wonderful. Now I've probably insulted her.

She laughed.

He breathed a relieved sigh.

"I'm twenty-two. And yep, I own it. My husband had money. When he died, I got it." Her tone sounded matter-of-fact. Not like that of a grieving widow. "Used it to buy this place."

"I'm sorry about your husband."

"Thank ya." She licked her lips. "He died early on in the war. I was sixteen when we married. Nineteen when he died." She gazed around the room. "This place helped me get over him. Gave me sumthin' to do. Hard when you know the one you love won't be comin' home."

Her openness caught him off guard. "I truly am sorry. But I'm glad you found something that makes you happy."

She smiled and nodded. "Doc tells me you're lookin' for work."

"Yes'm." His throat felt so dry he could barely respond.

"Call me Sylvia." She grinned. "I ain't much older than you. Doc says you're eighteen."

"Yes'm, *Sylvia.*" He liked her. "I'm Brian."

She tipped her head. "Ever wash dishes?"

"I—I don't know."

With an arm around his shoulder, she led him to the kitchen through a set of swinging doors. "I feel sorry for ya. Doc told me what happened." She pointed to a large stack of dirty pots and pans. "I got a lot needs cleanin'. Keep hot water on the stove in that there pot and soap over yonder." She nodded to a deep sink perched on top of a wood platform. "I'll show ya how to clean 'em. Think you can handle it?"

"You're giving me the job?" He had no idea she'd want him to start now.

"If you want it. Some folks don't like this kind a work. It ain't easy."

He hesitated, causing her eyebrows to rise, questioning him.

"I'm sorry," he said. "I have someone I need to look in on. I didn't know you'd want me to start today."

"I done forgot." She shook her head. "Doc told me 'bout the little boy. I reckon you can bring him with ya when you come to work, but he'll hafta stay back here. I can find sumthin' for him to do, but I can't pay him."

"He's only six. Is that a problem?"

"Reckon not. Long as he listens to ya and keeps outta trouble." A bell rang. Her head jerked to the sound. "Gotta check on my customers." She smiled over her shoulder as she scurried away. "If it helps your decision, you an the boy can eat for free."

"Thank you, Sylvia. I'll get Joe and be back before you have time to miss me." His heart danced. Something finally felt right.

"Good." She nodded to the back door. "Use that when ya come back with the boy. Sure you understand."

Yes, he understood. Back-door entrances were all he'd be allowed with Joe in his care. Maybe when his memory returned he'd be able to make sense of it.

Chapter 18

Tears blurred Angel's vision, but she'd write. She *had* to write.

January 25th, 1865. Billy's not coming home.

Staring at the words, she sucked in breath like it was water. Seeing it on paper made it real.

He's not coming home.

Her hand shook.

Mr. Denton and Jeriah rode in today from Clifton. They went back to ask more questions but didn't get any answers. Jeriah said the captain was upset and blames himself for Billy being gone. But Billy told him he had no family and wasn't using his real name. Why would he do that?

They went all the way to Mobile to a place called Fort Morgan. It was where Billy was supposed to be. He was never there. And now

She couldn't write the words. They couldn't be true. If they were, she'd feel it in her heart.

Billy can't be dead.

The book went back in her drawer, slipping from her trembling hands.

Flinging herself onto the bed, she buried her face into the old patch-work quilt.

Just before she'd left the main house, Mr. Denton brought the family doctor to give Mrs. Denton something to calm her. She'd never seen her so pale. Her wailing had echoed throughout the house.

Angel had tried to offer help, but the Denton's didn't want her anywhere near them. Seemed they were blaming her again. None of it was fair.

Though she'd told her mama she wanted to be alone to write, she realized she'd been wrong. She needed comfort.

She grasped the doorknob to her mama's bedroom. Ready to walk in, she stopped. Someone was with her. Normally, at this time of night, the only thing she could hear was her own breathing. The sounds coming from the room were unusual.

Her mama had a fondness for sweets. Every Christmas the Denton's would give her the same candy sticks they gave their children. The repetitive noise her mama was making was the same sound she made when she tasted the sweet candy. In response to that sound, a deeper reply mimicked her pleasure.

Angel pressed her ear to the door. It affirmed what she'd assumed was taking place. In a breathless whisper, her mama said his name. "Jeriah . . ."

They were lost in the comfort of each other's arms and *she'd* remain alone.

She envied them. Clinging to each other, sharing their love, and grateful they were no longer separated. They were breaking the rules, but the Denton's had enough of their own problems. Why worry about two slaves sharing a bed?

On the way to her room another sound stopped her.

She crept to the front door and silently opened it. "Biscuit." She covered her mouth, hoping she'd not been heard.

The cat ran to her. He snaked around her legs meowing all the while. She scooped him up. He'd been crying almost as much as she had since Billy left. He was, after all, Billy's cat.

She took him to her room, shut the door, and set him on the floor. He jumped on the bed.

"Alright, Biscuit," she whispered. "I reckon they don't want you 'round no more either. It's just you an me now."

She slipped under the blankets and lay back with a sigh. The moment her head touched the pillow, the cat nuzzled her chin with his wet nose.

Her mama wouldn't approve, but then again, *she* wasn't breaking the rules. Having a man in the house was another matter.

"She'll let me keep you here." She scratched under his chin, prompting a purr.

He lifted his paw and patted her nose, then licked her face. The uncomfortable roughness of his tongue surprised her. Relieved when he settled down to sleep, she put her hand across his belly. The rise and fall of his fur affirmed the warmth of his unconditional love.

Love.

Billy . . .

* * *

Am I really tryin' to be comforted by a cow?

Angel sat on the milking stool with her head rested against its plump belly. Having just finished milking her, Angel's tears flowed. The satisfied cow didn't move.

"Angel?"

She gasped, jerked her head up, and wiped away tears with the back of her hand. She almost spilled the bucket of milk.

Bo stood over her, holding a pitchfork. Why'd it have to be him?

"Angel, you a'right?" He held out his hand.

She hesitated before taking it, then allowed him to help her to her feet. "I'm fine." Quickly releasing his hand, she brushed off her skirt and picked up the pail.

"Don't look fine." He took hold of her chin. "Why you cryin'?" He pulled a handkerchief from his pocket and handed it to her. "Cuz a Billy?"

She took the handkerchief and blew her nose. "No." *Not this time.*

His brows rose. "No? I figgered—"

"I hate havin' them soldiers here!"

"What happened?" He led her to a hay bale and helped her sit.

She sniffled. "Nothin' happened, but I'm scared of 'em. They say things when I go by."

His face hardened. "What kind a things?"

"I—I can't tell you." Embarrassed, she covered her face.

"Miss Angel," he spoke with the same firm tone she'd heard from Jeriah. "I cain't hep you, if'n you don't tell me." He knelt in front of her. "If'n you cain't tell *me*, you needs to tell Mista Denton. He take care of it."

That was the last thing she'd do. "No! He can't know." Her face scrunched into a tight ball, forcing back tears.

"Tell me, Angel." This time he demanded an answer.

She trusted him, but didn't want to involve him. Causing problems at the estate seemed to be her new purpose in life. But the concern in his eyes indicated he wanted to help. Maybe it wouldn't hurt. "There's two of 'em that watch me every mornin' when I come to milk Spot. At first they just watched, but now they say things." She peered into his eyes. With a nod of his head, he encouraged her to go on. "They said I was pretty and don't look like other slaves."

He remained quiet and listened.

She looked down. "This mornin' they said I look fine cuz I have white in me. Then one of 'em asked me if Mr. Denton was my daddy."

She laid her head against her knees and sobbed.

"Don't cry, Miss Angel." He patted her back. "Pay 'em no mind."

Her head tipped slightly to look at him. "Why'd they say sumthin' so ugly? Mr. Denton would never do that. He loves Mrs. Denton."

"Some folks got mush in their heads." He stood and shoved the pitchfork into another bale of hay. "Promise me, if they keep on you'll tell Mista Denton."

"I can't!" She jumped to her feet and grabbed his arm. "I don't want him to know they're sayin' things 'bout him. He has enough dealin' with Billy bein' gone."

He crossed his arms. "They's sayin' things they gots no business sayin'. Thinkin' things they shouldn't. They might try doin' sumthin' to ya." His eyes grew more intense. "Understan'?"

Her tears stopped and she nodded her head. The way her stomach flip-flopped whenever they spoke to her, something about them threatened her.

She picked up the pail. "I gotta get to the house. Will you walk with me?"

"Course I will." He followed her out the stable door.

"I want things to be like they were before." She spoke in a whisper while looking sideways at the encampment.

"Before?" He kept in stride with her.

"Before Billy left."

He kept quiet until they reached the house. "I gots to get back to work, but member what I say."

"Thank you, Bo. I will." She opened the back door and went inside.

What would she do if the soldiers tried to touch her? Would they be punished if they did? Or did her status as a slave allow them to do whatever they pleased? *I can't believe that.*

She didn't want to involve Mr. Denton, but Bo was right. He'd take care of things. He might be angry over Billy, but he was a good man and he'd always taken care of her.

* * *

"Whew!" Brian wiped his brow. Washing dishes wasn't easy.

Joe had the task of scraping remnants of food into the trash and never grumbled. Each workday started at sunrise. A rooster perched outside their window woke them.

Since Sylvia fed them, Brian had told Miss Harrison that board was unnecessary, which reduced the rate of their stay. Even so, almost all the money he earned from Sylvia's would be used to pay for his room and to repay Dr. Mitchell. If he ever wanted to afford new clothing, he'd have to find a way to make more money.

He worked from sunup until sundown every day but Sunday, with only a few hours off after the midday meal. Most nights he carried Joe home clinging to his back.

It was almost time to go. He and Joe were finishing up some leftover pork roast from supper.

"You're a hard worker," Sylvia said.

"Thank you." Brian stared at his wrinkled hands. "You think too much water is bad for my skin?" He wiggled his fingers in the air.

She laughed. "Reckon not. You regret takin' the job?"

"No. But I'm not so sure about Joe." His little body was slumped over; sound asleep with a biscuit clutched in his fist.

"I don't wanna lose you. I might can raise your rate, if business keeps pickin' up. Folks've had a tough time with the war an all. Mobile has seen its share a hard times."

"I need to get Joe home, but I'd like you to tell me about it sometime. I've noticed a lot of soldiers around the city. When we tried to go to the bay, we were stopped. As if they were guarding the shoreline."

"They are. Union wants Mobile. Our men'll go down fightin' if they hafta. I seen enough bloodshed in August to last me a lifetime." A sad smile shadowed her face. "You're tired. Go home an get some rest. I'll see you t'morra."

He hoisted Joe into his arms and headed for the back door. He'd have to remember to ask her what she meant.

"Wait!" She stopped him, bustled from the room, then returned just as quickly. "Nearly forgot. There was sumthin' 'bout you in here." She handed him a newspaper.

"Take it with ya. It's on the second page. Hope it works out for ya, but I'd hate to see ya go."

His heart beat a little faster. If it weren't for Joe, he'd read it now. "Thank you." He tucked it under his arm and left. He was always the last employee to go home. Aside from him, there were two waitresses and two cooks who rarely said a word to him.

He put Joe in bed, then opened the paper. The glow from the hurricane lamp pulsed across the print. His heart pounded.

Your help is needed identifying a young man brought to Mobile City Hospital on the eleventh of January. He is five-feet-five inches in height, medium build, and has red hair and freckles. He is eighteen years old and was accompanied by a six-year-old male slave.

After being treated for a head injury, he has no memory of his identity. According to his slave, the man goes by the name of Brian. They were traveling to Mobile to see his uncle. If you have any information regarding this man, please contact Dr. Harvey Mitchell at Mobile City Hospital. Any help you can give in this matter will be greatly appreciated.

He read the article three times before setting it aside and turning out the lantern. His eyes were heavy but sleep wouldn't come. Why didn't Dr. Mitchell state that he lived at Miss Harrison's boarding house? Why contact the doctor rather than sending them directly to *him?*

A week had passed. Time to pay him a visit.

* * *

"I'm sorry, Brian." Dr. Mitchell shook his head. "No one replied."

Not what he wanted to hear. "No one?"

"Try not to be discouraged. The article was in Friday's Register. It's only Monday. Someone may still come forward with information."

"I just hoped . . ." His shoulders slumped and he stared at the floor.

"I understand. I promise if I hear anything, I'll get word to you." Dr. Mitchell led him down the hallway to a private room. Joe traipsed behind; always his shadow.

"Why didn't you say I was at Miss Harrison's?" Brian sat and waited quietly as the doctor took his pulse.

"Because I assume the men who hurt you aren't the men who brought you to the hospital, and it's likely they believe you're dead. Finding out otherwise might encourage them to come and finish the job." Looking at him through his glasses, the doctor's eyes could have pierced steel.

It hadn't occurred to him. "You believe whoever brought me here was some *Good Samaritan* who left me, but didn't want to make himself known?"

"Yes. Be grateful he brought you here." He gestured toward Joe. "*Both* of you."

"I am. I should have trusted your intentions with the article. I thought you were acting like a father—treating me like a child who can't take care of himself."

He rested a hand on Brian's shoulder. "I'd be proud to have a son like you. I know you're capable. Sylvia tells me you're a hard worker. And the way you look after Joe is commendable."

"I takes care a myself!" Joe said, standing.

"He does." Brian laughed. "But tends to fall asleep on the job. At least he's being fed well." He poked Joe in the sides and tickled him.

Joe wiggled away, bubbling with laughter. "No squirrels, neither!"

Brian thanked the doctor again with a promise of payment by the end of the following week. Though Dr. Mitchell told him he was in no hurry to be repaid, he insisted. In addition, they were invited to have dinner at the doctor's home on Sunday night.

Brian gladly accepted.

So did Joe.

Chapter 19

Three times. The knock on the door increased in volume.

It was midday, and they were preparing the evening meal.

Again, someone beat on the door. "Where's Mrs. Denton?" Angel asked.

Ada shrugged. "Though I know they wants to answer the door, you best go an see who it is."

Angel happily obliged. Anything to delay plucking chickens.

Before reaching it, there was another knock. Its intensity caused her heart to beat faster.

Maybe it's news 'bout Billy. She opened the door wide.

A young girl stood on the front step, with arms folded across her chest and a tightly-pinched mouth. Aside from that, she was pretty—a few inches taller than her and dressed in expensive-looking clothing. Her long, golden-brown hair had been pulled up into a matching hat.

"It's about time!" The girl threw up her hands. "I nearly froze to death waiting for you to answer the door!"

"Sorry 'bout that," Angel said, taken aback by the girl's behavior. "How can I help you?"

"Is this the home of Cora and Douglas Denton?" The girl tilted her head, her uptight air not diminishing.

"Yes'm."

Looking over her shoulder, the girl beckoned the driver of the carriage. He hopped down from his seat, then retrieved a large trunk. Grunting and groaning, he carried it to the door stoop and set it at the girl's feet.

"Thank you," she said flatly and waved him away.

Must be from the north. No one round here would be so rude.

"Aren't you going to ask me in?" The girl impatiently tapped her foot on the ground.

"I can't. I don't know who you are or why you're here." Angel wasn't intimidated. "The Denton's wouldn't want me to let just anyone in. Wait here and I'll get Mrs. Denton."

"You do that." The girl hissed out a long breath. "Hurry! I'm cold!"

"Yes,m." *Girl NEEDS some time in the cold.*

Regardless of how she felt, she hurried to Mrs. Denton's room and rapped on the door. "Mrs. Denton." She cleared her throat. "There's someone here to see you."

Blankets rustled. "Tell 'em to go away."

Angel closed her eyes and rested her forehead against the door. Even though a full week had passed, Mrs. Denton wasn't much better.

With Mr. Denton at work and Mrs. Wellesley with the children, she didn't have a choice but to persist. "It's a young girl, Mrs. Denton. Brought by carriage. The driver left her here."

Footsteps neared, so Angel backed away. The door opened a crack. "Why'd he leave her?"

"I don't know, ma'am. She asked to be let in."

The door opened wider. Mrs. Denton stepped into the hallway pulling her robe tightly around her. Her puffy eyes and sunken cheeks indicated how poorly she must feel.

"Want me to bring her to you, Mrs. Denton?"

The woman was stone-faced. "I wanna see who she is 'fore I let her in."

"Yes'm." The woman she'd become was *not* the one Angel had grown up knowing. She used to laugh—the most cheerful of them all. Billy *had to* come home so his mama could return, too.

Mrs. Denton took her time walking down the long hallway to the entryway, and Angel stayed right behind her, curiosity about the girl driving her. Besides, the chickens could wait.

"It took you long enough!" the girl shrieked the moment the door reopened. When she saw Mrs. Denton, her mouth shut tight. She froze in place and stared.

"That ain't polite," Mrs. Denton said. "If you want sumthin' from me, bein' rude ain't gonna get you far."

The girl's lips curled upward. "Mother told me you talk funny."

"'Scuse me?"

"Aunt Cora, I'm freezing!" The girl stomped her foot and hugged herself, shivering.

Good thing Angel had followed Mrs. Denton so closely. She stumbled back into her arms.

Obviously satisfied with the response, the girl stepped into the house and nodded toward her trunk. "Have someone bring that in for me."

"Mrs. Denton?" Angel helped her to a chaise. "Are you all right?"

"She doesn't look all right," the girl said, hovering over them. "She scarcely looks like my mother. I almost didn't recognize her."

Why had she called Mrs. Denton her aunt? She'd never said she had a niece.

Since Mrs. Denton remained silent, Angel decided to find out more herself. "Who are you?"

"I'm Emilia. Her niece." She pursed her lips and sat beside her aunt. "I've come a long way to get here. The war made traveling difficult."

Mrs. Denton clutched her chest. "You're Elise's daughter?"

"Of course I am!" Emilia laughed.

Angel knew of Mrs. Denton's twin sister, but they didn't speak kindly of her. They'd indicated she'd gotten into some sort of trouble with the law. It wasn't a subject anyone in the household ever wanted to discuss.

"Everythin' a'right?" Angel's mama walked down the hallway toward them.

Emilia jumped to her feet. "My trunk is right outside the door. Get it for me." She fluttered her fingers toward the entryway.

"My mama doesn't hafta do what you say." Angel defiantly crossed her arms. "'Sides, I saw your trunk. It's too heavy for Mama."

"Then help her with it," Emilia sneered.

Mrs. Denton sat motionless, but seemed more alert than ever. "Angel, get Bo. Have him bring Emilia's trunk inside."

"Who's Bo?" Emilia asked. "Another one of your slaves?"

She's stayin'? Hopefully not long. Angel leered at her. "Bo works in the stable. I'll get him."

"Thank you, Angel." Mrs. Denton smiled, making the girl's rude behavior worthwhile.

Angel sped from the room.

How will Mrs. Denton cope with another problem?

Racing past the encampment, she easily found Bo in the stable with Jeriah.

"Sumthin's wrong, ain't it?" Jeriah asked.

"Maybe. Mrs. Denton asked me to get Bo."

Bo questioned her with his eyes.

"Seems Mrs. Denton has a niece she didn't know 'bout. She just arrived by carriage. Has a trunk the size of a barn that needs brought in. She hoped you could bring it in for her, Bo."

"Course I can."

"Ms. Denton gots a niece, huh?" Jeriah asked, scratching his head.

She nodded. "Not a very nice one, neither."

"Elise's daughter?"

"Yes. Did you know her mama?"

"Shore did. Them was some bad times. Not my place to talk 'bout." Jeriah huffed. "If she be anythin' like her mama, we's in for a heap a trouble."

This wasn't encouraging. Angel wanted to know more. Maybe her mama would tell her.

She held the door open for Bo, as he drug the trunk across the threshold.

"Lawdy! She totin' bricks?" he grunted.

"The carriage driver lifted it." She eyed him playfully.

He stood from his bent position and gave her a look she'd not soon forget. He took her words as a challenge, bent down, and hoisted the trunk onto his shoulder. "Which room?" he groaned.

She didn't know, so she scurried down the hallway to find out.

"Hurry!" he yelled.

She popped her head into the kitchen. "Ada, where'd Mrs. Denton go?"

Ada chuckled. "Took that child to the second floor. Girl tried to go in Billy's room. Ms. Denton had a fit!"

"Oh, my," Angel said, and returned quickly to Bo. "Up the stairs."

He rolled his eyes, took a deep breath, and started upward.

"Need my help?"

She was answered with a grunt.

Voices came from the room on the far end of the hallway. By the time they reached it, sweat dripped from his face. He grimaced as he set the trunk on the floor.

"Good!" Emilia chirped. "I need to change."

He looked at Mrs. Denton. "Anythin' else you need, ma'am?"

"No. Thank you, Bo."

He nodded, then smiled at Angel before leaving the room. Instantly, she wished he hadn't.

"That man likes you. Doesn't he, Angel?" Emilia asked. Her words were accompanied by an annoying giggle.

"Bo likes everyone," her mama said. "Angel an me needs to fix supper. Long as you don't needs us no more, Ms. Denton."

"No. Thank you, Bessie. I'll help Emilia get settled, an then I'll be down to dress myself."

This was a *very* good thing. Mrs. Denton hadn't gotten dressed the past week. Maybe something good would come of this.

Angel and her mama left the room, though she wished she could stay and listen.

"Mama?" It couldn't hurt to ask questions. "How long's she stayin'?"

"Forever it seems."

"What?"

They'd reached the bottom of the stairs, and she was bustled into the kitchen.

Ada rubbed her hands together. "Tell me."

I'm not the only one anxious for gossip.

They all sat. It didn't take long for her mama to start rambling.

"Lawd hep us," she began, then reached across the table and took Angel's hand. "This is gonna be hard on you."

"Why?"

"I promised not to keep things from you no more. But I never 'spected this."

"It can't be so bad."

"Angel . . ." She placed a hand over her heart. "That girl be your sister."

What? Her mouth dropped. She gaped at her, speechless.

"Baby, I told you 'bout your daddy an how he like to have whatever woman he want. An I told you how he wanted Ms. Denton."

She nodded—too stunned to say a word.

"See . . . Ms. Denton had a sister who look just like her. Giles took her, thinkin' she was Miss Cora. He done things with her. Your daddy be Emilia's daddy, too."

I have a sister. A horrid *white* sister. "Does she know 'bout me?"

"No, baby. She don't. An I don't knows if'n Ms. Denton wants her to know."

"What happened to her mama?" Ada asked, leaning in.

"She be dead. Don't know how, but in the short time I was in the room with her an Ms. Denton, I found out she don't have no family left. That's why she be here. Ms. Denton couldn't turn her away."

"She has family," Angel whispered. "All the Denton's—an me." So many times growing up she'd prayed for a sister. *She's not what I wanted.*

"Baby . . ." Her mama stroked her hand. "She might come 'round. Maybe she ain't so bad."

"Or maybe she's just like my daddy." She stood from the table. "I got chickens to pluck."

She went out the back door and didn't look back. Her best friend was gone, and she had no one to talk to. Her mama always told her hard work would help get her mind off things, so that's what she'd do.

Pluck away the pain.

Chapter 20

Dr. Mitchell's house sat two blocks from the water. Brian breathed in the refreshing sea air, but the abundant presence of soldiers disturbed him.

Joe clutched his hand. "Why them soldiers hafta be everwhere?"

"To protect us." He tried to assure him with a smile.

"We need tectin'?" Joe's big eyes widened.

"Seems so." Two soldiers stood erect on the street corner with guns positioned at their sides.

Dr. Mitchell's home was three stories tall and had been fenced in with black wrought iron. The grounds—though bare from winter—were well-tended. Trees abundantly surrounded the house.

Hannah greeted them at the door, beaming like a ray of sunshine. She was finely dressed in a blue gown matching the color of her eyes.

His own attire seemed lacking. But thanks to Sylvia, he and Joe had clothes that fit—including winter coats. She'd given them on Saturday night as a bonus for a productive week of work. They were dressed in black wool pants and white cotton shirts, covered by heavy coats.

Hannah hung their coats on a rack, then took Brian's hand and led him through the house to the dining room. Joe traipsed behind, gasping at every turn. Truthfully, he'd felt the same—in awe of the spectacular home—but remained quiet.

The dining room looked brilliant. A large oak table had been covered with a lace tablecloth and laid with fine china. Overhead, a sparkling candelabrum flickered with warm candlelight.

Dr. Mitchell greeted them, then patted Joe's head. "You had no trouble finding us?"

"No trouble at all," Brian replied. "Your house is magnificent."

He smiled. "Thank you. We've been blessed."

"I'd like to be blessed," Joe said.

A giggle came from outside the room. "Constance," Dr. Mitchell said. "You may come in."

A little girl with hair redder than Brian's peeked around the corner, then ran into her father's arms. She buried her head into his shoulder and turned just enough to look at Joe.

"She's shy at first," Dr. Mitchell said.

"My name's Brian." He placed a gentle hand on her head. "And this is Joe."

Hannah hadn't left Brian's side. "Connie," she said, "Brian won't hurt you."

"What 'bout him?" Constance asked, wide-eyed, pointing at Joe.

Joe's eyes opened even wider. He placed his all-too-familiar hands on hips. "I won't hurt you."

Constance wiggled out of her father's arms onto the floor. She faced Joe nose-to-nose. They were almost the same size. Neither said another word. They simply stood there, staring.

A tall stunning woman entered the room carrying a bowl of mashed potatoes. She walked with such grace she seemed to be floating across the floor in her green gown. Like Constance, she had flaming red hair. But *unlike* Constance—whose hair fell in ringlets—the woman's hair was neatly spun on top of her head.

After setting the bowl on the table, she crossed to them with hands extended. "My husband has told me a lot about you." She grasped Brian's hands and smiled. Though he had no way to be certain, he believed she must be the most beautiful woman he'd ever seen.

"My wife, Margaret," Dr. Mitchell said. The pride in his voice was unmistakable.

"I'm happy to meet you, Mrs. Mitchell," Brian said. "Thank you for having us for dinner."

"Huh?" Joe exclaimed, ending his entranced stare with Constance.

Brian laughed.

"Don't fret, Joe," Mrs. Mitchell said. "We're having *turkey* for dinner."

Brian couldn't stop smiling. Joy filled the air. He wished he had a family like this.

Dr. Mitchell gestured to the table. "Margaret has dinner ready, so let's be seated. Hannah, please call your sisters."

"Yes, sir." Hannah grinned at Brian before leaving the room.

"There are more?" he asked.

Mrs. Mitchell excused herself to bring in the rest of the food.

"Two more." Dr. Mitchell motioned to a chair for him, then took his seat at the head of the table. "I've been blessed with four beautiful daughters."

"And a beautiful wife," Brian added, taking his seat.

"You noticed?"

"Yes." His cheeks warmed. Maybe he'd been out of line.

The doctor chuckled. "Don't be embarrassed. There's nothing wrong with saying a woman is beautiful. Should you try to steal her away from me, it would be another matter."

Joe stood against the dining room wall, nervously kicking his foot against the floor. "Brian don't need no wife."

Constance giggled.

Dr. Mitchell leaned toward Brian. "Joe doesn't understand jesting, does he?"

"No, sir."

"Joe," Dr. Mitchell said. "Why don't you take a seat?"

"At the table?" Joe wrinkled his nose.

"If you want to eat."

"Course I does!" He still didn't move.

"Then have a seat." Dr. Mitchell pointed to the seat beside him.

When he still didn't move, Constance took him by the hand and led him to a chair next to her. His stunned face caused both Brian and the doctor to laugh.

"You're right," Brian said. "Your daughter quickly overcomes shyness."

Hannah returned, followed by her sisters, who he was told were Rachel and Elizabeth. Hannah was the eldest at age thirteen. Rachel was eleven, Elizabeth was ten, and

Constance was only four. All the girls were pretty and very unique in their own right. Rachel and Elizabeth paid little attention to him, but Hannah seemed to find interest in every word he spoke. Constance had become Joe's new best friend.

The meal couldn't have been more spectacular. Aside from the turkey and potatoes, Brian filled himself with glazed carrots and hot biscuits with jam, much to Joe's delight. The Mitchell's had an ample root cellar and Mrs. Mitchell kept a large vegetable garden.

Dessert was something called *custard*, which Brian decided he loved. Even though this was all new to him, something felt familiar. If only he knew what it was.

"Have you lived here long, Doctor?" Brian asked, spooning out the last bite of custard.

"Quite some time. Margaret and I met while I was practicing in Memphis, Tennessee. We moved here before Hannah was born. I was offered a position at the hospital I couldn't decline."

"Memphis?" He looked upward, thinking hard. There was *something* about it.

"Yes. Do you know where it is?"

He thought even harder. Nothing came to mind. "No. But I'm glad you're here."

He glanced at Hannah and smiled, then grinned when her cheeks turned crimson. She'd been staring at him but quickly lowered her eyes.

Dr. Mitchell attempted to keep conversation light, changing its course when Rachel and Elizabeth fussed about the soldiers.

After the meal, Constance whisked Joe away, so Brian approached the doctor. "Can we speak privately?"

"Of course." He led him to the library and shut the door. "Is something wrong?"

"No, sir." Digging into his pocket, he produced four coins and handed them to the doctor. "It's not much, but it's a start."

"As I told you before, I'm in no hurry to be repaid."

"Yes, but I'm in a hurry to repay you."

"Very well, then." He put the coins in his pocket and took a seat in a large leather chair. "Has Sylvia talked to you about her latest endeavor?" He motioned to the seat beside him.

"Endeavor?"

"I'm certain she plans to tell you soon, and it's no secret. Everyone in Mobile knows."

"Except me."

Dr. Mitchell leaned back in his chair. "She's having a hotel built, adjoining the café."

"A hotel?" Her husband must have had an enormous fortune.

The doctor's brows drew in. "You know what a hotel is, don't you?"

"Yes."

"Good. I admire Sylvia for taking on a project like this despite the war. She's an ambitious woman. A hard worker like *you*. You may be more beneficial to her learning the construction trade. As I told you in the hospital, you might be surprised what you're already capable of."

Construction . . .

He liked the idea. "Maybe I was born with a hammer in my hand?"

Dr. Mitchell took his hands, turning them palm up. "Doubtful. Your hands would be calloused."

"I'm willing to try anything. Don't want to wash dishes the rest of my life. I'd like to have a home like this one day." He cast his eyes around the room, admiring the numerous shelves filled with books, a stone fireplace, and a large oak desk.

"I believe you will. I admire your determination and the way you're caring for Joe. Shall I assume he's not been allowed to eat at the common table at Miss Harrison's?"

"No, he hasn't. And he's not used to entering a home through the front door. Why should the color of his skin matter so much?"

"It doesn't to some of us." The doctor breathed deeply.

"I hope your wife knows how much we appreciate being invited here tonight."

"She delights in watching people enjoy her food. Besides, my daughter is fond of you."

"Hannah?"

He laughed. "Yes, Hannah. Although Constance seems to have taken to you as well."

"Constance likes Joe." He tried to change the direction of the conversation.

"Hannah's thirteen. She knows you're too old for her, but in time that'll change. I'm in no hurry to marry off my daughter, but decided to tell you her feelings so you won't mislead her."

"Mislead her?" His ploy hadn't worked.

"You have a lot you're coping with—trying to find out about your past. But in the meantime, you're creating new memories and making new relationships. If in time you find you care for her, then so be it. But for now, don't show her any outward indication that you *might*. Girls of her age tend to see things that aren't there." He peered at him over the top of his glasses.

Brian took everything in. He scratched his head. "I'm not interested in women right now. Especially not thirteen-year-olds. That is . . . I don't believe I am. Maybe I already have a wife."

"I'd never considered that. It's possible."

Brian swallowed hard. Wouldn't he feel it in his heart if he loved a woman? "Then I should wait until my memory returns before I pursue *any* kind of relationship."

"A wise idea." Dr. Mitchell stood and crossed to the window, looking out toward the bay. "Hopefully it will return soon. But if not, it'll give Hannah time to grow up. I don't want her to marry until she's eighteen, though by seventeen she'll probably insist on it." He let out a large sigh. "By then, this war should be over and we'll have our city back."

"Do you honestly think it'll end soon?" He was grateful the conversation had turned.

"Yes, but I fear more bloodshed before it ends," he replied in a whisper.

"Dr. Mitchell? What happened in August?"

The man looked over his shoulder. A pained look covered his face. "The battle of Mobile Bay. Something I wish I could forget."

"There was a real battle here?" Brian stood, crossed the room, and stood beside him.

The doctor nodded, then stared vacantly out the window. "When it became obvious tensions in the city were building and the war was being brought to our doorstep, I feared for my family. I sent Margaret and the girls to Memphis to stay with her family until things settled down. Even though I was uneasy with the idea of their return, they came home at Christmas."

The mention of the holiday warmed him. "They didn't want to be separated at Christmas."

Dr. Mitchell turned. "You remember Christmas?"

"Yes. And *no*. I know it's the celebration of Jesus' birth, but I don't know who I celebrated with." He rubbed his temples. "None of it makes sense."

The doctor patted his shoulder.

"Dr. Mitchell? In the battle, the Confederacy drove back the Union soldiers, but won't the Union make another attempt to take the city?"

Again, the doctor peered out the window as if searching for something not to be found. "Yes. I'm certain they will. The war isn't going well for the South. I hope we'll surrender before they destroy Mobile like they burned Atlanta. But even more than loss of property, I don't want to see more bloodshed here. When I think of the amount of blood that has covered my hands and the young men I've seen torn apart . . ." He turned from the window with misty eyes. "When you were brought in, I was relieved I didn't have to cut you."

David's words haunted him—*he holds the hospital record for cuttin' off limbs.*

"Does it make you regret being a doctor?"

Slowly, the man's head swayed from side-to-side. "No. Not regret. But this isn't how I imagined I'd practice medicine. It's difficult detaching myself from the men. Thinking of the lives they could have had, had it not been for the war. Yet I know our country has to change." His final words were barely audible.

"Do you side with the North?" Brian's heart raced. How could the doctor be in Mobile and not side with the Confederacy?

Dr. Mitchell grasped his arm, led him back to his chair, then sat beside him. "Don't repeat that ever again. Do you understand?"

He nodded, never having seen the doctor so intense. "Of course." Being he didn't know what side *he'd* been on, how could he question the loyalty of the doctor?

The room fell so quiet he could hear every breath they took. He'd never intended to create tension between them. He considered him a friend. "Doctor, why'd you take an interest in me?"

The man's shoulders lowered and the tension in his face dissolved into a smile. "Aside from the fact you became my daughter's special project?"

"Yes. I doubt you invite all your patients to dinner. Or help pay their rent."

Dr. Mitchell removed his glasses and polished them with his shirt. "You're the first. Yes, Hannah brought you to my attention, but after you began speaking and had no memory, you intrigued me. There's something about you I can't put my finger on. You remind me of someone, but I can't remember *who.*"

"My uncle?"

"I don't know." He chuckled. "Perhaps your memory lapse has plagued *me.*"

"Then it seems both of us will have to start remembering things." Luckily, the mood had lightened. "Should we go back to the others?"

"Yes, we should."

They rose and started walking toward the door.

"Brian?"

He knew that serious tone. "Yes, sir?"

"Wherever it was you came from, I know you came from a good home."

"How?"

"In the short time I've known you, I've seen a very good man."

"Thank you, sir." One day, when he found his family, he hoped his father was as kind as Dr. Mitchell.

When they joined the others, Joe ran to Brian and tugged on his arm. "I's ready to go!" His wide eyes were filled with horror.

It didn't take long to understand his urgency. Constance wanted him to have a tea party.

Dr. Mitchell let out a hearty laugh. "It seems there are limitations to their new-found friendship."

Brian knelt down and took the girl's hand. "I'm sorry sweetheart, but Joe and I need to go home."

Her lip protruded and her head dropped.

"I'll have a tea party with you, Connie," Hannah said. "Maybe Brian and Joe can come again another time." She looked longingly at Brian.

Remembering the doctor's words, he made a point not to return her gaze and instead addressed Mrs. Mitchell. "I can't thank you enough for the wonderful meal."

Joe nodded vigorously, while nudging Brian toward the door.

"I hope you'll both come back soon," Mrs. Mitchell said.

Hannah brought them their coats, then Dr. Mitchell escorted them out. He stood with them on the front porch admiring the brilliant colors covering the horizon. Lavender blended with blue and pink. The sun would set soon.

"I love it here." Dr. Mitchell sighed and leaned against the railing. "I pray for peace."

Brian stood beside him and gazed over the property. "I think it's coming, sir."

After a final goodbye, Brian took Joe by the hand and began the short walk home. Neither spoke, which was unlike Joe.

"Brian?" Joe perched on the edge of his bed.

"Yes?" Though it was time to sleep, he was relieved the boy had started talking again.

"What's gonna happen to me?"

"What do you mean?" He started to undress and waited for Joe's answer.

Joe sat silently without moving.

"Joe?"

The boy sniffled. "You gonna make me go back to the masta?"

He sat beside him and put an arm around his shoulder. "I thought *I* was your master."

"No. You're my friend. You take care a me."

"How long have I been caring for you?"

"If'n I tell you, can I stay with you?"

"Of course."

Joe hesitated, fidgeting. He took a large breath. "I found you a few days afore we got hurt. A bad man hurt us, Brian." He nestled his head against his chest. "A real bad man."

"Was he a soldier—like the ones we saw on the street tonight?"

Joe nodded. His body trembled.

"Was he wearing the same kind of clothing as the soldiers we saw?"

Again, he nodded.

"Same color?"

He tilted his head and looked up at him. "Uh-huh."

No need for more questions. If everything Joe said was true, then he hadn't been part of the Confederacy, he was a Union soldier. Why else would a rebel hurt them? This knowledge wouldn't make life in Mobile any easier.

What if the soldier who hurt us lives here?

Brian wouldn't recognize him, but Joe might. From now on he'd be warier around them.

Chapter 21

"You're a good girl, Spot." Angel patted the cow's side. The milk bucket was half-full.

"Spot?" Emilia's annoying voice ruined the quiet of the morning.

Angel stood and faced her. *Why'd she come out to the barn?* "Paulette named her." She picked up the pail, pushed past Emilia, and headed toward the house.

Emilia remained on her heels. "It's a silly name."

Angel stopped. "Why's it silly? It makes perfect sense. There's a large brown spot on her back. 'Sides, what's it matter to you?"

Lifting her chin in the air, Emilia smacked her lips. "I was raised in a fine house and thought I was coming to a sophisticated home. I was mistaken."

Angel looked beyond her. They were standing in the middle of the pathway beside the encampment. Stopping wasn't wise. The two soldiers, who constantly watched her, walked toward them.

"Emilia." Angel took her by the elbow. "We need to get to the house."

"Why?" The girl didn't budge. "I came to talk to you. Even put on my warmest coat."

Angel jerked her arm. "We can talk inside."

"No!" Emilia stomped her foot.

"New girl has a temper," one of the soldiers said with a sly chuckle.

Emilia whipped around. "Are you speaking to me?"

The men were young and didn't look old enough to be soldiers. Maybe they'd done like Billy and lied about their age. Even so, their eyes were filled with hunger. With so few women around, anything in a dress must look appealing. Emilia being pretty didn't help.

She had to try again. "Let's go, Emilia."

"Emilia?" The taller of the two raised his eyes. "Pretty name for a pretty girl."

"Thank you." She coyly tilted her head and batted her eyes.

Jeriah was right. They were in for a heap of trouble. Now both men were beside Emilia; one to each side. The most frightening thing of all, she seemed to be enjoying herself.

If Angel didn't get the milk to her mama, she'd be worried. But she couldn't leave Emilia alone with the men. She cleared her throat. "We *hafta* go."

The shorter man crossed to her. "You're always in a hurry. 'Bout time you stopped long enough to talk." He brushed his hand across her cheek.

She jerked back. "Don't touch me!"

The man cocked his head and returned to the others. The taller man had whispered something to Emilia, causing her to giggle. Making matters worse, Emilia's hand rested on his arm.

She'd had enough. Firmly holding the milk pail in one hand, she lurched forward, grabbed Emilia's wrist as tightly as she could, and yanked her away. "I said we gotta go home!"

"You're hurting me!" Emilia whined, and tried to break free.

Angel kept walking, dragging her sister, but turned her head just enough to look at the men. They followed right behind. She clenched her teeth. "Get any closer and I'll scream!"

With an even firmer jerk on Emilia, she faced the house again. Mr. Denton came out the back door and the men ran in the opposite direction.

"Is there a problem, Angel?" he asked, moving his eyes between her and Emilia.

"Well, sir—"

Emilia jerked her hand free. "Look, Uncle Douglas!" She displayed her wrist, revealing deep red lines. "Angel hurt me!"

"Angel?" His eyes narrowed.

Emilia stepped in front of her and blocked her from Mr. Denton. "I went to help her in the barn. She didn't want my help, so she *dragged* me back here. She thinks I can't do anything."

"Angel." He folded his arms across his chest. "If Emilia wants to help you, let her. She's trying to make herself at home here. I expect more from you."

"But . . ." Her mouth was so dry, she couldn't speak.

"This afternoon when you do the milking, take her with you. I'm glad she wants to learn." He smiled at Emilia, then passed by them.

Angel gritted her teeth, wanting to tear the smug expression from Emilia's face. The wretched girl sauntered through the back door and Angel followed her, ready to explode. Though she didn't know *why* Emilia had come looking for her, she didn't care. The more she could avoid her, the better off she'd be.

Two weeks putting up with Emilia had seemed like forever. She'd complained about everything; hated the food, didn't like her mattress, wanted to be on the first floor so she wouldn't have to climb the stairs. It went on and on.

The only good change was in Mrs. Denton, who got up every morning and dressed for the day. The children were curious about their new cousin and accepted her without question. Emilia acted kind to them, but Angel didn't trust her. Not one bit.

"Sorry, Mama." Angel scowled and handed her the milk pail. "Some of it spilled."

"What happened? That girl look like she won a prize." Emilia had strutted through the kitchen with her nose in the air.

"She's awful, Mama!" Anger bubbled out of her. "Made me look bad to Mr. Denton." She twisted her hands together wishing they were wrapped around Emilia's neck.

Paulette ran into the kitchen and flung her arms around Angel. Her tear-filled eyes tugged at Angel's heart. She scooped her up and held her close. "What's wrong?"

Paulette sniffled. "'Milia says Spot's name is silly."

"She's a little girl!" Mrs. Denton hollered from the hallway. "You didn't hafta be hateful."

Emilia stormed through the kitchen and out the door.

Mrs. Denton came in behind her and took Paulette. "Thank you, Angel." Pain covered her face.

"'Milia wasn't nice to me, Mama," Paulette said and nestled into her shoulder.

It hadn't taken long for Emilia to show her true self to the rest of the family.

"Pay her no mind, baby." Mrs. Denton stroked her hair. "No one could a given Spot a better name. Ain't that right, Angel?" She lifted her eyes from the girl and smiled.

"Yes'm." Her heart skipped a happy beat. Regardless of how it got there, Mrs. Denton's smile was a step in the right direction. She'd put up with anything from Emilia if it helped Billy's mama. "Mrs. Denton?" It had to be done. "Would you like me to go an check on her?"

Her smile dipped downward. "Reckon you should. Tell her to come in an have breakfast."

"Yes'm." She headed out the door.

Assuming Emilia went looking for the soldiers, she followed the path to the barn. *I may be lookin' for trouble, but I hafta find her.*

The chant of morning drills surrounded her and she sighed with relief. The men would be occupied for some time.

She continued on to the stable. It didn't take long to find Emilia perched on a hay bale talking to Bo. Her loud giggling filled the air.

"Well now," Emilia said. "Look who's here, Bo."

Bo nodded. "Hey, Angel."

"Bo." Angel bobbed her head, then motioned to Emilia. "Mrs. Denton wants you to come in for breakfast."

Emilia wrinkled her nose. "I don't *want* breakfast. I want to talk to Bo. He's been telling me about my cousin, Billy."

Angel questioned Bo with her eyes, then shifted her gaze to her sister. "Bo's got work to do. You shouldn't be botherin' him."

Emilia stood and took hold of his arm. "Have you ever seen such big muscles? His arms are larger than the arms of those soldiers we talked to."

Bo took a step back. "What soldiers you been talkin' to?"

"We weren't talkin' to the soldiers," Angel said, defensively. "They were talkin' to us."

Emilia tittered. "Angel, don't tease him. I saw that soldier touch your cheek. He likes you."

"Bo!" Jeriah's stern voice made Bo jump. "We gots work to do!"

Bo's brows drew in, forming a deep wrinkle between his eyes. "I gots to go." He frowned, stepped away from Emilia, then moved beside Angel. "Stay away from them soldiers." He spoke low so only she could hear. "They's trouble."

He didn't have to tell *her* that. She'd tried to save Emilia from them, yet now Emilia had led him to believe she'd been encouraging them. Unable to tell him what really happened, she stood there and watched him walk away.

Emilia spun in a circle and laughed. "Isn't this fun?"

"Oh!" Angel grabbed her arms, forcing her to look at her. "Why'd you hafta come here?"

Emilia pushed her away. "Grab me like that again and I'll tell Uncle Douglas."

"Go on an tell him!" Angel's heart beat so fast she could barely breathe. "An I'll tell him how you're leadin' them soldiers on. Can't you see they wanna mess with you?"

Emilia's eyes opened wide. "What do you mean *mess with me*? Is that some southern expression? They think I'm pretty. That tall good-looking one said I was *fine*."

Does she really not know? "Emilia, you talk like you're grown up, but I reckon you got a lot to learn. How old are you anyways?"

"I'll be thirteen in April." She stuck her nose high in the air. "I'm already a woman. I want to be married by the time I'm fifteen. I won't be an old maid like my mother. She was eighteen when my father died and never remarried."

Remarried? From everything Angel's mama had told her, their daddy was never *married*. But she couldn't ask Emilia anything about the man without creating suspicion. Could she?

Maybe a gentler approach would work. "I'm sorry, Emilia." The hardest words she'd ever said. "I was tryin' to protect you. Those men got one thing on their mind and it ain't marriage."

"How can you be sure? They seem nice."

"All you gotta do is look in their eyes. Or look where their eyes are *lookin'*." Hopefully Emilia was smart enough to understand.

The ignorant girl shrugged and pursed her lips. "I'm glad they think I'm pretty. Mother always told me so. So did Grandfather."

"What happened to 'em? I mean . . . How'd they die?"

Emilia frowned and returned to the hay bale. "After my father died . . ." She spoke in a whisper and stared at her hands. "Mother went a bit mad. I don't know what she did, but she got into trouble with the law." She looked up. *Tears?* "Grandfather said she was behaving just like my grandmother. He'd put her away into a mental hospital where she took her own life."

Though guarded, Angel's heart ached for her sister. But none of what she'd said made a lot of sense. "I'm sorry. 'Bout your gramma an all. What happened to your mama?"

"She went to prison. Grandfather raised me. He gave me everything." She lovingly stroked the fur collar of her coat. "About six months ago, mother got sick. The judge let her leave prison and sent her home. She died. Not long after, Grandfather died."

Moved by her story, Angel sat beside her. "Then you came lookin' for *us?*" She rested her hand on Emilia's arm.

"Not *you!*" Emilia shoved her. "I came looking for Aunt Cora. She and my cousins are the only family I have left." She'd reverted back to the Emilia Angel didn't like. "Besides, mother and Douglas were supposed to be married and Cora took him away from her. This house should have been hers. I belong here."

It couldn't be true. Angel had never known anyone more in love than Mr. and Mrs. Denton. "We've been out here too long. Breakfast should be ready by now."

"Go on then. I'm not stopping you." Emilia shooed her away.

Conflicted, she hesitated.

Emilia cleared her throat. "Since we've been talking about *dead* people, let's talk about Billy. Maybe you can tell me more about him than Bo could."

"He ain't dead!" Now she'd crossed the line.

"Then where is he? I overheard Uncle Douglas and Aunt Cora talking about it. She blames you. Did you two do something together? Hmm? Is that how you know what those soldiers want to do? Something *you've* done before?"

As if it had its own will, Angel's hand flew through the air and smacked Emilia's cheek. Without waiting for her reaction, she sprinted home. *What've I done?* Sooner or later she'd be punished for it.

She was tempted to tell Emilia all about their daddy. Knock a brick or two out of the high pedestal she'd set herself on. No one had ever roused her temper the way Emilia had.

Her room gave her comfort. Opening the drawer to her bed stand, she pulled out Billy's book and began to write.

February 15th, 1865. I have a sister.

The words nauseated her.

She doesn't know I'm her sister and seems to think our daddy was a saint. She's horrid. When I'm around her I want to scratch her eyes out.

She said Billy's dead, but I'll never believe it. And I'll never tell her how I feel about him. I love him and I know he loves me, too.

She stopped and blew on the ink, then felt compelled to write more.

When he gave me this book, he wanted me to write things to help us remember. Things about us. Here are some of those things ~

I was six when Billy taught me how to climb trees. He reached out to me from a higher limb and held my hand for the first time.

When I was eight, Billy talked his mama into letting me sit in on Miss Banks' lessons. Without him, I wouldn't know how to read. He laughed when I chose the thickest book in the li-

brary. I stumbled over almost every word. He helped me through it.

When I was nine, Billy and I held each other and cried while Mr. Denton shoveled dirt onto Mrs. Moss's grave. Not long after, he buried Mr. Wellesley. We learned about death together but also learned about life when Muffin had her kittens. Billy chose Biscuit from the litter. He's my cat now . . . until Billy comes home.

Best of all, I remember this past Christmas. He looked at me like never before. It made me tingle inside. Then he took me to the attic. It was cold but he kept me warm. He kissed me and I thought my heart would burst. I knew I loved him, but after that I knew he loved me, too.

The front door opened and she jumped—almost spilling the bottle of ink. Quickly she blew on the pages, then closed the book and placed it in the drawer. Her heart thumped.

"Angel?"

Not the voice she expected. Mrs. Denton rapped on her door.

"Yes'm?" She swallowed hard.

"We need to talk." She walked in.

Angel started to rise, but was motioned to remain. "I'm sorry, Mrs. Denton." Her chin quivered and tears came. She didn't fully understand *why.*

Mrs. Denton sat beside her on the bed and placed an arm around her. "You don't hafta cry. I've come close to hittin' her myself a time or two."

"I shouldn't a slapped her." She sucked in air, attempting to stop the tears.

"Don't know what made you do it but I wanna talk 'bout it so it don't happen again."

Angel faced her. "I know I ain't supposed to tell her she's my sister. But she thinks she's better than everyone else and she's hateful. She's causin' all kinds a trouble . . . an I'm afraid she's gonna get herself into a mess with them soldiers."

"Soldiers?"

"Yes'm." She looked away, embarrassed. "I didn't wanna say nothin', but two soldiers keep lookin' at me. Sayin' things, too. When Emilia came they started doin' it to both of us. She thinks they're the marryin' kind, but I don't reckon it's what they have in mind."

Mrs. Denton rested her hand against Angel's cheek. "You should a said sumthin' sooner. I know what it feels like havin' men act in a way that makes your belly twist an turn. I'll have Douglas talk to their captain. He'll take care of it."

"I don't wanna cause trouble."

"I know. You're tryin' to keep it from happenin'. But why'd you slap Emilia?"

Angel closed her eyes. She didn't want to look at her when she said his name. "She said Billy's dead."

A small whimper came from Mrs. Denton's throat. "Billy ain't dead."

"I know he ain't. Hearin' her say it made me mad." A pool of tears welled in her eyes. "She said other things, too."

Mrs. Denton insisted she tell her everything. But when she finished, the woman remained silent, then stood and paced the floor.

"You all right, Mrs. Denton?" *Please say something.*

Stopping sharply in the middle of the room, she placed her hand to her forehead and rubbed her temples. "I need to tell you the truth 'bout what happened." She licked her lips, then grabbed a chair and pulled it up beside the bed. Her legs trembled as she sat.

"You sure this ain't sumthin' Mama needs to tell me?"

"No." She gulped and twisted her fingers together. "Cuz this is 'bout me an my sister."

"Elise? Emilia's mama?" Angel sat upright. Having her confide in her, felt exhilarating.

"Yep. My twin. We was separated when we was born. Ma had a midwife, Lena Peck. She'd lost a baby, an when she learned Ma was havin' twins, planned how to take one. When Ma died, it made it easy. Pa'd been drinkin'. Didn't know Ma had two babies."

This was better than any book she'd read. She didn't say a word, listening to every detail.

"It wasn't 'til I was grown an married I found out 'bout Elise. I met Douglas in Harper's woodshop. He thought I was her 'til he saw my big belly. Had Billy that night. Douglas brought a doctor to the boat for me."

"You met Mr. Denton while you was still married to Billy's daddy?"

She nodded and sighed. "Yep. But I stayed true to my husband. Don't deny I felt sumthin' for Douglas the first time I saw him, but I didn't act on my feelin's."

Angel understood being faithful.

Mrs. Denton closed her eyes. "Forgive me. My story got a might off track."

"That's all right."

"Anyways. As you know, Billy's pa was hung for cheatin' at cards. After he died, I met up with Douglas again, an this time followed my heart. There's lots more to tell, but what I wanna get at is the truth 'bout Elise an Mrs. Peck.

Mrs. Peck didn't die in no hospital. She took her life in prison. Didn't take well to confinement. And it's true 'bout Elise bein' in prison, too. She an Mrs. Peck murdered some folks."

"Murdered?" It was worse than she'd ever imagined.

"They was tryin' all they could to have Elise marry Douglas. Mrs. Peck had it in her head this estate should a been hers. But that's another story for another day."

Angel wanted to know everything. She nodded and waited.

"On our weddin' night, Mrs. Peck helped Elise take my place at the hotel. Marcus Giles kidnapped me and took me away. They helped him. Elise pretended to be me, but Douglas figgered it out in time. 'Fore anythin' happened." She stared at her hands. "That was the night I shot an killed your pa."

Angel let out a long breath. "Does Billy know all this?"

"No. I was waitin' 'til he was older to tell him." She looked her in the eye. "I knew it was time to tell *you* cuz I don't want you believin' Emilia's lies. I feel a might sorry for her. Reckon she don't know they're lies."

"Should we tell her the truth?" She took Mrs. Denton's hand, hardly able to bear the pained look on her face.

"Someday. If you tell her now, she won't believe you."

"Especially if I told her Marcus Giles was my daddy, too. But I won't say nothin'. I'm just glad you told me." She squeezed her hand. It seemed she was regaining her trust.

"Can't believe they told that child Giles was *married* to her ma. It ain't right. Bad thing is she's exactly like him. Even looks like him. Makes it hard for me to be 'round her. I look in her eyes and see Giles."

"You used to say that *I* was like him."

Mrs. Denton pulled her close. "I was wrong."

They sat together for some time saying nothing.

"Your birthday's comin' up." Mrs. Denton broke the silence. "Reckon I best tell Ada to bake a cake. We're gonna celebrate for Billy, too. All right?"

She nodded. They'd always celebrated their birthdays together. "Mrs. Denton? I know it's hard for you to talk 'bout, but what do you an Mr. Denton think happened to him?"

She moistened her lips. "We reckon he was captured. Taken prisoner and sent to one a them war camps. It's the only explanation. May take 'til the end a the war 'fore we hear from him."

"Then we'll pray it ends soon." Angel hadn't stopped praying. "I know he'll come home. I feel it in my heart."

Tears trickled down the woman's cheek. "I feel it, too." She kissed her forehead, then stood. "For now, you an I are gonna keep our eyes on Emilia. I got no choice but to take care a her. An don't worry 'bout Douglas. He ain't as blind as you think. I'll tell him what you said."

Angel sighed. "I want you both to like me again."

"We ain't never stopped likin' you. Fact is, we've always loved you. We're just worried 'bout Billy." She turned to walk away. "Best get in the house for hotcakes. Ada saved some for you."

As Mrs. Denton left, an enormous smile spread across Angel's face like an out-of-control wildfire.

They love me. Nothing Emilia could do or say would take that from her.

Chapter 22

Sylvia pointed to the hammer in Brian's hand. "You seem to be even better at this than you was at washin' dishes."

He pulled a couple of nails from his mouth and laughed. "Thank you. I admit I like it better. So do my hands. My fingers don't look like prunes."

Joe extended a two-by-four. "Where's this one go, Brian?"

Brian nodded toward the wall, then helped him position the piece into place. "Joe likes this better, too. Once he got over the fear of holding the boards for me." With a few swift swings of the hammer, he nailed it tight.

"I's gonna be a carpenter, too!" Joe said. "Mista Bradley's learnin' us both."

Sylvia set down a basket filled with food and Joe dove in. "Nothin' wrong with that boy's appetite," she said with a laugh. "Better get some yourself or there won't be none left."

Brian's stomach rumbled appreciatively when the aroma of fried chicken filled his nostrils. Joe handed him a leg. "Delicious!" Though he found carpentry to be hard work, he'd never been happier.

A lot had happened in the past month. When Sylvia introduced him to Thomas Bradley, his life had taken on a positive change. Mr. Bradley had been contracted to build the hotel and had given him the opportunity to learn the trade. He also had no qualms about allowing Joe to help.

Mr. Bradley entered the room. "Brian, when you're finished eating I need you to go to Parker's for supplies." He peered into the basket, licked his lips, and nabbed a biscuit.

"Yes, sir." He'd been to Parker's Mercantile many times in the past few weeks. He'd learned quickly that Joe needed to be left behind. The owner, Jake Parker, had told him bluntly that his *nigger* had to stay outside. Not wanting Joe to be mistreated, Brian opted to leave him in Mr. Bradley's care. Luckily, the man didn't object.

Working kept Brian from dwelling on his uncle's lack of response to the ad in the *Register*. Oddly enough, for the most part he felt happy. And now that he had a job he enjoyed, he'd become content. He'd earned enough money to pay off his debt to Dr. Mitchell and even managed to purchase some additional items of clothing.

"Run outta nails already?" Jake Parker asked.

Brian approached the counter. "Well, I—"

"Be with you in a minute, Miss O'Malley," Jake yelled. He scratched at his full beard, then bent low over the counter. "Banker's daughter," he whispered. "One a my best customers."

Brian chuckled, then glanced at the girl. She could easily have been Margaret Mitchell's daughter. Same red hair and striking features. "She's very pretty."

"Just turned eleven." Jake shook his head. "She'll break hearts one day."

Brian agreed. To be that young and already well put together indicated she'd blossom into something extraordinary.

He wanted to get down to business, but Jake seemed more interested in gossip. "That dress," he said through the side of his mouth. "Twelve dollars. Came from overseas."

Brian gasped. *Twelve dollars for one dress?* Silk and lace. Not something any ordinary girl would put on for casual daywear. Even Hannah's attire wasn't this expensive-looking. *Impractical during a war.*

As if she knew they were talking about her, the girl came to the counter. She tipped her head coyly and batted her eyes. "Who's the new boy?" Her southern drawl was thick but refined, and though she posed the question to Jake, her eyes were on Brian.

Boy? I'm no boy.

Now that she'd moved closer, she was even more beautiful. Her eyes were deeper green than his.

"Miss O'Malley," Jake said. "This here's Brian. He works for Mr. Bradley over at that new hotel they're buildin'."

Brian nodded at her and smiled.

"A carpenter?" She stuck her nose in the air and grunted.

"Yes." He pulled his shoulders back. Her beauty rapidly diminished.

"Victoria!"

Brian faced the shrieking woman. This redhead was a grownup version of the girl. Dress *and* attitude. For all the women he'd met in Mobile who had his features, surely a relative had to be in the city.

"What, Mama?" Victoria rolled her eyes.

"Your father is waitin'." Mrs. O'Malley's Irish brogue caught Brian off guard.

"But I haven't had time to buy something," Victoria pouted.

Mrs. O'Malley took the girl by the hand. "There's always a first time." She smiled at Brian, then nodded to Jake. "Good day, Mr. Parker."

"Mrs. O'Malley." Jake dipped his head.

Relieved they were gone; Brian handed the man his order.

Jake gathered the supplies from the list, tallied them up, then added them to Mr. Bradley's bill. "Anything else?"

Brian reached into his pocket. "Have you ever seen anything like this?" He laid the carved bug on the counter.

Jake picked it up and examined the detail. "Hmm . . ." He scratched his head. "Nothin' *exactly* like it, but Widow Holloway has some pieces that's similar."

"Widow Holloway?"

"Yep. Her husband was a wood carver. Died a few years back."

"Where can I find her?" His stomach fluttered.

"Lives on St. Anthony. Know where that is?"

"Yes. The hospital's on that street."

Jake scribbled the address on a piece of paper and gave it to him.

Brian thanked him, and as he drove away, his spirits were high. As soon as he finished his work for the day, he'd be paying a visit to Widow Holloway.

* * *

Brain hated leaving Joe in the bedroom at Miss Harrison's, but had no other choice. Not knowing anything about Widow Holloway, he didn't feel comfortable taking the risk of Joe being demeaned again.

The description Jake gave him matched the house he faced. Tiny. White. Broken shutters.

Taking a deep breath, he strode toward the front door. The porch steps creaked under his feet.

This house needs a carpenter. He rapped on the door. Flecks of white paint fell away beneath his knuckles. *And fresh paint.*

An old rocking chair with a red upholstered cushion was on the front porch. Beside it sat a small table holding a partially carved block of wood. *This must be the right place.*

Hearing no one approach, he knocked again.

"I'm coming as fast as I can." Her timid voice grew louder as she neared the door.

It slowly opened and he breathed in a mixture of spices. Mostly garlic.

"May I help you?" she asked.

Though her white hair revealed her age, Mrs. Holloway was an attractive woman. Petite and simply dressed in a long blue dress, covered by a white knit shawl. The bun on the crown of her head had been covered with a net.

"Mrs. Holloway?" He folded his hands in front of himself and tried to remain calm.

"Yes?" Her eyes scanned him. Kind, but wary.

"Jake Parker told me where to find you. He said you might know something about this." He pulled the carving from his pocket.

She shivered. "It's cold out here, boy. Come inside."

Boy, again? Why couldn't anyone see he was a man?

It seemed inappropriate entering the home of a stranger, but he had to agree with her. It was cold, and the warmth of her home was welcome.

"Show me the piece," she said, and motioned for him to sit.

The small room had been stuffed full. The sofa took up an entire wall. It faced a stone fireplace that easily heated the tiny space.

Carved figurines were everywhere. An assortment of animals lined the mantel. A wooden chain hung from the ceiling and dangled all the way to the floor.

As he sat, a cloud of dust puffed into the air. *Not much of a housekeeper.*

"Here." He extended the figure.

She took it, then sat in a chair beside the sofa. Squinting, she turned the figure over and over in her fingers. "Hmm . . ."

"Do you recognize it?"

She shook her head. "My husband's work was much finer. This was done by someone inexperienced. It looks as if they were trying to carve an angel." Handing the carving back to him, her brows drew in. "What did you say your name was?"

I'd hoped you could tell me. "My name's Brian."

"My mind isn't what it used to be. I don't know what I was thinking asking you into my home without knowing your name. I'm a foolish old woman."

"You're not foolish. You were being considerate because of the cold."

She stood and moved toward the fire, then added another log. "Yes. It's cold. But before long we'll wish for this weather. I've never cared for the humidity of summer."

"I don't know what it's like. Is it *that* miserable?"

She shuffled to her seat once again and folded her hands in her lap. "You're not from here?"

It couldn't hurt to tell her the truth. Doubtful she was a Confederate soldier out to kill him. "I don't know *where* I'm from."

Having intrigued her, she wanted the entire story, so he told her what he knew.

"I hoped you might know who carved this," he said, looking at the angel. "I was holding it when I was brought to the hospital."

"I'm sorry, Brian. I truly wish I could help."

"It's all right. One day I'll remember." He returned the angel to his pocket. "Where are *you* from, Mrs. Holloway? You don't talk like other people here."

"I don't?" She chuckled. "I've traveled a great deal. That is—I *used* to. My husband was a traveling merchant. We went many places together before settling in Mobile. I was born in Massachusetts, then my parents moved to Memphis, Tennessee. I loved Memphis, but after I met Jason, I left with him."

"Memphis?" *An interesting coincidence.* "Dr. Mitchell used to live in Memphis. Did you know him there?"

She shook her head and smiled. "I lived there a very long time ago. You may not have noticed, but I'm a few years older than Dr. Mitchell." She winked and then laughed.

Brian cocked his head and sniffed. A foul odor caught his attention. "Is something burning?"

She jumped to her feet. "Oh, my! I forgot the chicken!" Her old form moved faster than he thought possible. In moments, she returned. "Burned the bird."

"I'm sorry. I feel it's my fault. I distracted you."

She waved her hand and sat. "I don't know why I bother cooking meals any longer. I'd just as soon have a bowl of oats." She leaned toward him. "Better for digestion."

He grinned. Though he'd not known her long, he liked her.

Time had flown faster than he'd realized. As the house darkened, he knew Joe would be worried. "Thank you for speaking with me." He stood. "I'd like to come back again sometime."

"I'd like that very much. I don't get many visitors. I was never blessed with children and have no living family."

"Would you mind if I bring Joe with me on my next visit?"

"The Negro boy you told me about?"

"Yes. I don't like leaving him alone."

"You may bring him. As long as he behaves himself. My husband's carvings are precious to me and I wouldn't want them damaged."

He assured her Joe would be careful.

"Before you go, I'd like to show you my favorite piece." She walked from the room. When she returned, she carried a wooden box. She placed it in his hands.

He turned it from side-to-side admiring it.

She chuckled. "It's what's *inside* I want you to see."

Returning to his seat, he placed the box on his lap and carefully opened it. The most intricately carved piece he'd ever seen lay on a piece of red silk fabric. A delicate flower with detailed leaves and petals. It had been sanded smooth and polished, bringing out the fine lines in the wood.

"It's beautiful, Mrs. Holloway."

"Iris," she said with a sigh.

"What?"

"The flower is an iris. And Iris is my name. Jason carved it for me on our first anniversary."

He closed the lid and returned it to her. "Thank you for showing me."

She wiped a tear from her eye, then carried the box out of the room.

When she returned, they said their goodbyes and he promised to come back soon. He'd made a new friend who he intended to keep. Even though her house was untidy and in need of repair, something about it felt like home.

Chapter 23

February 20th, 1865. I'm thirteen. A real woman. My birthday would have been better if Billy was here and NOT Emilia. I'm trying to like her. Since she's my sister I know I should love her. That will never happen.

The Denton's tried to make my birthday special. Ada made a cake with real sugar icing. And because we were also celebrating Billy's birthday we told stories about him.

Emilia ruined everything. She laughed and said it sounded like we were at a funeral. Mrs. Denton cried. Mr. Denton was so angry he sent her to her room. She huffed all the way up the stairs and slammed her door.

I didn't cry, but I was mad. I'll never forget this birthday. Not for good reasons.

"Angel?" Her mama knocked at the door. "Angel, baby. I'd like to come in."

Sighing, she put her journal away and opened the door. "I was about to go to bed, Mama."

"I know you was, but I need to talk to you." She led Angel to the bed and they both sat. "Don't let Emilia trouble you."

"Hard not to."

"You're thirteen now. A grown woman. Someday, you're gonna look back on today an laugh memberin' what Emilia was like."

I'll never laugh 'bout this. Not when she's bein' hateful 'bout Billy.

"Angel? What you thinkin' 'bout?"

"Billy. I can't *stop* thinkin' 'bout him." She braced for a scolding.

"I understan'." *What?* "I's just glad you stopped cryin'. It wadn't doin' Billy no good."

"I'm done cryin'. Time I start actin' like a grown woman. When he comes home, he'll see I'm all grown up." She stood, crossed to the window, and gazed at the soldier's tents. "Mama, Bo said there's talk the war's endin' soon. Reckon the soldiers'll leave?"

"If'n they ain't no war, they gots no reason to stay."

"Good. I want 'em gone." She stared vacantly through the glass. Mrs. Denton had said that Mr. Denton spoke to the captain, but because he didn't know which two soldiers she was referring to, no action had been taken. They needed names. As much as she hated doing it, she'd have to find out. Hopefully it wouldn't encourage them.

Her mama placed an arm over her shoulder. "My big girl. I ain't gonna be able to call you my baby much longer."

"You can call me your baby forever. I won't mind." She nuzzled her head into her mama's shoulder and smiled. "Mama?"

"Yes, baby?"

"Ain't Jeriah waitin' for you?"

Her mama drew back. "You know 'bout me an Jeriah?"

"Course I do. We live in the same house. Hard not to know what's goin' on in your room."

The woman's eyes widened. "I's sorry, Angel. I figgered we was bein' quiet 'nuff."

"Pay it no mind. I'm happy for you. 'Sides, I've always thought a him as my daddy. I hope this war ends and you can marry him."

"So do I." She hugged her. "Thank you for understandin'."

"I do. You love him." Angel sighed, then kissed her goodnight. "I best be gettin' some sleep. Tell Jeriah goodnight for me."

Her mama nodded, then left the room.

Maybe their discussion would prove how grown up she'd become and they could talk about such things. Besides, she had a lot of questions she hoped her mama would answer.

* * *

"What are you doing in my room?" Emilia shrieked.

"You scared the fire outta me!" Angel clutched her chest, gasping for breath.

"Good!" Emilia grabbed her arm and pushed her toward the door. "Get out!"

Take a deep breath. "Mrs. Denton asked me to change your sheets."

Emilia shoved her toward the bed. "Then do your *slave* work and strip my bed. I'll watch to make certain you don't take any of my things."

Angel had promised never to slap her again, but her hand twitched with desire.

It didn't take long to remove the bedding. She rolled it into a ball and headed for the door.

"Aren't you going to remake it?" Emilia tapped her foot against the floor.

"I'll be back with clean sheets." *No, you can't stomp on her foot.*

"Good. I'll be waiting. I may want to lie down for a nap. I have to get up *very* early in the morning." She smoothed her dress, tipped her head, and giggled.

She was up to something. "Why?"

"I don't know that I should tell you."

The only reason Emilia brought it up was because she *wanted* to tell. "Fine."

As she started to walk out the door, Emilia grabbed her arm. "Don't you want to know?"

"No." Again, she tried to leave.

"All right, I'll tell you."

Angel sighed, anxious to end the game. "I'm listenin'."

"That soldier—the tall, good-looking one." Emilia lowered her voice to a whisper. "He asked me to meet him in the stable before sunup. He said he has something for me." She giggled. "I love presents!"

"Oh, Emilia." Angel's chest tightened. "You can't go! That soldier wants to—"

"Don't tell me what to do! You're just jealous. The only *man* that ever gave you anything was Billy. And we both know he'll never give you another gift. It's impossible from the grave."

Angel couldn't breathe, unable to speak.

Emilia glared at her. "If you tell anyone, I'll make your life even more miserable."

How much more miserable could it be?

Angel wrenched free and dropped the sheets on the floor. She flew from Emilia's room, down the stairs, and out the front door. Wanting to be alone, she had no idea where to go. If she went home, eventually she'd be found.

She ran down the long path leading away from the house and continued along the road to the front gate. When she reached the tall iron structure she collapsed to the ground.

"I hate her," she mumbled. Tears readily fell. She leaned her head against the metal. The coolness eased the heat of her skin and her pounding head.

She gazed around the estate—her home. The ugly tents ruined the view. *They hafta leave.*

"She told me not to tell." Talking to herself seemed to help. "Fine. I won't tell. Let that soldier teach her a lesson." She breathed heavily and clenched a fistful of dirt. "I tried to warn her. She won't listen to anyone."

I don't care what he does to her. Closing her eyes, she lay back on the hard ground.

"Angel?"

Her eyes flew open and looked up into Bo's. She gulped. *Why'd he hafta find me?*

He knelt down on one knee and touched her face. "Angel? You a'right?"

"Hey, Bo." She didn't move.

"Hey Bo? That all you gots to say?" He sat on his bottom and drew up his knees, staring at her.

Suddenly feeling awkward lying sprawled out beside him, she sat up. She couldn't look at him.

"Angel?" He touched her arm. "You been cryin' again?"

She whipped her head around. "What do you mean, *again?* I ain't cried in a long time."

"I din't mean to make you mad." He pulled his hand to himself. "What you doin' out here?"

She wasn't about to tell him. Emilia said not to tell, so she wouldn't tell a soul. It'd serve her right. "I wanted to be alone." Standing, she huffed, then started to walk away.

"Why?" He followed her.

Why'd he keep asking questions? She stopped and stood her ground. "I'm a woman now. Sometimes women *need* to be alone. So stop askin' questions."

He had the nerve to chuckle.

"Oh!" She shook her fists, then continued on toward the house, marching with deliberation.

"Angel." He was no longer laughing. "I's sorry." He stayed on her heels like a puppy.

Planting her feet, she stopped. *I should be ashamed a myself.* "No, *I'm* sorry. You was tryin' to help. But . . ."

"But?"

"I don't wanna talk 'bout it right now."

"A'right. When you does, you knows where to find me." He offered a sad smile, then headed toward the stables.

She'd hurt his feelings. *What's wrong with me?* Bo didn't deserve to be hurt. Emilia was the one who needed to know pain. *She will . . . soon enough.*

* * *

After Angel's horrible day, she appreciated her mama's sweet smile. "Cat done took to you."

Angel was ready for a good night's sleep, but before it would come, her mind spun with questions. She stroked

Biscuit's fur, unable to look her mama in the eye. "Can I ask you sumthin'?"

"Course."

"'Bout my daddy . . ." She paused when her mama sucked in more air than necessary. Though talking about it was hard for both of them, she had to know. "You told me he took you cuz he liked havin' women. But I don't understand. Why would a man do that?"

Her mama fanned her face. "It's gettin' warm in here."

"No it ain't, Mama. I need to know." For more than one reason.

Her mama stood taller and swallowed hard. "Men does it cuz it makes 'em feel good."

"You told me that before. But *why* does it feel good?"

"Oh, lawdy . . ." She licked her lips and smoothed her dress.

"Mama, do *you* like it?"

"Reckon I could a gone my entire life 'thout you askin' me that."

"You're the only one I can ask. I wanna know."

Her mama wandered aimlessly around the room, twisting her fingers together. Then she rubbed her nose. "With your daddy, no. I hated it. He took me cuz he was my masta and say he had the right. But no man has the right to do that to a woman what don't want him to. He hurt me. But he gave me you. I thank God every day for that."

Through her discomfort, she'd touched Angel's heart. "I love you, Mama."

"That's the key, baby. *Love.* I loves Jeriah with all my heart. When we's together it feels good. When your heart's in it, it's right. When it's for pleasure only, it ain't. Somehow men get to feelin' good no matter how they does it. Sumthin' in nature I reckon. Drives 'em to it."

"Nature?"

"Animal in 'em. Good men has sense 'nuff to control it. Bad men don't."

The soldier's uniforms didn't make them good men. And the look Angel saw in their eyes affirmed it. "So one day, when I'm with the man I love, *I'll* like it?"

"Long as he's a good man." She studied Angel's face. "Sumthin' you needs to tell me?"

"No, Mama." She refused to tell her about Emilia. "I'm growin' up. I wanted to know."

"Don't grow up too fast."

"I won't."

After pressing a kiss to Angel's forehead, her mama left the room. Her footsteps crossed the hallway, then her bedroom door shut tight.

Most nights now, Jeriah shared her bed like a normal married couple. Only on occasion did sounds of pleasure come from their room. She tried to ignore them, but it was difficult. The sounds piqued her curiosity.

Love's the key. The soldiers couldn't be in love with Emilia, and Emilia didn't have an ounce of love in her body. *Hopefully I'm wrong 'bout what they want to do.*

Maybe the man actually had a gift for her. Or maybe Emilia would be the gift he'd give himself.

* * *

"Oh no!" Angel jumped from her bed and threw on her clothes. "How'd I oversleep?"

The sun was rising and the rooster would be crowing any moment. She had to hurry to the barn before it was too late.

Maybe she shouldn't have kept this to herself. She'd wanted Emilia hurt, but not like this.

How could I be so hateful? She scolded herself with every step. *What was I thinkin'?*

It wouldn't be long before Bo would be up to start his daily chores. The Denton's were still sleeping, as were her mama and Jeriah. Ada was the only one awake. She was in the main house stoking up the fire and preparing the morning bread.

I'm the only one who can save her. Hopefully she wouldn't need it.

As she neared the stable door, her heart pounded. With such a huge barn, finding Emilia wouldn't be easy. She entered as quietly as she could.

Emilia's giggle rang out. *Not as hard as I thought it'd be.* Laughter meant it might not be so bad.

Had it not been for curiosity, Angel might have returned home assuming all was well. Instead, she moved into one of the empty stalls and listened.

"What did you say your name was?" Emilia asked.

"Brett," the man said in one rasping breath.

"Brett." She giggled. "What about your surname?"

Probably thinkin' how it'd sound if she married him.

"You talk too much," he said. "Come over here."

Angel's heart beat faster. The swish of fabric kept her attention.

"I let you kiss me because you said you have a gift for me," Emilia said. "Where is it?"

He laughed. "I'm about to show you."

Angel could tell they were kissing. It didn't sound like the kind of kiss she'd shared with Billy—more like what she'd heard coming from her mama's room.

"What are you doing?" Emilia's voice trembled with fear.

"Shh . . ." he said. "Lay back."

"What?"

"We both know why you came here." His voice sounded desperate.

"For my present—"

Her words were cut off. Brett had obviously covered her mouth with his. He was moaning and the rustling of fabric grew even louder.

"What is *that*?" Emilia started to cry. "You're hurting me!"

Angel'd heard enough. She couldn't let this happen.

Grabbing a pitchfork, she raced to the stall. On a mound of straw, Brett lay atop Emilia, fumbling with her dress.

"Get off my sister!" She raised the pitchfork to strike.

Emilia's eyes widened with relief and horror.

"Sister?" With wild eyes, Brett looked over his shoulder. His lip curled into a snarl. "Put that thing away! Harold!"

Of course the other man was near. The two of them were inseparable.

Before Angel could react, Harold grabbed the pitchfork and flung it across the floor.

"I was gonna take my turn when Brett was done, but now I won't hafta wait." He laughed and took a firm hold of Angel, then tumbled with her to the ground.

The stench of manure filled her nose, but it was nothing compared to his foul breath. His mouth searched for hers and his hands roamed her body. She hit, kicked, and screamed, trying to push him away.

Brett was still on her sister, tearing at her dress like a vicious animal.

Just like Mama said. "Fight him, Emilia!"

The girl was crying, but lay there, defeated.

Harold wrapped his arm around Angel's neck and held her to the ground. "Don't ruin this for him. He needs it." He tightened his grip, and she lost her breath.

"You gonna kill me so he can have her?" She panted. "Mr. Denton will see you hung."

"Who's gonna believe a nigger slave? We're soldiers winnin' this war. You're nothin'." He spat the words into her ear.

"Let 'em go!"

Angel gasped. Eyes blazing with rage, Bo stood over them wielding the pitchfork, ready to spill blood.

Harold's grasp loosened, but he didn't release her. "Damn, nigger."

"I said, let 'em go!" Bo jabbed the sharp ends toward Harold.

"You won't do it," he snarled.

"Won't I?" Bo drove it into the ground, barely missing Harold's leg. "Next time, it goes through!"

Releasing Angel, Harold jumped to his feet. "C'mon Brett. Let's go." He leered at her. "When I tell the captain he tried to kill us, *he'll* be the one hung."

Brett didn't move. He remained atop Emilia, pinning her to the ground. "You would a liked it." He kissed her before rolling off her and onto his feet. With a smirk, he adjusted his pants.

Emilia didn't budge. She closed her eyes and cried.

"Get out!" Bo yelled, thrusting the pitchfork toward Brett.

"I'm going." Bold and cocky, Brett held his hands in the air. "She wanted it. They all do." He gestured to Angel.

Bo sneered. "You're filth. Now get out an don't come back!"

The air calmed the moment they were gone. Angel brushed off her clothing and rushed into Bo's arms. "Thank you." She firmed her jaw and didn't cry.

He held her for a brief moment, but then they turned their attention to Emilia who still hadn't moved.

Angel knelt beside her. "Are you hurt?" She pushed down Emilia's dress, which had been forced above her waist.

Emilia covered her face. "I—I don't understand. He was nice to me." She trembled.

Bo took off his coat and tried to place it around her shoulders.

She jerked away. "Don't touch me!"

"Bo," Angel whispered and took his coat. "Can you leave us for a spell?"

He nodded, but as he started to leave his shoulders drooped.

Angel rushed after him. She took his hand, then stood on her tip-toes and kissed his cheek. "I owe you more than I can ever repay. When Emilia's settled I'll come talk to you. All right?"

"A'right." He walked away. She couldn't worry about him right now. Emilia needed her.

The girl hadn't stopped shaking. Angel managed to get her to a seated position and placed Bo's coat around her shoulders. "Emilia, they're gone. They won't hurt you again."

"Why'd he do that?" Emilia sobbed. "I thought he wanted to marry me."

Angel pulled her close and stroked her hair. "You ain't even thirteen yet. But you're pretty, and they wanted you. Do you know enough 'bout men to know what I'm talkin' 'bout?"

Emilia nodded, but Angel wasn't convinced.

"Now, stop your cryin'. We should go to the house." Angel tried to lift her from the ground.

She wouldn't budge. "Why are you being nice? And why did you call me your sister? Is that some *slave* thing?"

Mrs. Denton wasn't going to be happy, but it wouldn't be the first time. Maybe she'd understand. "I called you *sister* because you *are* my sister. Marcus Giles was my daddy, too."

Emilia backed away. "Don't say that. You're lying!" Her tears stopped and her face contorted into something ugly.

"I ain't lyin'. Ask your Aunt Cora. She can tell you a lot 'bout your daddy. I've said enough already. I'll be in trouble for sure."

Emilia finally stood and attempted to adjust her clothing. Her dress had been torn at the waistline and ripped at the shoulder. "Yes, you'll be in trouble. You shouldn't lie about such a thing."

"I *swear* I ain't lyin'!" Angel's sympathy faded fast. "For once can't you be nice? If it hadn't been for me an Bo, that man would a had his way with you! Can't you see that?"

Emilia stomped her way out the barn door. "All I see is a little liar following me."

Angel stopped.

"Good! Stay there," Emilia sneered. "I'm going to change and throw away this old dress. Then I'll tell Aunt Cora what a horrid liar you are."

Angel fumed. "What 'bout the soldiers? Ain't you gonna tell what they done?"

"Why should I?"

"Why? Don't you want them punished?"

Emilia flipped her hair. "The only person who will be punished is *you*."

It was no use. Angel threw up her hands. For a brief moment, she thought she'd broken Emilia's shell, but the girl remained as hard as ever. It seemed nothing would change her.

* * *

Even before Angel could set down the pail of milk, her mama was at her side. "Mista and Ms. Denton is waitin' for you in the livin' room."

What did Emilia tell them? It didn't matter. She knew the truth—something foreign to her sister. The Denton's were always fair. Hopefully they'd listen to her.

Her heart thumped as she walked down the long hallway to the living room. To her relief, Emilia wasn't with them.

"You wanna see me?" Her spirit fell when she noticed the torn dress in Mrs. Denton's hand.

"Have a seat, Angel," Mr. Denton said, motioning to the sofa.

She did as he asked; doing all she could to keep her heart from beating out of her chest.

He took the seat across from her. "Emilia told us what happened."

"She did?" *Most likely all lies.*

"Yep," Mrs. Denton said, sitting beside her. "Now *you* tell us. How'd her dress get torn?"

Being allowed to tell her side of the story calmed her. They listened silently.

"I'm sorry I told her 'bout our daddy. I know you didn't want her to know." Angel swallowed the lump in her throat. Their silence was almost unbearable.

"Why didn't you come to us?" Mrs. Denton asked. Her brow dipped sharply—a new kind of pain.

"Yes, Angel," Mr. Denton added. "You knew there'd be trouble. Why did you take it upon yourself? Do you understand what could have happened?" He rubbed his temples.

Angel lowered her eyes. "I know what I did was wrong, but I wanted her to learn a lesson. She's been so hateful, an keeps talkin' 'bout Billy bein' dead." She softened her voice to a whisper. "I wanted her to be hurt. Like me."

"Come in now, Emilia," Mr. Denton said.

Oh God, was she listenin'? Angel's stomach twisted.

With her nose held high, Emilia walked in.

"Sit down," Mr. Denton commanded.

She plopped into a chair and defiantly crossed her arms.

"Emilia," Mrs. Denton said, calmly. "Angel told the truth. You're sisters. Your pa wasn't what you was told. He was a bad man an he was *never* married to your ma. I don't know what Mr. Peck told you, but from here on out we want the lies to stop. I reckon you don't even know what's true, but I aim to help you sort it all out."

"We don't want you creating *new* lies," Mr. Denton added. "We believe what Angel told us. She'd let us know there was trouble with the soldiers, and I intend to speak again with their captain. You're in my care and I won't have *anyone* harming you. But until I can trust you to have better sense, you're to stay in the house. You're not to go out unless you're accompanied. Don't make me lock you in your room."

"But . . ." Emilia squirmed in her seat. "Why do you believe *her*?"

"Are you saying she's lying?" He glared at Emilia.

"Well . . ." Emilia rapidly licked her lips.

"Shall I get Bo to confirm Angel's story?" His eyes remained glued to the girl.

"No." She sat back in her chair and gripped the seat cushion. Her knuckles turned white.

"Emilia." Mrs. Denton reached out to her. "You're my niece. My blood. We'll always give you a place to live, but you've made it hard to care for you. You could learn a lot from your sister. I want you to try an get along."

A single tear trickled down Emilia's cheek. Could it be real?

"You have anythin' else you wanna say?" Mrs. Denton asked.

Emilia's chin quivered and her eyes squeezed shut. "Uh-uh."

Mrs. Denton faced Angel. "Why don't you go tend to your chores? There's more Emilia an I need to talk 'bout."

Angel stood. "I'm sorry 'bout all the trouble. I can't seem to do anythin' right no more."

Mr. Denton crossed to her. "You helped Emilia. Though things should have been handled differently, in the end you did the right thing." He patted her on the shoulder and gave her a genuine smile. "I may need your help identifying them. I doubt they used their real names."

She nodded silently and left the room.

With a heavy heart, she returned to the kitchen and the comfort of her mama and Ada. The thought of facing the soldiers again terrified her. But if Mr. Denton needed her help, she'd do it. She doubted Emilia would.

Chapter 24

"I had that dream again." Brian was enjoying a piece of cherry pie after a hard day's work.

"One with the dark-eyed girl?" Sylvia flipped the sign on the door to *closed*.

He nodded, then lifted his plate and licked off a remaining dab of cherry filling. "Think she could be someone from my past?"

Sylvia grinned. "Glad ya like my pie." She winked and took his empty plate. "As for the girl, she could be. Reckon she's someone from your family?"

"No. She's too dark. I think my family would look more like me."

"She look like me?" Joe asked, holding his fork in the air.

Brian patted him on the head. "She's not as dark as you, but not as light as me."

The door flew open. Art Matthews stood there red-faced and panting.

Sylvia rushed to his side. "You all right?"

He leaned over and placed his hands on his knees, trying to catch his breath. "Sumthin's goin' on. Soldiers are ridin' outta town."

"Brian," Sylvia said. "Get Mr. Matthews a glass a water."

"Yes'm." He hurried to the kitchen. When he returned, Mr. Matthews was seated at the table.

"Thank ya, son." He gulped down the water, then wiped his brow with the back of his arm. "Sumthin's fixin' to happen. I just don't know what."

The door opened again and another man flew in. "Did ya hear?" His eyes were wide with excitement. "There's over thirty thousand Union troops headin' for Mobile!"

"Thirty thousand?" Sylvia gasped, raising her hand to her face. "They comin' in shootin'?"

Joe left his pie and stood, clinging to Brian's leg. "Brian? I's scared."

"It's all right, Joe." He placed his arm around the trembling boy.

"I don't know 'bout 'em shootin'," the man said. "But our men are leavin' in droves."

Mr. Matthews had finally caught his breath. "I'm gonna go see Mayor Slough. Find out what's goin' on."

"You come back an tell us when you do," Sylvia said, and wavered. "I need to sit down."

Brian helped her to a chair. "I'll get *you* some water." He returned to the kitchen with Joe attached to his leg.

Trying to comprehend thirty thousand soldiers, Brian's mind spun. There were a lot of Confederate soldiers throughout the city, but they were no match for such a large army. Were they fleeing from fear or surrendering?

"Thank you, Brian," Sylvia said, sipping the water. "I can't take much more a this."

Both men had left to get answers with a promise to return, and the café fell unusually quiet. Brian did his best to offer assurance to Sylvia, but he wasn't convinced they weren't in danger. Joe didn't help matters. He kept pulling on Brian's arm asking to go home.

"You go on," Sylvia said. "I'll be fine. I survived August. I can survive this."

"I'd like to wait until the men come back. See what they find out."

She frowned. "It's late. I reckon the mayor won't think too kindly of them botherin' him at home. Go on an get some sleep. You worked hard today."

He doubted he *could* sleep. Too much excitement.

Since Joe was tired and scared, Brian gave in. Certainly by the time they returned for work in the morning they'd know more.

Being late March, the air was cool. Even though the city was quiet, tension surrounded him. A shiver inched down his back.

"Is the soldier's really leavin'?" Joe asked, gripping his hand tighter than ever.

"It's what the man said."

"I want 'em gone but don't want more comin' in. Don't like guns." Joe touched the scar at his neck.

"When the war ends, things'll be better."

"What 'bout them men what hurt us?"

If only Brian could remember them. The only face he ever pictured belonged to the dark-eyed girl. "If they were soldiers, maybe they're leaving with the rest of them."

They arrived home—if he could call it that. The boarding house had never been welcoming, but seemed to be the only place that would allow both of them.

Joe pulled open the back door. The hinges creaked announcing their arrival. Voices came from the common room—unusual for this time of night.

"Stay here." Brian sent Joe into their room with a gentle pat on the back. "I'm going to see what they're talking about."

"I's scared." He looked up at him wide-eyed.

"I'll be right down the hall. I won't be long." He smoothed his hand over the boy's head. "You'll be fine. Sit on your bed and wait for me."

With his head hanging and shoulders drooping, Joe trudged to the bed.

Joining the other tenants in the common room wasn't what Brian wanted to do, but he hurried there nonetheless. He rarely had conversations with them. Yet somehow he'd managed to learn their names.

All eyes turned to him. "Good evening," he managed to say.

"He hasn't heard," Mr. Caster grumbled. "Nothin' good about this evening." Nearly blind, the old man had plenty to complain about, but appeared overly irritable.

"What I heard," Brian said, swallowing hard, "is that Union soldiers are heading for Mobile. A man at Sylvia's said as many as thirty thousand."

Miss Harrison fanned herself. "Lord help us."

"Don't you worry, Miss Harrison," Edward said. "I can still shoot. May only have one leg, but that don't hurt my aim. Any of them Yanks try an come in here, I'll take 'em down."

Brian had seen Miss Harrison and Edward conversing on several occasions. The woman obviously cared for him and sometimes called him *Eddie*.

She dabbed her eyes with a handkerchief. "Thank you, Ed—*Edward*. I pray it doesn't come to that."

Brian glanced at the newlyweds who shared the upper floor with Miss Harrison. They were huddled together on the sofa. Not much older than himself, they trembled as badly as Joe.

"I don't know much about all that's gone on with the war," Brian said boldly. "But from everything I've heard it's coming to an end. If our soldiers are leaving the city, it's likely Mobile will surrender. If we give up without a fight, maybe we won't see our city burned like Atlanta."

"Give up?" Edward rose from his seat. He leaned against a crutch and hobbled toward Brian. "How can you say that?"

Brian stared at the empty space that had once been his leg. "I know you gave a lot for what you believe in, but we can't fight forever. Haven't enough people died already?"

The man's eyes pierced into Brian's soul. "Are you a *Yankee?*"

Brian's heart raced faster and faster. "I—I don't remember."

Edward peered around the room before returning his attention to Brian. "Don't remember?"

"He—he was injured." Miss Harrison's voice quivered. "Lost his memory."

Edward didn't waiver. "I don't believe it. Reckon he's some kind a Yankee spy." His breathing intensified and his nostrils flared. "Him an his little nigger boy's been spyin' on us."

"I'm no spy." Brian stepped back. "I don't remember anything that happened before I woke up in the hospital in January." His mouth felt as dry as an empty well, and his heart pounded so hard it reverberated in his ears. He wanted to turn and run, but he wasn't a coward.

Every eye in the room met his with disdain. *I'm not welcome here.*

He'd stay tonight, but tomorrow he'd find a new place. One they could enter through the front door. "I'm sorry I interrupted your evening."

Silence.

He walked away.

"What happened?" Joe asked.

Brian shut and locked the door. "Nothing." He shoved the wardrobe across the floor and wedged it in front of the door.

Joe watched, wide-eyed. "Nothin'? Why you doin' that?"

"Those people don't like us. I don't want them bothering us."

"Good I gots a chamber pot." Joe pushed on the wardrobe. "Ain't strong 'nuff to move it."

"I'll move it in the morning. Then we'll find a new place to live."

"Good. Never liked it here." Joe hopped onto his bed. "Is it cuz a me?"

Brian lay back on his own bed and stared upward. "It's because of *me*. Now, go to sleep."

"'Night, Brian."

"Goodnight, Joe."

I won't be able to sleep anytime soon. His ears were attuned to the voices down the hallway.

"Brian?" Joe's little voice quivered.

"Yes?"

"I's still scared."

"Come here." Brian scooted toward the wall and lifted the blankets. Joe climbed in beside him. "Don't be scared. I'm right here."

The boy nestled his body against him and shared his pillow. Holding onto his tiny form, Brian calmed, listening to his slow steady breathing. His eyes became heavier as the hours passed, until he could no longer fight it. Maybe he'd dream of her. His dark-eyed girl.

* * *

"Why didn't you ask sooner?" Mrs. Holloway waved Brian and Joe into her home. She smoothed her hand over Joe's head. "I made cookies. You'll find them in the kitchen."

Joe scurried away.

"I didn't want to impose," Brian sighed. "But I know how fond you are of Joe, and I thought we could help each other. I can repair your porch in the evenings after work, and on my days off I'll do even more. Paint. Clean. Whatever's needed."

"I'll allow you to stay on one condition." She motioned to the sofa.

Brian sat. The familiar puff of dust rose into the air. "Yes'm?"

"I don't want your money." She folded her hands in her lap and pursed her lips.

"I can't stay here without paying. It wouldn't be right."

"You just said you'd repair my house. That and perhaps a bit of dusting . . ." She winked and chuckled. "Will be payment enough."

His heart danced. "I won't disappoint you. I'm an excellent carpenter."

"You don't have to sell yourself to me, Brian. I knew from the first day I met you that you were a fine boy."

That word again. "Mrs. Holloway, how old do you think I am?"

She studied his face. "Fifteen?"

"Do I really look that young?"

She patted his cheek. "A young face is nothing to be ashamed of. How old *are* you?"

"Eighteen. Or at least that's what Joe told me. I don't remember my birthdate, but Joe said I told him I was eighteen. I can't imagine why I'd lie about such a thing."

"Hmm . . . I don't know. But, no matter. Fifteen or eighteen, you're the finest *young man* I've had in my life in a very long time."

Brian smiled. "I like that better than *boy.*"

"I'm a boy." Joe entered the room with a cookie in each hand.

Mrs. Holloway laughed aloud. "Yes, you are. One who's had enough cookies."

"I likes 'em."

"I imagine I'll need to make more since you'll be living with me."

Joe's mouth dropped. "We's gonna live here?"

"Yes," Brian said. "Will you help me repair Mrs. Holloway's house?"

Joe shoved the cookies into Brian's hands, then ran into the woman's arms. "I do anythin' you say to live here."

She dabbed at her eyes.

They were home.

Chapter 25

March 31st, 1865

I had to go with Mr. Denton to identify the soldiers. Though they all look alike in their uniforms, once I got close enough I knew them. I thought I was going to be sick. If Mr. Denton hadn't held my arm I probably would've thrown up. I don't know what will happen to them, but Mr. Denton said they'd be sent away. I've never been so scared.

I thanked Bo again. He's been a good friend. He's older, but treats me like I'm his age. I'm afraid he might care for me. I'll never feel that way about him. I love Billy. Only Billy.

Angel closed her eyes and pictured him. She smiled remembering his Christmas-green eyes.

Startled out of her trance by a knock on her door, she set the journal aside.

"Yes?" Wanting to be alone, she tried to hide the disappointment in her voice.

"Can I come in?" *Emilia? In the slave house?*

Angel shoved the book into the drawer and jumped off her bed. She masked her shock and opened the door. "What's wrong?"

Emilia's red face gave every indication she'd been crying. "I need to talk to you."

Angel stepped aside, waiting to be criticized for her simple furnishings.

"Mind if I sit on your bed?" Emilia asked.

"No." Angel sat beside her.

Silence hung in the air. Emilia fidgeted with her dress, mindlessly looking around the room.

Angel couldn't bear the quiet. "Why'd you come here?"

Emilia stared at her lap. "Aunt Cora told me everything. I know about our father. I know how he died and why she killed him."

No wonder she'd been crying. She'd felt the same way when she'd been told. "Glad you know. I don't like keepin' secrets."

"I should have listened to you, Angel." She choked out the words. "You tried to warn me about the soldiers. He was going to put his . . ." She started crying again.

"I know what he wanted to do. You don't hafta say it. I'm sorry I didn't tell the Denton's before it happened."

Emilia sniffled. "I don't blame you. I've been horrid to you."

Angel gave her sister a sideways glance. Could she trust her now? Could everything that happened have made her . . . *nice*? "Yes, you have."

"You didn't have to agree with me." She scowled, then sighed. "But, it *is* true. I'm trying not to lie anymore."

"Good." Angel let out a long breath. "Maybe we can learn how to be sisters."

"We certainly don't look like sisters." Emilia wrinkled her nose. "You are *colored,* after all."

"I'm half white," Angel reminded her. "I'm willin' to try. Just don't get all nasty again."

"All right."

"One other thing." Angel looked her in the eye. "Don't ever say Billy's dead."

Emilia raised her chin in the air. "I thought I wasn't supposed to lie."

"It *ain't* a lie. He *ain't* dead. You hear me?" Angel stood and glared at the girl.

"Fine. Until we hear otherwise, I won't talk about him at all. I don't know why everyone's so upset about him. From what I was told he chose to leave."

"He did. But he's special. Everyone loves him." Heat rose in her cheeks.

Emilia grinned. "Especially you. Right?" She giggled, reminding Angel of the barn.

"He's like a brother. Course I love him." She was done talking about Billy. "It's late. You best get back to your room. If Mr. Denton knew you left without permission, he'd be angry."

"Aunt Cora knows. But you're right. I need to go to my room. It's much nicer than yours." She strutted out the door without another word.

So she hadn't *completely* changed.

About to retrieve her journal, she was disturbed by another knock on the door.

"Angel?"

"Come in, Mama."

She was already rubbing her nose. This couldn't be good.

They took their familiar spots on the bed. "What's wrong, Mama?"

"I have sumthin' to tell you." She laid her hands in her lap, then almost immediately started rubbing again.

Angel grabbed her hand. "You're gonna rub the skin plum off. Tell me what's wrong."

She blinked rapidly a number of times, then tried to break free of Angel's grasp. She finally gave in and stilled her hands. "Now that you understan' 'bout men an women, it won't be so much of a surprise" She blew out a long breath.

A grown up conversation. Angel couldn't be more pleased. She leaned in, waiting . . .

"I's gonna have a baby." Her eyes instantly filled with tears.

"A baby?" Angel couldn't contain her own tears. "When?"

"October. I din't think it could happen again. Jeriah's happy. I's happy. I just needs to know you're happy, too."

"Course I'm happy! I've always wanted a brother or sister." *Emilia.* "Well, I got a sister. Maybe you'll give me a brother." Angel gently hugged her "Do the Denton's know?"

"I was gonna tell you first. When Emilia came, I went to them. Ms. Denton cried. She be happy. They wadn't angry 'bout me an Jeriah."

"I can't believe we're gonna have a baby in our house." A broad smile covered her face. "If only you could get married."

"You know we cain't. That don't matter none. We loves each other. Least the good Lawd gave us mastas who lets us be together. But Ms. Wellesley don't know 'bout us. We's prayin' the war ends soon an we can be free to marry.

When we's free, it won't matter none what Ms. Wellesley think. No matter, Jeriah an I wanna stay here to raise our child. Free or not."

"Mrs. Wellesley will understand. She's always been good to *me*."

"We ain't takin' no chances. So, don't say nothin' to her. Least not now. She'll see my belly soon 'nuff."

Angel agreed to keep another secret. This one would be hard to hold inside. It was the happiest news she'd heard since Billy left. She longed to scream it out.

* * *

Spot let out a contented *maw*. Angel pulled her udders, humming all the while.

The first day of April brought joy she'd forgotten existed. The two soldiers had been sent away, Emilia was being nice, and her mama was going to have a baby. If Billy'd come home, her life would be perfect.

"Someone's happy this mornin'." Bo chuckled.

"I am." She let out a laugh of her own.

"Been long time since I heard you hum." He pulled up a stool and sat beside her, then leaned in close. "Jeriah told me."

She let out a relieved sigh. At least she could talk to Bo about it. "Ain't it wonderful?"

"Babies should be. If'n the war ends, it might just be the first free-born on this here estate." He gently pushed her hair back behind her ear, catching her off guard.

She couldn't look at him. Why'd he touch her that way? "I hope it ends. Then Mama and Jeriah can get married and they won't hafta worry 'bout Mrs. Wellesley bein' angry."

"Angel?" She hadn't heard her name spoken so soft since Billy . . .

"Huh?"

"Like hearin' you hum. You gots a nice voice." His breath brushed her cheek.

"Bo!" Jeriah yelled.

She hadn't noticed him approaching, but couldn't have been happier to see him.

"Yessa?" Bo jumped to his feet, knocking over the stool.

"Leave Angel be. She needs to finish milkin'."

"Yessa." Bo smiled at her. "I gots work to do. Keep hummin', a'right?"

As he walked away, Jeriah stepped up beside her. "Angel?"

She jumped up and hugged him tight. "I'm so happy, Jeriah!" She kissed his cheek, then hugged him again.

"Ain't mad?"

"Course not! You love Mama an she loves you. That's how it's s'posed to be. Sides, I've always thought a you as my daddy."

Her words produced an enormous smile. "I loves you, too."

"I know you do. Most important, you love mama. After what she went through with my daddy, she needed to know what real love is."

"Angel." She knew his serious tone well. "Bo's older than you is, but he sees you as a growed woman. You ain't. I aim to talk to him. I knows he'll respect you, but he don't need to be gettin' ideas. Leastways not now. Maybe when you're older."

A nervous laugh bubbled out of her. "Jeriah, Bo don't feel like that 'bout me."

He shook his finger at her. "I seen the way he looked at you just now. Made you uncomfortable. I ain't blind."

He'd always been able to see into her heart and mind. "Can't fool you, can I?"

"Nope." He grinned.

"My baby brother will have a good daddy."

"Brother?"

"I hope. Reckon you'd like a little Jeriah runnin' 'round."

He beamed. "That I would."

She sat on the milking stool. "I best get done."

"Good girl." He stroked her hair. *His* touch didn't make her jump.

Chapter 26

"It was kind of you to include me in Brian's supper invitation," Mrs. Holloway said to Dr. Mitchell. "He's told me so much about all of you."

Brian smiled. He'd enjoyed listening to them talk about Memphis. They'd remembered some of the same places. It sounded wonderful and he hoped to go there one day.

Hannah smiled at him from across the table. He immediately shifted his gaze. Trying to discourage her was becoming more and more difficult. Since there could already be a woman in his life, he needed to dismiss any thoughts of the young girl.

Loud shouts from the street turned their heads.

Dr. Mitchell rushed to the front window, followed by everyone else at the table. Mrs. Mitchell clutched her husband's arm. "Is it trouble, Harvey?"

"Stay here." He motioned for Brian to follow him. The moment he opened the front door, the noise grew.

They sped to the front gate. Brian recognized Art Matthews and waved him over.

"What's happening?" Dr. Mitchell asked.

"Wire just came in." Art scowled. "Lee surrendered to Grant. Damn it all!"

"What about the Union soldiers?" Brian hid his elation. "Will they leave now?"

"Unless the city surrenders, they're sure to try an destroy it." Art's face puffed up with anger. "Damn Yanks! They aim to ruin the south. Take away all we've known." He pointed down the road. "Gotta let Sylvia know what's happened." He sprinted away.

Dr. Mitchell squeezed Brian's shoulder. His unspoken words screamed relief.

Once inside the Mitchell's home, Brian finally let out a whoop. "It's over!" He lifted Hannah off the floor and swung her around. When he realized what he'd done, he set her down gently and apologized.

Her face flushed. "It's all right. I didn't mind."

Dr. Mitchell cleared his throat. "Thank God, Lee surrendered."

With tear-filled eyes, his wife embraced him. "Are you certain?"

"If it's true, won't it be in tomorrow's Register?" Brian asked.

"Yes, it should." The doctor kissed his wife's forehead. "There's hope for our city, but I'm afraid some of the rebels won't give up easily. You heard Mr. Matthews. His anger's mild compared to others."

"Why would they continue fighting? The war's as good as over if Lee surrendered. There comes a time when it's better to give in than lose everything."

"Some would rather lose everything than give up their principles," Mrs. Holloway said with a sad sigh.

Joe wrinkled his brow. "What now?"

"We wait and see," Dr. Mitchell replied.

Things calmed, so Mrs. Mitchell suggested they return to the dining room for dessert.

"C'mon Brian." Hannah took his hand. "Mama's cobbler's delicious."

He stared at her hand. Pulling away would be rude, but continuing would encourage her. Her soft skin kept his hand where it was; entwined with hers. He'd be sure to release it before they reached the dining room and the watchful eye of her father.

* * *

"I saw you holding that girl's hand," Mrs. Holloway said the moment they returned home.

He sat down hard on the sofa. "Do you think Dr. Mitchell noticed?"

"No. You were discreet. I was behind you with Joe. He saw it, too."

Joe laughed. "Why you holdin' her hand? She's too big."

Too big? It took a moment to make sense. *Hannah didn't need protecting.*

"Sometimes young men hold the hands of young women," Mrs. Holloway said. "But holding hands may leads to other things." She raised her brows.

"Like kissin'?" Joe puckered his lips, smacked them together, then grinned.

"What do you know about kissing?" Brian asked.

"I seen things." Joe rolled his eyes upward. "Ain't gonna say nothin' else."

Mrs. Holloway sighed and leaned back into the sofa. "I remember my first kiss . . ." Her voice drifted away. The memory lifted the corners of her lips.

"Your wedding?" Brian asked.

She giggled like a young girl. "No. Not even my husband. It was another young man."

The dreaminess in her eyes intrigued him. "What happened to him?"

"I shouldn't have mentioned it." She waved her hand in the air. "That was a long time ago and another life. I took a different path. But some things are never forgotten."

Brian's heart sank. *Many* things were forgotten. Had *he* shared a first kiss? Loved a woman? One thing was certain; he wouldn't be kissing Hannah anytime soon. Dr. Mitchell would never forgive him.

He set aside self-pity. There were important things to think about now. Tomorrow, he'd be able to confirm the rumors. If they were true, he prayed the city officials would have the sense to surrender. They *had* to. Mobile was too beautiful to go down in flames.

* * *

Mr. Denton burst through the back door, waving a newspaper. "It's over! Lee surrendered!" He flew into the hallway. "Cora! Mother! The war's over! Lee surrendered!"

The excited commotion brought the house to life. Everyone gathered around him.

A weight lifted from Angel's heart. *Maybe Billy'll be home soon.*

"What's all the fuss?" Emilia asked, entering the room.

"The war's over!" Angel exclaimed.

Emilia rolled her eyes. "Why is everyone screaming about it?"

Mrs. Denton wrapped her arm around the girl. "With the war over, they'll let the prisoners go. Billy can come home!"

"Billy's comin' home?" Paulette asked, clapping her hands together.

Her mama scooped her up. "Soon." She kissed her, laughed, and set her back down again.

Could it be true? Angel closed her eyes and prayed he'd not been hurt in captivity. She imagined he'd lost weight from being poorly fed. But it didn't matter. Ada could fatten him up.

"Angel." Mrs. Denton held out her hands. "We got good reason to be happy now."

"Yes'm." Their eyes locked. Her heart told her all had been forgiven.

* * *

Brian woke from the most restful sleep he'd had in a long time. Joe's heavy breathing indicated he was still asleep. The room they shared now was even smaller than the one at Miss Harrison's, but he didn't care. Mrs. Holloway's house was home.

He couldn't stop smiling. The city'd had sense enough to surrender, but what made him even happier was dreaming of *her* again. This time, she spoke. *But what did she say?*

Not all the news recently had been good. Sometimes having no memory of people and events was a benefit, making news less painful. When he'd heard Abraham Lincoln had been shot, he'd felt badly for the man's family, but had no other opinion of him—though Dr. Mitchell had said he was a fine man and a great president.

The country was changing. Even now with the Union Army declaring martial law, Mobile was uneasy. At least it hadn't been reduced to ashes.

"Shall I burn the breakfast?"

Mrs. Holloway's sweet voice made Brian chuckle. She scolded them for over-sleeping as only she knew how.

Joe jerked upright and rubbed his eyes.

"We'll be right out, Mrs. Holloway," Brian said. "C'mon, Joe. Let's not keep her waiting."

"Don't like her burned biscuits."

"Neither do I. So eat what you can and we'll eat more when we get to Sylvia's."

Joe grinned from ear-to-ear and hopped off the bed.

Although Mrs. Holloway had a tendency to burn food, they wouldn't want to live anywhere else. Brian was trying to learn how to cook so he could help in the kitchen. Even Joe had taken interest in it. Especially when it came time to bake cookies.

They graciously ate a few bites, then headed for work. Joe only worked half-days now and spent the afternoons with Mrs. Holloway.

Before going to the hotel, they stopped by the café for a golden brown biscuit with jam.

Sylvia held the morning *Register* in her hand, shaking her head. "It just ain't right." She extended the paper to Brian.

"What is it?" His answer stared him in the face. "An esti-mated sixteen hundred of Sultana's twenty-four hundred passengers died when three of the ship's four boilers ex-ploded and Sultana sank near Memphis, Tennessee . . ."

Reading it aloud made it even more painful. His heart felt as if it was being squeezed by an iron fist.

"They was goin' home," Sylvia said with tear-filled eyes. "I know they was Yankees, but they'd been freed. Made it through all the fightin' an bein' prisoners, an they was on their way home. It ain't right."

Brian scanned the rest of the article. A wrench in his belly made him short of breath. "It says the steamboat was overcrowded. Packed full. The worst maritime disaster in history."

"Serves 'em right."

Brian jerked around to see who'd said such a horrible thing. Seeing Art Matthews sipping a cup of coffee with a snarl on his face, didn't surprise him.

"How can you say that, Mr. Matthews? The war's over. They were going home." Brian returned the paper to Sylvia.

"Far as I'm concerned," Mr. Matthews grumbled, "they can all burn in Hell."

Sylvia cupped Joe's ears and frowned. "Don't talk like that in front a the boy."

The man mumbled something inaudible, and Brian took Joe by the hand. "We'll go on to the hotel, Sylvia. Thank you for the biscuits."

She smiled a sad smile and nodded.

Joe tightly gripped his hand. "Those men burned up, din't they, Brian?"

"Yes, they did."

"I's scared a burnin'. I seen my masta . . ." He stopped and covered his mouth.

Brian brought him to an abrupt halt. "What did you see?"

"I ain't sayin' no more." Joe stared at the ground, folding into himself.

Every time it seemed he'd open up and reveal something about his past, he shut down. It had to have been horrible. Did someone burn at the hands of his master? No wonder he was afraid of everything. In his short life, he'd probably seen more terrible things than any man ever should.

* * *

"Angel," Mr. Denton said. "Get my uncle a glass of water." He helped Harper to a seat at the kitchen table.

"Yes, sir." She did as requested.

Harper took it gratefully and drank it down.

Mrs. Denton entered the kitchen and sat beside him. "I settled the children with Miss Banks. Now tell me. What happened?"

All breakfast preparations stopped. Everyone awaited the news.

"I seen the glare from the fire," Harper said, shaking his head. "Lit up the night sky. One helluva inferno."

"I don't understand," Mrs. Denton said. "What's this got to do with Billy?"

Angel's heart thumped. Any other time, she'd have scolded him for cursing. Dread hung around her shoulders like a black cloak.

Mr. Denton sat beside his wife and took her hands. "The steamboat's boiler exploded. The boat was filled with released prisoners." His voice broke as he spoke. "Union soldiers. They estimated out of twenty-four hundred passengers, sixteen hundred perished."

Mrs. Denton gasped and clutched her chest. Her face turned white as a sheet. "But . . . why . . . you reckon . . ." She closed her eyes and fought back tears.

Angel wavered into her mama's arms. "Mama?"

"Shh . . . baby." She soothed her while leading her to a chair.

"Ain't no reason to believe Billy was on that boat," Harper said. "Don't know where he was. Shouldn't scare the women, Douglas."

"I don't mean to scare them. You brought the news. I felt Cora should know. But you're right. We don't know where Billy was being held."

Mrs. Denton cried openly now. "If he's alive, why ain't he wrote?" Her chin quivered, her entire body trembled. "If he was on that boat, there's nothin' left of him. They all burned . . ."

"I don't believe it!" Angel screamed. "I *won't* believe it! Billy ain't dead!" She jumped up and flew out the back door.

Rain came down in sheets, dampening her already dismal spirit. By the time she reached her house she was soaked to the bone. She peeled her clothing from her skin and lay naked on her bed. Though the house was warm, she shivered.

Biscuit jumped up beside her and nuzzled her face. Reaching down to the foot of the bed, she yanked on the quilt and covered them. He purred and nestled in beside her.

"He ain't dead," she muttered over and over.

"Angel?" Her mama rapped on the door, then pushed it open.

She couldn't answer—too numb to do anything.

"Baby. I knows you wanna keep holdin' onto hope. But Ms. Denton's right. If'n Billy's alive, he would a sent a telegram by now." She sat beside her and fingered her wet hair.

Her mama may have given up hope, but how could *she*? Filled with unstoppable pain, Angel lay there and cried.

"You go on an cry. It'll hep." Her mama's voice broke. "I miss him, too."

Angel wanted to sleep and never wake up. The tightness in her chest was unbearable. Every part of her being ached and her mama's words gave no comfort. She closed her eyes and tried to picture Billy. But all she could see were flames.

Chapter 27

Brian stretched and arched his back. He'd been bent over too long working on floorboards. It felt good to get out in the fresh air, though the heat of summer seemed to be coming early. Only the twenty-fifth of May and already eighty degrees in the early afternoon.

As he straightened, he noticed an unusual pillar of smoke rising into the northern sky. He tilted his head studying it. *Odd . . .*

A loud blast dropped him to his knees. *Oh, God!* He covered his ears. Another blast rumbled the ground beneath him. His heart pounded. Within minutes, complete bedlam ensued. People were screaming and running into the street. *The war's over. Why . . .*

Composing himself, he ran to the café, shoving past people going the opposite direction. "What's happening?"

Sylvia grabbed him by the arm. "Where's Joe?" Her eyes were wide with panic.

"Home. With Mrs. Holloway."

"Go see to 'em. Whatever's happenin' ain't good. Make sure they're safe." She pushed him toward the door. "I'm stayin' here. I ain't goin' out there."

"Yes'm." He raced into the street. The fear in her eyes was nothing compared to the looks on the faces he passed. His own fear drove him faster.

The smoke over the city grew thicker as another explosion boomed through the air and rattled inside his chest.

Bursting through the front door, he found Joe shivering in Mrs. Holloway's arms.

"Brian," she said with tear-filled eyes. "We heard the blasts. I've never been so frightened."

"You'll be fine." Breathing hard, he placed a gentle hand on her arm. "The fires are further north."

"But how did this happen? We surrendered. Why are they burning our city?" She cried openly, rocking Joe back and forth.

"I don't know, but I'll be back as soon as I find out. They may need my help."

"Be careful." She dabbed her eyes with a handkerchief. "I'll tend Joe."

He nodded his appreciation. With adrenaline pumping through his veins, he left and headed north toward the flames. People frantically ran amok.

"Don't go up there," a woman said, gasping for air. She cinched Brian's arm. "There's bodies everywhere!" She released him, then stumbled down the road; dazed and confused.

Torn over whether he should take her to the hospital or continue on, he chose the latter. He assumed his help would be more important elsewhere. *Bodies everywhere?*

The smoke became denser. He had to be close.

A bloody detached arm dangled above him from the branch of a tree. To his right, a gory mass he determined to be the partial body of a horse lay in the road surrounded by shattered glass, bricks, and other debris.

He dropped to his knees and retched. Screams and moaning filled his ears.

"Help me!" A shrill voice cried out.

Keep your head straight. He jumped to his feet and ran toward the screaming woman. Her hands—covered in blood—held the limp body of a child. "Please, help me."

He extended his arms and took the little girl. To his relief, she moaned. "We need to get her to the hospital," he said to the woman, who blankly stared at him. He nudged her with his shoulder. "Come with me."

She shook her head as if to awaken, then followed him.

"What's her name?" he asked.

"I don't know."

"Isn't she yours?"

"No. She fell into my arms when the city blew up." She stumbled and sat down hard on the ground. "I can't go any further."

He couldn't wait for her. The child's need was urgent. He pressed on . . .

The steps leading to the hospital were a welcome sight, but he wasn't the only one bringing wounded. Mobile may have survived the war, but she was burning and people were dying.

The chaos that followed made his head spin. Nurses barked orders, barely audible over the turmoil. He caught the eye of Nurse Primrose and ran to her, cradling the child. "Please help her."

"Oh, my dear, Brian." The sparkle in her eyes had disappeared, replaced by fear and sorrow.

"She's still breathing." He licked his dry lips. "Please . . ."

"In here." She motioned to a large room.

People battered, burned, and bleeding surrounded him. He'd never heard such wailing.

He placed the girl on the end of a bed beside a crying little boy. Her long blond hair was matted with blood, and her face had been cut. She was tiny—smaller than Joe.

"Brian?"

His heart eased, hearing the voice of his friend. "Dr. Mitchell. I found this girl—"

With a raised hand, the doctor cut him off. After feeling the girl's pulse and giving instructions to Nurse Primrose, he motioned for Brian to follow him. "I need your help."

Brian hesitated, staring at the still body of the child. "But—"

"She'll be fine. There are others in worse condition. I don't have enough help."

He didn't need to hear anything else. He followed the man to the entrance of the hospital. People were everywhere. "What do I do?"

"Help the nurses sort the injured. Take the most critical to that room on the left." He nodded down the hallway. "Try to keep everyone calm."

Taking a deep breath, Brian stilled his heart.

Cries of *help* filled the air and set his body in motion. A man was brought in, held between two others. His leg had been nearly cut in half. They'd pieced it together crudely with rope.

Brian pointed left. Dr. Mitchell would once again show his skill at amputation.

In a blur, he continued on, deciding quickly which way to send each person. His head ached, but he wouldn't quit. Thankfully, no one questioned his authority.

By the time the sun set, he was exhausted. It was all he could do to set one foot in front of the other and keep his mind straight. The entire northern half of the city had gone up in flames.

Stories circulated the hospital until finally the facts were revealed. A munition's depot said to have over two hundred tons of explosives had caught fire. The explosions were caused by mines, gunpowder, and artillery shells. The building was obliterated, replaced by a thirty-foot-deep hole.

The burning debris filled the air and fell onto other buildings, trees, and houses, setting everything ablaze. Hundreds were dead. More were injured and dying.

With the facts also came rumors. Some said a Confederate soldier had purposely set the depot on fire, but that couldn't be true. *Why would he want to harm his own people?*

Most said it had been an accident. A horrible *deadly* accident. Whatever was true, Brian would never forget it.

Things had calmed, so he returned to the little girl. She blinked slowly but didn't speak.

"No one's claimed her," Nurse Primrose whispered. "We'll keep her here until she's well, but if she's not claimed she'll be turned over to the city orphanage."

Orphanage?

The nurse rushed away before he could question her. Feeling compassion for the girl, he longed to take her home. But how could he? Joe was already his charge. He didn't have the means to take in another child. *Maybe her parents will come.*

He smiled at her, then returned to the hospital steps. They were finally empty.

He sat on the uppermost tier and gazed at the city. Heavy smoke lingered in the sky. The darkening night created an ominous view.

He finally realized how much blood covered his clothing. The bitter smell filled his nose, making him nauseous.

"Are you all right, Brian?" Dr. Mitchell laid a hand on his shoulder.

He jerked, startled by the touch. "Sorry. Yes, I'm fine. As fine as I *can* be."

"You did an excellent job." The doctor sat beside him. "Union soldiers tried to help, but no one would listen to them. Even wounded, pride kept them from taking help from the enemy."

"It was horrible." Brian swallowed a lump in his throat. "All those bodies, and—"

"Yes. It was." He let out a long breath. "I've seen it before. I thought I'd seen the last of it."

"No one expected this. You were incredible. Those people are lucky you took care of them."

"There were many more *unlucky* today." The doctor raked his hands through his hair. "I'm tired. I need to go home."

"*Can* you?"

"For a short time. I've done all I can for now. Some will make it. Others won't. But if I don't get some rest, I won't be able to help anyone. You should go home as well."

Brian nodded. "Joe's probably worried."

"Mrs. Holloway, too." Dr. Mitchell stood and extended his hand. "I need to hold my wife and hug my girls."

Taking the doctor's hand, Brian gratefully accepted his help. Every muscle in his body ached. "I'll come back in the morning if you think you'll need me."

"Thank you. But first, get a good night's sleep."

"Yes, sir."

"I'll let Hannah know you're all right."

Not knowing how to respond, Brian simply smiled, then headed toward home.

* * *

"No one claimed her, Mrs. Holloway," Brian said, shaking his head. "They've taken her to the orphanage. She won't have a chance there. It's already over-crowded."

Mrs. Holloway handed him a cookie. "Eat this. It'll make you feel better." She smiled with that motherly smile he'd grown to love.

He stared at it, but couldn't eat. What bothered him more? The churning of his stomach or his reeling mind? Something pushed him to take responsibility for the girl.

"She's only four." He sat on the sofa. "Younger than Joe."

"You can't care for every needy child you meet." She placed her hand against his cheek. "You have a very loving heart."

"Is that why it hurts?" He studied his hands trying to erase the memory of her face. Big blue eyes looking up at him through a mist of tears. "She clung to me when I went to check on her at the hospital. She cried when I left. How do I know she wasn't part of my former life?"

"From what you've told me of her, she looks nothing like you. It's unlikely she's family."

"Joe doesn't look like me either." He forced himself to chuckle, then covered his face with his hands. "What do I do?"

Mrs. Holloway walked toward the front door, then turned and faced him without speaking.

Her silence troubled him. "I'm sorry. I hope I didn't upset you."

"No." She took a deep breath. "I'm old, but not *too* old. Dr. Mitchell said for a woman my age I'm doing quite well. I hope to live at least another ten years . . ." She twisted her hands together, looking more uncomfortable than he'd ever seen her.

"I hope you live longer than that," he interjected, before she could continue.

She looked upward. "God willing. But, no matter. Ten years will be long enough to bring that child into womanhood."

His heart thumped. "Are you saying what I think you are?"

"I've always wanted a daughter." She stared at him with tears trickling down her cheek. "I've not stopped thinking about her since you shared her plight."

He sprung from the sofa and hugged her, dropping the cookie on the floor. "Thank you!"

She erupted into nervous laughter. "I'm scared as can be! I've never been a mother."

"Trust me, Mrs. Holloway. You're already a mother. Your love for me and Joe is proof."

She took hold of his hands. "You've made an old woman very happy. Aside from repairing my home and removing dust from my furniture, you've dusted off my heart."

What could he say? Until now, he'd just wanted to remember his past so he could go back to how things were. Everything had changed. He loved his life now and couldn't imagine it any other way.

He smiled at her. "I'll go to the orphanage and see what's needed to bring Becky home."

"Becky . . ." the woman sighed. "Becky Holloway."

Yes, Rebecca would take the last name of Holloway once the adoption was finalized. It was one detail that troubled him. *What's my last name?*

In time, he'd have to choose one. Something fitting. Perhaps *Carpenter.*

Chapter 28

"Push harder Mama!" Angel urged. She could see the top of the baby's head. It needed to come out.

"I's waitin' for the doc!" Her mama clenched her teeth and grimaced.

"He ain't gonna get here in time. The baby's done made up its mind. It's comin' now!"

Angel knelt on the bed between her mama's legs. Her heart throbbed out of control. Scared beyond words, she'd made up her mind she could do this. After Ada had fainted at the first trace of blood, she was the only woman left to help. Mrs. Denton was sick with fever. The doctor had seen her the night before and told her to keep her distance.

The baby had decided to come early. No one was prepared.

"How's she doin'?" Jeriah yelled through the door.

"Fine!" *I hope.* "Go see if Mr. Denton's back with the doctor!"

Jeriah's heavy footfalls were followed by the slamming door.

"You're a liar," her mama grunted. "I ain't fine." She pressed her head into the pillow. "Oh!"

"Good, Mama. It's time to push again." Angel positioned her hands over the baby's head. Her mind wandered from the task at hand and focused on the size of the head protruding from between her mama's legs. *Ain't no way it don't hurt.*

She swallowed hard, shook her head, and bit her bottom lip. *I never wanna go through this.*

"Lawdy!" Her mama dug her fingernails into the blankets.

"Mama, the head's out!" Angel grabbed a towel and wiped the blood from the tiny face.

"I want it *all* out!" She rose up and pushed so hard the baby's shoulders popped through.

"You're doin' it, Mama!" Tears welled in Angel's eyes at the reality of this miracle.

With one more contraction and a burst of renewed energy from her mama, Angel's baby brother came into the world. "It's a boy!" Angel laughed and cried at the same time, while lifting the perfectly-formed infant from the bed.

"Swat his behind!" Her mama commanded. "He ain't cryin'!"

Swat him? She couldn't swat him. It wouldn't be right.

"Swat him, Angel!"

"All right!" She draped his body over one hand, and struck his bottom with the other. Immediately, he let out a wail.

Ada sat up rigidly. "What was that?"

"Mama's baby boy," Angel said, giggling with nervous laughter. "You done missed it, Ada."

Breathing heavily, her mama reached out. "Give him to me, baby."

Angel gladly complied and placed him on her mama's chest. She tucked a blanket around him to keep him warm. "I'll get some water to clean him up. But, what do we do 'bout that?" She pointed to the cord still attached to the boy.

The door opened. "I'll take care of it." The long-awaited doctor stepped into the room. "I'm sorry I missed all the excitement, but it looks like you did fine without me."

"I had an Angel watchin' over me," her mama said. "But I's glad to see you, Doc."

"I'll get that water," Angel said, and left the room. She found Jeriah pacing the floor, and wrapped her arms around him. "She's fine, Jeriah. Tired, but fine. So's my little brother."

Jeriah stumbled, but she grabbed him before he fell. His face contorted. "I gots a son?"

"Sure do. One that needs a good bath. Help me with the water." She took his hand to steady him, then led him to their small kitchen where water was already boiling on the stove. She'd never seen him so out of sorts. His face revealed elated fear—something she'd just experienced herself.

They tested the temperature of the water and poured some into a pan. With trembling hands, Jeriah carried it to the bedroom door. Angel pushed it open for him and he stumbled through.

Finally a reason for joy. Angel closed her eyes and leaned against the wall. After all these months since the news of the accident, for the first time, she felt truly happy.

"Is everything all right?" Mr. Denton poked his head through the front door.

"Yes, sir. It's a boy. He's strong and healthy." Angel beamed.

"Did *you* deliver him?" He nodded toward her dress, then stepped into the house and closed the door, keeping out the cold November wind.

Looking down, Angel gasped. "Oh, my! Didn't know there was so much blood. I'll go change." She hurried into her room, leaving him alone.

As she stripped off her clothing, it struck her hard. *I delivered a baby.*

She wavered and plopped down on her bed. What would have happened if she hadn't spanked him? *It was like a punishment for bein' born.* She never knew babies needed it to make them start crying as well as *breathe. Oh, my.* His little life had relied solely on her.

A soft smile worked its way from the bottom of her heart and onto her lips. *I did good.*

By the time she got ready for bed that night, she was exhausted. Emotionally drained, but ready to write her thoughts in Billy's book.

November 17th, 1865. My baby brother was born today. They named him Uziah. I'd never heard the name before, but Mama said it's in the Bible.

I delivered him. All by myself. The doctor came in time to cut the cord, but I did everything else. Well - Mama pushed. It was a miracle. I don't know how he ever came out of her.

I've decided I'm going to put my attention on Uziah and try to let Billy go.

She stopped. Had she truly written those words? Her eyes misted over, and made continuing difficult.

I've not wanted to believe he's dead, but there's no other explanation. I'll never forget him, and I'll always love him. But Uziah proved life goes on. I can't stop living waiting for someone who won't be coming back.

With the corner of a blanket she wiped the tears from her eyes.

The grounds are empty with the tents gone, but I'm glad they're not here. Maybe if the soldiers had never come, Billy wouldn't have left.

I overheard Mr. Denton say laws had been signed to free us slaves even before Billy left. Some of the owners of the cotton plantations asked the government for our release to be delayed until after the summer harvest. Billy left to free me, but I was already free.

I'm afraid to ask if Mrs. Wellesley knew all along. If so, does she blame herself for Billy?

My family needs me. I'm going to do all I can to be a happy and loving big sister.

If she was so happy, why were tears trickling down her cheeks?

She dipped the pen and swallowed to moisten her dry throat.

I'm letting you go, Billy. It hurts but it's something I have to do.

* * *

"Lookie, Brian!" Becky pointed to the gate, beautifully decorated with fresh boughs and large red ribbons. Candles lined the walkway and flickered in the cold December air.

Even with Rebecca added to the family, the Mitchell's had continued having them over for Sunday supper at least twice a month. They'd welcomed Becky with open arms.

To Joe's relief, Becky became the playmate Constance needed to share her tea parties.

She wiggled out of Brian's arms. "Mama?" She reached a hand to Mrs. Holloway.

"What is it sweetheart?" Her face lit up every time Becky called her *Mama* and it warmed Brian seeing how easily they'd found their way into each other's hearts. Though scared and confused when he'd first brought her home, it didn't take long before she slept through the night. Usually in the arms of Mrs. Holloway.

"Will Santa bring me presents?" Becky asked.

"Me, too?" Joe held Mrs. Holloway's other hand. It had taken him several months to get over having to share his family, but he, too, had grown to love Becky.

"Of course he will." Mrs. Holloway chuckled, then winked at Brian. They'd worked together to make certain the children had presents under the tree.

They were welcomed at the door by Dr. Mitchell and Hannah. She took their coats and hung them in the cloak-room. After casting a brilliant smile at Brian, she excused herself to the kitchen. Mrs. Holloway followed her.

Constance whisked Becky away and Joe gladly stayed with Brian.

"Shall we have a seat until Margaret calls us to supper?" Dr. Mitchell asked.

Brian nodded, then followed him to the living room.

"Look at that tree!" Joe shouted and raced toward the Christmas tree. Crystal ornaments sparkled beside glowing candles. Hand-painted multi-colored balls were scattered around it and strung popcorn encircled it. "That real pop-corn?" Joe touched it and wrinkled his nose.

"Yes, it is," Dr. Mitchell said with a laugh. "The girls string it every year."

"I'd ruther eat it."

"I have to agree with Joe," Brian said. "But it looks nice on the tree." He glanced to the top of the evergreen and admired the glass star perched perfectly at the pinnacle. "The star of Bethlehem," he muttered, and shook his head.

"You remember?" Dr. Mitchell took his arm and motioned to a chair.

"I remember the Christmas story—*clearly*. So why can't I remember who told it?" He refused to get depressed on such a wonderful day.

"I wish I knew. It's been almost a year since your injury. I'd hoped by now you'd have at least a glimmer of your memories."

Joe sat on the floor staring at the tree. "All he members is a girl."

"What?" Dr. Mitchell tilted his head. "What girl?"

"It's not really a memory," Brian said. "Well, I don't believe it is. I dream about her. A dark-eyed girl who appears in my dreams over and over again. She seems real to me."

"Perhaps she is. Your mind may be recreating your memories, bringing them out in your dreams. It's possible if you saw her again while awake, she could trigger *all* your memories."

Brian crossed to the tree. "I can't see her if I don't know where she is." An angel ornament caught his eye. When he touched it, something tugged at his heart. "It's beautiful."

The doctor joined him. "I gave it to Margaret a number of years ago. Every ornament has a story to tell." He turned his head and looked at him. "Brian, I believe you've grown."

"What?"

"I'm quite certain you've grown at least an inch." He chuckled. "You told me you wanted to be taller. You're getting your wish."

A bell tinkled and Joe jumped to his feet.

"Supper must be ready." Dr. Mitchell motioned out of the room. Joe was already well on his way.

"You truly think I've grown?" Brian asked.

"Yes, I do."

Brian grinned from ear-to-ear. "Good." His height wasn't *that* important, but Hannah had been growing and he didn't want her to pass him.

* * *

"Grandfather Peck's tree was much taller than this one," Emilia said, gazing upward at the Christmas tree. "And we had a lot more ornaments."

Angel bit her tongue. She wouldn't say what she wanted to. She and Emilia had become close over the past months. There were times she reverted back to her old snobbish self and Angel had to fight the urge to slap her.

"I like our tree," Christina chimed in. "Daddy chose it special. Right, Daddy?"

"Yes. Height isn't as important as shape. Your mother likes me to choose a *full* tree, not necessarily a *tall* tree." Mr. Denton smiled at his wife, who shifted her sad eyes downward.

The ache in Angel's heart leaped to the surface. Seeing Mrs. Denton this way on Christmas made the pain return as though it'd never left.

Angel had done well since Uziah's birth. Smiled and even laughed. However, Mrs. Denton's face had remained almost emotionless. The only trace of feeling in her eyes was sorrow.

Mr. Denton had done his best to keep the family from spiraling downward. He'd been taking Donald and Richard to work and encouraged Christina to entertain Paulette and Emilia.

Now that Angel was free, she, too, was allowed time away from daily chores. In her spare time, she'd taught Emilia how to knit. They'd not only made booties for Uziah but also gloves to be given as Christmas presents. Of course they reminded her of Billy.

He was everywhere . . . and nowhere.

Every year prior, Angel had spent Christmas Eve at home with her mama and Ada. This year, Emilia asked if Angel could celebrate with them at the estate house. Busy tending Uziah, her mama didn't object.

Christmas morning was another matter. When they'd been given their freedom, Mrs. Wellesley deeded the houses to them for *services rendered.* It'd be their first Christmas in a home they owned and they'd planned a special celebration.

Angel was grateful they didn't have to leave the estate. Finally allowed to legally marry, Jeriah had moved into their home. Bo lived by himself in his little house now that the mill slaves who'd shared it left the estate. Not every free Negro wanted to stay on the property of a former master.

"Hot chocolate?" Donald extended a mug to Angel, bringing her out of her thoughts.

"Thank you." She sighed and took the steaming cup.

Donald looked a lot like Mr. Denton. Though his hair was darker, he had the same cleft in his chin. Same smile. He'd always been a friend, but not like Billy.

"I'd like some, too," Emilia said, protruding her bottom lip.

Donald graciously returned to the kitchen and came back with a cup for Emilia.

"Mama?" Cautiously, Paulette wandered to her side. "Will you read the Christmas story?"

Mrs. Denton had already made it clear she wasn't up to reading *A Christmas Carol*. She'd recovered from her illness but remained frail and tinier than ever. With a blanket draped across her lap, she looked more like Mrs. Wellesley, who'd already retired to her room. "I reckon I can manage that one." With great effort, she sat upright.

Richard placed the Bible in her hands. "Here you go, Mama."

Angel shared their pain. Their eyes revealed horrible loss. In time, it *had* to get better.

She gazed upward at the star set atop the shimmering tree. *You're in my heart, Billy.*

"In those days, a decree went out from Caesar Augustus that all the world should be enrolled." Mrs. Denton was almost inaudible. She cleared her throat. "She gave birth to her first-born son . . ." Her face went ashen. She sucked in a large amount of air and sputtered out the words. "An wrapped him in swaddlin' clothes, an . . ."

Tears spilled from Angel's eyes.

Mrs. Denton dropped the Bible and fled the room with her hand clutched to her mouth.

Mr. Denton quickly followed.

Donald picked up the Bible. He thumbed through the pages. Looking toward Angel for encouragement, she gave him a simple nod, along with a gentle smile.

"And laid him in a manger," he read. "Because there was no room for them in the inn."

Paulette snuggled beside him on the sofa and the rest of them gathered at his feet. He continued until the story ended. Then they all sat motionless and listened to the crackle of the fire and the sobs filtering down the hallway.

* * *

"Was it that bad?" Bo stood over Angel as she milked Spot.

"Worse. You should a seen Mrs. Denton. I've had a hard time acceptin' Billy bein' gone, but I'm scared it could kill her."

He grabbed a bale of hay, placed it next to her, and sat. "She be fine in time."

She looked sideways at him. "Don't you got work to do?"

Though free, they were employed and had made arrangements to continue on with their work as they always had. In addition to their houses, each month they were also given pay.

"Yep," he replied, but didn't move.

She pulled her hands free from Spot's udders, stopping the rhythmic pulse of milk going into the pail. "Then why are you sittin' here talkin' to me like you don't have a thing to do?"

"Cuz talkin' to you is what I'm doin' right now." He grinned. "I din't like seein' you so sad."

"I'm fine. It's Mrs. Denton I'm frettin' over."

He grabbed one of Spot's udders and gave it a tug. The cow jerked and let out a loud protest.

Angel smacked his arm. "That's not how you do it. Your hands are cold. You can't just yank on her. You gotta be gentle." She breathed on her hands to warm them. "Like this." Once again, milk squirted into the pail.

He placed his hand over hers. "You're good at it." With his face so close to hers, his warm breath misted across the frigid air.

Her stomach flipped and her mouth went dry. His rough hand felt nothing like Billy's. "I—I've had lotsa practice."

"I could learn to be gentle," he whispered.

"Reckon you could." She choked out the words, wanting to run. "That should do. Got plenty for breakfast." Standing, she took the pail, patted Spot, then turned to leave.

"Angel?" He was directly behind her.

"Uh-huh?" The barn door beckoned her. Only a few steps and she'd be outside.

"You be fine, too, in time. I's willin' to wait."

She bobbed her head, then fled toward the door.

Chapter 29

Angel rushed down the long hallway to the front door. *Who'd be knockin' on Christmas?*

The Denton's house was much too quiet, so she didn't mind they were getting visitors. After waking at dawn and exchanging gifts, they'd all gone back to bed. It seemed an odd thing to do on Christmas day, but her mama told her depression made folks tired.

She wasn't tired. She was still trying to shake what had happened just hours before in the barn with Bo.

When she opened the door, two unfamiliar faces stared back at her. The woman was stunning—long dark hair and dark eyes surrounded by full flowing lashes. She was petite. Compared to the man standing beside her—who stood well over six feet tall—she looked tiny.

The woman's face lit up with a broad smile. "Merry Christmas."

"Merry Christmas," Angel replied, dumbfounded. "Can I help you?"

"Yes," the man said. "We're looking for Mr. and Mrs. Denton. Are they home?"

Though the woman intrigued her, Angel was impressed with this well-spoken man. Obviously much older than the woman, by the looks of the gray streaks in his hair, he was handsome in his own right. He talked like a Northerner and was dressed in a sophisticated suit.

"Yes, they're home. But they're asleep. I hate to ask you to wait here in the cold, but I ain't allowed to let strangers in. If you don't mind waitin', I'll be right back."

"We understand." He wrapped his arm around the woman's shoulder. "Don't we, my dear?"

"Yes, we do." Again, she smiled.

"All right then." Angel pushed the door shut.

Heading down the hallway to the Denton's room, she mumbled, hating to wake them.

A one-knuckle tap on the door should do. No response.

Two knuckles with a bit more force. The bedding stirred.

"Yes?" Mr. Denton's groggy voice doubled her guilt.

"It's me, Angel. There's folks here to see you." She leaned toward the door. They were talking to each other, but she couldn't make out the words.

The door inched open. "Who are they?" Mr. Denton asked, rubbing his forehead.

"I don't know, sir. They seem nice."

From the look on his face, she doubted he'd gotten much sleep. "Give me a moment," he said, and shut the door. In no time he came out alone.

"They was askin' for Mrs. Denton, too."

"She needs to rest. I'm certain you understand." His mouth formed half a smile.

When he opened the door, the couple still stood in the same spot. "May I help you?"

"Mr. Denton?" The woman tilted her head, looking up at him. "Billy Denton's father?"

Angel's heart thumped. *How's she know Billy?*

"Y—Yes."

"May we come in?" the man asked. "It's bitterly cold. I don't want my wife to become ill."

"Yes, please. Forgive me." Mr. Denton motioned them inside.

Angel stepped back but wasn't about to leave. She'd stay unless asked to do otherwise.

"I'm Hugo Cornwallis and this is my wife, Jessica," the man said with a slight bow.

Mr. Denton's brow drew in. "Should I know you, sir?"

Jessica stepped forward. "No. But I knew your son."

Angel's hands shook.

Mr. Denton closed his eyes, then reopened them in one slow movement. "Let's go to the living room and sit by the fire."

"Thank you," Jessica said, and followed him.

As soon as they were seated, Mr. Denton excused himself. "I know my wife will want to hear what you have to say. I'll be but a moment." Before he left the room he pulled Angel aside. "Stay with them. Please?"

"Yes, sir." Exactly what she *wanted* to do.

Jessica kept looking her way as if she knew her, making her uncomfortable. She knew she'd never seen her before. She'd have remembered someone so pretty.

Angel swallowed the lump in her throat. "Mrs. Denton hasn't been well. I hope you haven't brought more bad news."

"Bad news?" Jessica asked. "Today is Christmas. How could there be bad news?"

Angel gazed beyond her into the pulsing fire. "Seems it's all we've had 'round here this year. 'Cept for my baby brother bein' born."

Mr. Cornwallis smiled. "A baby brother? That's wonderful." He glanced at his wife and his eyes lit up even more. Then he returned his attention to Angel. "You haven't told us *your* name."

"Her name is Angel," Jessica said before she could answer. "Isn't that right?"

She nodded. "How'd you know?"

"It is a long story."

Angel leaned in ready to hear it.

"This is my wife, Cora," Mr. Denton said, entering the room.

She clutched his arm, looking timidly at their guests. Though Angel was glad to see her out of bed, the timing couldn't have been worse.

Mr. Cornwallis stood. "I'm pleased to meet you, Mrs. Denton. This is my wife, Jessica."

Jessica rapidly crossed the room and kissed her on the cheek.

Mrs. Denton pulled back. "Why'd you do that?"

"I am sorry," Jessica said. "I didn't mean to offend you. But I am forever grateful to you. Without you, Billy would have never been born and my life wouldn't be the same."

"What?" Mrs. Denton appeared to be wavering, so Mr. Denton helped her to the sofa.

Jessica returned to her seat and folded her hands in her lap. "What I have to say is—*delicate*. May I speak openly?"

"Do you mind, sweetheart?" Mr. Denton asked, looking at his wife.

She shook her head. "I wanna know what she has to say 'bout Billy."

Jessica looked at her hands, then slowly raised her head. "Where do I start?"

Fear over what this beautiful woman had to do with Billy kept Angel's heart pounding.

"I would have never met Hugo if I hadn't met Billy," Jessica began. "I met your son in Clifton. At the encampment."

"You was in Clifton?" Mrs. Denton's eyes widened.

"Yes'm." Jessica's cheeks turned a darker shade of red. "I was *working* there. Brought to the camp from Nashville. I *serviced* the men."

Mrs. Denton became rigid. "Serviced? You tellin' me you was a prostitute?"

Angel gasped, but quickly covered her mouth. This was worse than she could have imagined. Oddly, the word hadn't offended the couple.

"Yes." Jessica lifted her chin. "I believed it was all I could do."

Mrs. Denton stood. "Douglas, take me back to our room. I ain't gonna believe Billy . . ." She covered her mouth.

"No." Jessica waved her hands. "Billy did not. Please, Mrs. Denton. Sit."

Angel's heart rested.

Mrs. Denton lowered herself down again. "I don't understand. How'd you know Billy?"

"I knew him as *Will*. He was brought to my tent the night before he left camp." She stopped and studied Mrs. Denton's face, obviously choosing her words carefully.

Angel didn't like the image of him in Jessica's tent—something out of character for Billy.

"He'd befriended a man named Duffy," Jessica continued. "Duffy believed he needed my services and paid me for a full night. He told me to take good care of him. I didn't know Will would be the one to take care of *me*. He was kind. He wanted to talk and nothing more."

Angel breathed a relieved sigh.

Jessica shifted toward her husband. "Will convinced me to leave camp to find real love. Not the kind I'd been giving. He mentioned a woman named Francine who had done the same."

Mrs. Denton gasped. "My Francine?"

"Yes. He said she'd been in my profession and found a man who loved her and overlooked her past. Hugo knows what I did, but he loves me."

The man touched her cheek and accompanied it with a loving smile.

She returned her attention back to Mrs. Denton. "Will gave me money so I could leave. I tried to refuse it, but he insisted. I owe him everything."

"He was a good boy." Mrs. Denton wiped away tears.

Jessica moved to her and knelt down. "I'm sorry for your loss. I sought out Captain Granger when the war ended and asked him about Will . . . *Billy*. He told me about the misunderstanding and about sending him to Fort Morgan. He said he'd contacted you inquiring about Billy and was told he'd never returned home. It broke my heart." She took Mrs. Denton's hands and held them in her own. "He saved my life."

Angel couldn't control the tears streaming freely down her face. She sniffled, drawing Jessica's attention. She once again smiled knowingly, but this time the smile seemed sorrowful.

"Jessica?" Mrs. Denton's voice trembled. "You said you're from Nashville, but you don't talk like it. There's sumthin' familiar 'bout the way you speak. Where you from?"

Jessica returned to her seat. "I was born in New Orleans. My mother *worked* there."

Mr. Denton cleared his throat.

"Yes, Mr. Denton, it is what you are thinking."

"Did your ma know Francine?" Mrs. Denton asked. "She grew up there."

"No. We left New Orleans soon after I was born. Mother wanted to move away from my grandmother. She was a seer and Mother grew tired of her telling her what to do. She wanted to go far away and live her own life. We went north and eventually moved to Nashville. She died there and I did the only thing I knew how to survive."

Mrs. Denton's body shook. She clutched her husband. "What was your gramma's name?"

Jessica's brows drew in. "Are you unwell, Mrs. Denton?"

Her head bobbed up and down. "Tell me. What was her name?"

"It was Beaumont. Everyone called her *Madame Beaumont.*" Jessica's eyes filled with fear. "Why?"

Mrs. Denton crumbled and laid her head on Mr. Denton's lap. He soothingly stroked her hair, while she sobbed and clung to him.

"What did I say?" Jessica asked.

Mr. Denton's eyes were pooled with tears. "My wife knew your grandmother."

"How?" Jessica swallowed hard.

He shook his head. "This is all too remarkable. Having you come here like this."

"Tell her Douglas," Mrs. Denton muttered.

Angel scooted to the edge of her chair.

"Francine took Cora to meet your grandmother in New Orleans. You see, my wife has a mark—a *birthmark*—on her abdomen."

Jessica sat completely upright. "Grandmother told her its meaning?"

"Yes. She frightened her. From what Cora told me, your grandmother was unusual."

Jessica nodded.

"After telling Cora a strange tale about the origin of her mark, Madame Beaumont went on to say she was with child. That she would have a *good* son. Most importantly, she told Cora to protect him at all cost."

"She was right forceful 'bout it," Mrs. Denton said, sitting upright. "Now I know why. She knew Billy'd help you one day. She must a loved you as much as I love him."

Now, Jessica cried. "I only saw her once. I was fifteen. She was dying and Mother took me to New Orleans to see her. After we buried her, we left. A few years later I buried my mother."

Mr. Cornwallis hugged his wife. "She's had a difficult life. When we met, I looked beyond her pain and into her heart. I loved her instantly."

Angel placed her hand over her heart. What Billy had done for Jessica had changed her life forever. It was meant to happen. She didn't believe in seers, but couldn't deny the coincidence.

"Mrs. Denton?" Jessica took a deep breath. "Are you certain Billy is dead? Have you seen his name on the list of soldiers?"

"We've seen many lists," Mr. Denton answered for her. "But we've not seen his name. However, we're not certain what name he used, which makes it more difficult. And the inefficiency of the military in regard to the Sultana made it impossible to know what men died on her. They neglected to create a record of the prisoners put on board."

"There's still hope," Jessica whispered.

Mrs. Denton shook her head. "No. Billy would a wrote. He ain't the kind a boy who'd keep us wonderin'. I don't wanna believe it, but I hafta accept he's dead." She shifted her eyes to the floor. "Born on a steamboat and died on one."

A chilling silence followed. Angel hugged herself trying to get warm. She felt as though she wasn't even in the room, but had been a ghostly presence hovering over them, listening to their words.

Mr. Cornwallis stood. "We should be going. I'm sorry if we've troubled you. Jessica hoped telling you about your son would lessen your grief. I know it's odd for us to come at Christmas, but it was the first opportunity I had to leave my work."

"Your work?" Mr. Denton asked, rising to his feet.

"I'm an attorney. As you can imagine a name like Cornwallis keeps some from trusting me, but I've established a successful firm."

"I wasn't going to mention it. No one should judge character by a name alone."

"Or by one's past," Mr. Cornwallis said, smiling at his wife.

Mrs. Denton dabbed her eyes with a handkerchief. "Please stay for dinner. Ada's fixin' a feast. Thought I wasn't hungry, but I reckon I could eat now."

Angel found her voice. "I should go help in the kitchen."

"Miss Angel?" Jessica said. "May I speak with you privately?"

Angel looked to Mrs. Denton for approval.

She nodded. "We gotta get the children up. We'll leave you to talk." She took her husband's hand and left the room.

"I'm going outside for a smoke," Mr. Cornwallis said.

Jessica watched her husband leave, then patted the spot on the sofa beside her.

Angel gazed around the room feeling out of place. This beautiful woman who knew how to please a man in every way possible had spent a night with Billy. How'd he resist her?

"Angel, please sit." She patted again.

"All right." Had Jessica seen her legs quiver beneath her dress?

Jessica studied her face. "Billy talked about love. *True* love."

Angel couldn't breathe. "What'd he say?"

"He told me he loved someone. Someone named Angel." She smiled the same warm smile that lit up her face at the door.

"He said he loved me?" She worked her bottom lip and forced back tears.

"Oh, yes. And because he loved you, he never considered having me. He was saving himself for you." She brushed her hand across Angel's cheek.

Angel couldn't speak. Billy loved her. She knew it in her heart, but to hear someone else say it . . .

"You are young," Jessica whispered. "You'll never forget him. He'll always be in your heart. I know it hurts now, but give it time." She pulled Angel into an embrace and let her cry.

Angel didn't hold back. She sobbed in the arms of the woman whom Billy had shared his secrets with. He'd just given her the best Christmas present ever. An affirmation of love.

Chapter 30

"Mrs. Holloway, I believe we're in for snow this year."
Brian adjusted his scarf. He raised his hand in the air and
breathed deeply. "It smells like snow."

"How does snow smell?" Becky asked, giggling.

"Cold." He laughed, amazed at what a pretty young
woman she'd become. Nine years old and as tall as Mrs.
Holloway.

"You reckon Ms. Mitchell will make custard?" Joe asked.
"It's my favorite."

"Whatever she makes will be good," Brian said. It was
their fourth Christmas Eve with the Mitchell's, and bound
to be the best ever. *Will Hannah like her gift?*

The thought made his stomach knot, but it was time for
this. Time to move forward.

After almost five years, he'd given up hope of regaining
his memories. He'd made new memories he cherished.
Watching Becky and Joe grow, ranked at the top of his list.

Mobile had rebuilt since the fire, which kept him constantly busy. Once the hotel had been completed, he'd never lacked for work.

Joe was always by his side. There'd been a few times he'd not been permitted on a job site, which resulted in him turning down the project. They were a team never to be separated.

The boy had never opened up about *his* past, but it didn't matter any longer. The scars on Joe's heart had faded, and Brian did his best to keep people at bay who might try to create new ones.

"Merry Christmas!" Hannah exclaimed, opening the door.

She looked radiant in her shimmering red dress. He couldn't help but appreciate how it fit her form—no longer a trace of a little girl in it. She'd become a full-fledged woman.

He hugged her and buried his face in her hair. A mixture of cinnamon and vanilla filled his nose. Sweet and a little spicy. "Merry Christmas, Hannah," he whispered in her ear.

She released him but didn't take her eyes from his. "May I take your coat?"

Did her voice tremble? He let out a small chuckle. "As long as you give it back."

"Here's *my* coat," Joe said, handing it to her. He then nudged Brian.

"Becky," Mrs. Holloway said. "Let's go to the kitchen and help Mrs. Mitchell."

"Yes, Mama," Becky said. "C'mon, Joe."

"I don't wanna go to the kitchen," Joe said.

Becky's eyes widened.

"All right." Joe begrudgingly followed them down the hall.

Hannah took a step closer to Brian. "Merry Christmas."

"You already said that." He let out a contented sigh when she moved into his arms and rested her head on his chest. "Merry Christmas, Hannah."

Grateful he'd continued to grow, he now stood a full five-feet-eight-inches tall. Hannah was three inches shorter and fit perfectly against him. He kissed the top of her head. "You smell wonderful."

She giggled. "It's Mama's cooking you smell, not me."

"No, it's you." Should he kiss her lips? He'd never done it before but had often considered it. As she raised her head to look into his eyes, it appeared she wanted him to.

"Brian?" Dr. Mitchell's tenor voice brought the idea to an abrupt halt.

"Yes, sir?" He released her and her body deflated.

"Merry Christmas," the man said.

"Merry Christmas, sir."

Dr. Mitchell guided them toward the living room.

The tree looked more brilliant than ever. As the girls had grown, their ability at decorating had improved. The simple popcorn chains now included strung cranberries, giving them more color. The ornaments were well-placed, rather than in clusters.

Brian gazed at the star on top. Feeling Hannah's presence close behind him, a shiver inched down his back. It had taken years to allow himself to care for her, fearing he'd be betraying the love of another woman. *The dark-eyed girl in my dreams.*

He couldn't wonder for the rest of his life.

He shifted his gaze to the doctor and found him staring. "What's wrong?"

"I don't know." He rubbed his chin. "Something about you troubles me. More so now than ever. I always said you remind me of someone but could never place it. Looking at you now, I feel I could almost reach out and touch the memory."

"It's been almost five years, Dr. Mitchell. What's different now?"

"You're older."

"Yes, and so are you." Brian laughed and faced the tree. The star slightly tipped to the side and needed to be set upright. "I can fix that," he said, pointing to it.

"Let me get you a chair," Hannah said. Before he could object and do it himself, she returned with a wooden chair.

He scooted it close to the tree, making every effort not to disturb the decorations. Especially the lit candles. Even atop the chair, he had to stretch to reach the star.

"Careful now," Dr. Mitchell said. "I'd like to have supper this evening, not perform surgery."

Brian glanced at him, shook his head, then returned his attention to the star. He reached it with his fingertips and adjusted it upward. "Dang!" He jerked back.

One of the candles had singed his shirt at the elbow, nearly catching it on fire. Realizing he'd cursed, he covered his mouth, then hopped down from the chair. "I'm sorry," he said, looking at Hannah. When he turned to apologize to the doctor, the man's face was pale.

Dr. Mitchell dropped into a chair and put his head in his hands. "Oh, God."

Hannah rushed to his side. "What's wrong, Daddy?"

"Are you all right, sir?" Brian knelt beside him. "I didn't mean to curse. But . . ."

The doctor placed a hand on his shoulder. "Brian . . ." He whispered the name.

"Daddy?" Hannah's eyebrows drew in, looking to Brian for help.

"O'Brien," Dr. Mitchell uttered. "Not Brian. *O'Brien*."

"Daddy, you're not making sense." Hannah frowned. "Brian, get Mother."

He started to rise, but Dr. Mitchell grabbed his arm. "No. I'm fine. But . . . Oh, God. You look so much like her. Why didn't I see it sooner? They must be devastated with worry. Believe you're dead . . ."

"Who?" Brian swallowed the enormous lump in his throat.

"Your parents." The doctor grasped his hands. "Your age was wrong. If I'd known your true age . . . Brian, I delivered you."

He shook his head in disbelief. "How could you? I'm twenty-two. You haven't been practicing medicine that long."

"No. You're eighteen. I delivered you on a steamboat in 1851. When you said that word, I heard your mother's voice as if it were yesterday."

Eighteen? He had to be mistaken. "Word? You mean *dang*? Saying dang reminded you of my mother?" He sat down to compose himself.

"Yes," Dr. Mitchell laughed. "She had a tendency to curse. But it was part of what made her so charming. Her name is Cora. Does that sound familiar?"

"Cursing made her *charming?*" Something he couldn't fathom. Cursing was highly improper, especially for women.

He closed his eyes. "Cora?" Nothing came to mind. "Did she have dark eyes?"

"Her eyes were brown, and her hair dusty-blond. Your green eyes and red hair came from your father, William O'Brien. He died shortly after you were born." He leaned in. "She's one of the finest women I've known. She married a dear friend of mine, Douglas Denton. He raised you and loved you like his own child."

Brian's head reeled. "So my name isn't Brian?"

"No. You were named after your father. They called you *Billy.*"

"I can't believe it," Brian said. "I *won't* believe it until I have proof. I'm sorry. Though you say I look like *Cora*, you could be wrong. When was the last time you saw them?"

"At least ten years. On one of our visits to Memphis." Dr. Mitchell stood and began to pace. "You gave me little regard, but then again you were only eight. You were too busy playing with your brothers and sister. There was also a slave girl . . ."

"I'm from Memphis?" Brian's stomach churned. "If all this is true, wouldn't it spark some kind of memory? Because nothing's coming to mind."

"Maybe in time. And—not that money matters to you —but your family is wealthy."

Hannah placed her hand on his shoulder. "Are you all right?"

Lifting his head, he looked into her beautiful blue eyes. All the plans he'd had for today would have to wait. He needed answers. "I'll be fine. I just need to know." He jerked his head around to face the doctor. "Can you send a telegram? Ask them if their son's missing?"

"I already thought of that. I may be able to send it after supper, but with the holiday it could be difficult finding someone to deliver it."

"If I'm wealthy, I'm certain we can find a way to pay someone to do it." Brian raked his fingers through his hair. "I don't care what it costs."

"We'll eat, then we'll see to the wire." Dr. Mitchell helped him to his feet. "That is, if you *can* eat."

"He can eat," Hannah said with a smile. "I've seen him do it many times."

She took his hand and he stared at their entwined fingers. Only minutes before, he'd thought about kissing her, but now all he cared about was finding out if Dr. Mitchell was right.

Dang . . .

* * *

"That was the best meal I ever had, Ada," Bo said, patting his stomach.

"Bessie an Angel hepped." Ada grinned at her. "Angel's a might fine cook."

"I helped, too," Emilia added. She smoothed the front of her dress and batted her eyes at Bo.

"Yes, Bo," Angel said. "Emilia put the potatoes in the bowl. She's an enormous help."

Everyone at the table broke into laughter, including Emilia.

Angel sighed with contentment. Looking from face to face, she realized joy no longer had to be forced. It had taken years to return, but now it surrounded them like a warm blanket.

"Oh, my!" Mrs. Denton placed her hand on her belly. "The baby kicked so hard I reckon he bruised my rib!"

"Can I feel, Mama?" Paulette rushed to her side. "Please?"

"Course you can. Put your hand right here."

Mrs. Denton's baby was due any time now. When Angel asked her if she hoped it was a boy, she said it didn't matter. Boy or girl, she'd love it just the same. Uziah hoped for a boy—wanting someone to play with—but Angel told him it would be a while before the baby would be able to.

She glanced at Bo and their eyes locked. He'd told her earlier in the day he had a Christmas present for her. She couldn't explain why she'd been fighting her feelings for him all these years. He'd been patient, but she doubted he'd wait forever. *Maybe it's time.*

If she agreed to marry him, it'd help their living arrangements. Everyone expected her to share his house. Then Uziah could have his own room. For a little while.

But that didn't seem like the best reason for marriage. Whenever she searched her heart, an ever-present remnant of Billy held onto a corner and wouldn't let go.

"You gonna name that baby after me?" Uncle Harper asked.

"Hmm . . ." Mrs. Denton looked upward. "Harper Denton. What do *you* think, Douglas?"

"I don't know. Hard to imagine another Harper."

"I won't be 'round forever," Harper said. "I'm gettin' old."

"You're not old," Mrs. Wellesley said. "If you're old, then *I'm* old. And I refuse to be old."

"*I* think you're old," Richard said and shrugged. Donald socked him in the arm.

Again, everyone laughed.

This is how Angel remembered their Christmas dinners. Laughter, family, and a lot of love. Soon Mrs. Denton's baby would come, and in the spring her mama would give her a new baby brother or sister. Yes, she needed to move out. But should it be into Bo's house? Into his bed?

Her heart fluttered. She'd not even allowed him to kiss her . . . *yet.*

"Angel?" Bo stood beside her.

"Huh?"

"Wanna go for a walk?"

The silence around the table was disturbing. They needed to start laughing again. *Now.*

"It's cold out, Bo." She looked up at him but didn't stand.

"Get your coat," her mama said with a twinkle in her eye.

Angel glanced nervously around the room. *Do they all know sumthin' I don't?*

Mr. Denton winked at her. Instantly her cheeks warmed.

To save herself from further embarrassment she rushed to the kitchen and grabbed her coat. Bo helped her slip her arms through the sleeves then buttoned it as if helping a child.

She gulped. "Where we gonna go?"

"You'll see," he replied with a devilish grin.

As he pulled her eagerly down the path toward the barn, the cold stung her face. He swung the heavy door open and motioned her inside, then closed it behind them. "Gotta keep the cold out best I can."

The horses pawed the ground. Their breath blew out in bursts. The air wasn't much warmer inside the stables.

"Why'd we come out here?" she asked, shivering.

"Come here." He pulled her to him. "I'll keep you warm."

Was this why? To put her some place frigid and give him an excuse to hold her?

Rigid at first, she allowed herself to mold into his body. His muscular arms surrounded her, and his heart beat strong beneath her cheek.

"Angel," he whispered. "I been waitin' long time for this."

Oh, my.

She knew what was coming, but what would she say? She kept her mouth shut and waited.

"You're seventeen now. A woman in every way." He ran his hand down her long hair. "I done asked your mama an Jeriah. They say I can marry you." He swallowed hard.

Her heart raced. *Oh, my, oh, my . . .*

"But I ain't asked *you* yet. So I's askin'. Will you marry me, Angel?"

Her tongue froze to the inside of her mouth. She couldn't utter a word.

"Angel?" He took her face in his hands and lifted it. "You're the most beautiful woman I ever knowed. I loves you. I'll take care a you an be good to you. Please marry me."

"I . . ." She couldn't catch her breath. She wanted to say *yes* but it wouldn't pass her lips. What reason did she have for refusing him? Only one. *Billy . . .*

"Angel! Bo!"

Their heads jerked around, stunned by the interruption.

Donald flung the door open. "Come quick! There's news!" He waved frantically, beckoning them to follow. "Hurry!"

Angel stepped away from Bo. "C'mon. Sumthin's wrong."

"But . . . Angel?" He held onto her hand. "Cain't you give me an answer fore we go?"

She shook her head and wrenched free from his grasp. She then lifted her skirt, broke into a sprint, and followed Donald.

"You won't believe it!" Donald yelled over his shoulder.

"What?"

His reply was an ear-to-ear grin.

When they entered the house, she saw Mrs. Denton, crying.

No . . .

Then it struck her.

These weren't sorrowful tears. *She's happy.*

"Angel." Mrs. Denton reached out her hand. "We've had a miracle!"

Angel looked to her mama, who was rubbing her nose with her finger. "Sit down, baby." She motioned to a chair at the dining room table.

Bo came in and took his place beside her. Her mama gave him a sad smile. *Why?*

"Read this," Mrs. Denton said and handed her a telegram.

As the words sunk into Angel's mind, they made their way to her heart. The small corner that belonged to Billy took over, filling it entirely. "He's alive?" She burst into tears.

Mrs. Denton nodded rapidly, dripping tears of her own.

"How?" Angel couldn't still her heart. "What does it mean he's lost his memory?"

Mr. Denton took the paper from her. "Telegrams are impersonal and to the point. I have questions myself. Until I see him with my own eyes I'm not completely convinced it's Billy."

"Oh, Douglas," Mrs. Denton said. "I know it is! If Dr. Mitchell says it's him, then I believe it. 'Sides, I feel it in my heart." Her eyes popped open wide and she clutched her belly. "His baby brother knows it, too."

"When's he comin' home?" Angel wanted to jump up and down and scream at the top of her voice, but she sat in her chair forcing herself to remain calm.

"He's not," Mr. Denton said.

"What?" Angel stared at him.

"I'm going to Mobile as soon as there's a train. I need to make certain it's Billy before we even *consider* bringing him here. I won't have this family torn apart again with disappointment. Donald, I'd like you to go with me."

"Me?" Donald asked. "You want me to go on the train with you?"

"Yes, I do. Your mother can't travel in her condition and I'd prefer not to go alone. I'd appreciate your company."

Donald puffed out his chest. "I'd like that. Thank you, Father."

Almost in unison, Christina and Richard protested.

"Christina," Mr. Denton said, "I'm counting on you to look after your mother. And Richard, you'll be the man of the house while we're away. I need you both here."

There were no more protests.

"Is he the big brother that used to tuck me in at night?" Paulette asked.

"Yes, he is," Mrs. Denton said. "An he loves you very much."

"Then I hope Daddy brings him home." She rested her head on her mama's shoulder.

Angel wished she could go to Mobile, but it wasn't an option. Like Mrs. Denton, she knew in her heart it was Billy. It explained why he'd never written. But if he'd lost his memory, did it mean he'd forgotten *her*?

She turned to look at Bo, but he was nowhere in the room. "Mama, where's Bo?"

"He left long time go." Her sad eyes said everything.

Angel jumped to her feet. "'Scuse me." She fled from the room.

Assuming he'd gone home, she raced to his house and beat on the door. "Bo!"

The door opened with hesitation. He blinked slowly. His smile had vanished.

"Bo? Why'd you leave?"

"Din't have no reason to stay."

"But it's Christmas. Emilia's gonna sing."

"Don't wanna hear no singin'."

She licked her dry lips. "Bo, I . . ."

"Billy be comin' home. You don't hafta say nothin'. I knows how you feel 'bout him."

"But . . ." Her heart broke in two. Hurting Bo had never been her intention.

"Angel, I waited years for you. Waited 'til you was growed. I've loved you for long time, but there ain't no room in your heart for me if'n Billy's there."

He was right, but it still hurt. Her heart had celebrated, but now it ached. It hadn't hurt like this since the day she'd heard about the steamboat catching on fire. "It's been years since I seen Billy. He may not be the same no more. May not even know who I am. Until he comes home, I won't know *how* I'm gonna feel."

He cleared his throat. "I'll wait a little longer. Ain't gonna stop lovin' you. After he goes, you can answer my question. For now, I needs to be alone. Don't wanna see ya."

"All right." She took a step back and he closed the door. Not feeling like returning to the Denton's, she went home.

December 25th, 1869. As Mrs. Denton said to me tonight, we've had a miracle.

It's hard to know what to write because there's so much I still don't know.

The Denton's got a telegram from Dr. Mitchell in Mobile, Alabama. He said a man was left on the steps of the hospital in January of 1865 with a head wound. He'd lost his memory. Somehow the doctor realized it was Billy even though he's been using a different name. Mr. Denton says until he sees Billy he won't be convinced it's him. But I know in my heart it is. I've never wanted to believe he was dead.

Bo asked me to marry him tonight. Before I could answer, Donald came with the news about Billy. I was relieved because I didn't know how to answer Bo. I love him, but not like I love Billy.

Yes, I still love Billy. I just pray he'll remember he loves me, too.

Chapter 31

Sweat covered Brian's entire body. He jerked upright in bed and gazed around the pitch black room. She'd spoken to him again. This time he remembered. She'd said his name. *Billy.*

He lay back against his dampened pillow. It all must be true. If only he could remember them: *Cora*, his mother, *Douglas*, his stepfather, brothers, sisters, and . . .

A slave girl? Possibly the dark-eyed girl of his dreams? *Why would I dream about a slave?*

Giving Hannah the locket should have been the highlight of their day, making their courtship official. Instead, he'd given her the necklace with a wish of *Merry Christmas*. No kiss on the lips. She'd smiled at the gift, but her upturned face indicated she'd wanted something more. He couldn't do it.

Douglas Denton would arrive in two days. The telegram indicated he'd be bringing Donald with him. Donald Denton, Douglas's son and *his* brother. Would seeing them help?

He closed his eyes, doubting he could sleep again. *Please, God. Let me remember.*

* * *

"Brian!" Mrs. Holloway hollered through the door. "Dr. Mitchell will be here in thirty minutes. You need to hurry!"

"I'm coming." He adjusted his string tie. He'd dressed in his finest suit. He'd even shaved. Though he'd been trying to grow a beard, the time had come to shave it off. Besides, he didn't have whiskers when they saw him last and he wanted to be recognized.

Lack of facial hair should have been an indication of his immaturity back then. The fact he'd grown three inches since his arrival in Mobile was also a sign. Only fourteen at the time, yet he'd believed himself to be eighteen. Now that he actually *was* eighteen—nearly *nineteen*—he'd become a man by all accounts. *People have finally stopped calling me boy.*

Again, he adjusted the tie. *Stop being so nervous.*

"Mrs. Holloway." He opened the door. "Please, help with my tie."

She gladly obliged. A large smile covered her sweet face. "You'll be fine, Brian."

"Are you sure you don't want to go with me?"

"Bring them here after you've had time to talk. I don't want to be in the way."

"You'd never be in the way." He turned to Joe, who hadn't spoken all morning. "Joe, you can come with me if you'd like."

"Uh-uh. I'll stay here. Reckon I'd be in the way, too."

"*None* of you would be in the way." He looked toward the ceiling, shaking his head. "You're my family. That's not going to change."

Joe crossed his arms. "You gots other family."

"Brian." Mrs. Holloway took his arm. "Go *now*. Dr. Mitchell's buggy has arrived."

"But . . ." He gestured toward Joe.

"I'll take care of Joe," Mrs. Holloway whispered. "Now go."

Brian grabbed his coat and headed out the door. He'd been relieved when Dr. Mitchell had agreed to take him to the train station. At least he'd have someone familiar by his side.

* * *

Brian's pounding heart kept him glued to the platform. Two men stepped off the train. The younger of the two was a copy of the elder—tall, handsome, and extremely well dressed.

Dr. Mitchell embraced the man. "Douglas, it's good to see you!"

"Thank you, Harvey." The man patted his back. "Do you remember my son, Donald?"

Donald dipped his head. "It's good to meet you, Dr. Mitchell."

"You've grown," the doctor said with a chuckle.

Brian stared at them. *Complete strangers*. Why should he have expected anything more? The lack of familiarity stung and struck with undeniable pain all the way to his heart.

Mr. Denton's eyes shifted. His expression changed from joy to elation. The man who supposedly raised him rushed to him. His arms wrapped around Brian's body so tightly it took his breath. "Billy," he whispered. "It *is* you." Pulling back, he examined his features and ran his hands down his shoulders as if to make certain he was real. And then, his face fell.

Brian didn't want to hurt him, but couldn't pretend he'd felt something.

"Don't you know me?" Mr. Denton asked. His brow furrowed deeply; his elation gone.

"I'm sorry, sir. Dr. Mitchell told me who you are, but I have no memory of you."

"Harvey?" Mr. Denton looked to his friend for help.

"As I told you in the telegram," Dr. Mitchell said. "The blow to his head caused memory loss. It may never return."

Mr. Denton silently nodded and faced Brian. "But you're alive and you've grown! You look well. That's what matters most."

"I'm Donald," Donald said, stepping beside him. "I'm seventeen. Almost as old as you."

Brian gazed up at his *little* brother, who towered over him by at least six inches. "Nice to meet you."

The turmoil in Brian's belly made him wish he'd convinced Mrs. Holloway to join them. He needed the comfort of his family.

"My buggy is over there," Dr. Mitchell said, pointing. "I'm certain you're hungry. Why don't we have a bite at Sylvia's? There's much to talk about."

"Can we go by your home and pick up Hannah so she can join us?" Brian blurted out. He needed someone close who knew him as he was now, not what he once was.

"Hannah?" Mr. Denton asked.

"*My* Hannah," Dr. Mitchell replied. "You remember the little girl with long blond ringlets? She's no longer *little*. And she's rather fond of your son."

Brian loosened his collar. Heat crept up his neck.

"I see," Mr. Denton said with a grin. "Then by all means have her join us."

"Very well." Dr. Mitchell motioned them off the platform. "I'll have to return to the hospital after we eat, but we have time to get Hannah."

"Let me help you with those." Brian pointed to Mr. Denton's bags.

"Thank you . . . *Brian*." His hesitation using the name was all Brian needed to hear. It'd be a very long meal.

* * *

"Joe has never liked Connie's tea parties." Hannah clutched her hand to her breast, laughing. "I'll never forget the first time she dragged him in. When we went in Connie's room, there sat Joe, with a napkin across his lap, sipping water from a china teacup. She'd placed a sunbonnet on his head!"

Donald erupted with laughter. "She and Paulette would have gotten along very well."

Brian listened, but couldn't join in their merriment. The entire meal had been a series of *do you remember when* and *certainly you recall that*. None of which he did.

The only enlightenment from their conversations had been learning why there'd been confusion about his age. Mr. Denton explained that he'd left home to join the Union army and had lied about his age to enlist. He'd been sent on a mission to Fort Morgan. After that, no one seemed to know how he'd ended up in the hospital. And somewhere along the way he'd acquired Joe. He must have lied to Joe about his age to continue the façade.

Other than that, he'd been made aware that there was too much he *didn't* know.

He definitely didn't like the way his *brother* had been looking at Hannah. Hadn't he ever seen a pretty girl before? *She shouldn't have worn that dress exposing her neckline.* Had she forgotten it was winter? And why did Donald have to be so damned good looking? All six-feet-two inches of him.

Brian poked at his food.

"Brian?" Hannah finally looked in *his* direction. "Aren't you hungry?"

"No. We should be going. Mrs. Holloway and Becky are making cookies. I know they're waiting for us."

"I'm anxious to meet her," Mr. Denton said. He rose to his feet, followed by Donald, who rushed to help Hannah with her chair.

She tipped her head coyly and smiled up at him. "Thank you."

So this is what jealousy feels like. He wanted to punch the smile off Donald's perfect profile.

Brian hurried to Hannah's side and took her hand. "I'll help you to the buggy."

She giggled. *She's enjoying the attention. How dare she?*

He gave her hand a gentle squeeze. "Remember me?"

It prompted another giggle.

He continued holding her hand all the way home, making certain Donald noticed.

Dr. Mitchell stopped the buggy. "I'll send your wire before I go back to work."

"Thank you," Mr. Denton said. "Three words should do it."

"*He is Billy,*" Dr. Mitchell said, shaking his head. "Cora's going to cry."

"I know. But they'll be good tears."

Brian might as well have been invisible. Everyone talked about *Billy* as if it meant something to him. He liked Mr. Denton—believed him to be a fine man—but didn't *feel* anything. Aside from wanting to whop his new-found brother upside the head.

"I'll see you tomorrow night for supper," he said to Hannah, then leaned in and gave her a kiss on the cheek.

She smiled, but brightened even more waving goodbye to Donald.

"It was nice meeting you!" Donald yelled, as the buggy rolled away.

Brian stepped up beside him. "She's mine."

"Yours? You're courting then?" Donald folded his arms across his chest.

"Not exactly. But it's assumed."

Donald's eyebrows rose. "You're fortunate. She's beautiful."

"Yes, she is." He jerked up Mr. Denton's bag. "I'll help you take your bags to the hotel after you meet my family."

"Thank you," the man said, but frowned.

Maybe I shouldn't have called them my family. But they were the only family he knew.

Mrs. Holloway greeted them with open arms. Becky bubbled over, offering cookies and hot cocoa. She, too, noticed his handsome brother.

Why didn't he stay in Memphis?

Brian's respect for Mr. Denton grew when he showed no disapproval in regard to Joe. He treated him with as much warmth and courtesy as he gave both Mrs. Holloway and Becky. The man who'd raised him obviously had good principles.

"Mr. Denton," Mrs. Holloway said. "Are you aware your son repaired my home? He and Joe did a marvelous job. You've no idea what a wonderful young man you have. Handy with a hammer, but more importantly, he's a man of good character."

"Your home is beautiful. I wasn't aware of his carpentry skills, but was well aware of his character. I've always been proud of him."

Brian looked him in the eye. "Thank you, sir." They exchanged smiles. The longing for recognition tugged at him. *I want to remember this man.*

Mr. Denton glanced around the living room. "Brian mentioned your husband was a wood carver. Donald's been admiring his work. He also carves."

"Do you?" Mrs. Holloway asked.

"Yes." Donald crossed the room and fingered the wooden chain. "My great uncle taught me."

"I'll be right back," Brian said, and went to his room. He grabbed the carving from his dresser and returned to the living room. "Do you know anything about this?" He placed the figure into Donald's hand.

"My angel." Donald laughed. "Or, *bug,* as everyone called it. How'd *you* get it?"

"It was in my hand when I was taken to the hospital. It's what brought me to Mrs. Holloway. I was told her husband was a carver so I came here hoping she might know where it came from." He took it from Donald and returned to his seat. "So, *you* carved it?"

"Yes. I know it's not very good. I was just learning. But I didn't give it to *you*." He shook his head. "I should have known *she'd* give it to you."

"Who?"

"Angel, of course." Donald looked at him as though he should know who he was talking about. How could he? They were all strangers.

"The slave girl?" Brian's heart thumped. *Why?*

"She's no longer a slave," Mr. Denton said. "And she's a grown woman. She was your best friend, Brian. She's missed you terribly."

"Your best friend was a slave?" Joe finally spoke. He'd been sitting in the farthest corner of the room munching on cookies.

Brian shrugged. "I don't remember her." How many times had he said a form of that sentence in the past few hours?

"You were raised together," Mr. Denton said. "She and her mother work for us."

"They din't leave when they was freed?" Joe asked.

"No." Mr. Denton smiled at him. "Many of our slaves left, but not them. We've given them a good life at the estate. They were free to go but chose to stay."

"Oh." Joe stuffed another cookie in his mouth.

Brian turned the tiny carving over and over inside his palm. *Why'd she give this to me?* "Has your carving improved?" He directed the question to Donald. Maybe it wasn't nice, but Donald had already managed to rub him the wrong way.

"Uncle Harper says I'm almost as good as him now." Donald lifted his chin. "Though I've never attempted a chain like this."

Mrs. Holloway inched closer to him. "Did you say, *Harper*?"

"Yes. He doesn't carve much any longer, but he's taught me all he knows."

Mrs. Holloway bustled over to Mr. Denton. "Harper isn't a common name. I knew a Harper when I lived in Memphis but he wasn't a wood carver. His last name was Hadley."

"That would be my uncle. Harper Hadley. My mother's Mary, his sister. Did you know her?"

Mrs. Holloway looked like she might buckle at the knees, so Brian jumped to his feet and helped her to a chair. "Becky, get your mama a glass of water."

Becky rushed from the room.

"What's wrong, Mrs. Holloway?" Brian knelt in front of her.

"Harper Hadley," she muttered, and touched her fingertips to her lips.

Brian turned to Mr. Denton for help, only to find him staring at her. His eyebrows knit together in deep concentration.

"I don't understand why she's upset," Brian said. "I've never seen her like this."

Becky handed her the water. "Drink, Mama."

Her hands trembled. "Fate brought you to me, Brian." She drank the water down.

"What do you mean?" He took the empty glass.

She smiled at Mr. Denton. "I think *he* knows."

He bobbed his head. "Iris?"

She giggled. "He told you?"

"No. Mother told me. Harper doesn't say much."

Brian stood, tired of all of it. How did even Mrs. Holloway know things about his family and his past? Why was he the only one in the room lost in a dense fog? "What are you talking about? How'd you know her name's Iris?"

"Oh, my dear, dear, Brian," she said. "I know how hard this is for you. Please forgive us." She motioned for him to sit. "Do you remember when I told you about my first kiss?"

"Of course I do. I remember everything that happened *after* my injury."

"Yes, dear." She gave him a look he knew well. His tone had been too sarcastic for her liking. "That man was Harper Hadley. Mr. Denton's uncle." Her brow furrowed. "But when did he become a wood carver?"

"After he lost the woman he loved to a man who swept her off her feet with his beautiful carvings." Mr. Denton lifted a sculpted water crane from the mantel. "From what mother told me, he never stopped hoping she'd return one day."

She'd calmed enough for the color to return to her cheeks. "How is he? Well, I hope."

Mr. Denton nodded. "He's slower than he used to be, but is otherwise in good health. Everyone is much better since we got the news about Billy. That is . . . *Brian*."

"It's all right, Mr. Denton," Brian said. "You've called me Billy for eighteen years. I know it's difficult for you."

Mrs. Holloway smiled, showing her appreciation of his improved manners. "I'm glad to hear Harper is well. And . . . his family?"

"We're all the family he has. Mother's fine. Anxious to see Billy." He leaned close to Mrs. Holloway. "Harper never married."

Her mouth twitched and she clutched her breast. "Never?"

"No. Seems he couldn't find another woman who captured his heart."

"Oh, my." She fanned herself. "Becky, please bring me more water."

"I didn't know Uncle Harper ever loved anyone," Donald said. "I mean—a woman that is."

"He's private," Mr. Denton said. He leaned back in his chair and crossed his legs. "Mrs. Holloway, how do you feel about traveling?"

Becky handed her the glass filled with water and sat, listening wide-eyed to the conversation.

"I used to all the time," Mrs. Holloway said. "Jason was a traveling merchant after all."

Mr. Denton added another log to the fire. "I have a fantastic idea."

Brian watched him stoke the fire. "You want her to go with us to Memphis, don't you?"

He spun around to face him. "You read my mind?"

"No. It makes sense. I know you want *me* to go. But understand . . . my life's here. I have a job, a home, a family. And Hannah." He glanced sideways at Donald. "I'll go with you to Memphis, but I don't intend to stay."

Though he could tell his words once again hurt Mr. Denton, they had to be said. He didn't want any misconceptions about how he'd live his life. He'd become a grown man, not the boy they remembered. The Denton's would have to accept that he'd moved on and made a new life for himself.

"I understand," Mr. Denton said. "I'm grateful you're willing to go. And what about you, Mrs. Holloway?"

She lit up like the Christmas tree perched in the corner. "It sounds like an adventure! Becky? Joe? What do you say? Shall we spend the New Year in Memphis?"

"Yes!" Becky said. "I've never been outside Mobile. It sounds wonderful!"

Joe kicked at the floor. "Reckon so."

It was settled. They'd arrange their tickets tomorrow and be in Memphis by New Year's Eve. Brian had something more in mind. He planned to ask Hannah to join them. With her at his side he could cope with the unfamiliar. And then on their way back home to Mobile, he'd do what he'd put off far too long. He'd ask her to marry him. Skip the courtship and go directly to the altar. The perfect plan.

Chapter 32

He is Billy.

Angel read the telegram at least twenty times. Three short words lifted her off her feet.

Of course, Mrs. Denton cried, laughed, and cried again. Ever since the message arrived, the house bustled with activity preparing for Billy's arrival. No one spoke about his memory being gone. He'd remember all of them when he walked through the door. Wouldn't he?

The only one *not* celebrating was Bo. Even Emilia had gotten caught up in the elation and she didn't even know Billy. Most likely she was happy because they were planning a party—a reason to dress up. Her favorite thing to do.

Sleet pelted down outside Angel's bedroom window. A glaze of ice frosted the already frozen ground. She much preferred snow.

Biscuit sat at her feet pawing her leg. She lifted him into her arms and scratched under his chin prompting his internal motor to rumble.

"Don't get your hopes up too high, Biscuit. They say he won't remember us."

Setting him on the bed, she opened the drawer that held her journal. "Billy told me to write to help us remember. Reckon he never knew he'd need this much help."

She thumbed through the pages. It was all here. Every thought she'd had since he left. Some were too personal for him to see. Especially when she wrote about Bo. Maybe she could read parts of it to him. *Will he want to hear it?* What if he wasn't the same Billy at all anymore?

Bo was waiting for Billy to come and *go*. Waiting for her to agree to marry him.

She stretched out on her bed. Life with Bo wouldn't be so bad. He was a good man, and she'd never tire of his looks. Her life could be much worse. She could move into the other house and it would be theirs alone. Until the babies started coming. Bo's babies. *Oh, my . . .*

* * *

"Before we go to supper, I'd like to speak with you." Mrs. Holloway gave Brian that motherly look.

He was about to get a talking to. "Yes'm." He joined her on the sofa. What had taken her so long? He'd felt this coming since yesterday.

"Brian." She folded her hands and looked him in the eye. "Don't forget who you are."

His eyes popped wide and his mouth dropped. "That's just it. I *don't remember.*"

She shook her finger at him like the pendulum on their clock. "I don't like that tone. I heard it yesterday and again now. You're too good a man to feel sorry for yourself."

"Sorry for myself?"

"I know how badly you wanted to recognize Mr. Denton. Even your brother." She pursed her lips. "And that's something else I want to address."

Donald was the last thing he wanted to discuss. However, he wasn't about to cross Mrs. Holloway. She'd been good to him and he'd never hurt her. "You want to discuss my brother?"

"Yes. I've never known you to be unkind to anyone. Yet the way you spoke to him—"

"I know." He sighed. "But if you'd seen how he doted on Hannah."

"Oh?" Her brows rose to her hairline. "I see. He's a handsome young man and Hannah noticed. Hmm?"

He nodded and stood. "Yes, she noticed. And he told me he thinks she's beautiful. It bothered me. I don't intend on sharing her with anyone."

"Even your family?"

"He wasn't looking at her like a family member. More like . . ." He gazed upward trying to find the perfect word.

"A man looking at a woman?" She tipped her head and smiled.

"Exactly!" He returned to the sofa and sat down so hard it jarred her. She had to steady herself with her hands.

"Jealousy is an ugly thing. If Hannah loves you and you love her, then nothing your brother says or does can change that." She patted his leg.

"I know you're right. But it's all part of what's tearing me up inside. I assumed when someone came to *claim* me it'd make everything better. But all it's done is make things worse. I know I need to go to Memphis, but I want to get it over with so I can get back to my life here. I don't know those people, yet I can see in their eyes that they love me. It

hurts not to feel the same way about them. Even Donald."
He blew out a large breath and frowned.

Her sad eyes told him she shared his pain.

He locked into her gaze, then stood again unable to remain still. "Do you understand how much it hurts when I can't tell them I remember their stories?" He moved to the fireplace, soaking in its soothing warmth. "It hurts so badly I get angry. And that's what comes out of me. It's all so . . . *hard*."

"I know, dear." She moved beside him, and circled his waist with her arm. "But you have the ability to handle it well. You've faced difficulties before. Remember how you helped Joe and Becky? You have an enormous heart. Give your family time. You'll learn to love them again."

The flickering firelight danced before him calming his nerves. "Even if I only stay in Memphis a few days?"

"You may decide to stay longer. A few days may not be enough time to make up all the years lost. Stop trying so hard to remember your past and simply get to know them. I believe you'll fit in just fine. Besides, you have your mother to consider."

"My mother?"

"Yes. Of all the people you'll meet, you must be gentle with her. A mother's heart is a delicate thing. Becky has shown me that."

He turned to the woman who'd become the mother he'd sought from the moment he'd left the hospital. He kissed her on the forehead. "Thank you."

"What for?"

"Caring. And not being afraid to set me straight. I'll do better tonight. If Donald upsets me I'll close my eyes and count to ten before planting my fist in his jaw."

"Brian!" She took his chin in her forefingers. "Don't think such thoughts."

"I'm teasing," he chuckled. "I'll be a perfect gentleman."

* * *

One, two, three . . .

Brian held his breath. He would *not* break his promise to Mrs. Holloway.

The evening had started well, but then everything fell apart when Donald took a seat beside Hannah at the supper table. Of course Brian took the seat to her other side, but it didn't matter. Her attention had been on Donald throughout the meal.

She'd never found the things *he* told her as amusing or entertaining as everything that flowed from Donald's mouth. His *brother* ate it up. Feasted on Hannah with more enthusiasm than he'd had for the food on his plate.

But this was the last straw. He'd asked her to show him the bay and she'd agreed.

"It's too cold outside to be walking to the bay at this hour," Brian said, taking her arm.

"I didn't intend to go tonight," Donald said. "Perhaps tomorrow. Hannah said there's often wood washed up on the shore perfect for carving. I'd like to gather some to take home."

"Oh." Brian swallowed hard and unclenched his fist.

"You're welcome to join us," Donald added with a sly smile.

Brian's fist tightened again as Hannah's lips moved upward into a warm smile for Donald. She knew very well he had a job to complete tomorrow. He had no time to comb the beach for wood. Since they'd be leaving the following day, he had no choice but to go to work.

Maybe I don't want her to go to Memphis.

"Brian?" Mr. Denton had taken to using the name Brian preferred, much to his relief.

"Yes, sir?" Had he noticed the way his son was pursuing Hannah?

"Dr. Mitchell agreed to accompany us to Memphis. And you'll be happy to know Hannah will be joining us as well."

Brian jerked around to look at Hannah and Donald. Both were beaming. How had this happened without him suggesting it? "How can you leave the hospital?" He tried to shift his gaze toward the doctor, but his heart made his eyes remain on Hannah and *him.*

"I'm overdue for some time away," Dr. Mitchell said. "But I have to return by the fourth of January. A new doctor—fresh out of medical school—is joining our staff. I'll be taking him under my wing."

"He'll be in excellent hands," Mr. Denton said. "Aren't you pleased, Brian?"

"Of course he is," Hannah said, scooting against him.

He welcomed the warmth from her body. Perhaps he'd been reading too much into her behavior with Donald. "Yes. I'm pleased. Overwhelmed, but pleased."

"I have a professional interest in this," Dr. Mitchell said. "You're my patient. I have great hopes that being in familiar surroundings will trigger your memory. I'd like to witness it."

Brian tried to smile. He'd given up hope a long time ago.

* * *

"Billy, when you look at it, think a me."

Brian woke with a start, jerking in his seat. His heart thumped so loud, Hannah had to have heard it.

"Brian," she whispered. "You're drenched with sweat."

He blinked at her, trying to bring her into focus.

The dream had seemed real again. The same dark eyes haunted him. And this time, she'd placed the wooden angel in his palm. Was this a memory or something created in his subconscious after being told the slave girl was the one who'd given it to him? Patting his front pocket, he sighed, relieved to feel it. It wasn't his, and he had no reason to keep it. He'd return it to its rightful owner.

The train ride had been exciting for Joe and Becky, but Brian hadn't been able to relax and enjoy it. His eyes had been kept on Hannah and Donald, and only now could he sleep. Crammed into the Denton's carriage, Donald was with Jeriah, the driver. Joe was also up there, suddenly not caring that the weather had turned bitterly cold. *At least someone's having a nice time.*

"Brian," Mr. Denton said. "We're getting close. Look out the window."

He parted the curtain. They'd just passed through a black iron gate and were headed down a winding path.

"Jeriah usually drives to the stables and we walk to the house, but I asked him to take us to the front steps," Mr. Denton said, smiling. "I didn't want the ladies to walk so far in the cold."

Mrs. Holloway tittered. "You're being kind. You could have said you were saving the *old woman* from walking so far." She fidgeted with the bow at her neck. "Will Harper be waiting?"

"I'm not certain. I don't know what Cora planned for a homecoming. If Emilia has any say in the matter, I imagine we'll be stepping into the middle of a large party. Lots of food. That being said, more than likely Harper will be present. I know how much he's missed Billy."

Brian tried to ignore that Mr. Denton used *Billy* rather than *Brian* for the first time since they'd left Mobile.

"That can't be your house," Brian said. His heart pounded, working overtime. This humongous structure looked more like an elaborate hotel than a home. Three stories high and wider than his view from the tiny window would allow.

"It's your house, too," Mr. Denton said with a gentle smile.

Brian hoped he wouldn't do anything out of line to ruin what was to come. He didn't want to disappoint this kind man.

"Mama, look at it!" Becky exclaimed. "I ain't never seen nothing like it!"

"You *haven't* seen *anything* like it," Mrs. Holloway said.

"That's what I said, Mama. It's beautiful!"

Hannah peeked out the window. "I've been here before. I remember it, Daddy."

"You were little," Dr. Mitchell said. "But it made an impression on you. Very few people forget something as grand as the Wellesley estate."

Brian looked directly at him, unable to hide the hurt his remark prompted.

"Forgive me, Brian," Dr. Mitchell said. "I should have thought—"

"It's all right. Most people don't have their memories altered with a bash to the head."

Stop feeling sorry for yourself! He'd promised Mrs. Holloway he'd try harder. Washing away the dour expression on his face, he replaced it with a smile. "That makes me unique."

"Yes, you are," Mrs. Holloway said, and squeezed his kneecap. She then began fanning her face. "I'm as nervous as a hen in a den of foxes!"

"Oh, Mama," Becky laughed. "Don't be. This is too exciting!"

"I'll stay close to your side, Mrs. Holloway," Brian said. "You'll be seeing someone whom you haven't seen for many years, but you should probably recognize. I won't have any idea who I'm looking at. I'm nervous, too."

"Don't worry, Brian," Mr. Denton said. "I'll introduce you to everyone."

"Thank you, sir." He was relieved. The man was gracious and understanding. Hopefully the rest of the family would be as kind.

* * *

Angel gazed into the mirror, turned sideways, and then back again to face it squarely. She'd chosen a blue dress. Billy's favorite color. She'd been saving it for a special occasion. The cotton material was warm, but not confining. And the delicate lace that trimmed the neckline and sleeve cuffs gave it a feminine flair she hoped he'd appreciate.

He'd only ever seen her in the plain clothing she wore as a slave with the drab gray scarf covering her head. Today she wore no scarf, but tied a wide blue satin ribbon in her hair, matching the color of her dress. She left her hair down, flowing all the way to her waistline.

She leaned in and touched her face, then ran her hands down her sides and rested them on her hips. When Billy left, she didn't have the curves reflecting back from the mirror. Or a bosom to speak of. She'd been a girl then. Now, she'd become a woman. She prayed he'd notice.

"Angel!" Her mama's voice rang through the house. "Billy's gonna be here any minute!"

"Yes, Mama!" Angel primped her hair one last time and walked out of her room.

Uziah stood there holding their mama's hand. "Angel purty," he said with a grin.

She bent down and gave him a kiss. "Thank you, Ziah." Her brow wrinkled as she stood. "Mama, *do* I look all right?" She smoothed her dress and turned in a circle.

"Uziah's right. You's beautiful." She took her hand and squeezed it. "But Billy ain't the same no more. May not member you. I don't wanna see you hurt."

Angel nodded, but frowned. "I'll do my best."

They'd been working all day preparing food and setting up the ballroom for his homecoming. Emilia had flitted around the house singing. Angel preferred this side of her, remembering what a hateful young girl had once walked through the front door.

"I love the smell of cinnamon bread." Angel inhaled the fantastic aroma. "It was always one a Billy's favorites."

"I know," Ada chuckled. "That's why I made it."

"The carriage is here!" Richard yelled. He popped his head through the archway. "C'mon!"

After almost five years, it was the moment Angel had been waiting for. Yet her feet froze to the floor. What would he look like? Would he be taller? She'd grown a few inches, but had stopped at five-feet-two.

Forcing herself to move, she grabbed a glass, filled it with water, and gulped it down in an attempt to wet her dry throat. All the water in the river wouldn't calm her racing heart.

Oh, Lord, please let him know me . . .

She sped away with the rest of the family to wait for Billy.

* * *

Lead weights seemed to be pulling down Brian's legs. Each step became more difficult. Why was he so nervous? He just had to meet them. Then, in a few days, he'd go home.

He tilted his head backward and looked up at the enormous house. *What was it like growing up here?*

Jeriah raced effortlessly up the steps and opened the door. His eyes were full of excitement. What was *he* so happy about?

Mr. Denton laughed. "Leave the carriage for now, Jeriah. I want you to be a part of this."

"Yessa." Jeriah rubbed his hands together and let out a laugh. "Welcome home, Billy." He fanned his hand through the air and motioned them inside.

Brian took a deep breath and stepped through. Joe and Becky chattered non-stop behind him but he didn't listen to their words. The only words he was attuned to were the ones playing over and over in his mind. *Be a gentleman and soon you'll go home.*

Mrs. Holloway clung to his arm, trembling. He did his best to steady her. "He's just a man," he whispered through the side of his mouth.

"No. He was more than that." She fanned her face. "Oh, dear . . ."

Mr. Denton motioned to a large open doorway. "The ballroom."

Brian's heart skipped a beat. *Where's Hannah?* He whipped his head around and found her at Donald's side.

"Let it go, Brian," Mrs. Holloway said, squeezing his arm. "He's simply escorting her."

Escorting her? Not likely. More along the line of courting her. Once the introductions were over, he'd make a point of speaking to him. This had to be resolved one way or another.

He gulped. A line of people faced him, smiling as though they'd just received the greatest gift ever given. If only he felt the same. He searched their faces hoping for a tiny glimmer.

His breath caught and his thumping heart seemed to have stopped completely. *It's her.*

Beautiful wasn't a good enough word. The girl from his dreams—no longer a girl.

Her eyes locked with his and he couldn't shift his gaze. Her skin was the color of chocolate; flawless and smooth. Her hair fell down her shoulders in waves of rich satin. Once his eyes were free from her spell, they moved downward. His body warmed taking in her form.

"Brian?" Hannah pressed his arm with her fingertips. "What's wrong with you?"

"Huh?" He shook his head and turned to look at her. "Nothing. I'm fine."

"Your father was speaking to you." She nudged him. "Go over there."

His face heated as he crossed the room to Mr. Denton. "Sorry, sir. I'm a bit overwhelmed."

"I see that. Let me introduce you."

Mr. Denton cleared his throat. "I'm aware how much you all want to welcome him home, but I want to introduce you to Brian Carpenter. He knows you care about him, but please give him time to get to know you again. This hasn't been easy for him."

"It ain't been easy for any of us," a noticeably pregnant woman said. "I gotta hold my son."

Brian was pulled into the sincerest embrace he'd ever felt and immediately dampened with tears. He didn't resist her. No doubt she was his mother. Much tinier than he'd imagined—with the exception of her large baby bulge—but he definitely looked like her. Even though he had no memories of her, somehow his heart warmed with love for her.

"Billy," she repeated over and over. She hugged him, kissed him, and hugged him again, unwilling to let go.

"Cora," Mr. Denton said gently. "Let me introduce him to the rest of the family."

She let go of every part of him except his arm. "All right. But I ain't goin' nowhere." She wiped her face with the back of her hand, but clung to him as if letting go might mean she'd never touch him again.

Brian smiled down at her—a genuine smile—not even bothered by her use of the name *Billy*. Dr. Mitchell had been right; she was charming.

"First," Mr. Denton said, "I want you to meet *Brian's* family. This is Joe, Becky, and Mrs. Holloway." They took their places beside Brian. Mrs. Holloway took the arm Mrs. Denton wasn't attached to.

"And now," Mr. Denton went on. "Brian, this is the rest of your family."

He went down the line, starting with his other brother and sisters. Brian decided Richard looked more like him and his mother. The girls, Christina and Paulette, favored their father. They were pretty girls. They didn't say anything, simply stared at him as if he was a foreigner, but smiled nonetheless. His belly churned and his throat tightened. *They're just as confused.*

"This is Ada," Mr. Denton said, pointing to a large Negro woman. "Our head cook. And Bessie, who also cooks for us and keeps house. In addition, she's Jeriah's wife and Angel's mother. The little boy with the big brown eyes is Uziah, their son."

Brian nodded to each person in turn. His eyes kept shifting to Angel. *An appropriate name.*

"This is Bo," Mr. Denton said. "He works in the stables with Jeriah."

"It's good to meet you, Bo," Brian said.

Unlike the others, Bo didn't smile. He nodded, but said nothing. Brian found it odd, but dismissed it. Obviously the man wasn't as friendly.

Then, they reached Angel. His heart thumped and he choked out the words. "I'm happy to meet you, Angel."

A grunt from Bo caught him by surprise.

Angel elbowed him and reprimanded him with her eyes before shifting her gaze back to Brian. "I'm glad you're home—*Brian.*" Her voice was soft as silk.

He stood close enough now to become lost in the dark eyes of his dreams.

"Ahem! Excuse me!"

Brian hadn't noticed the attractive young woman standing beside Angel. But now that she'd started waving her hands in his face, it was impossible not to.

Mr. Denton chuckled. "Brian, this is Emilia. Your cousin."

He gave her his full attention. "I'm pleased to meet you." *So she's the one who likes to entertain.* It showed. Her dress looked expensive. Pink satin and lace. He'd seen a similar dress on Victoria O'Malley.

"Yes, I'm your cousin." Emilia leaned in. "But I'm also *her* sister!" She bumped her shoulder into Angel's and giggled. "Try to figure *that* out."

Brian turned toward Mr. Denton for an explanation.

"I'll explain later," he said, then shook his head at Emilia. "Behave yourself."

She giggled again.

Mrs. Holloway tugged on his arm. "I don't see Harper."

Mr. Denton scanned the room. "He must be lying down."

"Your ma went to get him just before you came in," Mrs. Denton said. "There they are now." She pointed to the doorway.

"Oh, my." Mrs. Holloway buckled.

"There she goes again," Becky said.

"What's wrong with her?" Mrs. Denton asked, as they helped her to a chair.

Mr. Denton patted her shoulder. "A little surprise, my dear. You'll see soon enough."

The elderly couple crossed the floor. Though gray-haired and slow, they were an attractive pair. Unmistakably brother and sister.

So this is the man who first kissed Mrs. Holloway? Maybe some sparks remained.

"Uncle Harper. Mother," Mr. Denton said. "This is Brian Carpenter."

Brian smiled.

"Huh?" Uncle Harper said. "Looks like Billy."

"It *is* Billy," Mrs. Wellesley said. "But he's called *Brian* now."

"Makes no sense." Harper scratched his head, then pointed to Mrs. Holloway. "That *Mrs.* Carpenter?"

Mrs. Holloway let out a loud nervous laugh. "Oh, Harper! You've not changed one bit!"

He inched closer to her, then he, too, buckled at the knees.

Mr. Denton grabbed him and sat him beside Mrs. Holloway.

The two stared at each other—speechless. Brian's heart warmed.

"Iris?" Harper whispered. Tears filled his eyes.

"Yes. How are you, Harper?" She reached out to him. He studied her hand as though he'd never seen one before. With a slow quivering hand of his own, he finally took hers.

"How am I? Dang, woman. How long you got for me to tell you?"

Mrs. Wellesley beamed. She moved to Iris and touched her shoulder. "You've come back after all this time."

"I wouldn't have had it not been for Brian," Mrs. Holloway said.

Mrs. Wellesley turned toward him. The concern on her face broke his heart. She'd not come to him as easily as his mother. *Why?* "You're my grandmother?"

She placed her palm against his cheek. "Yes. I thought I'd never see you again. And now, not only do *you* return home but you bring with you a treasure. Harper's Iris."

Mary Wellesley carried herself like a refined woman. No wonder she hadn't showered him with the same affections as his mother had. In many ways, he was relieved. He preferred to work his way into her affection. "I'm glad I've made you happy."

She took his hand, patted it, then slowly walked away. Watching her saddened him. Something about the way she'd looked at him . . .

His dampened spirit was quickly revived by loud laughter. The children were devouring the food. It hadn't taken long for Joe and Becky to befriend his brother and sisters, and little Uziah was the center of everyone's attention.

Brian's mother latched onto his arm again.

"Mrs. Denton?" Hannah said. "I'm certain Brian's hungry. Do you mind if I steal him away for a few minutes so we can eat?"

The woman gazed up into his eyes. "Reckon so. You've got a might pretty woman there." She stood on her toes and kissed his cheek. "I love you. Ain't never stopped."

"Thank you." *Thank you?* The appropriate thing would have been *I love you, too, Mother.* But he couldn't say that to a woman he'd just met.

Hannah led him to the food tables. He glanced over his shoulder and caught a glimpse of the back of Angel's dress as she fled from the room.

Chapter 33

"What'd you 'spect?" Bo stroked Angel's hair. "He ain't Billy no more."

She covered her face and cried. "But, he *is*." And he'd found someone else to love. Someone pretty and whiter than snow. She couldn't bear it. "Bo, I wanna be alone right now. Please?"

He hovered over her. "A'right. But I be waitin'. I'd never hurt you like he done."

"It wasn't his fault! Billy'd never hurt me on purpose!"

Bo's nostrils flared. He stood firm with clenched fists. "His memory's hurtin' you. Let him go, Angel. He ain't Billy!" He left, slamming the door behind him.

How could she let him go now? He'd come home. Right where he belonged. And if the look she'd seen in his eyes gave any indication, maybe she still held a piece of his heart.

* * *

"We appreciate the offer, Cora," Dr. Mitchell said. "But my mother-in-law would be upset if Hannah and I stayed here."

"Just come back soon. Brian's gonna miss her. It's hard on him bein' 'round all us strangers." She rubbed her hand over his head. "I'll leave you to tell her goodbye."

"And I'll help Jeriah with the buggy," Dr. Mitchell said. "Thank you again, Cora, for the wonderful meal."

She beamed. "Thank *you* for bringin' my boy home." She gave the doctor a hug.

Her boy. Brian hadn't been called *boy* in some time, but it didn't bother him coming from her. Watching her walk away, he was caught off guard by the tug at his heart. Maybe Mrs. Holloway was right. A few days wouldn't be long enough.

"Brian?" Hannah moved into his arms.

"Yes?"

"That girl. The slave girl—"

"She's not a slave."

"You know what I mean." She tilted her head and gazed at him through her long lashes. "The way you looked at her—as if you recognized her. Did you?"

"How could I?" Had she noticed their eyes lock together?

"I don't know." She licked her lips and lifted her face. "She's very pretty."

"Pretty?" He decided to make light of it. "I didn't notice."

She squeezed him tighter. "Brian?" She moistened her lips again, this time her tongue lingered. "Why haven't you ever kissed me?"

"I've kissed you." His words were defensive, but he knew exactly what she wanted.

"Not on my lips." Again, her tongue flicked out of her mouth.

His mouth watered with desire. He glanced around the hallway making certain they were alone. Then he bent down, closed his eyes, and kissed her. Her moist lips drew him in and caused his heart to race. His body ached for more. He stood erect and raised his eyes.

Her lids slowly opened and a smile spread across her face. "That's what I've been waiting for," she sighed.

He lifted his eyes higher and his heart stopped. *Angel?* Grateful he'd not spoken her name aloud, she was gone as quickly as before.

"Brian?" Hannah rested her hand on his chest. "You didn't say anything. Didn't you like it?"

"No. That is, *yes*." Focusing on her right now took complete concentration. "It was nice."

"Nice?" She backed away. "*Nice?*"

"*Really* nice," he stammered. "I'm sorry Hannah. I'm tired, and confused, and—"

"Fine." She crossed her arms. "Get some sleep. Maybe the next time you'll actually *feel* something." She turned to walk away.

"Hannah . . ."

"Yes?" She stopped and huffed. Her face contorted, becoming unattractive.

"Goodnight."

She rolled her eyes. "Goodnight." She exited in one swift motion.

Spying a chaise in the hallway, he plopped down and buried his face in his hands. "That went well," he mumbled.

"I didn't mean to interrupt you."

His stomach flipped. Angel stood over him, close enough to touch. Why did he *want* to? "I . . . Uh . . ." Heat rose from his neck. His face was probably as red as his hair. "Angel?"

She laughed. "You all right?"

"I . . . I think I am." He raked his fingers back through his hair.

"I see you still do that." She pointed to his head.

"I do?" He swallowed hard. "Oh, yes. I do."

"Can I sit?" She motioned to the vacancy beside him.

He scooted over and nodded. "I thought everyone was getting ready for bed."

"They are. But I wanted to talk to you. I'm just sorry I walked in on you an Hannah."

He was sorry, too. After all this time—waiting for the right time to kiss her—then to have it go so poorly. *So much for planning.*

He twisted his fingers together. Something about her presence made him uneasy. "Angel?"

"Yes?"

"Everyone tells me we were best friends." He turned his head slightly to look at her, fearing the eye-lock from earlier in the day. He doubted his heart could take it.

"Yep. Always told each other everythin'. I know more 'bout you than your mama." She laughed softly, but then placed her hand over her mouth.

"Were we . . . *more* than friends?"

This time she giggled nervously. "We were children. How could we be more than friends?"

"We weren't *that* young." Bravely, he looked her in the eye. "If you were half as pretty as you are now, I'm sure I was taken with you. How could I not be?"

She stared at him. Her breathing became labored; her chest rose and fell with every breath, taking away his.

"Brian?" Paulette's voice drew both of them from their trance.

"Yes?" He cleared his throat and scooted away from Angel.

"Mama said you used to tuck me in at night." She bit her lower lip. "I know I'm not a baby anymore, but will you tuck me in?"

He stood, though it was difficult. What was it about Angel that drew him to her?

"Of course I will." He took the child's extended hand. "Angel? Can we talk more later?"

"Course. Night, Paulette."

"Goodnight, Angel." She led him down the hallway to her room.

* * *

Brian settled into his *old room,* as Mrs. Denton had called it. They'd kept it exactly as he'd left it. However, she'd told him they intended to turn it into a nursery. Not knowing whether to decorate in pink or blue had been a good excuse to leave it as it was.

His bedroom prompted no memories, but he liked it. It suited him. Who wouldn't like a bed filled with soft down? It begged him to sleep, but he couldn't. Not yet. He sat on the edge thinking about what had happened since his arrival.

Mrs. Holloway had gone off somewhere with Mr. Hadley. She'd appeared no longer nervous, chattering nonstop as she'd linked her arm through his and walked away. Obviously, no matter one's age, love could be rekindled. Not only did it make *them* happy, but his grandmother was also elated. Even so, she'd retired to bed shortly after supper, complaining of a headache.

Joe had bonded with Jeriah instantly and was staying in their house. He'd declined the Denton's offer and jumped at the idea of sleeping on Bessie's sofa. Uziah was most likely keeping him awake wanting to play.

Becky, on the other hand, couldn't be more thrilled to have her own room and settled down in a bedroom next to Emilia.

His brothers were another matter. Richard acted almost irritated to have him home. Jealous perhaps of the attention their mother had shown him? As for Donald, his only interest was Hannah. Or so it seemed. *Maybe in time I'll like him. Maybe . . .*

Christina was the quiet one. She'd smiled at him more than once, but kept to herself. Young women, he'd decided, were very complex.

Ada and Bessie were exceptional. Having found him too thin, they'd offered to cook anything he liked. No burned biscuits at this house.

Mr. Denton was exactly the kind of man he'd presumed him to be upon their first meeting. He'd made him feel comfortable and answered every question he'd had.

Of all of them, he wanted to get to know Mrs. Denton better. Aside from Angel. But Angel was dangerous. Spending time with her might not be wise.

He lifted a lantern from the bed stand and grabbed a quilt from the base of the bed. He'd forgotten to pack his robe, so the blanket would have to do. The huge rooms and high ceilings made for a very cold house.

The fire in the living room called his name. *Which* name remained a point of confusion.

"Mrs. Denton?" He wasn't disappointed to find her also enjoying the comfort of the fire.

"Brian?" She lit up brighter than the flames and patted the spot beside her on the sofa.

"I can't sleep." He took a seat and tucked the blanket around himself.

"I can't neither." He'd grown fond of her accent.

He looked around the room while searching for the right things to say. "Your house is spectacular."

"Yep. It is." She wrinkled her nose. "You should a seen the house I grew up in. It would a fit in this here livin' room."

"Tell me about it." He drew up one leg and folded it under himself. "I want to know all about you and Mr. Denton, and my real father, too."

"Dang!" She laughed and covered her mouth. "I reckon that'll take all night."

There it was. *The word that changed my life.* "I don't mind. I can't sleep anyway."

She started to talk and he listened to every word. How he came into the world. How she met Mr. Denton. It was their story, but it wasn't fiction. It was his life. Her life. His mother. His home.

"You always called me *Mama*." She ran her fingers through his hair. "Never *Ma* or *Mother*."

Her tenderness made him close his eyes. A tingling sensation crept down his spine. He remembered this feeling. Remembered her touch. His heart pounded. *Is it possible?*

He opened his eyes. The tingle faded—the memories with it.

"Why do you think this happened to me?" he asked. "Am I being punished for something I did?"

"Oh, baby." She touched his cheek. "You ain't bein' punished." She took his hands in hers. "I know you don't remember her, but the woman I told you raised me? Mrs. Moss? She used to say, God has a plan for all a us. Everythin' happens for a reason."

"What reason could there be for my loss of memory?"

Her face softened. "Think a the lives you've changed cuz a what happened."

"What lives?"

"If you hadn't a left here, you never would a gone to that Union camp. That woman I told you 'bout—Jessica— she'd a never changed her life. An what do you reckon Joe might be doin' right now? Or Becky? You was in the right place at the right time. You saved them children."

"How do you know someone else wouldn't have saved them?"

"All I know is their lives are better cuz a *you*. Then there's Uncle Harper. I ain't never seen him so happy. Mrs. Holloway's life changed for the better cuz a you. See what I'm sayin'?"

"But why did I have to lose my memory for it to happen?"

"It happened the way it was s'posed to. If you hadn't forgotten everythin' you would a come home 'fore you ever did the things you was s'posed to. Iris would a died a lonely old woman, but now she has a family. Maybe even a new husband."

He took a deep breath. She made sense. So much sense it scared him.

"Don't forget 'bout Hannah. You'd never a met her. We was so worried you an Angel—" She stopped mid-sentence, becoming rigid.

"Angel and me *what*?" Until then she'd talked freely. Now her lips were pinched tight.

"Nothin'. Forget I mentioned her."

"I know you like her. And from what I've seen, she's a fine young woman. Why were you worried?"

"Pay it no mind. It was in the past. We ain't got nothin' to worry 'bout no more. You have Hannah, an Angel has Bo. It's how it should be."

Angel has Bo? His assumption earlier had been correct. Bo was jealous of Angel's reaction to him. "Do Angel and Bo plan to marry?"

"Yep. He asked her Christmas Eve."

"When's the wedding?" He stared at his hands, waiting for her reply. Suddenly, *he* was the jealous one. But it made no sense.

"Don't know just yet." Her brows wove together. "Seems Angel's still thinkin' on it."

He couldn't help but smile. "She hasn't said *yes* then?"

"Not yet. I reckon she's fixin' to."

"Cora?" Mr. Denton entered the room, yawning. "Do you know what time it is?"

"Nope," she replied with a laugh.

"It's three a.m. You need your rest. You've got to think about the baby."

She rubbed her large belly. "Hard not to. Brian an me was catchin' up. I'll be there soon."

"All right." He gave her a kiss on the lips. "I love you."

"I love you, too."

Warmth enveloped Brian. This was the home he'd grown up in. The people who'd raised him. He'd been very blessed.

Chapter 34

"He's still sleepin'?" Angel asked Ada, while setting the morning milk pail on the counter.

"Yep. Mista Denton been in for breakfast. Had to go to the mill. Said Brian an Ms. Denton was up past three."

"Three?" Angel shook her head. She'd also been wide awake then. Sleep wouldn't come. Her mind had been unable to rest realizing the truth. Even if she had to go the rest of her life calling him Brian, it wouldn't change her feelings. She was still in love with him.

She'd closed her eyes and tried, but her thoughts brought images of him to mind. Long ago he was shorter. Smaller. Younger. The vision of what he'd become had popped her eyes wide open; a man who was tall, very handsome, and . . . *My, oh my, how he'd filled out.*

She'd tried not to look. She couldn't help but notice his muscular arms through the fabric of his shirt. His chest appeared broader, though he still had a small behind.

I probably shouldn't a been lookin' at it.

When he'd kissed Hannah, she knew Bo was right. She had to let him go. It was that terrible thought that kept her up. She'd stared at her journal for hours, but couldn't write a word.

Maybe there was one last hope.

"Did I miss breakfast?" Brian asked, poking his head into the kitchen.

Angel covered her mouth to keep from laughing at his mussed hair.

"Shore did," Ada said. "But I'll fix you anythin' you like. Hotcakes? Oats? Bacon?"

"Got any more cinnamon bread?" He jiggled his eyebrows.

"Shore do! Boy always did like my bread." She moved to the counter and uncovered the remainder of the loaf. As she sawed with the knife, her bottom wiggled in its familiar fashion.

Angel glanced in Brian's direction. His head tipped to the side, watching. He was grinning. She cleared her throat and he met her gaze. She muffled a laugh.

"Thank you, Ada," he said, then scolded Angel playfully with his eyes.

"Nothin' like Ada's cinnamon bread," Angel said.

Ada faced them with her hands on her hips. "What you children up to? Was you laughin'?"

"No, Ada," Angel said. "An we ain't children."

"Far from it," Brian whispered. His eyes passed over Angel, and she nearly lost her breath. He wasn't making this easy.

He buttered his bread. "Would you like some, Angel?" He broke off a small piece.

"I already ate. I got work to do." She fled from the kitchen. She had to get away from him. Even though she had something to give him, it had to be done privately.

* * *

Since Brian hadn't fallen asleep until five a.m., he was extremely tired. After he'd left Mrs. Denton, he'd lain on his bed and stared into the darkness until he'd finally drifted off. All the things he'd learned about his life had spun through his mind. In the middle of it all was Angel.

When Mrs. Denton filled in the details about Angel and Emilia's father, his heart went out to both of them. They hadn't had the advantage of a father like Douglas Denton, though Jeriah appeared to have stepped into Angel's life. He'd found Emilia intriguing, but since the party she'd not given him the time of day.

Angel filled his dreams once again. No longer a young girl. She was the grown version, complete with breasts and curves. Even his dreams had become dangerous. He woke, completely aroused. That'd never happened before. Not even with thoughts of Hannah.

Strangely enough, Hannah was the last person on his mind. He'd set aside his disinterest, believing it to be the need to get to know his family and reconnect with his past.

He'd heard Angel's voice before he'd entered the kitchen. It had made his heart race over reminders of the night's dreams. He'd kissed her. Nothing like the kiss with Hannah. It had been formed out of love and burned with desire.

Why'd she run off so quickly? He'd hoped to spend time with her. She couldn't be *that* dangerous.

With that in mind, he returned to his room, washed, and dressed in clean clothes. Glancing in the mirror, he finally understood the look she'd given him in the kitchen. His hair stood on end. From now on, he'd check the mirror *before* leaving his room.

As he tucked his shirt into his pants, a hard knock rattled his door.

"Brian?" Angel's unmistakable sweet voice.

He checked the mirror one more time, then breathed into his hand to check his breath.

Pulling his shoulders back, he opened the door. "Angel? Can I help you?" *That sounded ridiculous.*

She giggled. It wasn't an obnoxious giggle like Emilia's; Angel's giggle charmed him. Soft. Sweet. Like Angel herself.

"Wanna go for a walk? I know it's cold outside but this house is big enough we can walk the halls. I doubt you've seen it all."

"I'd like that."

She grinned. "We might need this." She picked up the blanket he'd wrapped himself in the previous night. "Thought I'd show you the attic."

The attic? A little odd, but he'd go anywhere with her. "What's that under your arm?"

"You'll see." She teased him with another grin and nodded down the hallway.

Was he betraying Hannah by spending time with Angel? Certainly not. But the fact he was questioning his intentions made him question his intentions. *Get your head on straight. She's your long-time friend. Nothing more.*

It was a long walk to the attic. As they climbed the final staircase, the air turned crisp.

"Over here," she said, thumping her hand against an old wooden chest. She sat down and waited for him with a smile that warmed the frigid air.

"Why'd you want to come up here? We'd have done as well to go outside. It's just as cold."

Her eyes softened. "This place is special." She blew out a long breath. "You asked me if you an I were more than friends. I hafta tell you the truth." She twisted her mouth and closed her eyes. "You kissed me here. This is where you told me you was leavin', an then you kissed me." Her eyes opened, but filled with tears. "It's my fault you left. You said you wanted me to be free. That you had to fight for me." She struggled to keep from crying and it broke his heart. "I didn't want you to go . . ."

Compelled to comfort her, he wiped away her tears with the tips of his fingers. He wanted to do more. Every part of him begged to draw her close. "Don't cry, Angel. Please? You can't blame yourself. Mrs. Denton said I *wanted* to go."

The tip of his nose already suffered from the cold, but he didn't want to leave. And she'd given him every indication she felt the same. She inched closer to him. Their hips touched, and the blanket she held was partially around his body.

She asked him about his life in Mobile and he told her everything. Talking to her was effortless; as easy as drawing breath.

"So, when you heard about the Sultana," he said, "everyone thought I'd been on it?"

"You never wrote home so it made sense. We figgered you had to be dead."

"I can't imagine what Mrs. Denton must have gone through." It tore at his heart, but it was something beyond his control.

"It's hard hearin' you call her *Mrs. Denton*. She's your mama after all."

"She's also a stranger." He looked away from her.

She placed her hand on his knee, as if feeling his pain. "Here." She handed him a book. "It's all inside. You gave this to me for Christmas five years ago and told me to write in it. You said to write things to help us remember growin' up here. Some of it's personal, but I don't care. I want you to read it. Maybe it'll help. Maybe you'll remember."

His hands shook. "Are you sure? If the thoughts are personal—"

She placed her hand to his lips. "I want you to remember."

He set the book aside, took her hand, and held it to his chest. "So do I."

Her eyes widened. She pulled away and jumped to her feet.

He wasn't about to let her leave this way. He stood and grabbed her hand. "Angel . . ." He dared not say what he was thinking. "Why are your hands so soft? I've seen how hard you work, yet your skin is soft as satin."

Though hesitating this time, she again pulled free. "Mama makes cream from lanolin. Said it's important for a woman to be soft all over."

He gulped. Where else had she used the cream? "It works," was all he could squeak out.

She stooped to pick up the blanket. "We best be gettin' downstairs. I reckon you'll wanna warm up by the fire. Memphis is colder than Mobile. Or so I've heard."

"It is, but I'm not cold." She'd said he had kissed her here. Was it a kiss like the one in his dream last night? It couldn't have been. They'd been too young for such a kiss.

"C'mon, Brian." She motioned to the door.

"You go on. I'll be down soon."

She cocked her head, and her brows drew together. "All right. I'll see you later then."

He could only nod. He needed to have her gone. Otherwise he'd be tempted to find out about that kiss.

Once she was out the door, he returned to the trunk and picked up the book. Before opening it, he glanced around the attic. With her absence, he was able to look at other things.

The room was full of dusty furniture, stacked wooden crates, and a few latched trunks. Several mattresses were leaning against one wall. Tempted to pull one out onto the floor in order to lay back and read, the cold air changed his mind. Though he wanted to read in private, his room would be wiser.

Standing still for a few moments, he breathed deeply to compose himself. Excited and scared about what she'd written on the pages, he went as fast as he could down the many stairs to the first floor. Ignoring everyone he passed on his way, he went to his room and shut the door.

* * *

"Angel." Her mama stood over her shoulder. "You done peeled that potato to nothin'."

"Sorry, Mama." She set the knife aside.

Her mama chuckled, then took a seat on a stool and placed the butter churn between her knees. Uziah sat comfortably on the floor beside her, building a house from wooden blocks. "You been happier since *Brian* came home," she said, moving the paddle. Her voice held the serious tone she'd been expecting. "But Bo's been mopin' 'round like someone died. Don't hurt him, baby girl. He loves you. He been waitin' a long time for you."

"I know, Mama." Angel sighed. She didn't want to hurt Bo, but she wasn't ready to marry him. Every time Brian looked at her, she got those old familiar feelings deep down inside that stretched all the way to the tips of her toes. Looking into his eyes, he was Billy. Every handsome grown-up male part of him. And still the best friend she'd ever had.

"Take some a that cornbread to Bo." Her mama motioned with her head toward the counter. "I's shore he's hungry."

How could she tell her no? Bo could go without cornbread. Her mama was just trying to force them together. Seeing Bo now—while Brian was reading her book— seemed wrong. She'd much rather wait to see Brian's reaction, hoping it would bring Billy back to her. And then, she'd *have to* hurt Bo.

After wrapping a large portion of cornbread in a cloth napkin, she put on her coat and headed toward the barn.

"He's big!" The exclamation came from Joe, who sat atop Brown Boy, the newest stallion in the stable. Jeriah stood on one side of the horse holding the reins, and Bo was on the other, patting the horse's side to keep him calm.

"Not as big as Cotton was," Jeriah said shaking his head. He then caught Angel's eyes. "Hey, Angel. What brings you out in the cold?"

She lifted the cloth napkin. "I brought cornbread for Bo. Thought he might be hungry."

"Din't you bring me none?" Joe asked.

"I didn't know y'all would be out here. There's more in the house."

"Get me down!" Joe exclaimed. "I'm hungry!"

Jeriah laughed and helped him down. Though Joe was no small boy, Angel sensed his nervousness around the animals. Jeriah seemed to be doing his best to ease his fears.

"I's a might hungry myself," Jeriah said, smiling at Bo. "We be back."

She watched them leave, wishing they'd stayed.

"I best put Brown Boy up," Bo said. He led the horse to a nearby stall.

She followed him and remained quiet while he removed the horse's halter. The pit in her stomach grew as the silence lingered. She cleared her throat. "You hungry?"

"Nope." He began brushing the horse.

"Oh." She traced a pattern with her foot in the loose straw on the ground. "Reckon I should a let Joe have this then." She opened the napkin and picked at the bread.

"Brown Boy might like it," he said dryly.

Stepping forward, she gave the horse the bread. "Yep. He likes it."

Silence again.

"Why you here, Angel?" He closed the gate on Brown Boy's stall and moved to her side.

"To bring you the bread."

"That all?"

"Yep."

"Then go back inside where it's warm." He grabbed a rake and pulled it through the straw.

"Bo. I . . ." She owed him so much. He'd saved her and Emilia in this very spot. She loved him, but was it the kind of love that would hold her heart forever? What could she say to him?

"What, Angel?"

"Bo?" She swallowed hard. "Would you mind so much kissin' me?"

"Huh?"

"I want you to kiss me." It might not be the smartest thing she'd ever done, but she hadn't been able to come up with another way to know.

A soft smile covered his face.

This was a horrible idea. Depending on the outcome, it could hurt him even more.

He set aside the rake, then erased the distance between them with one quick stride. He pulled her to him. He'd been working hard that morning. She breathed in his musky scent.

"Angel," he rasped with his mouth against her ear.

Oh, my. Terrible, terrible idea.

His lips brushed across her cheek before finding their way to her mouth. They were full, warm, and extremely wet. He tightened his grip on her waist with one large hand and clasped the back of her head with the other. After kissing her, he didn't release her. Instead, he rested his bristly cheek against her smooth face.

"Angel, my Angel," he whispered. "I love you."

She closed her eyes, unable to reply. She'd wanted to feel something more than the wetness of his mouth. Her life would be simpler if she felt about him the way he felt about her. Now she knew for sure. She could never marry him.

Pulling back as easily as she could, she placed her hand on his chest. "I gotta get back."

His smile showed he hadn't seen into her heart. "I know. But I be waitin'. There's many more kisses to come." He cupped her face with his calloused hand.

She forced a smile and left. *I'm sorry, Bo . . .*

Chapter 35

She loves me. Brian thumbed through the pages quickly at first, then started at the beginning and read every word. While reading her private thoughts, he'd considered closing the book. Did he have the right?

She'd willingly given it to him, so he pressed on. Her love sprang from nearly every page

Yes, I still love Billy. I just pray he'll remember he loves me, too.

Her final entry might as well have been branded on his forehead. He'd never forget it.

I'm so tired. He placed the book under his pillow, then nestled his head into the comforting down. Dreams were easier to cope with than his life. His lids were heavy and easily closed.

* * *

"Ugh! What have you been eating?" He pushed the cat away and opened his eyes. How long had he slept? It had been late afternoon when he'd fallen asleep, but the room was dark now.

"Biscuit?" His heart thumped. He fumbled for a lantern. After lighting it, he pulled the cat into his arms and was rewarded with another lick in the face. The cat's breath could have easily singed every hair on his head. "You're Biscuit. My cat." *Oh, God . . .*

He hopped from the bed. His breathing became panting and his legs wobbled. Covering his face with his hands, he took in large amounts of air and tried to calm down.

Had Angel's book placed all this in his mind or were these actual memories?

She'd written about Biscuit. He thought hard attempting to come up with something he hadn't read. Something she wouldn't know.

Missy Ingalls. Angel didn't know about Missy. He'd never told her. Missy had tried to kiss him under the mistletoe at her parent's Christmas party when he was twelve.

Dang! He laughed aloud. Sweat beaded on his forehead. What else could he remember?

Jessica. No. He shook his head. His mother—his *mama* —had mentioned her last night.

Jessica's breasts. She hadn't mentioned *them.*

I'm remembering!

He sat down. How could it happen so quickly? Just like the lantern he'd lit. Everything had been dark, but now light surrounded him.

I'm Billy Denton. I was William Casey O'Brien before Douglas adopted me.

He jumped up and paced. His heart beat out of his chest. Wanting to scream, he held it in.

I'm Billy Denton, and I . . .

He froze. *I love Angel. Oh, God, I love Angel.*

He had no doubt. She filled his heart and every part of his being. She'd never left him. It explained why she'd haunted his dreams and why he couldn't commit to Hannah.

Hannah. Dang! What do I do now?

He knelt beside the bed and buried his face into the cat's fur. "I remember, Biscuit." He closed his eyes, silently thanking God for the memories of his life.

"How'd you get so fat?" He poked Biscuit's side. "And where've you been hiding?" The cat patted Billy's nose, prompting a laugh. "You may be fat, but I'm starving!"

He stretched his arms high to the ceiling, then bent down and touched his toes. He finally felt alive—as if his body had just woken from a very deep sleep.

The door creaked as he pushed it wide. The harsh sound brought the silence of the house to his attention. *Is everyone asleep? Glad I didn't scream.*

He tiptoed to the kitchen, guided by the pulsing light from the lantern. The last of the cinnamon bread beckoned him. *I'm home.*

Ada's pots and pans hung where they'd always been, ready for another day of cooking. He lifted the light and peered around the rest of the room.

New curtains? The floral print that had been there when he left had been replaced by red and white gingham. He smiled. They looked nice.

With the stove unlit, he shivered. Mrs. Holloway's house had been warm. Not so here. But his parents put large logs on the fire in the living room before going to bed. If he was lucky, they'd still be burning.

He couldn't stop smiling. Tomorrow he'd share the news. Could he wait that long? Yes, it would give him time to figure out the best way to do it. Perhaps have a little fun.

He ate the cinnamon bread in a few quick bites and made his way down the hall.

The back of his mama's head brought him to an abrupt halt. The control he'd gained in his room vanished at the sight of her. Tears pooled in his eyes.

"Mama?" The word barely came out. He bit his bottom lip, swallowed hard, and wiped away a tear that trickled down his cheek. "Mama?" He took another step toward her.

She seemed to grow two inches just sitting there. Her head rose and tilted to the sound. "Richard?" She said the name, but the quiver in her voice revealed the truth.

"No, Mama." He moistened his lips. "It's me. *Billy.*"

Her body shifted. She turned with slow caution to face him. "Billy?" She placed her hand over her heart, breathing rapidly.

He ran into her embrace. With no control whatsoever, he sobbed. "I remember, Mama."

Instantly her tears joined his. She stroked his hair and held him, letting him cry on her shoulder. "*Billy.*" She said his name over and over again, intermingled with motherly kisses.

There was so much he wanted to say to her, but all he wanted right now was the feel of her. He knelt at her feet and rested in her arms for a very long time. So long, that his knees became numb. He chuckled.

"Why you laughin', Billy?" She sniffled and placed her hand against his cheek.

"I can't feel my knees, Mama." Holding his hands against the sofa, he pushed himself up from the floor and sat beside her.

She laid her head on his shoulder. "I've been prayin' for this. Prayin' every day for the last five years." Raising her head, she looked into his eyes. "How'd it happen?"

"I woke up and it was there." He faced the fire. "I think Angel's book helped. Dr. Mitchell said it takes a trigger. Something familiar. I read her journal and it sparked something."

"You read her book?" She let out a long breath.

"Yes, Mama."

"So you know how she feels 'bout you?"

He nodded. "And how I feel about her. Truthfully, I felt something for her before my memory returned. I don't think love can ever be forgotten. I felt the same for you."

Her body stiffened. This wasn't something she wanted to hear. Even being told he felt love for *her*, knowing how he felt about Angel upset her.

"Since you read her book, you know 'bout what I did to her pa." She folded her hands over her belly. Her eyes remained focused downward.

"Yes." He let out a long sigh. "There were things I wished I'd never read, but I needed to know. It must have been horrible having to kill a man."

She closed her eyes and shuddered. "Sumthin' I had to do, but wish I could forget." She opened her eyes. "Let's not talk 'bout that right now."

"All right." He tenderly rubbed her arm. "If it helps, I understand. You had no choice."

"Choices." She cleared her throat. "Makin' the right choice is what I want for you. What 'bout Hannah? An Bo?"

He stood and laid his hand on the mantel, while staring at her carved figurine. "I love Hannah, but not the way I love Angel. I didn't realize it until I kissed her."

"Angel?"

"No. *Hannah*. I believe she felt it, too. The lack of love."

"Billy, you gotta marry Hannah. An Angel's gotta marry Bo. That's how it's s'posed to be. Give it some time an think 'bout it. Don't make the biggest mistake of your life."

Sitting beside her once again, he took her dainty hand. "Marrying Hannah would be the mistake. I'd live my life regretting it. I want to be with Angel."

"You can't. The law won't allow it."

His fist tightened around the sofa cushion. "It's a ridiculous law. Angel had a white father. There's no reason why she shouldn't be allowed to marry me."

"By law she's a Negro. It's sumthin' we can't change." Her voice softened. "I'm sorry, but you can never marry her."

What could he say? Changing the law would be impossible. Interracial marriage would never be allowed. But how would marrying Bo be any different for her? He'd be marrying a woman who was half *white*.

He wanted to scream. This time happiness had nothing to do with it.

"Is this going to be a habit?" His father asked, entering the room.

Billy dismissed his frustration and jumped to his feet. He rushed to him and gave him a bear hug that took the man's breath. "I'm home, Father."

The moment he spoke, his hug was returned with a fierceness that made them both lose their breath and laugh. "Billy?"

"Yes, sir."

"He remembered, Douglas," his mama said.

As she stood to join them, she placed her hand on her lower back and groaned. Billy put his arm around her, helping her. This was the sixth time she'd been through the discomforts of pregnancy, and he couldn't recall ever hearing her complain.

New tears formed in their eyes.

Instead of going back to bed, his father pulled a chair close to the sofa and they all sat.

"I thought I didn't like Donald," Billy said. "Then I remembered he and Richard were always a pain." He laughed, but then gave his brother a second thought. "If Donald truly cares for Hannah, maybe that's what's supposed to be."

"What?" his father asked.

"Billy says he's in love with Angel," his mama replied with a frown.

"After only two days?" The man's eyebrows rose.

"More like eighteen years," Billy said. "As I told Mama earlier, my love for her never died."

"But you were children then."

"No." Billy wouldn't hear it. "We were children when we used to climb trees and catch frogs. We stopped being children long before I left."

"Kissin' don't make you grown up," his mama whispered.

"No, it doesn't. But the kind of love we feel for each other does. It's a love like the two of you share. One I know will be there forever. She's my best friend, but I want more. I want to live with her. Have a family with her—"

"You can't!" His mama's head shook rapidly. "Douglas, tell him. He won't listen to me. The law won't allow it!"

"Calm down, honey." His father rested his hand on the unborn child. "Think of the baby."

"I am. My *first*-born. I don't want him hurt."

"Billy." His father spoke with a tone he'd not forgotten. "She's right. Do you honestly think you can marry her, live in Memphis, and raise a family together?"

"I—I don't know. I hadn't thought it through." He looked away from them. "I have a lot of thinking to do." He stood, looking down on them. Their eyes reflected their concern. "Don't worry about me. I grew up these past five years. I'm capable of making adult decisions. I'm grateful I know who I am and found out before I made the wrong choice."

"Don't discount Hannah," his father said. "She's a lovely girl. I know she loves you."

"Does she?" Billy didn't need a response. He bent down and kissed his mama on the cheek, then hugged his father's neck. "I love you both. What I love most is that even if I hadn't regained my memory, I have no doubt you'd have still loved me. You'd have called me Brian even though it wasn't the name you gave me."

"Yes, we would have," his father said.

"Dang!" His mama sat up straight, breaking the solemn moment.

"Is it the baby?" His father placed his hand protectively over her abdomen.

"Yep. But don't fret. He ain't comin' yet. He's just tryin' his darndest to break my ribs."

"Can I feel?" Billy asked.

"Course you can." She placed his hand on her belly.

"Paulette never kicked this hard." He moved his hand to another spot. "It has to be a boy."

"You remember Paulette?"

He nodded. "I remember everything."

Chapter 36

Maybe putting Biscuit in Brian's room hadn't been the best idea, but Angel was at her wits end. She had to do all she could to help him regain his memories before he left for good.

Even if he went away and married Hannah, she could never marry Bo. It wouldn't be fair to him. She doubted he'd want to share their bed with Billy's memory.

Sleepless nights were taking their toll. And now the obnoxious rooster was already crowing. With eyes half shut, she dressed, then trudged through the yard to the barn.

"Mornin', Spot," she mumbled and took a seat on the milking stool. She rested her head against the cow's warm belly while her hands mindlessly yanked and pulled.

"Need some help?" Brian's voice brought her fully awake.

She looked over her shoulder. "Nope." He'd combed his hair this morning. She turned her attention back to Spot and couldn't help but grin. It was an improvement.

"I'm sure Spot appreciates the lanolin cream." He tossed a hay bale on the ground beside her.

"Spot likes warm hands." Her heart beat out of her chest. She closed her eyes. Not only had he combed his hair, he'd also bathed. The fresh scent her mama added to the lye soap overpowered the earthy aroma of the barn.

"Most cows do." He sighed. "Buttercup hated your cold hands."

She giggled. "Buttercup kicked over the pail a time or two because of it. I learned quick." Her heart stopped. "How'd you know 'bout Buttercup?"

"I remember." He breathed the words directly into her ear.

She swung around to face him, heart pounding. Before she could say a word, he took her hand and pressed something into it. She opened her palm. "My angel?"

"I'm giving it back to you."

"But . . ." Her breath hitched and her vision blurred from the sea of water covering her eyes.

"You gave it to me to remember." He smoothed her tears with his thumb. "And you said you wanted it back one day. Now I want the *real* Angel."

"Billy?"

"I love you, Angel. More than ever." He inched closer and closer.

"I never quit lovin' you." She made no attempt to stop him.

His warm breath covered her face. She closed her eyes waiting for the kiss she'd ached for. His lips molded to hers, then parted to go even deeper. It took her back to that kiss she'd held on to for all these years. His arms encircled her waist. He pulled her body closer while their tongues danced, creating a kiss unlike anything she'd remembered.

Her body tingled with no trace of a chill. They briefly came up for air, then kissed again with hungering fervor.

"It's New Year's Eve," he whispered, drawing his fingers through her hair. "We'll be playing hide and seek."

They remained cheek-to-cheek. She wanted this moment to last forever. "I wanna hide with you. Hide and never be found again."

"I want that, too." He placed tiny kisses across her face, then returned to her lips for another deep kiss.

"What are we gonna—" *Oh Lawdy, that feels good.* His mouth had moved to her neck, sucking gently; warm and hungry. "What are we gonna do?"

He worked his way back up, and kissed her again. "I love you." He wasted no time unbuttoning her coat, then slipped his hands inside and moved them to her back. They were warm, caressing her with tenderness. He slid them along her sides, gliding over her curves.

"What 'bout Hannah?" She didn't want him to stop, but had to know.

"I'll tell her," he rasped, then nuzzled into her neck.

"And Bo? What 'bout Bo?" With closed eyes, she tilted her head back and allowed him access to her neck and chest. He buried his face into her body and moved his lips downward toward her breasts. Even through the fabric his hot breath penetrated her skin. "Oh, Billy . . ."

A violent jerk wrenched him away.

Bo flung him across the stable floor and sent him tumbling to the ground. "What you doin' to my woman?" he screamed and went after him again.

"Stop it, Bo!" She jumped to her feet and grabbed his arms.

Billy shook his head and stood, but then dropped down wincing with pain.

"You hurt him!" She pushed Bo to the side and knelt beside Billy.

"I'll hurt him even more!" Bo brought up his fists. "Stay outta this, Angel!"

"Stay outta this?" She fumed. Her chest heaved as she tried to catch her breath. "I love him!"

"You love *him?*" Bo scowled. "Why'd you ask *me* to kiss you?"

Billy's head spun around to face her. "You kissed him?"

"I had to know. You kissed Hannah. Didn't it tell you sumthin'?" The hurt in Billy's eyes turned instantly to understanding.

"Yes, it did." He let out a long sigh. "It did."

Bo's mouth drew into a snarl. "You should be shamed a yourselves. Playin' with hearts like they was toys. I waited five years for you to become a woman, an this is what I get? You deserves each other. I's done with you." He waved his hands dismissing them, then walked away.

"Oh, Billy." She sat on the cold ground. "What'd we do?"

He inched his body next to hers. "What had to be done. He's hurt. I know how *I'd* feel if I lost you. It would've been easier if you hadn't kissed him."

"I wish now I hadn't. This is gonna get harder. You hafta tell Hannah."

"I will. But I believe she'll take it better than Bo. And Donald will have a good reason to celebrate the New Year."

She looked toward the barn door, half expecting Bo to return. Maybe she should have followed him. Tried to talk to him.

No, this was best. He'd hurt for a time, but in the end he'd realize she'd done him a favor.

"Can you walk?" She helped him to his feet.

"With your help." He rolled his eyes. "I've twisted my ankle."

"That's what you get for kissin' me." She nudged him in the ribs.

"Is it?" He turned her in his arms and pulled her close.

Their bodies fit perfectly together. Standing in an embrace was even finer than sitting on the stool and kissing. As if her thought prompted his action, they kissed again, and again, and again.

* * *

"It seems you've already made up your mind, Brian," Mrs. Holloway said. "That is . . . *Billy.*" She shook her head. "Oh, my. It will take some getting used to."

"Yes. I want to stay here." After the blow-up in the barn, Billy decided to break the news to Mrs. Holloway before everyone in the house knew. She'd given him a home all these years. The least he could do was to give her an explanation.

"I understand why. And I promise I won't tell a soul about Angel. But you need to follow your heart. I imagine Dr. Mitchell will be disappointed. He cares for you and made assumptions about you and Hannah."

"I'll tell him when the time's right. Besides, this is my home. I belong here."

"I'm rather fond of it here myself. But, *my* home will always be in Mobile."

"What about Uncle Harper?"

Her dreamy eyes revealed her heart. "We have some decisions of our own to make. He's asked me to marry him." She chuckled. "I'm old, but I'm not dead. And Becky needs a father."

"That's wonderful! But how? If he's here and you're in Mobile?"

"I'm persuasive." She winked. "When you get to be our age, your old bones don't care for the cold. Harper wants to move to Mobile. He's speaking to Mr. Denton about it now. Making arrangements for the sale of the woodshop."

Billy folded his arms over his chest. "That must have been some kiss all those years ago."

She coyly tilted her head and grinned. "All those years ago?" Her eyes opened wide. "As I said, I'm not dead."

Was she implying they'd kissed again? "I'm happy for you. And Becky, too."

"What about Joe?"

"I have a feeling he'll stay here. He's taken to Jeriah. Not to mention Uziah. I think he's finally found his family."

"You're wrong about that." Mrs. Holloway pursed her lips. "*We* are Joe's family. All of us. But I believe you're right. That little boy would miss Joe if he went away."

He put his arm around her shoulder. "Can you help me to the kitchen?"

"An old lady helping a young man?" She shook her head. "Fate *is* smiling on us."

"I'm going to miss you." He hobbled beside her.

"Let's not talk about that right now. I've shed enough tears already."

* * *

It didn't take long for everyone to learn Billy had regained his memory. Emilia found it *fascinating* and picked his brain about family tidbits that might have been withheld from her.

He'd kept his distance from Angel in anticipation of Hannah's arrival, though they'd shared several steamy glances at the supper table. After their kisses in the barn, he'd thought of little else. But what would he do if he couldn't marry her? There had to be a way.

Still early in the evening, almost everyone had gathered in the living room waiting for the traditional game of hide-and-seek. Joe would be coming over as soon as Uziah was in bed. Billy had missed him since their arrival. But with all he'd been coping with, he was grateful Joe had so easily fallen into place with his family. He'd smiled more in Memphis than he ever had in Mobile.

With a full belly, courtesy of Ada's fine cooking, and an urge to shut his eyes and sleep, Billy sat with his leg propped up on a stool close to the fire. His foot was so swollen that his boot wouldn't fit and his socked foot appreciated the warmth.

Angel stood on the far side of the room talking to Christina and Emilia. Even so, he felt her presence as if she was right beside him. He had one important thing to do before he was free to love her. Then regardless of the law, he'd find a way.

"See," Paulette said. "I told you. Billy's back." She tugged on Dr. Mitchell's arm.

Hannah followed right behind. After depositing the two of them directly beside Billy, Paulette fled the room, giggling, with Becky shadowing her.

Billy attempted to rise, but a stabbing pain kept him right where he was.

"What did she mean, *Billy's* back?" Dr. Mitchell asked. "And what did you do to your foot?" He knelt down and examined his ankle.

"I took a tumble in the barn. It's not broken. Just twisted."

"I'm the doctor." He looked over the top of his glasses. "Mind if I make my own diagnosis?"

"Please do." Billy waved his hand toward his ankle and bowed his head in playful submission.

His mama waddled over to them holding her belly. "I told him he should prop it up." She placed her hands on Billy's shoulders, rubbing in a way that intensified his desire to sleep. He closed his eyes and sighed with contentment.

Hannah moved beside him and rested her hand on his arm. "This is what happens when I'm not here to take care of you."

All the attention overwhelmed him. He briefly opened his eyes to gaze at Angel, then closed them again, retaining her image in his mind. "It was an accident," he muttered. Luckily Bo hadn't told anyone what truly happened. For now, he and Angel had a secret.

"You're right," Dr. Mitchell said. "It's not broken."

Billy opened his eyes and grinned with a very obvious *I told you so.*

"But it's swollen," the doctor added. "Best to stay off it as much as you can. Ice would help bring down the swelling."

After an, *I told you so* of her own, his mama motioned for Richard, then instructed him to have Ada prepare an ice bag. He sprinted from the room.

Dr. Mitchell stood, but gave Billy another firm glance. "Stay off it as much as you can. I mean that, Brian. You don't want to make it worse. There could be a hairline fracture. Stress could cause it to actually break."

"*Billy.*" Billy said.

"What?" Dr. Mitchell pulled back and tipped his head.

"I'm Billy. I remember."

Hannah gasped. "How?" She bent down, hugged his neck, and started to cry.

He proceeded to explain how he'd woken up with his restored memories.

"We were up late last night," his father said. "He told Cora first. We had a lot to talk about." He patted Dr. Mitchell on the back. "I'm sorry you weren't here to witness it for yourself."

"And it happened just like that?" The doctor snapped his fingers. "I'm amazed. Nothing out of the ordinary happened?"

"Well," Billy looked toward Angel. "I think a lot of unusual things have happened since I've been home." He didn't want to mention the journal with Hannah present and hoped his mama wouldn't either. "Oh, and my cat woke me up. I knew his name."

Dr. Mitchell tapped his index finger on his chin. "Hmm. This is remarkable."

"Remarkable?" Hannah was giddy. "Daddy, for once stop being a doctor! It's a miracle!" She flung her arms around Billy and kissed his cheek.

This would be harder than he realized. She acted loving and attentive. *How will I do it?*

"It's not going to be easy for me to call you Billy," she said. "But I'll do my best. I may slip now and then." She fingered the locket at her neck.

"I understand." He took her hand. "If you slip, I'll forgive you."

"That's right, Hannah," his mama added. "Billy's very patient."

He'd simply been nice to Hannah, but Angel must have misunderstood. She rushed from the room without looking back. Following her was impossible. Not only would it raise suspicions, but his foot wouldn't allow it.

Emilia scowled at him, then hurried after Angel. What had Angel told her?

Richard returned with a cloth sack filled with ice and handed it to Billy.

"Thank you." Billy smiled the best he could. The cold might help his foot, but that was the least of his troubles.

"You're welcome." His brother returned the smile and walked away. Eventually, Billy needed to spend time with him. Maybe they could learn how to be brothers again.

"Did we miss the game?" Uncle Harper asked, clapping his hands together. He paraded into the room with Mrs. Holloway on his arm.

"You're going to play?" Billy asked.

Mrs. Holloway chuckled. "Harper's feeling his youth." She led him to a sofa. "But I believe we'd do best to sit and watch. I prefer to limit the number of times I climb those stairs."

"Long as I'm with you." Harper patted her cheek. He then pointed to Billy's foot. "It broke?"

"No. But I still have to stay off it."

"Shame." Harper shook his head. "Where's Mary?"

"Mother is having another one of her headaches," his father said. "She's gone to bed."

"Would you like me to take a look at her tomorrow?" Dr. Mitchell asked. "I don't mind."

Billy leaned his head back and closed his eyes. The extreme cold from the ice numbed his ankle in a painfully pleasant way. He listened as his father agreed to have Dr. Mitchell examine his grandmother. She'd been having a lot of headaches and Billy feared the worst.

Why'd he have so much to worry about? It was New Year's Eve. He wanted to celebrate with Angel. Yet she'd left the room—undoubtedly upset—and he was stuck in a chair with a bad ankle.

"Hannah?" Donald's voice prompted Billy to open one eye.

"Yes?" Her sugar-sweet voice intensified.

"Did you enjoy visiting your grandparents?" He moved closer, blocking the heat from the fire.

"Yes. But I'm glad to be here. I wanted to spend the New Year with you. *All* of you." She giggled nervously.

Billy played possum. Closed his eyes tight and listened.

"Have you eaten?" Donald asked. "There's plenty left in the kitchen. Even chess pie."

"I love chess pie." The swish of her skirt skimmed Billy's ear. Without giving him a second thought, she left. Though he'd secretly wished this would happen, he almost found it offensive. Didn't she know Donald was interested in something more than her appetite?

Billy considered making an attempt to follow them, but the warmth from the fire and his heavy lids kept him seated.

Too much trouble.

* * *

Billy woke with a start, jerking in his chair. He stared upward, bringing into focus whoever shook him.

"Are you all right, Billy?" Dr. Mitchell pulled up a chair beside him.

Billy glanced around the now-empty room. "A little tired. Did I miss the game? Where is everyone?" He sat upright, then stretched and yawned, trying to animate his stiff body.

Dr. Mitchell let out a laugh. "You were snoring so loudly they decided to leave you alone. They found other things to occupy their time until the game." He pulled on the chain of his pocket watch, flipped it open, and sighed. "Nine o'clock. Three more hours until midnight. When do you normally start?"

"Ten." Billy grinned. "I remember that, too."

"I'm happy for you." Dr. Mitchell removed his glasses and polished them on a handkerchief. "I'm in awe of how rapidly your memories returned."

"Rapidly? It's been five years."

"Yes, but when they came back, it was all at once. Remarkable." He returned his spectacles to his face, crossed his legs, and gazed at the fire.

"Doctor . . ." The time to tell him had come.

"Please, Billy. I've considered you a friend for a long time now. Call me Harvey."

Billy's stomach knotted. "Harvey? It doesn't seem appropriate."

The man laughed. "It's been my name all my life. I think it's quite appropriate. You're the one who keeps everyone guessing." He wiggled his brows and grinned.

"All right then. Harvey." Billy readjusted himself. He'd been sitting too long. "This won't be easy." He whispered the words, and it pained him to say them. "I'm not going back to Mobile."

The grin on Harvey's face disappeared. "You're staying longer then?"

"No, sir. I'm staying for good. I—I don't know how to tell Hannah."

"You plan to break my daughter's heart?" He stood. "Why did you ask permission to marry her? Regaining your memory of the past shouldn't affect your new memories. Did you forget you love her?" His final words stung. He turned his back on Billy.

"Sir, I . . ." He was utterly helpless. *Dang ankle.* "I'm sorry. But do you remember when I told you all those years ago that I wanted to wait to court her? At least until I knew for certain there wasn't another woman who held my heart?" He took a deep breath. "It's good I waited."

Harvey whipped around. "You may not have been *courting*, but she expects to marry you."

"If that's true, why'd she leave so readily with my brother? Haven't you noticed their attraction to one another?"

"Donald?" His brows drew in so far that his glasses slipped down his nose. "I . . ."

"You noticed." Billy motioned to the chair. "Please sit down."

"I'd better. When Margaret learns there won't be a wedding anytime soon, she'll be sorely disappointed. She cares for you." He sat and leaned back.

"She may not be disappointed for long. Donald seems rather eager." Billy leaned toward him. "I don't believe I'll break her heart. If I'm not mistaken, we've *both* come to realize our love is more like that of family. As if she was my sister. I love her, but I'm not *in* love with her."

Harvey rubbed his chin. "But, you *are* in love. Someone else holds your heart."

"Did your examination of my ankle reveal that?" Billy laughed.

"No. But I'm not blind *or* deaf. You said yourself it was good you waited. Are you going to tell me who she is?"

Harvey Mitchell had been his best friend for five years, so why was it hard to tell him? Of course, up until two days ago he'd had every intention of marrying his daughter.

"You're hesitant," Harvey said. "If you don't want to tell me, I'll guess."

Billy arched an eyebrow. "Yes?"

"Your dark-eyed girl." Harvey's voice softened in a manner Billy didn't recognize. "Angel."

Billy nodded. "I didn't tell you everything about how my memory came back."

Harvey folded his arms over his chest. "Go on."

"Angel'd been keeping a journal all these years. I gave it to her before I left. Asked her to write down things to help us remember growing up here. She did an excellent job." He paused to observe the change in Harvey's expression. Once again, he became the analytical doctor examining his patient. "I fell asleep after reading it. When I woke—well —I already told you about that."

Harvey tapped his chin with his finger. "Remarkable."

"You think her journal made the difference?"

"I'd say so. It sounds like a logical trigger." Harvey smiled, then patted his leg. "I may need to write a paper about your case."

Billy calmed, relieved to see him smile. "Harvey, I could use some advice."

"Medical advice?"

"Not exactly. Mama's not happy about my feelings for Angel. She begged me to marry Hannah. But I have to follow my heart. Considering the racial issue, it won't be easy."

"No, it won't. The South isn't ready for what you're suggesting. I doubt it ever will be." He stood, paced a few times, then faced him. "I can't advise you what to do regarding Angel. Though I wish you'd reconsider. Mobile won't be the same without you."

"You want me to reconsider my decision to stay, or my decision *not* to marry Hannah?"

"I don't want you to marry my daughter if you don't love her that way, but I doubt I'll ever have another friend like you. I'll miss you."

"If I promise to come for a visit will that suffice?"

"For now. Besides, I have family here. We won't be strangers." Harvey nodded toward the hallway. "They're returning. I won't say anything to Hannah. I'll leave that to you."

Billy breathed a relieved sigh. Telling Hannah would be hard, but he'd dreaded telling Dr. Mitchell. *Harvey,* his friend. Realizing he'd miss him more than Hannah solidified his decision.

Chapter 37

"Why didn't he tell her?" Angel sat on a wooden bench facing the dormant gardens. She didn't want to be out in the cold, but with twenty people inside, privacy was impossible.

"He's still a silly boy," Emilia said. "That's why. You should marry Bo."

"She's right, Angel," Christina said. "Billy's my brother, but he's got a lot a growin' up to do. Bo's a man. And I know he loves you."

The three of them had grown close the past year. Coming into womanhood had made the difference. They'd shared many secrets. So when Billy kissed her, and she'd made up her mind not to marry Bo, it seemed appropriate to tell them. She wished she hadn't.

"Did you see how he looked at her?" Angel blubbered and covered her face with her hands.

"*I* did," Emilia said. "He's lovesick. *And* Aunt Cora loves her. I saw that, too."

"Marry Bo," Christina urged. "You'll have beautiful babies."

Angel sobbed even harder. She didn't want to have Bo's babies. She wanted Billy's.

As Emilia paced, Christina moved beside Angel and placed an arm around her. "You know it wouldn't have worked out anyway."

Angel's chin quivered. "I ain't white enough." She turned her body and buried her head into Christina's shoulder.

"Shh…" Christina held her and let her cry.

"I'm getting cold!" Emilia fussed. "I'm going in. You two stay here as long as you like." She knelt in front of Angel. "Go find Bo. Tell him you're sorry and marry him." She giggled as she stood. "He's fine to look at. Maybe even finer with his clothes off."

Angel's head jerked upright. "Shame on you for sayin' such a thing, Emilia!"

"Don't tell me you haven't thought it," Emilia smirked.

Angel cinched her lips tight. "I . . ."

"Knew you had." Emilia strode away, humming all the while.

"You know how she is," Christina said. "Don't let it bother you."

What bothered her was Emilia was right. She'd thought about it. Curiosity more than anything. But since Billy'd arrived, he was the only man on her mind. She couldn't wash away the memory of their heated kisses.

They were far from being children. She finally understood what her mama had told her about men. Billy wanted more than a kiss. The bigger problem was, she wanted it, too.

"You think I should marry Bo?" Angel sniffled and dabbed her tears with her coat sleeve.

"Yes. Go find him. If he's as mad as you said, he might decide to leave for good."

Angel shook her head. "I'm so confused."

Christina patted her back. "Go find Bo." She stood. "Maybe the two of you will play your own game of hide-and-seek. I'll tell everyone you're sick and you went home to bed. Then no one will come looking for you."

"I know Billy won't." Angel pouted and sat up. "Happy New Year, Christina."

"You don't *sound* happy. Maybe Bo can fix that." Christina smiled, then walked away.

Since it was getting dark, Angel decided she'd better act quickly. She hadn't stopped scolding herself for being so blinded by love for Billy. What if he'd become one of those kinds of men her mama had warned her about? Those kisses in the barn were leading up to what he really wanted from her. He'd take it, then marry Hannah and forget about her.

Bo had been patient. He wanted to marry her. Maybe in time she'd come to love him the way she loved Billy. The *real* Billy. Not the one holding Hannah's hand.

She'd go find Bo. But what would she say to him. A simple, *I'm sorry*, wouldn't be good enough. She'd have to tell him *yes*.

* * *

"Jeriah made this for you." Joe handed Billy a wooden crutch. "I hepped."

Billy had never received a more useful gift. "Thank you." He carefully lifted his foot from the stool. "Will you help me stand?"

"Course," Jeriah said. "Figgered you'd be needin' to use the outhouse. You been sittin' in this here chair for long time."

"You're right. So please don't make me laugh." He propped the crutch under his arm and leaned into it, holding his injured foot off the ground. "This is wonderful, Jeriah."

"Glad you like it. Though I reckon you'd best not play no hide-n-seek."

There was only one person Billy wanted to seek. Angel. Nearly ten o'clock and she hadn't come back. "You're right. I'd better not play, but I do need to use the outhouse."

"Need hep?" Joe asked.

"No. I can do *that* myself. Stay here and enjoy yourself. And thank you again."

He limped down the hall, then paused and glanced over his shoulder. It warmed him seeing Jeriah with his arm around Joe, laughing.

"Hannah?" Billy was about to go out the back door and there she was, sitting in the kitchen with Donald. "Hey, Donald." He forced a smile at his brother.

"Billy?" Her eyes were wider than the pie tin in the middle of the table. "You're *walking*."

"Thanks to Jeriah and Joe. Did I interrupt something?"

Donald awkwardly stood. "N—No. We were *talking*."

Talking in a room far away from everyone else, believing he'd never be able to walk in on them. *Convenient.* "And eating pie." He pointed to the empty tin. "I'll be back in a few minutes, then *I'd* like to talk to you, Hannah."

"You know the game is about to start," Donald said. Laughter erupted from the living room.

"Yes, I know. But this is important."

"All right," Hannah said. Her brows dipped slightly. "I'll wait here for you."

"I'll go," Donald said. He offered Hannah an encouraging smile, then an apologetic eye to Billy. He walked away without looking back.

Billy took care of business as quickly as his impairment allowed and returned to find Hannah waiting as she'd promised. He hobbled to the wash basin and cleaned his hands.

"It was nice of them to make that for you." She pointed to the crutch. Her voice sounded foreign—her words forced.

"Hannah, I have to tell you something."

She looked down and drew invisible lines on the table. "I have something to tell you, too."

"Please let me go first." He made his way to the table and sat.

She nodded, but wouldn't look at him.

"I'm staying in Memphis. I won't be going back to Mobile." He leaned back in his chair, waiting for her to lash out. Cry, perhaps?

Silence.

"Hannah, did you hear me?"

She nodded.

"Aren't you going to say something?"

She lifted her head and met his gaze. "I knew. When you kissed me, I knew."

"Was it that bad?" She'd hurt his pride, but he wished he hadn't asked. *So immature.*

"You've changed." She spoke flatly while nervously wringing her hands. "You truly aren't Brian any longer. It started when your family came to Mobile."

He'd changed? "When you met Donald." He defensively crossed his arms.

She looked away. "Yes, when I met Donald."

He stood and turned his back on her. Why was he angry? This was the last thing to take care of before seeking out Angel and getting on with his life. Somehow, it still hurt.

I'm a better man than this. I can't fault her for caring about someone else when I was doing the same thing.

"Brian?" Her voice quivered.

He faced her.

She undid the locket and extended it to him. "I know it was expensive. I can't keep it."

"No." He folded his hand over hers. "Keep it. You've been a good friend." Looking in her eyes he saw the same girl he'd seen all those years ago. "You were the first person I saw when I woke up in the hospital. You cared about me even then."

"Daddy always let me help." Her face softened, and she took his hand. "When I saw you looking so lost it hurt my heart."

"I *was* lost." He rubbed her hand with his thumb. "And now I'm where I belong." He released her knowing everything would be all right.

"I'll never forget you, *Brian.* And hopefully I'll get to know *Billy* as a very good friend."

He nodded. "Who knows? You could be my sister-in-law."

Her cheeks flushed. She coyly dipped her head downward. "I'm sorry if I hurt you. I've been confused this past week." Pulling a handkerchief from her sleeve, she dabbed at her eyes.

"So have I. I'm sorry, too."

She peered down the hallway. Voices and laughter grew even louder.

He could tell she wanted to be elsewhere. "You said you had something to tell me, but if I'm not mistaken it's already been said." She silently nodded. "Go on, then. Please. Enjoy yourself. And don't feel badly about Donald. He's a good man."

She stood, hugged him quickly, and left.

Was it wrong not to tell her about Angel? And where was she? Since he couldn't play and didn't feel like being in the middle of it all, he stayed where he was to gather his thoughts.

Have I changed? He rested his head on the table.

Hannah had slipped easily out of his life. Almost too easily. Though his pride had been hurt, his heart was relieved.

"Are you pouting?" Emilia's voice raised his head.

"No. Resting."

"You slept all evening." She laughed. "You snore very loud. I pity the woman you marry."

He reached for his crutch. He had no intention of talking to her any longer than he had to. "Have you seen Angel?"

"Hmm . . ." She pointed a finger into her chin and rolled her eyes upward. "Not for some time. I assume she's off with Bo somewhere." She pierced Billy with her eyes and a satisfied grin.

"Bo?"

"Yes. You remember him don't you? Tall, muscular, *colored.*"

Billy's heart pounded. "Why's she with Bo? She and I—"

"She and you, what?" She placed her hands on her hips. "She saw through you, Billy. She saw you with Hannah. Hugging her. Holding her hand."

"But I'm not with Hannah any longer. I'm staying in Memphis. I love Angel." Fear rose within him, turning his stomach. How could she have thought there was more to his actions than simple courtesy? "She doesn't love Bo. I know she loves me."

"Then you have a problem, cousin." She released a haughty sigh. "She's gone to accept Bo's proposal. You should leave her alone. She's better off with someone of her own kind."

Good thing she walked away. Otherwise, he might have said something unkind. He needed to find Angel now more than ever. To tell her the truth before it was too late. He wasn't about to lose her again.

Chapter 38

Propped up on his crutch, Billy pounded on Bo's door. He'd started by simply knocking but got no answer. *What are they doing in there?*

Finally, the door opened. He peered over Bo's shoulder. "I need to talk to Angel."

Bo scowled. "What makes you think she's here?"

"Don't do this, Bo. Emilia told me she was with you. Please let me talk to her."

"Emilia? Reckon you ain't been here long 'nuff to know not to listen to her." He kept his hand on the door, un-moving. "Angel ain't here."

Maybe Billy didn't know Emilia very well, but he also knew little about Bo. He could be hiding her inside. "Have you seen her?"

The scowl on Bo's face hardened. "Why you messin' with me? I ain't seen Angel since you had your lips all over her." He backed away and started closing the door.

"Wait!" Billy pushed against it.

"What for? I ain't got nuttin' I wanna say to you."

Billy's heart thumped in anticipation of a fight. "I need to find her."

"Ain't my problem. She made it clear she chose you. Leave me be." He pushed the door shut and locked it.

Emilia had been wrong. Angel hadn't gone back to him. But she wasn't at her own house. Unless Bo was a good liar, she wasn't in his. There was only one other possibility.

He stared at the path leading to the stables. *Dang. Why does it have to be so far away?*

Harvey would scold him tomorrow, but he wasn't about to go through the night not knowing where she was or being able to explain his actions. Maybe she hadn't had time to talk to Bo and was working up the courage. If so, he had to find her quickly.

Without the crutch, he'd never have been able to make it to the barn. Determination kept him plodding along one crippled step at a time. A frozen crystal melted on his face. He lifted his lantern and looked upward. *Snow?* Tiny flakes fell around him, sparse but steady. No matter where she might be, he hoped she was warm.

The barn door was heavier than ever with only one hand to open it. As he stepped through, the undeniable sound of Angel crying filled his ears and broke his heart.

He followed it to a stall in the center of the stable. Crying so hard, she hadn't heard him hobbling across the barn floor. Huddled in the corner with her knees drawn up to her chest and her head resting upon them, her shoulders jerked with every sob.

As carefully as he could, he leaned the crutch against the side of the stall and slowly knelt beside her. He set the lantern on the ground, but it wasn't until he placed his hand on her knee that she noticed him.

She pulled back; startled. "Billy?" Her chin quivered. "What are you doin' here?"

"Looking for you." She shivered, so he scooted closer. "You need to go inside. You'll freeze out here."

She shook her head. "Don't want to. You go back. I know Hannah's waitin' for you."

"No, she's not." He took her hand. When she tried to pull away, he held it even tighter. "I told her I'm staying in Memphis."

"You did?" She sucked in her breath and sniffled.

"Of course. I told you I would." He moved around and sat on his bottom next to her. "I know you saw me with her earlier, but it meant nothing. She hugged me, and yes, I held her hand. But it was out of friendship and nothing more." His words didn't appease her. She cried even harder. "Angel, it's over with Hannah. I promise you. We both knew it wasn't meant to be."

"I want to believe you." She wiped her eyes with the heel of her hand. "I thought . . ."

"Angel," He moved his fingers into her hair. "I love *you.* That's never going to change."

"Oh, Billy!" She wrapped her arms around him. "Emilia and Christina told me I should go back to Bo. But—I couldn't do it!"

Thank God.

He buried his face into her hair, breathing in the essence of her. "Please don't ever leave me."

"But what are we gonna do? I may be free, but the law won't allow us to be together." She placed her hands on the sides of his face, forcing him to look at her.

"Maybe we can't get married under the law, but in my heart I'll be yours forever." He stared deeply into her dark eyes. "Tell me you feel the same."

Breathing deeply, her chest heaved. "I—I do. But, I'm scared."

He took her hands and kissed each one in turn, then cradled one against his face. "Say you love me and I'll swear my love to you. We'll make marriage vows with our hearts."

Her hand trembled against his cheek. "I've always loved you, Billy."

He pulled her hand to his chest. "Do you feel my heart? It's never beat harder. Until I walked in and saw you face-to-face, I wasn't able to understand why I couldn't commit to Hannah. But when I looked into your eyes, I knew *you* were in my heart. No one could ever take your place."

"I feel it." She flattened her hand against him, then tentatively moved it over his chest.

He couldn't hold back any longer and brought her to him with a hungering kiss.

She melted into his body without reservation, just as she'd done earlier. He kissed her over and over again until they were no longer cold and every trace of fear had disappeared from her face.

"We need to go inside," he said, then kissed the tip of her nose. "They'll wonder what happened to us."

"Christina was gonna tell everyone I was sick so they wouldn't miss me." She lowered her eyes. "She thinks I've gone to Bo."

"So let's go back and show them what a *remarkable* recovery you've made. As Dr. Mitchell would say." He chuckled, then lifted her hand to his lips and kissed it. "Besides,

Mama's expecting me. She's probably frantic by now thinking I fell into the well."

"Let me help you," she said, rising to her feet. After hoisting him up, she handed him the crutch, then put her arm around his waist.

"I like this part." He encircled her tiny waist with his arm. "Angel." He swallowed hard, uncertain how he should say this. "I want you as my wife in every way." His heart thumped. He watched her face, making sure she understood.

She blinked twice before nodding her head. "I want that, too." She nestled against his chest.

He brushed his lips across the top of her head. "You were in my dreams almost every night. An angel I never imagined could be real. But nothing imaginary could make me feel the way you did. I never should've doubted your existence."

Standing on her tip-toes, she placed her hand behind his head and pulled him to her. She kissed him deeply, drawing him into her with a fierceness he hadn't expected. "Can a dream kiss like that?" Licking her lips, she waited.

He caressed the side of her face. "Once. A dream I'll never forget."

She quivered. "Next time we're alone, we'll go beyond your dreams."

The implication of her words caused heat to explode through his veins. Had she not been born a slave, he'd marry her immediately. He'd take her away somewhere wonderful and private to consummate their love. Their situation wasn't typical, but their desires were that of every couple in love. Why should they be denied?

"Where?" He had to control the rate of his breathing.

Her brows wove and she bit her bottom lip. She pointed to his foot. "If it weren't for your ankle, we could go to the attic. No one would bother us there."

"If that's the only place we can be alone—aside from this barn—then I'll get up there. Even if it kills me." He'd climb the highest mountain if it meant making love to her.

"That wouldn't be good for either of us." She laughed softly. Then her head dropped and she sighed. "What we're plannin' ain't right. It's not how it's s'posed to be."

"Neither is the law." Her doubt tugged at his heart. He'd never consider having her unless she willingly gave herself. He loved her too much to have her regret it.

She studied his face. "Then, we'll make our own vows. I'll marry you without the law. We'll swear our love and let God hear our words."

Relieved, he thought hard, weaving a plan. "After midnight, when everyone's asleep, meet me in the attic. Bring Mrs. Moss's Bible with you. And bring some blankets. We'll need them."

They faced each other silently; their breath mingling in the cold air. His heart thumped out of control, anticipating what was to come. Maybe they were rushing things, but he didn't want to wait any longer. Tonight they'd vow their love and she'd become his wife in every way.

* * *

Angel crept as quietly as she could into her house, tip-toeing to her bedroom. Her mama was sleeping, most likely with Uziah by her side. Jeriah and Joe were at the main house playing hide-and-seek, waiting for midnight.

Her mind reeled. She'd come close to going to Bo. She'd stood on his doorstep for nearly thirty minutes contemplating whether or not to knock. But she hadn't been able to do it. She didn't love him that way. She never would.

Why'd I doubt Billy?

She closed her eyes, fearing what they were about to do. Making love to him would be easy, but the repercussions could scar them forever. They'd never be accepted. Would they have to go the rest of their lives hiding in the shadows?

She poured water into her wash basin and cleaned herself thoroughly. Then she cleaned her teeth and rubbed her mama's rose-scented cream over her entire body. Tonight she'd become a woman in every sense of the word. She'd finally know the pleasure she'd heard her mama and Jeriah share so many times.

What's so different 'bout me an Billy?

Jeriah hadn't been able to marry her mama until the law changed. But they'd always loved each other. They'd become man and wife long before the state recognized their union.

Billy an me are the same. Maybe in time, the law would change for them, too.

It was time to return to the house to bid everyone *Happy New Year.* She'd linger in the kitchen—easily finding something to occupy her time—while waiting for everyone to go to bed. Once there was complete silence and no possibility of being seen, she'd creep up the stairs to the attic. The place of their first kiss. The place where she'd given him her book. Most importantly, the place where she'd give *herself* to him and leave her innocence behind.

* * *

Mrs. Holloway's head rested on Uncle Harper's shoulder. But then she brought it up abruptly, stood, and crossed the floor to the fireplace.

Billy had returned to the same chair in the living room, waiting for the games to end and his time with Angel to begin. Seeing the look on Mrs. Holloway's face, he sat upright. "Is something wrong?"

Harper stirred from his dozing on the sofa. "Iris?"

She glanced over her shoulder. "I just noticed Jason's figure. When did Mary acquire one of his carvings?" She lifted the wooden angel from the mantel and examined it closer.

"That's *my* angel." Billy's mama stood from her chair and joined Mrs. Holloway. "My pa made it for me."

Mrs. Holloway shook her head. "No, it's most definitely Jason's work. You see, his initials are here on the bottom."

"Can't be." His mama turned the figure in her hands. Her eyes opened wide. "J. H. Dang. I never seen that before." Her face crinkled, ready for tears. "I don't understand. Pa said *he* made it. I've treasured it all my life."

"Mama," Billy said. "You need to sit down." Her face had turned ashen.

"Oh, my dear." Mrs. Holloway guided her to a chair. "I'm very sorry. I had no idea . . ."

"Course you wouldn't know, Iris," Harper said. "Where you reckon he got it?"

Mrs. Holloway returned to his side. "Jason traveled everywhere, as you well know. It's likely he met Cora's father on one of his many trips. He could very well have taught him to carve."

Billy wanted to reach out to his mama, but his leg kept him seated. At least she hadn't cried.

Her face changed. A realization worked her brow. She clutched the figurine to her breast. "Everythin' happens for a reason," she mumbled, then looked up and smiled. "All these years I carried this with me. An angel made by a man I never met. Don't y'all see what it means?"

Billy couldn't be more confused. "What, Mama?"

"Mr. Holloway made this here angel. My pa passed it off as his. Because a this carvin' I was drawn to the angel outside Harper's woodshop. That's where I met Douglas. Then Harper taught Donald to carve, an he made the angel Billy carried with him when he left here. Cuz a that angel Billy found Iris. An here we all are together again." She chuckled, then covered her mouth. "Mrs. Holloway, your late husband did sumthin' wonderful."

Billy leaned toward her. "You're not angry?"

"No. I'm grateful. We had us a guardian angel."

Mrs. Holloway wiped tears from her eyes. "Harper, I believe Jason is giving us his blessing."

Harper grinned, but then his expression changed, looking upward.

"Billy?" His father stood over him; his brow wrinkled with concern.

"Yes, sir?"

"Are you able to walk a short distance?" He placed his hand on Billy's shoulder.

"I can manage." He glanced at his mama before leaving the room. A sad smile followed him.

His father motioned to his grandmother's room, then took a step back. "She's not well. She asked to speak with you."

She'd not been well since his arrival. She'd been cautious with him. Now he understood why. His chest tightened at the realization. "You're not coming in with me?"

"No. She wants to speak with you privately." The man's forced smile wasn't convincing. His heart was breaking.

Billy nodded and stepped into her room. The door clicked shut behind him.

A dimmed lantern pulsed light through the room. Her bed canopy had been pulled back and she was propped up on several pillows. The hair she usually kept up on her head hung loose around her shoulders. Her sunken cheeks and drooping eyes revealed her diminishing health.

"Billy?" She sighed and attempted to pat the bed.

He wouldn't cry. Her strength was failing, but he'd be strong *for* her.

"I'm here." He took his place beside her.

She covered his hand with her own. Her skin felt cold and dry. "I remember when your mother first brought you here. You were a tiny baby. I fell in love with you immediately."

Holding back tears wouldn't be easy. "I love you, too." He lifted her hand to his lips and kissed it.

"I could always see into your thoughts. You and I had a bond unlike any other." She placed a trembling hand to her breast. "I carried you in here even when you were gone."

Shutting his eyes, he squeezed them tight. If he looked at her, he'd break.

"Billy." She slowly pushed herself up higher on the pillows. "I know what's in your heart. That is, *who* is in your heart."

He managed to look at her then and questioned with his eyes.

"She's always been there. Your Angel."

"How'd you know?"

"It wasn't difficult. I know you too well. I also know how your love for her has been discouraged. You left because of her. To fight to free a slave I held captive." She coughed, and motioned to a glass of water. He gave it to her, but she struggled to tip it to her lips.

"Let me help you." He lifted the bottom of the glass.

She smiled as he took the glass from her quivering hand. "Was I wrong? All I'd ever known was slavery. It was our way of life. Sometimes I'm ashamed. But I can't change the past."

"You gave them their homes and did your best to make amends. I know Angel loves you."

"Maybe so. More importantly, she loves *you*." She pointed a shaking finger toward her bureau. "There's a small box in the top drawer. Bring it to me."

He crossed the room and opened the drawer.

"Under the garments." A deep cough rattled in her chest. "In the back right corner."

Pushing aside the delicate cotton underclothes, he found a small wooden box with a single rose carved on the lid. "Did Uncle Harper make this for you?" He sat beside her once again.

"Yes. Many years ago. Isn't it beautiful?"

"Yes, it is." He traced the intricate design with his finger. "Open it."

He lifted the lid. "Your wedding ring?"

"I want you to have it."

The gold band held a solitary diamond. An expensive gem for the wife of a wealthy man. Billy held it toward the light and it sparkled with undiminished radiance. "I don't understand. Why give it to me? Why not Christina?"

"So you can give it to *her*." She rested a hand on his leg. "A symbol of your promise to her. The poor girl had no control over her parentage. She's as much white as she is Negro. Damn the government for not seeing that."

"How'd you know our intentions?"

"Because there's no other way. But mind you this . . ." Her tone changed, becoming stern and earnest. "You can't stay here. Take her north . . . or west. I'm leaving you the means to do it. I won't have you starve, or my great-grand-children either."

Leave? He'd not thought that far ahead. The only thing on his mind was what would happen tonight. But she was right. They couldn't stay in Memphis or anywhere in the south.

He leaned forward and kissed her cheek. "Thank you. You've no idea how much this means to me. But Angel will cry when I give it to her."

"Happy tears, Billy. They're the best kind." She winced and rubbed her temples. "Tell her I'm sorry and I hope she understands."

"I will." Her eyes pinched tightly together, and her face drew up from pain. Reaching out, he touched her hair with heartfelt tenderness. "Get some rest. We can talk more to-morrow."

Her head bobbed, and she nestled down into the bed-ding. "I love you, Billy."

"I love you, too." He kissed her one last time.

As he exited the room, his father stood quietly waiting with Harvey beside him. It seemed they'd decided that to-morrow would be too late for the examination.

Billy limped down the hall to the living room, with the ring held tightly in his fist.

Chapter 39

Beating spoons against pots and pans brought in the New Year. 1870.

Though Billy's heart was heavy with worry over his grandmother, everyone attempted to mask their concern to keep the spirit in the house lifted for the children.

Exhausted, one-by-one everyone went to their rooms. Bidding goodnight wishes, they passed by him like a New Year's parade. Being an invalid had its advantages. As each person departed, the growing anticipation of his night with Angel set his heart racing.

"I can't stay up with you tonight, Billy," his mama said, yawning. "It's nearly one. I gotta take your baby brother to bed." She cupped her hands under her belly. "Don't worry 'bout your gramma. Dr. Mitchell's doin' all he can."

"I know he is. But it's hard seeing her so sick."

"Even so, seein' you again helped her." And just like she'd done since he was very little, she raked her fingers through his hair.

He forced a smile. "I won't be up much longer. I'd like to sit here by the fire for a while and enjoy the New Year." He looked up into her loving eyes. "It's going to be a good one, Mama."

"You're home. It's already good."

As she bent down to kiss him goodnight, guilt covered him. If she knew what he was about to do, she'd be heart-broken. "I love you, Mama," he whispered.

Her face brightened. "I'll never get tired a hearin' that. I love you, too." She waddled away, then waved her hand over the top of her head. "G'night."

His father had remained with his grandmother and had come out only for a brief moment at midnight. When Harvey left her room, his expression had been grim. He'd opted to take his mama's invitation to stay. Both he and Hannah had settled into rooms on the second floor.

Billy closed his eyes, leaned his head back, and listened. His mama's door clicked shut. The fire popped and crackled. No other sounds. His heart thumped.

After waiting several long minutes, he got up and limped his way to the washing room.

The water he poured from the pitcher into the basin was cold, but he didn't care. He wasn't about to waste time to heat it. He removed his clothing and briskly moved the dampened washcloth over his skin. Then he cleaned his teeth and thoroughly rinsed his mouth.

As he dried off and put his clothes back on, he made certain the ring was in his coat pocket. Though smiling at the thought of giving it to her, he grumbled at his foot. All would be perfect if not for the pain in his ankle. But that wouldn't stop him. They'd be lying down after all.

Lying down. Fear crept in. He'd never done this before. How would he know what to do? Knowing she'd never done it either gave him some comfort. But he was the man. It was up to him to lead the way. Wherever that might be.

More guilt erupted when a vision of Jessica came to mind. One thing he wished he'd never remembered. But aside from holding her, he'd not done anything *to* her.

Recalling the feel of her skin against his made him shiver. She'd wanted him, and his body had responded to her, but he'd resisted. Waiting for Angel. Waiting for this moment.

He released his shallow breath in a slow steady stream, then as quietly as possible headed for the stairs. With a dimly lit lantern in one hand and his crutch perched under the opposite arm, the painstaking process would take time. But they had all night. She'd wait for him.

He took the steps one at a time, briefly resting the crutch against each wooden step. Thirteen steps to the second floor, around a corner, and another twelve steps to the third floor. He hobbled down a short hallway to the stairwell ascending to the attic. As far as he knew, no one had heard him. He'd scarcely heard himself.

Angel would be taking the stairs built for the servants. They were hidden in the farthest corner of the house with the intention of keeping the slaves away from the residents and guests. They were much narrower, but also more private. She'd have no difficulty being unseen.

As he pushed the attic door open, the room was dark. It seemed *he'd* be waiting for *her*. Wishing he'd brought water to aid his dry throat, he shuffled across the floor to where the mattresses rested against the wall. After setting the lantern down and turning the flame a little brighter, he pulled one toward him. It thumped onto the floor and a mist of dust arose into the air. Thankfully, no one roomed on the third floor. The sound shouldn't have been heard.

He patted the mattress, sat, and made himself as comfortable as possible. Then, he waited . . .

* * *

Watching Billy perched by the fire all night had been almost unbearable. Angel had tried not to look at him, but every time she'd heard him speak, her eyes were instantly drawn to him.

I love him, and he loves me. Nothing else mattered.

She'd bustled around the kitchen long enough. Every pot had been scrubbed and put away, every counter wiped down, every corner dusted. She moved the broom across the floor not even looking at what she was sweeping.

Her mind remained on Billy. She was about to give herself to him. What if she didn't please him?

What if I do it wrong? She shook her head to dismiss those thoughts. *We love each other. That's all that matters.*

The house had become completely silent.

She lit a candle and crept to the hallway to retrieve the Bible. Tonight it'd be used to sanctify their union. She prayed God would accept it even if the laws of Tennessee wouldn't.

She'd set aside a few blankets and placed them in the stairwell earlier. Grabbing a wicker basket, she set the Bible inside, then filled a jar with water and tightened down the lid.

She threw on her coat. With blankets under one arm and the basket on the other, she made her way up the narrow stairs with the flickering candle lighting the way.

The icy cold stairwell made her shiver. Her heart thumped harder with each step and caused her hands to shake. Eerie shadows danced on the walls.

Billy better be waitin'. She needed his arms to warm and comfort her.

As she pushed open the door, a soft glow welcomed her. Her heart rested momentarily at the sight of him lying on a mattress in the far corner. *Is he asleep?*

After blowing out the candle, she set it aside and crossed to him. She placed the items on the floor, carefully setting the Bible atop the blankets.

"Billy?" She shook his shoulder.

"Mmm, hmm?" The corners of his mouth rose into a playful grin. He pulled her down.

She giggled as he rolled her on top of him, then stifled it when his mouth took hers in a passionate kiss. He wasn't wasting any time.

"Billy." She arched her back and stared down at him. "We have things to do first." She pursed her lips in a teasing way, then succumbed when he drew her down again.

It seemed they'd skip the marriage and go straight to the honeymoon. After a few more kisses, she didn't raise any objections.

As quickly as he'd started, he stopped, sat up, and moved her to sit beside him.

Disappointed, she sighed.

It made him laugh. "Angel." He took her hand. "I love it when you pout. But unless you've forgotten, we have things to take care of first."

She smacked his arm. "Billy Denton, that's what I just said."

He wiggled his brows. "And I listened. When I was ready."

This was the Billy she'd always loved. Playful. Her best friend. "I reckon you're ready now."

"I am." He nodded to the items she'd placed on the floor. "You remembered everything."

"*I* wasn't hit in the head."

"Not fair." He grinned and picked up the Bible.

As he opened it, his face became solemn. He raised his eyes and looked at her—a look of utter devotion. "When God made Adam He knew he needed someone to love. Someone to hold. Someone to share his life and give him children. I'm going to read something my mama showed me when she explained about marriage. It's from Genesis."

He brought the lantern closer. "Therefore a man leaves his father and his mother and cleaves to his wife, and they become one flesh. And the man and his wife were both naked, and were not ashamed." He closed the book and gazed deeply into her eyes. "Angel, put your hand here with mine." He placed his hand on the Bible and she set hers upon it.

Her moist eyes offset her dry throat. He placed his other hand over hers and inhaled deeply. "Angel, I promise to love you forever. I'll take you as my wife, cherish you, care for you, and never stray from you."

Tears trickled down her cheeks. "Billy, I'll love *you* forever. I take you as my husband. I'll give you all the love I can. I'll take care of you, an I swear I'll never leave you."

She shivered. Not so much from the cold, but from the beauty of it all. This felt right. Surely God was looking down at them. He'd heard their vows and she prayed He'd accepted them.

Billy removed one hand from the Bible and fumbled into his coat pocket.

She gasped. The ring in his hand glittered in the lamp-light. "Billy?"

"This ring is a symbol of my love. I want you to wear it. Wear it as my wife." He took her hand, kissed it, then slid it onto her finger.

She shook uncontrollably and stared at it. "Where'd you get it?"

"Grandmother. She wanted you to have it. She asked me to tell you she's sorry."

"Sorry?" With emotions overwhelming her, she couldn't grasp it all.

He set the Bible aside, grabbed one of the blankets, and placed it around her shoulders. "She regrets keeping all of you as slaves. It was all she knew, but now she understands it was wrong."

"She was good to us. Like I told you all those years ago, I never felt like a slave. This has been my home."

"*Home* is wherever we're together."

* * *

Billy stared at his wife. The most beautiful woman God ever created. She'd blessed every life she'd touched, and now she was his to love completely.

"We can use these as pillows," he said, helping her with her coat. He then removed his own, rolled them into balls, and patted them into place. "There." When he turned to look at her, her dark eyes glistened with tears. "Please tell me those are happy tears."

She nodded without speaking, then lifted her hand and gazed at the ring.

"Do you like it?"

"Like it? I ain't never seen anythin' so beautiful. I don't recall her wearin' it."

They lay back against their *pillows*. He took her hand, fingering the ring. "She hadn't for some time. Her hands had gotten so thin it didn't fit properly."

"I'll thank her tomorrow." She rolled onto her side facing him. "Am I your wife now?"

He moved his hand into her long silky hair. "Yes. No matter what anyone else ever says, in my eyes you'll always be my wife."

"Then . . . love me, Billy." She whispered the words against his face.

"Angel," he rasped, and kissed her lips. He'd waited a long time for this moment.

His hands worked without thought, assisting her with her dress. He watched every movement of her body, as he removed the cloth from her skin. The dim light held no color, only form. She captivated him.

He lifted her chemise, exposing her breasts. He buried his face into her bosom and inhaled the scent of roses. Her erect nipples beckoned him and he didn't hesitate moving his mouth onto her.

When he tasted her, she moaned and tugged at his shirt. Her cold skin brought him to his senses, so he tore himself away from her long enough to pull the blankets over them.

Hunger filled her eyes. She grasped the buttons of his shirt, trying to work them with trembling fingers. They breathed heavily, quickly removing their garments and casting them aside until they were lying naked. Naked and unashamed beneath the warmth of old quilts.

He attempted to move onto her, but a shot of pain forced him onto his back. "My ankle," he muttered, disgusted by the interruption.

She leaned over him. Her sleek body distracted him from the pain. "Don't fret, Billy." She ran her hand over his chest. "Let me." Rising up, she kissed his lips, then moved her mouth along his chin and down toward his neck.

His body shook. He closed his eyes, savoring every moment. Every touch. Her fingertips wandered aimlessly down his body. Her breasts pressed against him. She inhaled deeply and moved her hand down further until . . .

He gasped. She touched him in a way he'd never imagined; boldly and without reservation. Yes, she was taking him beyond his dream.

With confidence and fearlessness, she climbed atop him and sheathed him into her as if they'd always been one. The sensation took his breath. He pressed his head into the fabric of his coat and squeezed his eyes tight, relishing the feel of her.

With great effort, he opened his eyes and looked up, meeting her gaze. Her eyes were half-closed as she began to move. Taking him deeper, they closed completely. Rich sounds of pleasure emerged from somewhere inside her.

Seeing her like this mesmerized him and caused his heart to race. Her hair cascaded over him, framing them like a fine piece of art.

He slid his hands along her waist and they came to rest on her full bottom. He assisted with her movement, much to his own benefit.

This wasn't how he'd envisioned it. He believed he'd be the one making love to *her*. She was so much more than he'd ever dreamed she'd be. He'd never tire of this. Never tire of her.

She arched her back, pulling up and away from him, then swiveled her hips and breathed even harder. Her movement drew him in, taking him to some other place.

He couldn't hold back. Grabbing her firmly, he helped her move up and down, faster and faster until he released with a cry that undoubtedly woke everyone in the house.

She made a sound like that of a whimpering puppy, then fell down breathless upon him.

He stroked her back, and when she calmed, he lifted her face and kissed her tenderly. "I love you, Angel."

Her eyes were still half shut. "I love you, too, Billy."

* * *

Nestling into Billy's body, Angel was home. Loving him had come as naturally as breathing. The same thing her mama had with Jeriah. It was how love should be.

She brushed her fingers over his chest, lingering in the small patch of hair in the center. Content beyond words, she wanted this night to never end. She now understood the sounds her mama made. Sounds of happiness and complete gratification.

"How'd you know how to do that?" His arm circled behind her, and his hand cupped her breast.

She hesitated, almost too embarrassed to answer. But he was her husband now. *No secrets.* "One night when I had a bad dream, I went to talk to Mama 'bout it. Back when Jeriah wasn't livin' with us. I didn't know he was with her." Billy's fingertips skimmed her nipple, making it impossible to concentrate. She gulped hard, and the movement stopped.

"Yes?" he said playfully and kissed her forehead.

"You make talkin' difficult." She tilted her head up and looked at him, while biting her lower lip. He winked, and she laid her head back down on his chest. "Well . . . I opened the door a might and heard them. Before I backed away, I saw Mama on him. Her back was arched, an she was movin' . . ." She placed her hand over her face. "I was so embarrassed. I reckon they never knew I was there. But I never forgot it."

"There were times I heard *my* parents, but I never *saw* them. It's one of those things you know is happening, but you don't like to imagine your parents doing."

She sighed. "I thought it was beautiful. But I still felt uncomfortable havin' seen it."

The movement of his hand resumed, warming her through and through. Their night of love-making was far from over.

"What *we* did was beautiful," he said. "Something we'll share with each other and *only* each other. No one can take this from us."

She rested her hand on her flat abdomen. "What if we made a baby?"

"Then we'll have a baby. And we'll love it as much as we love each other."

"What color do you think it'll be?"

"It doesn't matter. I don't even want to think about it." He let out a loud breath.

She hadn't meant to spoil his mood. Yes, they were married—or as married as they could be—and yes, they'd made love. But now what?

"Billy, where are we gonna live?" His body deflated under her.

"I'm still working on that."

"But . . ."

"Angel." He rose up on his elbows. "Let's not talk about this tonight. Let's forget about everything else just this once and simply love each other. We have the rest of our lives to work things out."

He was right. In every way it was their wedding night. She had a lot more love to give him. "I'm sorry, Billy."

"It's all right. I understand." He lay back and pulled her against him. His hand drifted along her body and came to rest on her upper thigh. "You used the lanolin cream, didn't you?" He returned his hand to her breasts.

"Everywhere." She shivered from his touch.

"Show me." He brought the lantern closer, then raised the blankets to look beneath. Licking his lips, he gave her the most devilish grin she'd ever seen.

"Billy Denton," she scolded, and tugged the blankets down. They were done talking.

Chapter 40

Sunlight streamed through the small attic window and Billy rubbed his tired eyes. It couldn't be morning already. They'd slept little, but he'd do it all over again in a heartbeat.

Angel was still sleeping; lying on her side with an angelic expression fitting her name. Her long hair lay fanned across the coats, and a peaceful smile turned the corners of her mouth.

Though the blankets were pulled up high, a glimpse of bare skin dried his throat. He'd been grateful she'd brought water.

He wanted to stay, but after realizing what time it must be, he had to go. He dressed quickly.

Leaning on his crutch, he bent down and shook her gently. "Angel."

Her eyes opened slowly at first, but then popped wide. "What time is it?" She sat up straight causing the blankets to drop to her waist.

He could have done without seeing her like this and wavered against the crutch. Knowing he had to leave, arousal wasn't wise.

She followed his gaze, then tipped her head and grinned. "Sumthin' wrong?"

Playing already? He dropped the crutch and pounced on her with the agility of a crippled tiger. "You're evil, Angel." He laughed, and tickled her. Not what he wanted to do, but the only thing safe at the moment.

"Me?" she teased, laughing with him. Then she became rigid. "Billy, stop! You gotta go! I can go down the back way, but you can't. If anyone sees you—"

"I'll make an excuse."

"Then . . . don't go. We can make love again." She lifted her eyes and fluttered her lashes.

Pushing her into the mattress, he draped his injured limb over the top of her. "There's nothing I'd rather do. But I'm already limping. I'm afraid a certain doctor will notice I'm having an even harder time walking today." He narrowed his eyes. "And not just from a bad ankle."

She giggled. "He won't be able to tell." Her face fell. "Will he?"

"No." He took one finger and circled her face, then touched it to the tip of her nose. "My beautiful wife." He lifted her ringed finger. "Don't worry about anyone knowing, but you'd better take this off. Why don't you put it on some yarn and wear it around your neck under your dress? I want you to keep it close, but I don't believe either of us is ready to let anyone know."

She froze. "Billy, did you hear that?"

"What?"

She grabbed his arm. "I thought I heard cryin'."

He tilted his head, but heard nothing.

"We gotta go, Billy. I don't wanna get caught." Springing from the mattress, she grabbed her clothes and threw them on.

"I'll go. Wait a few minutes, then *you* go. Be sure to put the Bible back." He stood and kissed her. "There will be more to come, I promise."

She handed him the crutch, then frowned. "How long will we have to hide from folks?"

"Not long. After the Mitchell's and Mrs. Holloway leave, we'll get our families together and tell them. In the meantime we can meet here." He put his hand behind her head, then pressed his forehead to hers. "It won't be easy, but we can do it." After placing a tender kiss on her temple, he turned and hobbled away.

"Be careful," she said in a loud whisper.

"You, too." He left her, though his heart begged him to stay.

* * *

Billy made it all the way to the bottom of the stairway without incident. But as he placed his foot on the final step, he stopped. The unmistakable sound of her tears filtered down the hallway.

Mama? He swallowed hard and took the last step. Why was she crying?

"Billy?" Harvey walked briskly toward him.

"Yes, sir?" His throat tightened. Was his hair mussed? Were his clothes buttoned correctly?

"Were you out walking?" Harvey asked, with a furrowed brow.

"Y—Yes. I know it wasn't the wisest thing to do, but I was restless. What's wrong?"

He put his arm over Billy's shoulder. "Your grandmother passed away."

Feeling as if someone had punched him in the stomach, Billy wavered against him. "No . . ."

"She died without pain, but your parents aren't taking it well." He helped him to the chaise in the hallway. "Sit for a moment, then I'll take you to them."

It wasn't fair. He'd not had enough time with her. He put his head in his hands and cried. How would Angel thank her now? Assure her she'd been happy?

She can't be dead. Not now.

The household came to life around him, as doors opened and shut overhead. Soon they'd all know she was dead. She'd died on the happiest night of his life.

"Harvey?" Billy swallowed hard and stood. "I need to see her."

He put his arm around Billy's waist and helped him down the hallway. "Walking wasn't wise. After you see her, I want you to sit down and put that foot up. Understood?"

"Yes, sir."

The canopy had been pulled around his grandmother's bed. His mama sat to one side and his father on the other. Billy nearly stumbled through the door, upheld only by Harvey's strength.

"Billy." His mama's chin quivered as she reached out to him.

He went into her embrace, then felt his father's hand on his shoulder. Standing, Billy wrapped his arms around him. "I'm sorry, Father."

"She died peacefully. I was with her when she took her last breath."

"When did it happen?"

"We heard her cry out about three a.m. I sat with her and held her hand. She passed twenty minutes ago."

Twenty minutes? The pit in his stomach grew. If only he'd been there.

"I'm surprised you didn't hear her," his mama said. "You musta been sleepin' real sound."

He nodded, but couldn't look at her. "May I?" He motioned to the canopy.

"Of course." His father pulled back one side.

Billy perched on the edge of her bed and stared at her lifeless form. Only hours ago she'd been talking to him. Now she was gone.

He placed his hand against her face. Death had not yet chilled her.

Tears came readily as he laid his head against her. "I love you," he muttered. "I'm sorry I wasn't here."

His father patted his back. "She knew you loved her. You don't have to be sorry. She was content after speaking to you last night. I believe she knew it would be the last time."

"Douglas?" Billy's mama stood from her chair, holding her lower back. "I need to lie down."

The sound of her voice brought Billy out of his grief. "Are you all right, Mama?"

"Reckon so . . . *Dang!*" She plopped back down in the chair.

Harvey's face appeared in the door. "I know that *dang.*"

"Yes, you do." His father hovered over her. "How would you like to deliver another baby?"

"I've gotten better at it over the years."

This couldn't be happening. Billy was in no condition to help his mama, but Harvey and his father had her on her feet and out the door before he was able to hobble across the room.

The chaos that followed had the entire house in an uproar. Harper left with Jeriah to get the mortician, while everyone else gathered in the living room to wait for the baby to be born.

* * *

Hurrying much too fast, Angel nearly took a tumble down the back stairwell. She caught herself just in time, but dropped the Bible with a loud thump. Sitting down on a narrow step, she took a breath, then clutched the Bible to her chest.

Her body tingled, reliving last night. Billy had been everything she'd imagined and more.

Only six more steps and she'd come out the door at the back of the kitchen.

What if Ada's already there? Worse yet, Mama?

Quickly, she formed a story. They'd believe her as long as she didn't look directly at them. Lying had suddenly become necessary. *Sorry, Mama.*

She took the final step and grabbed the doorknob.

The ring. She placed it in her coat pocket. As soon as she was able, she'd get a piece of yarn and put it around her neck as Billy suggested. It would be horrible to lose it.

She pushed the door open.

"Angel?" As she'd feared, Ada was there stoking the fire.

"Hey, Ada." She acted as casual as possible. She forced a smile, then hung her coat on its peg and set the Bible on the table.

"Where was you?" Ada's words were filled with pain.

She's been cryin'. Angel flew to her side. "What's wrong?"

"Figgered if you was in the house you'd already knowed." She lifted her apron and wiped away tears. "Ms. Wellesley be dead."

Air was sucked from Angel's lungs. "Dead?" She shook her head in denial. "She can't be."

"She be dead a'right," Ada sniffled. "Mista Harper went for the mortician. An now Ms. Denton be havin' her baby." She sobbed. "Ms. Wellesley won't never see the new granbaby."

Angel stumbled to a chair. "I need to go to Billy."

"Oh, Miss Angel." Ada cried harder. "Ms. Wellesley was good to me. I's gonna miss her."

Angel forgot her own troubles, and returned to her, pulling her into a hug. "Me, too, Ada. Does Mama know?"

"Shore does. Jeriah told her before he left with Harper. She was lookin' for you." Ada stepped back. "Where was you?"

Angel licked her lips and pointed to the Bible. "It may sound odd, but I've been havin' a hard time since Billy came home. I borrowed Mrs. Denton's Bible and wanted to be alone. So I went up the stairwell. I thought readin' it might make me feel better." What was she thinking? Lying and using the Bible to authenticate it? *I'm goin' to hell.*

Ada didn't help her guilt when she reached out and stroked her face. "You're such a good girl. They's all gonna need your prayers."

Good girl? If she only knew. "Will you be all right, Ada?"

"I's gonna cook breakfast for everyone. Least I'll be heppin'."

Angel kissed her cheek, then hurried from the room to find Billy.

* * *

Angel . . .

Billy sensed her presence the moment she entered the room. The look on her face revealed she knew. All the happiness in her eyes had melted into grief. He wanted to hold her—to comfort her. Yet he couldn't touch her.

Hannah paced nearby, close to Donald. Maybe they had secrets of their own.

The air in the room hung heavy. Sorrow mixed with anticipation of the new life emerging in the room down the hall.

"Why's it taking so long, Mama?" Becky asked, huddled against Mrs. Holloway's bosom.

"These things take time." Mrs. Holloway ran her fingers through Becky's hair.

A loud *dang* made them alert. They all turned their heads to the sound.

"Having babies hurts, doesn't it Mrs. Holloway?" Paulette asked. She was on her other side, resting her head on the woman's shoulder.

"I've heard it does, though I've never had one of my own. But I also know there's nothing more wonderful a woman can do."

"It may hurt now, Paulette," Angel said. "But once your mama holds the baby in her arms, she'll forget the pain." She pulled up a chair beside them only a few steps away from Billy.

He swallowed the lump in his throat. Her essence covered him like a warm quilt. "You helped deliver Uziah, didn't you?"

She nodded, and for a moment their eyes locked. "I did everythin' but cut the cord."

"And *push*," he said, trying to ease the tension in the room. He spoke low, not intending to make anyone laugh, but rather take away a small amount of pain.

"Yes, Mama did that." Her face softened into a smile. "Billy, I'm sorry 'bout your gramma." She leaned toward him, but wasn't within reach. Her eyes glistened with tears. "I wanted to tell her . . ." She stopped and covered her mouth.

He knew exactly what she'd wanted to tell her: Thank you for believing in our love. Thank you for entrusting me with your ring. Thank you for giving me a home. Words she could never say. "I know, Angel. You loved her."

She nodded. "Very much."

Christina and Emilia approached. They were solemn, but he detected something devious behind Emilia's eyes.

"Hey, Billy," Emilia said. "Sorry about your grandmother. Though she really wasn't your grandmother you know."

"She was just as much his gramma as Christina's or the boy's." Angel jumped in before he could reply.

Emilia rolled her eyes. "Not by blood. You and I know all about blood, don't we Angel?"

"Blood isn't everything," Mrs. Holloway interjected, her face hard and angry.

Becky's eyes widened. "What does she mean, Mama?"

"Miss Emilia is confused, Becky. Sadly, her mother died years ago and it's difficult for her to cope with Mrs. Wellesley's death. Isn't that right, Emilia?"

"Hmph!" Emilia crossed her arms, and lifted her nose in the air. "Angel, Christina and I need to talk to you. *Privately.*"

Angel jerked her head around, looking to Billy for help.

"Now, Emilia?" he asked. His blood boiled. It was all he could do to remain civil.

"Why not now? Aunt Cora sounds as if she's *dying* in there. It could take a while."

Billy'd had enough. He swung his foot off the stool and pushed himself up from the chair. Tempted to swing the crutch and knock her on her backside, he placed it under his arm instead. He hobbled to face her. "Never say that again."

Christina took Emilia's arm. "Emilia, he's right. It wasn't very nice."

"How can you tolerate her?" Billy asked, looking at his sister. "I've not known her a full week and I already want to turn her over my knee!"

Emilia covered her mouth and giggled. "Oh, cousin. I wouldn't give you that pleasure."

"Billy!" Mrs. Holloway sat up straight. "If you don't turn her over *your* knee, I'll turn her over mine!"

"C'mon, Emilia," Christina said, tugging at her arm. "Let's go to your room. We can wait there just as well as here."

"Only if Angel comes, too." Emilia smirked at Angel.

Angel stood. "I'll come."

Billy remained, helpless. The two girls left the room with his *wife*. One he could only hold in seclusion.

* * *

Angel trudged reluctantly behind the girls. The further away from Billy, the more her heart ached.

Emilia's room had become a sea of pink. Her wood-framed bed was covered in a pink and white quilt, accented with tiny roses. A heavy canopy hung over it. It, too, was white with pink roses. Angel wasn't afforded such luxuries in her room.

The canopy had been pulled back to the walls on each side. Emilia immediately lay down with her hand extended behind her head. Christina perched beside her; hands folded quietly in her lap.

Angel knew Christina well enough to understand she felt the pain of her grandmother's death. But she'd followed Emilia regardless. The two had become inseparable.

"Sit," Emilia said, patting an empty spot on the bed.

Angel sat, wanting to get this over with. She stared at the far wall, focusing on the climbing rose-patterned wallpaper. Imported. Something Emilia had been given for her sixteenth birthday.

Angel caught sight of her reflection in the standing mirror and nearly gasped. Her dress was badly wrinkled and her hair needed a good brushing. After leaving Billy, she'd instantly joined the family in the living room. She'd not had a chance to groom herself.

"So," Emilia giggled. "How was he?"

Angel's heart fell into her shoes. "What?" It returned to her chest and thumped. *Hard.*

Christina placed a hand to her face, covering cheeks that were turning a shade darker than the roses on Emilia's quilt.

"Angel . . ." Emilia huffed. "We know you spent the night with him. What was it like?"

Angel couldn't breathe. How'd they know? "I don't know what you're talkin' 'bout." They *couldn't* know.

Christina cleared her throat. "Your mama couldn't find you this morning. You stayed late in the kitchen last night. We assumed you went back to Bo after you left."

Angel's heart rested. *They don't know I was with Billy.* "Why would you think that?"

"Because, silly," Emilia tittered. "You told us you were going home after the game. But you didn't. And this morning, you still weren't home and no one has seen Bo."

"But . . ." Angel thought fast. She didn't want to say anything that might get her deeper into a lie she couldn't work her way out of.

"But nothing," Emilia said. "When we left you outside, you were going to him. You came in and told us he wasn't well, and that's why you didn't stay with him. But you must have gone to *nurse* him back to health. From the looks of you, you nursed him well." She bit her lower lip and tipped her head.

How could she say such a thing? She'd never, *ever* do that with Bo. She had to set them straight. "I didn't go back to Bo. I . . . fell asleep in the stairwell."

Emilia erupted into laughter. "Fell asleep in the stairwell?" She nudged Angel's shoulder. "You don't expect us to believe that do you?"

"It's true," Angel persisted. "I—I was readin' the Bible and fell asleep."

Emilia jumped off the bed. "Reading the Bible?" She looked at Christina, rolled her eyes, then placed her hands on her hips. "That's the most absurd thing I've ever heard.

What *I* believe is that Bo bed you last night, but you're too ashamed to admit it."

Angel turned to Christina for help, but Christina looked away, cheeks glowing red.

"There's nothin' to admit," Angel said. "Now, I'd like to go downstairs and wait for the baby to come. Billy . . ." She stopped. *Why'd I say his name?*

"Billy?" Emilia clapped her hands together. "There's another mystery. Did you see his *Hannah* last night?"

"What about Hannah?" She was the last person Angel wanted to talk about.

"I saw her kissing Donald," Emilia grinned. "And then, she kissed Billy. Billy's going to have an awful time with her if he has to share her with his brother. Then again, maybe he deserves it after the way he treated you."

"You're wrong about them," Angel said. "I know for a fact Billy broke things off with her. He's staying here in Memphis."

Emilia's brows drew in. "When did you find out about that?"

"Last night."

"Last night?" Emilia folded her arms over her chest. "How would you know? You were never alone with him and I certainly didn't see you talking to Hannah."

"That's right," Christina said. "After we left you, you went to see Bo. When you came back in, you were with us. I never saw you talk to Billy *or* Hannah."

Angel was trapped. What could she say? Her heart started thumping again, and her mind reeled. This was the problem with lying. Everything wove together like a mitten with a loose string. One pull and the entire thing would come unraveled.

"Hey!" Richard yelled up the stairs. "The baby's here!"

Thank you, God!

Angel hopped off the bed, raced for the door and didn't look back. Emilia's disgusted grunt followed her.

Chapter 41

Billy smiled broadly. His father walked toward him carrying a blanketed bundle.

As everyone gathered around to see the new baby, the sorrow of his grandmother's death was set aside. She'd want them to be happy. He just wished she'd lived long enough to see him.

"Did you choose a name for him?" Billy asked from his never-ending seated position.

He nodded. "*Mary.*"

"Mary?" Richard asked. "That's not a boy's name."

"You're right. *She* isn't a boy." He moved the blanket away from her face. At her age it was difficult to tell the difference.

"You named her after Grandmother," Billy said. "It would've made her happy."

"I have a baby *sister*?" Paulette screamed and took Becky's hands. They both jumped up and down until Mrs. Holloway told them to mind their manners.

"No boy?" Uziah pouted and raised his arms to his mama.

Bessie scooped him up. "No boy, Ziah. Maybe mama's baby be a boy."

"You still got me, Ziah," Joe said. "I ain't goin' nowhere."

So, it was settled. Billy was glad Joe would be staying at the estate, but would *he* be staying?

Everyone took turns looking at baby Mary. Billy sat quietly and waited.

He'd been grateful when Angel returned, even though Emilia was right behind her. Emilia had glanced his way and given him an all-too-familiar smirk. She was up to something. Tonight, in the comfort of Angel's arms, he'd find out what it was.

"Your mother's doing well," Harvey said, smiling at him. "Her cursing may have indicated otherwise, but this delivery went smoother than yours."

"I'm glad you were here to help her." He smiled at his friend.

His father knelt beside him. "Would you like to hold her?"

Her tiny face mesmerized him. Utterly perfect and beautiful. Extending his arms, he took his baby sister.

Richard stood over his shoulder. "Sure she's a girl? Mama's called him a boy for months."

"Very sure," their father said, and Harvey nodded his agreement.

Billy cradled baby Mary, but then returned her to their father. "May I see Mama?"

"Soon. She needs rest."

"Let me know when she's up to it, please?"

He nodded, then walked away with the baby.

"Someday *I'll* have a baby," Emilia said, loud enough so everyone could hear. "And so will Angel. Won't you, Angel?"

Knowing the discomfort his wife must be feeling, Billy chose to answer for her. "As will Christina and Paulette, I'm sure." He scooted up in his chair as tall as he could. "And one day, little Mary will probably have a baby. It's what women do."

Emilia wrinkled her nose, then grabbed Christina by the arm. "Let's go to my room. You're coming with us, aren't you, Angel?"

"No," Angel said harshly. She looked toward Billy and softened. "I can't, Emilia. I have work to do. Ada needs me to help with breakfast."

"We'll finish our conversation later then." Emilia flitted from the room with Christina trailing behind her.

Mrs. Holloway approached him. "Things will get better, Billy." She bent down and hugged his neck, then took Becky and Paulette's hands and walked down the hall toward the kitchen.

Angel knelt beside him and encircled him with her arms.

"Angel? What are you doing?" He spoke as low as he could, burying his face in her hair. He breathed in deeply, wanting more of her.

"Huggin' my friend." Her lips brushed his ear and her voice dropped to a whisper. "And tonight I'll hold my lover." Her warm breath—combined with her sensual words—made him shudder. "Billy, I'm sorry 'bout your gramma. We'll talk 'bout it later."

As she stood, he thanked her as he would any friend, then she walked away.

Was it appropriate to think about making love to her so soon after hearing about his grandmother's passing? Maybe since his grandmother had been the one person who'd given them her blessing, she'd understand.

He needed Angel now more than ever. If only their houseguests would leave early.

* * *

The mood in the house remained somber throughout the day and became even more so when the mortician arrived and carried out Mrs. Wellesley. Her body would be prepared, placed in a casket, then returned to the estate for burial next to her late husband.

Mrs. Wellesley had always been very private, so Angel doubted she'd want to be fussed over. Mr. Denton was making arrangements to have Reverend Rogers perform the funeral for family only.

Standing in the kitchen amidst the bustle of activity preparing for dinner, she spied her coat hanging on the wooden peg. Her eyes popped open.

My ring! Her mind had been preoccupied and she'd forgotten about it.

She rushed to the coat and felt the pocket. Relief replaced a moment of panic, when she found it in the lining. A small hole in the pocket had caused the ring to drop through.

With the excuse of nature, she put on her coat and went to her room. She selected a strand of blue yarn from her knitting basket. Nervously looking over her shoulder, she threaded the ring onto the string, then tied it around her neck. Her high-neck dress and long hair covered it well.

The cold metal pressed between her breasts. Close to her heart. *Just where it should be.*

"Angel?" Jeriah's voice boomed through the house.

This can't be good. "In here, Jeriah."

He poked his head into her room. "We needs to talk."

"What's wrong?" Smoothing her skirt, she walked out. "Is it Mama? Uziah?"

He shook his head. "Bo's gone."

"Gone?" She gulped.

"Gone. Look like he won't be back. His things ain't in his house. You know sumthin' 'bout it?" He crossed his arms over his chest and stood with his legs slightly apart.

She couldn't lie to him. It was bad enough lying to everyone else. But could she tell him about Bo without bringing up Billy? "Yes, sir." She took a seat on the sofa.

Jeriah grabbed a chair and sat in front of her. "Tell me."

"I told him I couldn't marry him." It was true. Hopefully it'd satisfy him.

"Why?" Again, he crossed his arms.

"Cuz . . . I don't love him." *I love Billy.* "I know it hurt him, but I didn't think he'd leave."

"Then I reckon he ain't comin' back." He stood, hovering over her. "He was a good man, Angel. He loved you. I know he did. He'd a been good to you."

She rose and took his hand. "Jeriah, I know you wouldn't a wanted me to be with a man I don't love. He was my friend. I loved him that way, but not the *other* way."

He squeezed her hand, but then pointed a finger in her face. "Don't you get no ideas 'bout Billy. Hear me?"

"I hear you." What else could she say? *I'm sorry, but I already gave myself to Billy an there's nothin' you can do 'bout it?* No. Not yet.

"Good." He patted her face. "Your mama's worried sumthin' awful 'bout it. I told her you gots more sense."

She forced a smile. "I gotta get back to work. Lotsa mouths to feed."

"You're a good girl, Angel."

She walked toward the door, but stopped and turned. "I'm sorry 'bout Bo. I know he was a big help to you. Reckon you can teach Joe?"

He smiled. "I's been teachin' him already."

She threw on her coat and went out the door.

Bo was gone, and she was relieved. But now, even more questions would be raised. How would she ever keep Emilia away from her? With Bo gone, she'd know she wasn't with him last night. And Emilia didn't believe her story about falling asleep in the stairwell.

She'd make herself sick with worry. She decided not to think about it and avoid Emilia.

Now I hafta figure out how to sneak away with Billy tonight.

* * *

Billy had dimmed the light, but not completely. Satisfied beyond belief, he lay against his pillow; one arm around Angel and the other behind his head. She'd brought the pillows with her this time, sneaking them from storage in the laundry room behind the kitchen.

Their *bedroom* seemed more complete with them, but still a long way from the kind of room he wanted to share with her. She deserved the best—not a place where cobwebs clung to the ceiling and mice skittered about in the walls.

Even with their poor conditions, he couldn't have been more content. They'd made love for hours. He should be sleeping, but sleep wouldn't come.

The slow rise and fall of her body soothed him; her warm skin pressed to his. Watching her breathe was no different than watching *his* chest rise and lower. They were part of each other.

"Mmm . . . Billy," she murmured, half asleep. Her fingers came to life, caressing his skin.

Knowing they couldn't stay here all night was part of the reason he couldn't sleep. They'd need to leave soon and return to their own beds, but he couldn't bring himself to let her go.

Running his hand along her face, he pushed away a strand of hair.

So beautiful. Do I deserve someone like you?

"I don't wanna leave," she whispered.

His kissed the top of her head. "I thought you were sleeping."

"I was." She lifted her head and propped herself up, leaning on his chest. "I love you."

He grinned and ran his index finger along her lips. "I love you, too." When he chuckled, she pouted.

"Why are you laughin'?"

"Aside from being happy, I was thinking about your journal."

"It made you laugh?"

He wrapped both arms around her and squeezed. "It wasn't a *funny* kind of laugh. It was a laugh of endearment."

"What?"

"I was thinking about how many times you wrote *I love Billy.* Every time I read it, my heart beat faster. Even before I regained my memories, my heart remembered you."

"That laugh was because you're happy?" She placed tiny kisses on his chest.

"More than you know." He pulled her up to him and kissed her lips.

They sighed in unison, then she snuggled down into the crook of his arm. She'd probably been thinking what he had, but they were both too exhausted to make love again.

"Did you know that Richard is the same age as I was when I left?" he asked, and even though he was tired, he couldn't seem to keep his hands off her breasts.

"He's fourteen. You was thirteen when you left. *Nearly* fourteen." Her breath hitched, as his fingers teased and taunted.

"And you were only twelve."

"Nearly *thirteen.*"

"We were so young." He pushed his head deeper into the pillow. "When I look at Richard, I see a child. If he decided to leave home like I did, I'd think he wasn't in his right mind."

"Richard *is* a child. You was grown up for your age." She lifted her head and tilted it in concern. "What's got you thinkin' 'bout all this?"

"I'm just thinking." Leaning to the side, he brightened the lantern. "Thinking about how much we've grown in the past five years. How much we've changed."

She ran her hand down his arm and squeezed his muscle. "I like how you've changed. Now that you got your mind back and remembered you want me."

He turned on his side and rolled her over onto her back. "I'll always want you. But I believe *you've* changed more than I have."

"How?" She licked her lips, which only enticed him more.

"You're not a girl anymore. In any way."

"And you're not a boy." She said the words matter-of-factly, but then brushed his manhood with her fingers, causing him to jump.

He could play this game. He breathed deeply, cocked his head, then moved his hand over her breasts, caressing and squeezing. "I'm rather fond of the way you changed."

She giggled. "I noticed."

"And . . ." He slid his hand down her body, along the curve of her waist, then went lower until it came to rest between her legs. "You've become more of a woman than I deserve."

"That's always been there." Her body writhed against his touch.

"Maybe so, but I had no idea what it could do." He couldn't bear it any longer. He had to try. Even if it hurt more than he could endure, he'd make love to *her*.

He rolled over onto her and she gasped. "Billy! You'll hurt yourself."

"I won't. I need to do this." He winced only once. The moment she opened to him, he forgot everything else.

He looked down and watched her expressions change as he moved. He started slowly, wanting to savor every second. Her simple smile turned to utter pleasure. She rapidly licked her lips, tilted her head into the pillow, and closed her eyes.

He increased his pace. Her mouth moved as if trying to form words, but unable to utter more than soft sensual moans. As he thrust harder, she arched into him and her eyes squinted tightly shut. Her hands grasped his back and she whimpered, quivering beneath him as he groaned with his own gratification. Finally, he stilled himself within her.

Her mouth regained its smile, and her eyes opened, blinking slowly. He'd pleased her.

Though they'd both found pleasure the other way, he needed this. Needed to know he could make her as happy as she'd made him. Rolling onto his back, he heaved a heavy sigh.

Instantly, she draped herself over him and kissed his chest with renewed energy. "Billy that was . . ." She kissed him again, rising up to his lips. "I can't describe it." She stared at him. "I love you so much."

"I love you more." He pressed his lips to her forehead.

"Did it hurt you?"

"Only at first. But watching you was worth it."

She tipped her head down, then he raised her chin to look at him.

"Did I embarrass you?" It was the last thing he wanted to do.

"No, but . . ."

"But?"

"Are you glad you chose me? With all the troubles we've got ahead of us?"

He ran his hands along her back, hoping to soothe her. "We'll get through whatever may come, *together*. And I'll never, *ever* regret choosing you. I've loved you all my life."

Her long lashes moved in slow animation, warming her face.

"And," he continued. "When I said we've changed, the one thing that *hasn't* changed is who we are inside. You're still my best friend and the one I know I can share everything with. We complete each other."

She placed her hands behind his head and kissed him long and hard, as if hungry and looking to him to be fed. "Then, I hope you never get tired a watchin' me."

He held her firmly in his arms, wanting to be so close there would be no distinction between the point where one of their bodies began and the other ended. He wanted to crawl inside her and never leave.

Running his fingers along the strand of yarn that encircled her neck, he reached the ring and put it on the tip of his finger. "In two days they'll be gone and I'll put this back on your finger for good." Earlier in the night it had dangled above him, glimmering in the lantern light. A shimmering reminder of the vows they'd taken.

"And our folks are gonna hate us." She placed her hand around his.

"No. They love us too much to hate us. We'll give them time. They'll understand."

Though unsure how many hours had passed, they needed to part. Reluctantly, he pushed the blankets from his body and began to dress. Should he tell her what he'd decided?

He looked at her, lying there, watching him. No. He wouldn't tell her now. She was worried enough about revealing their marriage. Leaving the estate would only cause her more pain.

Chapter 42

It wasn't easy burying a body in the frozen ground of January. Using picks and shovels, Billy helped his father and Jeriah dig the hole where his grandmother's body would rest. He believed in his heart her soul had already gone elsewhere.

Reverend Rogers gave a brief eulogy. It astonished Billy when Emilia broke into, *Shall We Gather at the River.* Her voice sounded surprisingly lovely, and the song was heartfelt. Perhaps she had one after all. She looked slightly out of place in her black satin and lace, but at least she'd shown enough respect to wear the appropriate color.

Angel stood at his side holding his arm, as she'd done when his grandfather died. Hannah gave them a brief glance and a soft smile. He doubted she suspected anything. Besides, her mind was on Donald, evident by the way she huddled close to him. She shed tears, but he believed her grief was over leaving Donald behind tomorrow.

Light flakes of snow drifted to the ground. His father wrapped his arm around his mama and led her and the baby down the path toward home. Billy admired them. He was part of both of them, making him the man he'd become. Baby Mary would have an exceptional life, even if he wasn't here to see it.

"You go on to the house," he said to Angel. "I'll be there soon." He wanted to kiss her, but now wasn't the time.

"All right." She kissed his cheek and joined her mama on the path to home.

Snow dusted the loose earth over his grandmother's grave. Uncle Harper knelt beside it with Mrs. Holloway and Becky at his side.

"Uncle Harper?" Billy rested his hand on his shoulder.

Harper lifted his tear-streaked face and looked at him. "Gonna miss her."

"I will, too." Billy knelt beside him. "She loved you very much."

Harper cried even harder. He raised his hand toward Billy, then opened it, exposing the wooden ring box. "It's empty. Don't know what happened to the ring."

Billy's heart thumped. He couldn't tell him where it was. "I'm certain we'll find it."

Becky stepped in front of Harper and took one of his hands. "Don't cry, Mr. Hadley. You have *us* now. Soon you'll be my daddy. Mama and I will take care of you."

Mrs. Holloway's face changed from a frown to a soft smile.

Knowing his uncle was well tended; Billy paused one last time to gaze at the grave then wandered away, leaving them to their grief. Would Harper forgive him for his deception?

* * *

The train would be leaving the station at eight. Everyone rose early to either be on the train, or see off those who were traveling. With that knowledge, Angel and Billy chose to forego a night in the attic. One of the hardest things she'd ever done.

At least her mama hadn't noticed she'd been gone the past few nights. Since she slept with her door closed and her mama was preoccupied with Uziah, she'd avoided suspicion.

With the inevitable discussion with their parents looming, her nerves had gotten the best of her. While helping Ada with breakfast, she'd burned a batch of hot cakes and spilled milk.

"You all right, baby girl?" her mama asked, while helping mop up the milk with a rag.

"Yes, Mama." *Liar.* She kept her eyes glued to the sea of milk; far from her mama's gaze.

"I gots more hotcakes ready." Ada held out a plate. "Angel, you takes these to them children."

Grateful for the distraction, Angel took the plate to the dining room, where everyone had gathered for their last meal together.

Joe dove into the hotcakes—spearing three with his fork —and received a reprimanding look from Jeriah. He returned two to the platter. "Cain't hep it if I's hungry."

"You're always hungry," Jeriah chuckled.

"Anyone need anythin' else?" Angel asked, looking around the table.

"I can't eat." Becky poked at her food. Paulette sat beside her as glum as could be.

"Aren't you glad you'll be home soon?" Angel asked, kneeling beside her.

"Yes, but I'm gonna miss Paulie." Becky turned to her new friend. The girls embraced, then burst out crying.

"They've been doing that all morning," Mrs. Holloway said. She wiggled her fork at Becky. "Don't you worry, Becky. Mr. Denton invited us to come back whenever we'd like."

"He has?" Becky sat up straight. Her eyes twinkled, smiling at Paulette.

"Yes, he has," Mr. Denton said, entering the room. "Anytime."

Becky and Paulette hugged again, then Becky began eating, suddenly finding her appetite.

"Would you like some breakfast, Mr. Denton?" Angel asked. "There's plenty a hotcakes, but if you'd like sumthin' else, I'll get it for you."

"No thank you, Angel, I'm not hungry this morning. But I'd like a cup of tea."

"Yes, sir." She curtsied, as she'd done many times, then left to get the tea. What was he going to think of her? Would she lose his respect forever?

As she hastened from the dining room, she nearly ran over Billy. He teetered on his crutch, so she grabbed him around the waist. "I'm sorry, Billy!"

He laughed and held onto her, then bent close and whispered in her ear. "*I'm* not. It's the first chance I've had to hold you since the night before last."

"Billy!" She scolded him in a hushed whisper, her skin warmed from his touch.

Hannah cleared her throat. "Did I miss breakfast?"

Angel stepped away from him. "No!" The word came out in a panic.

He placed his hand on her arm. "Be more careful next time, all right?"

She nodded. "Sorry, Billy." She rushed to the kitchen. Her heart pounded. She leaned against the wall with her ear attuned to the hallway.

"She nearly toppled me," Billy said, laughing.

Hannah giggled. "Have you had breakfast?"

"No. I was on my way there when I ran into Angel."

"Well then, let's eat."

Angel peered around the corner.

Hannah linked her arm with Billy's and helped him hobble to the dining room.

Though he'd become her husband—her *lover*—she ached with jealousy.

"Angel." Her mama tapped her shoulder. "They's work to do."

"Yes, Mama." She took a deep breath and crossed to the stove where Ada kept water boiling in a tea kettle. After preparing Mr. Denton's tea, she returned to the dining room and set it down in front of him.

Billy met her gaze. Why'd he look so sad? Did he have regrets? Hannah sat beside him comfortably engaged in conversation with Mrs. Denton. Did Mrs. Denton hope Billy would change his mind? Surely she knew Hannah cared for Donald.

Angel clutched her hand to her breast, feeling the ring beneath the fabric. After scolding herself for doubting Billy, she returned to the kitchen. Hard work would help.

* * *

The train whistle blew, announcing it would soon leave the station.

"I *am* sorry," Billy said, holding Hannah's hand. He lifted it to his lips and kissed it.

"Me, too. But we'll always be friends." Her eyes shifted to Donald.

"I'll leave you two to say goodbye." Billy smiled at his brother, who returned it with one of his own.

He limped away from them and moved toward the doctor. "Goodbye, Harvey."

"Goodbye, *Billy.*" He patted him on the back. "I'll be writing that paper. You'll have to let me know if there's anything else you neglected to tell me."

Billy sighed. "Actually there is. I told you I remember everything, but it's not true."

Harvey tipped his head. "How would you know there's something you *don't* remember?"

"Because I don't remember how it happened. I can recall everything that led up to it. The encampment, meeting Joe on the road, and . . ." He placed his hand to his temples and frowned. "The fox is coming home."

"What?" The doctor looked at him as if he'd lost his mind. *Again.*

"A phrase I was told to remember in order to be allowed to speak to General Canby at Fort Morgan. I failed them all. I was carrying a message. A message they never received."

"Canby?" Harvey gazed upward, his brow wrinkling in thought. "General Canby led the Union troops to Mobile Bay. There were more than thirty thousand. I know you remember that stage in the war. It was just before the end. Rebel soldiers fled the city in droves. You may not have gotten your message to Canby, but he had no difficulty helping the Union win the war."

Not knowing what had been in the message bothered Billy. It was something he'd *never* know. Perhaps the man who injured him read it and because of it may have been one of the first Confederate soldiers to flee.

"I know I need to let all that go, but—I don't know *how* I was injured. Or who did it. And I wish more than anything I knew what happened to Cotton. Why can't I remember that *one* day?"

"It was too traumatizing. Obviously your mind has chosen to block it. You may never regain that piece of your puzzle." He patted Billy's shoulder. "But the memories you've recalled have made you happy. I know they have. You're back where you belong."

Billy let out a large breath. "Yes, I am. But as you know I have some challenges ahead."

"That you do. Aside from that ankle. Give your parents a chance to understand. They're good people. I know I don't have to tell *you* that. And don't worry about Hannah. I forgive you." He peered at him over the top of his glasses. "But your brother had better not break her heart."

Billy looked down the platform to where he'd left Hannah and Donald. "I don't think you'll need to worry about that."

Harvey turned his head, following Billy's gaze. "I need to have a talk with that girl." The two were locked in a kiss completely inappropriate in such a public place.

"She's not a girl any longer."

"No, she's not," Billy's father added. "I don't fully understand what happened this past week, but as long as you're fine with the way things have transpired, then so am I."

"I am," Harvey said. "And so is Billy."

Billy smiled and hobbled away. Mrs. Holloway was waiting for him. The whistle blew again, tugging at his heart. Saying goodbye to her would be the hardest of all.

"Uncle Harper," Billy said. "Take care of her." He put his arm around Mrs. Holloway's waist and gave her a squeeze.

"Aim to marry her," Harper said. "Soon as we get to Mobile. Gotta keep her honest."

"Oh, Harper." She laughed, but then her face became instantly somber. "I'll miss you, Billy!" She began to cry and pulled him into her arms for a final hug. She squeezed him so hard he almost dropped his crutch.

"Please, don't cry. I want to remember your *happy* face."

"You brought my happy face back to me." She wiped away tears, then patted his cheek.

"You talkin' 'bout me?" Harper asked.

She giggled. "You were part of it, but Billy changed my life when he knocked on my door."

"And when he brought me to you," Becky added. "Right, Mama?"

"Yes, my dear," Mrs. Holloway said. "Billy made us a family."

The conductor called for final boarding.

"Look after Joe," Mrs. Holloway said. "I know he's happy here."

"I will," Billy said. "Now, go. I'll see you again one day."

She hugged him once more, then Becky wrapped her arms around his neck and kissed him on the cheek. "I love you, Billy. I'll never forget you saved me."

He returned her kiss, then she walked away with Mrs. Holloway on one side and Harper on the other. Before boarding the train, she stopped, turned, and waved.

Paulette slipped her hand into Billy's and squeezed.

"She'll be back, Paulette," he said.

Paulette said nothing. Tears trickled down her cheeks.

The carriage ride home was somber. Billy understood why Joe chose to stay behind with Bessie. He'd said his goodbyes and didn't want to have to say them again. Besides, the carriage could only hold a handful of them and they'd squeezed in tight as it was.

Donald fidgeted with the window curtain looking as though he'd lost his dearest friend. "How could you so easily let her go?" he asked Billy. "You were with her for five years. I've only known her a week and telling her goodbye has left a hole in my heart as big as a barn."

"When I realized I didn't love her that way, it was the right thing to do." Billy turned to his father. "When we get home, I need to speak with you and Mama. It's important."

He nodded, while raising a brow. "Would you like to talk about it *now*?"

"No, sir. I need to speak with both of you together."

"Very well." He pulled Paulette against his chest. "Don't cry, sweetheart. Mobile isn't far away. Maybe we can go for a visit this summer. I've heard the bay is beautiful then."

Billy closed his eyes and rested his head against the back of the seat. He thought of Mobile and what he'd left behind. He'd sent a letter with Harvey to be given to Mr. Bradley regarding his unfinished business; certain Mr. Bradley would appreciate the work. He also included a letter for Sylvia, thanking her for all the opportunities she'd given him over the years.

Sealing those letters tucked away Brian Carpenter forever. And now, he'd take the next step in his life.

Jeriah stopped the carriage in front of the house and they exited one-by-one.

"I still don't understand why Bo left without saying a word to us," his father said, as they ascended the steps.

"I do," Billy said. "Look at Donald. He's got heartache the size of Tennessee. Bo was no different. Angel broke his heart turning down his marriage proposal. He didn't want to stay here if he couldn't be with her."

Donald's head hung so low that for once Billy stood taller than him—even while leaning on his crutch. He placed his arm over his brother's shoulder. "Maybe you should make plans to go to Mobile soon."

Donald nodded, but said nothing.

"I'm grateful I don't have to relive my youth," their father said. "And even though getting your mother to the altar wasn't easy, it was well worth it. Don't worry, Donald. If it's meant to be, she'll wait for you."

Billy considered his words. They couldn't have been truer. Angel had waited for him, even after everyone believed he'd died. She never gave up hope. They were meant to be.

* * *

Angel fidgeted with the ring at her neck. Twice she'd slipped it on her finger, but both times she'd returned it to the strand of yarn. *Soon I'll be able to wear it for good.*

Billy had given back her journal, but she'd not written in it since. Now seemed appropriate.

January 4th, 1870.

I'm waiting for Billy to come home from the train station. When he does, we plan to tell our folks we're married. I'm scared, but I know we need to tell them. I don't want to go on for the rest of our lives hiding our love.

We've been meeting in the attic since New Year's Eve. I gave myself to him that night after we'd placed our hands on Mrs. Moss's Bible and exchanged vows. It was beautiful. All of it. Making love to Billy is like nothing I ever dreamed. I'm his wife now and will be forever.

She blew on the ink and waited for a few moments before placing the journal in her drawer.

Biscuit wove himself around her legs; rubbing and purring. "Don't know why you didn't stay in Billy's room, silly cat." She grinned answering her own question. Billy was rarely there. At least here, Uziah gave him some attention.

"Angel." Her mama knocked on her door.

"Yes, Mama?"

"The carriage is back."

Oh, my . . .

Angel opened her door. "Mama." She took a deep breath. *Be brave.* "I need you to come with me to the Denton's. Jeriah, too. I have some things to talk to you 'bout."

"Why don't we talk here?"

"Cuz I need to talk with the Denton's, too."

Her mama's finger rubbed along her nose. "What'd you do, Angel?"

"N—Nothin', Mama."

"Mmm, hmm." She crossed her arms.

"Please come with me." Angel scooped up Uziah, then took her mama's arm and led her toward the door.

* * *

Billy stood propped on his crutch, with one hand on the fireplace mantel.

"What's this all 'bout?" his mama asked, while patting Mary's tiny back.

"I'll explain when Angel gets here." The look his mama gave him made him shiver. He added a log to the fire.

When he turned around, he let out a long stream of held breath. Angel approached with her mama trailing behind and Jeriah close by carrying Uziah.

She looked like she might fall over; scared beyond words. Billy moved to her side, took her arm, and escorted her to the fireplace.

Jeriah helped Bessie sit, then took his place beside her. Looking from parent to parent, their looks were the same; fearful something bad was about to happen.

Billy cleared his throat. "We wanted you all here—"

"What about me?" Emilia flitted into the room.

Billy shook his head in disbelief. "Emilia, this doesn't concern you."

"Why not?" She lifted her chin and placed her hands on her hips.

"We want to talk to our folks," Angel said.

Emilia plopped down in a chair. "Go on. I won't stop you."

The girl had a lot of nerve. Billy wanted to pick her up, throw her over his shoulder, and remove her from the living room. Two things stopped him; his leg and Angel.

"It's all right, Billy," Angel said. "Let her stay. I don't care anymore."

Emilia grinned and sat fully upright. "You heard her. Go on now."

With great effort, Billy avoided eye contact with Emilia, resisting the urge to glare at her. "The reason we wanted you all here is Angel and I . . . well . . ." He turned toward his wife. Her brown eyes sparkled. She nodded, giving him the encouragement he needed. "We love each other."

The moment he said the words, his mama sighed and Bessie groaned.

"We do," Angel said. "We always have. It ain't gonna change."

Billy took her hand. "And even though the law won't allow it, we married each other."

"Oh!" Emilia shrieked. "It was *Billy* you were with all night!"

Bessie stood and glared at Emilia. "What'd you mean? All night?"

"Married?" His mama's hand flew to her mouth.

Billy didn't want to lie anymore. "Yes, Mama. I married Angel. We've vowed our love."

"You can't just *say* you're married. You gotta get a license an a preacher!" She stood from the sofa and handed Mary to their father. "What were you thinkin', Billy?" She faced him squarely, tears glistening in her eyes.

"I love her, Mama." He wouldn't release Angel's hand. He looked toward his father for help. "Father, you said if love is meant to be, the person you love will wait for you. Angel waited. She never stopped believing I'd come home to her."

"What'd you do to her, Billy?" Jeriah stood and moved toward him. Fury filled his eyes.

"Don't." Angel lifted her hand to stop him. "He didn't do anything I didn't want him to."

"You tellin' me you an Billy …" Bessie stared at them in horror.

His mama's eyes opened wide. "Billy, you didn't?"

Emilia clapped her hands together, drawing everyone's attention. "I knew she was doing it with *someone*! I just thought it was Bo."

"Emilia!" his mama yelled. "Go to your room!"

Mary began to cry. His father tried to calm her *and* his mama. "Yes, Emilia, for now, please go to your room."

Emilia huffed. She walked out and stomped up the stairs. Her door slammed shut.

Angel started to cry. "She makes it sound ugly. But it's not. We love each other. It's no different than what you have with Jeriah, Mama. Or what you have either." She directed her last remark to his parents. Billy pulled her closer, his heart aching from her tears.

"Please," he urged. "Everyone sit down." Fortunately, they complied. "I know you all love us and you're concerned about how we'll live together as man and wife. Angel shouldn't be punished because of her parentage. The only one in this house who understood was Grandmother." The mention of her brought tears to his eyes. "Before she died, she gave us her blessings. She also gave me her ring and told me to give it to Angel."

"*You* have mother's ring?" His father stood, but when Billy motioned him down, he returned to his seat.

"I did. But I gave it to Angel." He smiled at her. "Show them."

She unfastened the top buttons of her dress and slowly withdrew the strand of yarn, producing the diamond ring.

Billy lifted the strand up and over her head, then drew it out from her hair. Untying it, he removed the ring and placed it on her finger. "This is where it'll stay."

"Billy." His father drew his attention. "Saying you're married and giving a ring doesn't make it so."

"In our hearts we're married. And in every aspect she's my wife." Billy didn't shift his gaze.

"What do you plan to do?" His father sat back, but with a look on his face of complete disappointment. A look he'd never seen from the man. He'd always wanted to make him proud, and this hurt. More than he'd imagined it would. Making it worse, both their mama's were crying.

"We'll have to leave Memphis."

"What?" Angel asked, stepping back.

He faced her, taking hold of her hands. "It's the only way. We'll never be accepted here. Grandmother suggested we go north. Or west. I've been thinking Kansas might be a good place."

"Kansas?" She frowned.

"I wanted to say something sooner, but you've been so worried about all this. I'm a carpenter. I can find work any-where. And Grandmother promised she left us the means to go. I love you, Angel. We can do this. We can make a life for ourselves." He shut out everyone in the room but her. He didn't care any longer what they thought, but he had to know she'd go anywhere necessary to be together.

Her frown disappeared. She reached out and touched his face. "I love you, Billy. My home's with you. I'm scared as can be, but I'll go."

"Can I go?" Uziah lifted his hands toward Angel.

With tear-filled eyes, she picked him up and held him close. "No, Ziah. You hafta stay with Mama an Daddy."

Billy's heart rested. With Angel, he believed he could do anything. "Mama?" He swallowed the lump in his throat. "I'm sorry you're disappointed in me, but you've known for a long time how I feel about her. And Father, please understand. I've never wanted to let you down, but I've made up my mind. Nothing you say will change what we've done or how we feel."

"Billy's right," Angel said. "Mama, think 'bout what it was like for you an Jeriah. When you had to hide your love. An when the law changed an you could marry, you did. But were you any less married to him before the law allowed it?"

Bessie lowered her head, shaking it slowly. "In my heart, he was always my husband."

"An Billy's mine." Angel moved to her mama and knelt at her feet. "I love him, Mama. More now than the day he left. We ain't children no more. He's a man, an I'm a woman, an—"

"Don't say no more, baby." Bessie cupped Angel's cheek and gazed into her eyes.

Billy knelt beside her. "Bessie, I'm able to take care of her. For the past five years I've made my own living. And I swear we'll come home as often as we can."

"I was there when you was born," Bessie said, sniffling. "I loved you then, an I loves you now. Take care a my baby." She grabbed his hand and gripped it tight. "It's gonna be so hard . . ." She cried again, tearing another piece from his heart.

"Billy?" His mama reached out to him.

"Yes?" He moved to sit beside her, praying to hear what he wished she'd say.

"You just came home. I don't want you to leave again." Her chin quivered. She moved her fingers through his hair. "This is the hardest thing I've ever had to say, but you can't live together under this roof. It'd confuse folks. We can't live like that."

He took no offense. "I understand." He looked from her to his father. "The last thing I want is to bring shame on our family. What matters most to me—to *us*—is you all accept us. Regardless of how the rest of the country sees us."

Angel placed her hand on his shoulder. "We need to know you love us. We never meant to hurt y'all. Love's not supposed to hurt."

Silence hung in the air. Billy stood, using Angel for support. She no longer appeared to be scared. Her body had relaxed; the tension gone from her shoulders.

Bessie rose and faced the others. "All them years ago, when Angel was in my belly, I hated the man what done it. I wondered why God would let that happen to me. But He knew my Angel would bring joy. She done brought me more joy than I reckon I deserve. She an Billy's special. I ain't gonna deny them their love. I won't turn my back on 'em."

Angel wrapped her arms around her and they both cried. "Thank you, Mama."

Billy looked at his mama, who hadn't moved while Bessie spoke. And then, her head lowered. She studied her entwined fingers. When she lifted her head, she faced his father. The two shared a silent stare. *What are they thinking?*

His father stood. "We love you. *Both* of you. And though it seems this happened quickly, we know it's been in the making for many years. Having your memory restored brought back the reason why you left. It was always for Angel. Because you love her."

"I do."

His father took Angel's hand and gazed at the ring. "Mother knew the troubles you'd face. I didn't understand why she allotted such a large sum to Billy in her will, but now I know. If she of all people could accept this, so can I. All my life I fought my father over his treatment of our slaves. Telling him they weren't pieces of property, but real human beings. Humans with feelings. With *love*. I'd be a hypocrite if I tried to pretend the two of you are incapable of loving each other."

"I'm scared for you," his mama said, standing beside him. "Folks can be hateful and cruel."

"She's right," Jeriah said, joining them. "I sees it all the time. It ain't gonna be easy."

"We know," Angel said. "But if we have your blessin's, then we'll have a good start."

Instantly, the air in the room warmed as if a heart that had stopped beating had been brought back to life. Tears turned to hugs and kisses.

They'd been accepted.

Chapter 43

I don't ever want this feelin' to end . . .

Angel lay on her side with eyes half open. With Billy's body pressed behind her and his arm around her; she felt safe. His chest rose and fell. Slow and steady in a peaceful slumber.

Bo's house was warmer than the attic. She'd been grateful when Mr. Denton offered it to them. But it was temporary. Once they packed, she and Billy would be going to Topeka, Kansas.

She knew little about Topeka. Rumors were that a lot of freed slaves had moved there. The city was growing and had opportunities for a skilled carpenter. They'd settle there as husband and wife. Maybe no one would notice a white man married to a woman who wasn't *entirely* white.

They might assume her to be part Indian. They'd ask questions if overly nosy, but she might be lucky enough to meet people who saw through her color and accepted her simply as *Angel*.

He's awake . . . His fingers roamed her breast.

"Angel," he whispered.

He shifted his weight and pushed her hair away from her neck. His lips brushed her skin, causing her to shiver.

Rolling onto her back, she looked up into his tired green eyes. "Mornin', Billy."

"Morning, Mrs. Denton." After propping himself up on one elbow, he studied her face as if he'd never seen it before.

"Why are you lookin' at me like that?" She blinked slowly, then squirmed when his hand cascaded down her body.

"You're beautiful. Even in the morning."

"Your vision's blurry. You didn't get enough sleep. I must look a sight." She placed her hand over her mouth. "I need to clean my teeth." Her words came out mumbled beneath her fingers.

"What?" He pulled her hand away. "What did you say?"

"I said I need to clean my teeth."

"Oh." He grinned. "You don't offend me." To prove his point, he kissed her thoroughly.

Her mind spun in a million different directions. Torn between another round of love-making, and needing to get up and fix breakfast. What was a wife's most important duty?

"Billy?" She scooted up against the pillows. "Are you hungry?"

"A bit." He buried his face into her neck and nibbled.

"That's not what I meant." She giggled, then gently pushed him back. "Do you want *food*?"

He sat up and folded his arms. "Hmm. Food or you?" Tapping his finger against his chin he stared upward, then flopped back down on top of her. "I'd much rather have you."

She gave in, disregarding her breath and appetite, and focused on satisfying his.

When they finished, he lay back and closed his eyes.

"Don't go to sleep now, Billy. We've got lots to do." She nudged him with a gentle prodding. "We gotta get things packed, and sometime today we gotta eat."

She jumped from the bed and hurriedly dressed. Since the fire had died down, the room had turned cold. After stoking it, she lifted the angel figurine from the mantel. "I can't believe your mama gave this to us."

"It meant a lot to her to do it. She feels it's protected her for a long time. Seems she thinks we need it now more than she does."

"I hope Kansas won't be *that* dangerous." She set the angel down and began rummaging through Bo's small kitchen, trying to find pans to cook breakfast.

"I'll protect you."

"I know you will." She smiled at him, then placed a frying pan on the stove.

"What are you doing?"

"Gonna fix breakfast." When she looked his way, he met her with the same sad eyes she'd seen the morning everyone left for the train station. "Billy?" She knelt on the bed beside him, then reached her hand to his face. "Why do you look so sad? You looked at me the same way the other day in the dinin' room."

He brought her into his arms and cradled her against him. "That morning, I saw you as you'd always been. A slave in my parent's house. It tore my heart in two."

"I was doin' my job. I didn't mind."

"I know. But I don't want you to feel like you have to wait on me." He stroked her hair as he spoke. "You're free, Angel. Not a slave."

She propped herself up on his chest and smiled. "I know. But I'm your wife. And as your wife, I'm gonna take care of you. Whether you like it or not."

He chuckled. "Fine. And I'll take care of you. Whether *you* like it or not."

She jiggled her brows. "I'll like it."

"You don't burn biscuits, do you?"

"Nope. Only hotcakes." His lips formed into another playful grin. "I'm not *that* hungry, Billy." She licked her lips and waited . . .

"Neither am I."

His eyes were glued to her as she removed her robe. "Still watchin' me, Billy?"

He lifted the covers, and she slid in beside him. "Always." He hushed her with a kiss.

THE END

Acknowledgments

When my mom started reading a first draft of this book, she told me she had to stop at one point and put it aside because it made her nervous. She was so concerned over what was going to happen to Billy, she had to quit reading until she became brave enough to pick it up and start again. Thankfully, she did. From what she's told me, this has become one of her favorite books.

The 1860's were a terrible time in our nation's history. Statistically, 620,000 soldiers lost their lives in the Civil War. We recently visited a cemetery in Frankfurt, Kentucky, and I noticed numerous graves of young men who'd died between 1862 and 1865. No doubt, they'd been in the war. I told my husband that those men had a story to tell. That's what drives me to write about this time in history. It's not glamorous, but incredibly moving. Though my stories are fiction, my hope is that they reflect true feelings and the emotion of the time period.

I wrote this book during a difficult time in my life, but one I'd never trade for anything. I'd been caring for my mother-in-law, who suffered from Alzheimer's disease, which caused dementia. She sat quietly beside me while I wrote, unable to walk, but content in her easy chair watching game shows on TV. She passed away the day after I typed *the end*. I'll never forget her, and am thankful for the time I had with her. I'm especially grateful for the things she taught me about life *and* death.

I hold this particular book close to my heart. With the exception of some historical figures, my characters are fictitious. But I've intertwined real historical events. I'd like to thank Johnnie Williams and Fred Frazier for taking the time to read this book and help me with the historical accuracy. They're both Civil War experts and had incredibly valuable input.

Thank you to my other expert, Diane Gardner, who gave me insight into horse behavior. She also continues to be one of the best 'typo' finders around. And speaking of horses—you'll be happy to know that the mystery of Cotton will one day be revealed. Stay tuned ...

Special thanks go out to my team of fabulous cohorts! My books wouldn't be the same without them. Topping that list is my editor, Cindy Brannam. She knows my voice *and* my style and keeps me moving forward.

I believe the request for my cover design made Rae Monet pull some of her hair out this time, but she came through with flying colors. Thank you Rae, and thank you also to Karen Duvall for designing the flat. Jesse Gordon did another fantastic job formatting. I count my blessings every day, knowing I have such talented people to work with.

Finally, thank YOU! Without readers, I'd not be able to continue doing what I love. You're all included in those blessings I'm counting.

If you enjoyed *Forgotten*, you'll want to read...

From the *Ashes of Atlanta*
A Novel by Jeanne Hardt

After losing his Atlanta home and family to the war, Confederate soldier, Jeb Carter, somehow wakes up in a Boston hospital. Alone, desperate, and with a badly broken leg, he pretends to be mute to save himself from those he hates—Yankees.

Gwen Abbott, a student at Boston Women's Medical College, is elated when she's allowed to study under the guidance of a prominent doctor at Massachusetts General. While forced into a courtship with a man she can scarcely tolerate, her thoughts are consumed with their mysterious new patient. If only he could talk.

Two strangers from different worlds, joined by fate. Perhaps love can speak without words and win a war without a single shot being fired.

Coming Soon!

The Southern Secrets Saga
by Jeanne Hardt

A little more than six years have passed since the end of the War Between the States, and life in Mobile, Alabama isn't easy. Many loved ones were lost and folks simply want to piece their lives back together again.

But one thing hasn't changed ... The ability to love.

Follow the lives of five families. Many secrets will be kept, and some will be painfully revealed.

* * *

Deceptions: Southern Secrets Saga, Book 1

Claire Montgomery is twenty-five and single. After years of listening to her mama caution her about men, she's determined to stay that way. However, when Dr. Andrew Fletcher arrives in her little town, she's smitten.

Andrew tends the elite at Mobile City Hospital, but also cares for the poor Negroes in a less desirable part of town. Despite criticism from the hospital administrator, he's determined to stand by his principles and help anyone in need. Regardless of the color of their skin.

Andrew proposes marriage. Claire agrees and moves with him to Mobile, where they begin making plans to wed. Her world crashes around her when she discovers a letter that reveals a painful truth. Knowing she can't marry him, but not wanting to cause him pain, she holds the secret and runs away, only to discover she's carrying his child.

Every decision made, changes the lives of those she loves. Secrets and lies become a way of life, and she finds that in protecting her child, she's lost sight of her values and endeavors to find them again.

* * *

For information on upcoming releases,
be sure to follow Jeanne Hardt:

facebook.com/JEANNEHARDTAUTHOR
jeannehardt.com
amazon.com/author/jeannehardt
goodreads.com/jeannehardt

Made in the USA
Middletown, DE
26 June 2015